W9-BKG-256

MORNING STAR

Moon Hunt

BY W. MICHAEL GEAR AND KATHLEEN O'NEAL GEAR FROM TOM DOHERTY ASSOCIATES

NORTH AMERICA'S FORGOTTEN PAST SERIES

People of the Wolf
People of the Fire
People of the Earth
People of the River
People of the Sea
People of the Lakes
People of the Lightning
People of the Silence
People of the Mist
People of the Masks
People of the Owl
People of the Raven
People of the Moon
People of the Nightland
People of the Weeping Eye
People of the Thunder
People of the Longhouse
The Dawn Country: A People of the Longhouse Novel
The Broken Land: A People of the Longhouse Novel
People of the Black Sun: A People of the Longhouse Novel
People of the Songtrail

THE MORNING STAR SERIES

People of the Morning Star
Morning Star: Sun Born
Morning Star: Moon Hunt

THE ANASAZI MYSTERY SERIES

The Visitant
The Summoning God
Bone Walker

BY KATHLEEN O'NEAL GEAR

Thin Moon and Cold Mist
Sand in the Wind
This Widowed Land
It Sleeps in Me
It Wakes in Me
It Dreams in Me

BY W. MICHAEL GEAR

Long Ride Home
Big Horn Legacy
The Athena Factor
The Morning River
Coyote Summer

BY WILLIAM GEAR

This Scorched Earth

OTHER TITLES BY W. MICHAEL GEAR AND KATHLEEN O'NEAL GEAR

The Betrayal
Dark Inheritance
Raising Abel
Children of the Dawnland
Coming of the Storm
Fire the Sky
A Searing Wind

www.Gear-Gear.com
www.gear-books.com

MORNING STAR

Moon Hunt

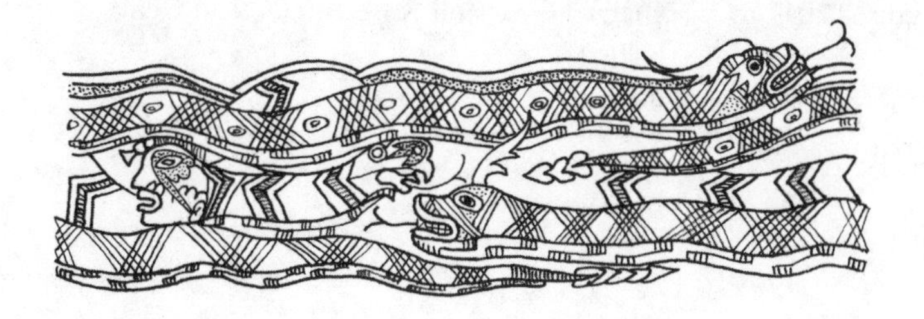

W. Michael Gear and
Kathleen O'Neal Gear

A TOM DOHERTY ASSOCIATES BOOK · NEW YORK

This is a work of fiction. All of the characters, organizations, and events portrayed in this novel are either products of the authors' imaginations or are used fictitiously.

MOON HUNT

A Forge Book
Published by Tom Doherty Associates
175 Fifth Avenue
New York, NY 10010

www.tor-forge.com

The Library of Congress Cataloging-in-Publication Data is available upon request.

ISBN 978-0-7653-8059-3 (hardcover)
ISBN 978-1-4668-7460-2 (ebook)

First Edition: November 2017

Printed in the United States of America

0 9 8 7 6 5 4 3 2 1

Brian O'Neil

For friendship, for fire in the belly,

And the constant

Joy

That is archaeology.

Acknowledgments

So much of the Morning Star series owes its existence to the works of Dr. Timothy Pauketat, Dr. Susan Alt, Dr. Carol Diaz-Granados, Dr. James Brown, Dr. John Kelly, Dr. F. Kent Reilly III, Dr. Bill Iseminger, and so many of the dedicated archaeologists who have slowly and surely been prying Cahokia's secrets from its resistant soils.

To understand more about Bundles, astroarchaeology, and the cosmology that made Cahokia tick, see Dr. Pauketat's excellent *An Archaeology of the Cosmos,* published by Routledge Press, 2013. Descriptions from the Sacred Cave can be found in *Picture Cave: Unraveling the Mysteries of the Mississippian Cosmos,* edited by Carol Diaz-Granados, James R. Duncan, and F. Kent Reilly III, published by the University of Texas Press, Austin, 2015. An additional introduction to the Cahokian world can be found in Tim Pauketat and Susan M. Alt's *Medieval Mississippians: The Cahokian World,* published by the SAR Press, Santa Fe, 2015.

And finally, as keepers of the Cahokian world, our deepest appreciation goes out to Mark Esarey, Bill Iseminger, and the remarkable staff at Cahokia Mounds State Historic Site. As stewards of one of the most important archaeological properties in the world, they have skillfully preserved, directed productive research on, and promoted Cahokia and its remarkable heritage. Learn more at cahokiamounds.org.

Our sincere thanks are offered to our editor, Claire Eddy and her capable assistant, Kristin Temple. To our copy editor, Deanna Hoak, thank you for keeping us from looking silly.

As always, we are again indebted to Theresa Hulongbayan for her wonderful *Gear Fan Club: book series First North Americans* on Facebook. Theresa, you are a gem.

And finally, to our publisher, Tom Doherty, Associate Publisher Linda Quinton, and the good folks at Tor/Forge Books, thanks for your continued dedication to telling the story of our country's fascinating precontact heritage.

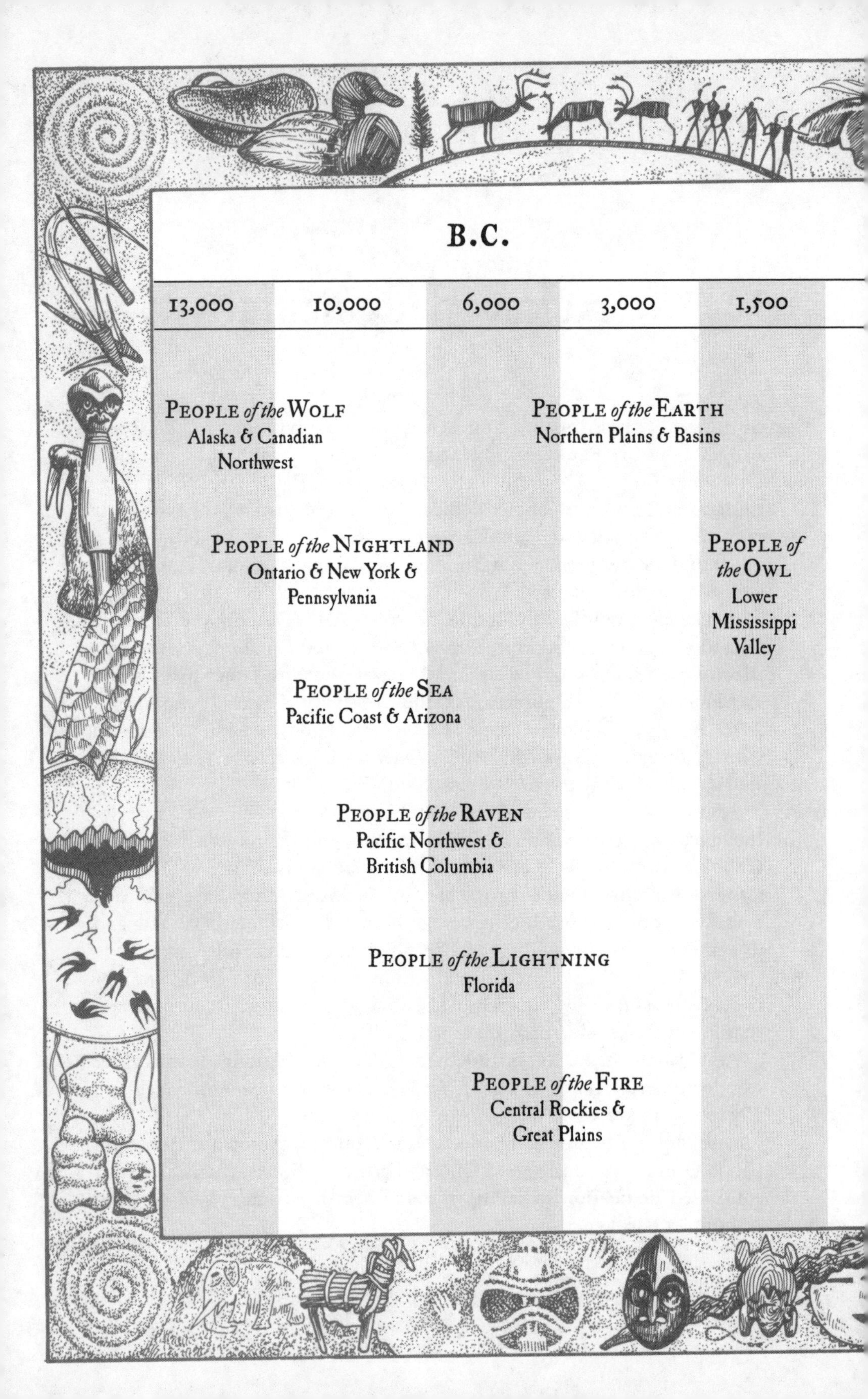

B.C.
13,000
10,000
6,000
3,000
1,500
PEOPLE of the WOLF
Alaska & Canadian Northwest
PEOPLE of the EARTH
Northern Plains & Basins
PEOPLE of the NIGHTLAND
Ontario & New York & Pennsylvania
PEOPLE of the OWL
Lower Mississippi Valley
PEOPLE of the SEA
Pacific Coast & Arizona
PEOPLE of the RAVEN
Pacific Northwest & British Columbia
PEOPLE of the LIGHTNING
Florida
PEOPLE of the FIRE
Central Rockies & Great Plains

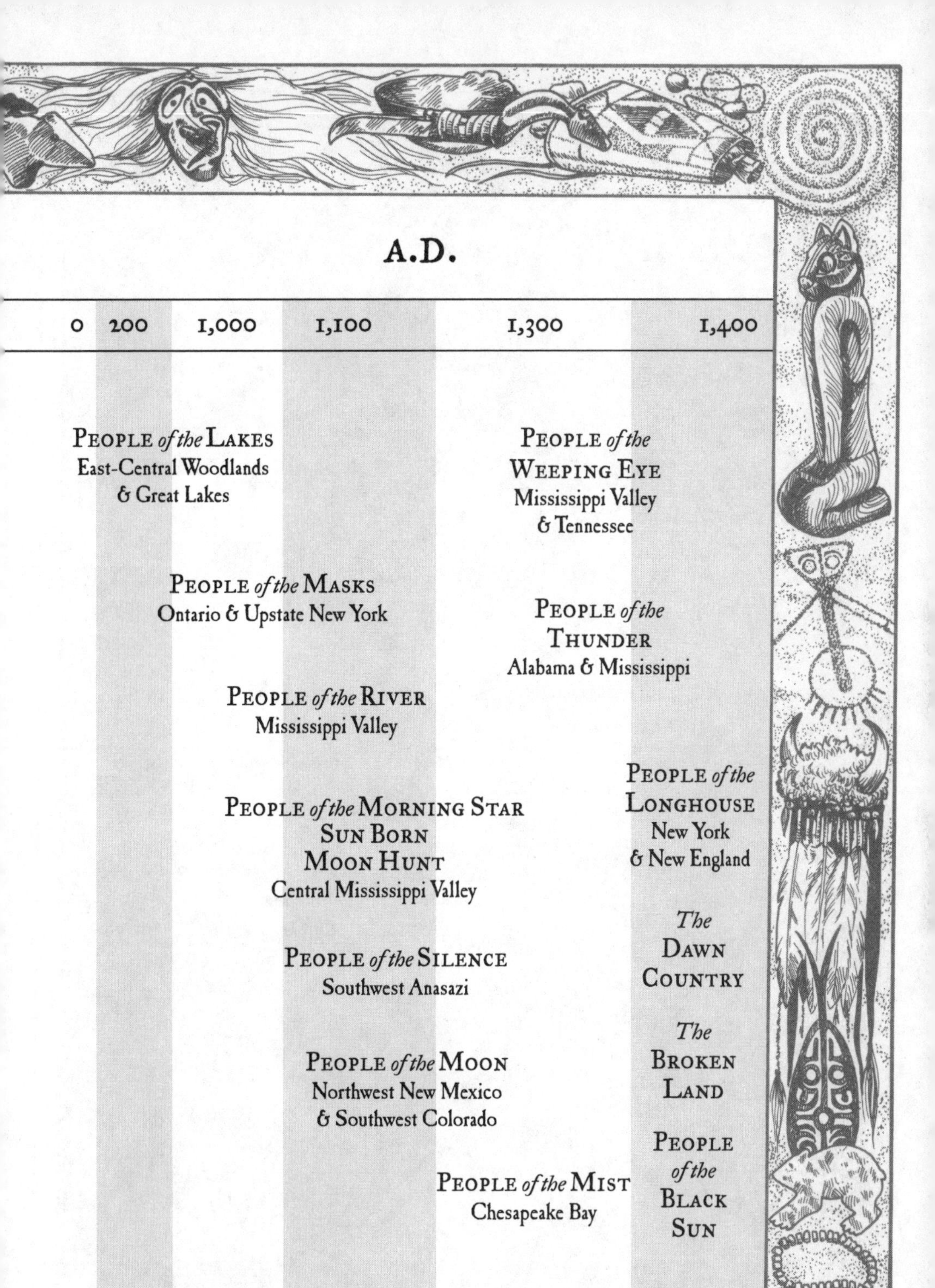
A.D.
0
200
1,000
1,100
1,300
1,400
People *of the* Lakes
East-Central Woodlands
& Great Lakes
People *of the*
Weeping Eye
Mississippi Valley
& Tennessee
People *of the* Masks
Ontario & Upstate New York
People *of the*
Thunder
Alabama & Mississippi
People *of the* River
Mississippi Valley
People *of the*
Longhouse
New York
& New England
People *of the* Morning Star
Sun Born
Moon Hunt
Central Mississippi Valley
The
Dawn
Country
People *of the* Silence
Southwest Anasazi
The
Broken
Land
People *of the* Moon
Northwest New Mexico
& Southwest Colorado
People
of the
Black
Sun
People *of the* Mist
Chesapeake Bay

Serpent Woman Town
North
To the Sacred Cave
Marsh Elder Lake
Black Tail's Tomb
CAHOKIA
Evening Star Town
River
Water
Father
Avenue of the Sun
Avenue of the Moon
Canoe Landing
River Mound City
Horned Serpent Town

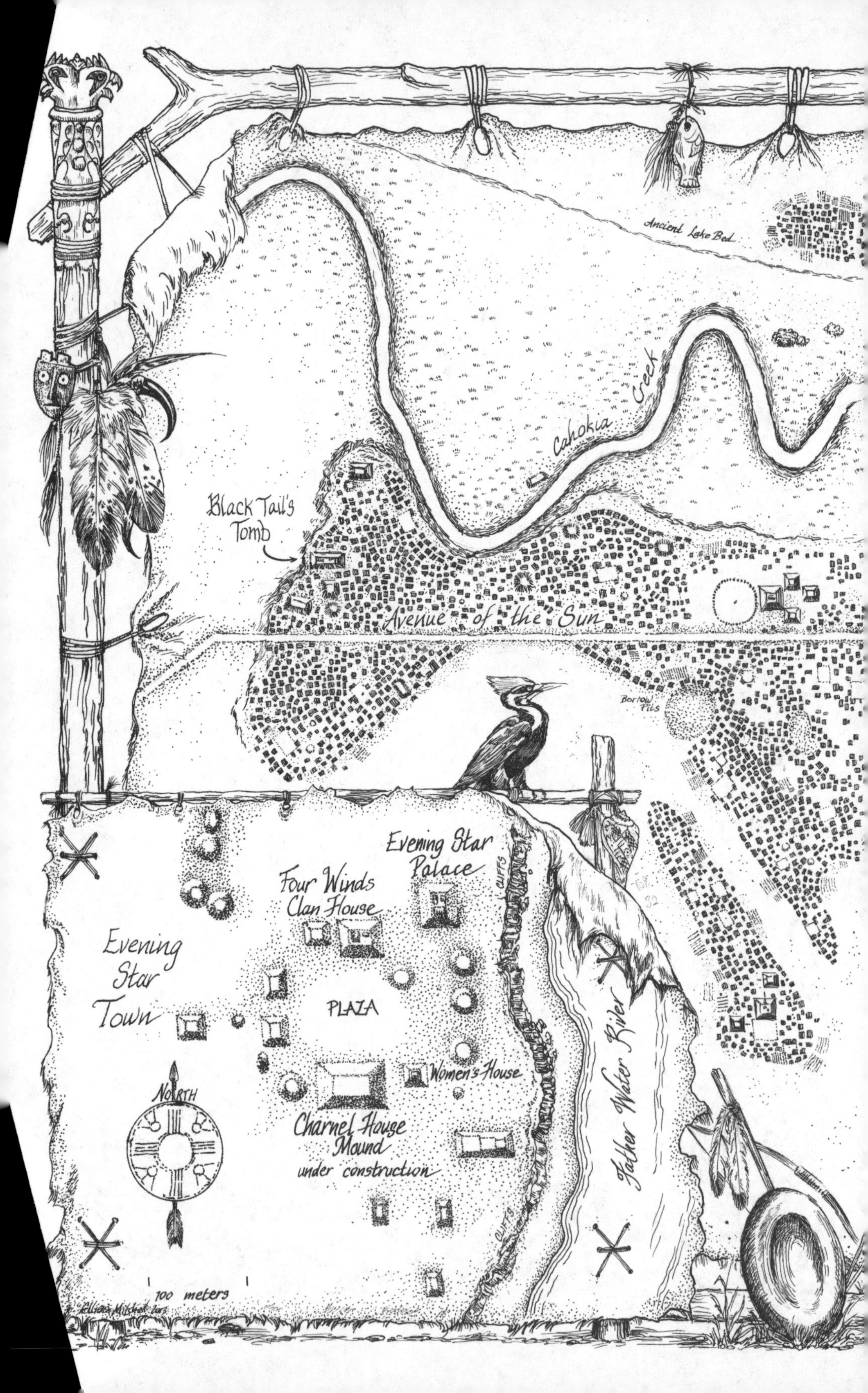

Ancient Lake Bed
Cahokia Creek
Black Tail's Tomb
Avenue of the Sun
Borrow Pits
Evening Star Palace
Four Winds Clan House
Evening Star Town
PLAZA
Women's House
Charnel House Mound under construction
Cliffs
Father Water River
North
100 meters

Old-Woman-Who-Never-Dies' Temple
Cahokia Creek
Avenue of the Sun
1 Morning Star's Great Mound
2 Night Shadow Star's Palace
3 Tonka'tzi's Palace
4 Four Winds Clan Palace
5 Rides-the-Lightning's Temple
6 Record Keeper's Temple
7 Four Winds Burial Mound
Avenue of the Moon
North
Cahokia

MORNING STAR

Moon Hunt

Prologue

Years of hardship, danger, and war had imbued War Leader Five Fists with the instinct of a forest-hunting cat. Perhaps it was just a stirring of the air that brought him awake, for the Morning Star made no sound as he padded silently from his personal quarters in the great palace's rear.

Though the eternal fire had burned down to coals it cast a faint orange glow through the gloom. Just enough illumination. Five Fists was able to recognize the living god's familiar walk and posture as he headed for the artistically carved double doors that opened out into the walled courtyard.

Wincing because it was the middle of the night, Five Fists threw back his blanket, pulled on his breechcloth, and reached for his war club.

"Wasss wrong?" Foxweed asked as she stirred and clawed her long hair back. She had been sharing his bed for more than a month now. A Panther Clan woman from one of the outlying lineages, she reveled in her newfound status, and didn't mind that Five Fists was older, ugly with his poorly healed and off-centered broken jaw, or that he had problems with his sexual abilities.

"He's up," he whispered. "Go back to sleep."

"It's the middle of the night."

"He's a living miracle. The hero of the Beginning Times brought to earth in a human body. What does he care?"

Five Fists gave his head a toss, as if to shake sleep's cobwebs from his thoughts. Then, hefting the club, he started across the mat-covered floor, his steps as silent as his master's.

Outside the night was dark: Occasional clouds blotted the starry heavens. A chill lay heavy in the air and sent a shiver down Five Fist's sun-darkened and scarred hide. He ran a hand over his tattooed cheeks.

Where was . . . ? Ah, yes.

He saw the Morning Star's shadowy form as it climbed the ladder up to the bastion that dominated the southwestern corner of the clay-covered wall. The Morning Star often retreated to the high bastion, where he could look down from his monumental mound, see his remarkable city, and perhaps touch the essence of the Sky World from which his Spirit had been called.

Five Fists, from long practice, took his position at the foot of the ladder and wished he'd brought a blanket to cut the chill.

"You need not inconvenience yourself, War Leader." The Morning Star's words carried a wistful note.

"You shouldn't be out here alone, Lord."

"She's still on the river, War Leader. I can feel her."

"Who, Lord?" Five Fists stepped out so that he could see the Morning Star's shadowy form against the midnight sky. The living god stared intently off to the southeast, the smoke-laden breeze fingering the strands of his long hair where it hung down his back.

"She's so . . ."

Five Fists waited, then couldn't stand it. "So what, Lord?"

Another silence from above, then Morning Star asked, "Do you think she understands?"

Safe in the darkness, Five Fists made a face. All these years of service to the living god, and half the time he couldn't make head nor tail of what the Morning Star was talking about. Despite knowing that any answer probably wasn't going to make sense, he asked, "Understands what, my lord?"

"That all of Creation is the One, War Leader. Life is death, creation is destruction . . . hatred is love."

"I don't . . ." He took a breath. Why bother?

The ensuing silence stretched for nearly a finger of time; then the Morning Star softly said, "I am giving you an order, War Leader. You must not execute her."

"Execute who?"

"She's only a piece in the game. But a necessary one. Poor thing hasn't a clue about what is at stake."

"Lord? If you'd give me a better idea about what—"

"The balance has to be maintained, War Leader. Lady Night Shadow Star will understand. Aid her in any way you need to."

"Yes, but, what are we talking about, Lord?"

"And the woman? Hear me, War Leader. She is to be *unharmed*! Especially afterwards."

"Afterwards? After what?"

"After she achieves my death, War Leader."

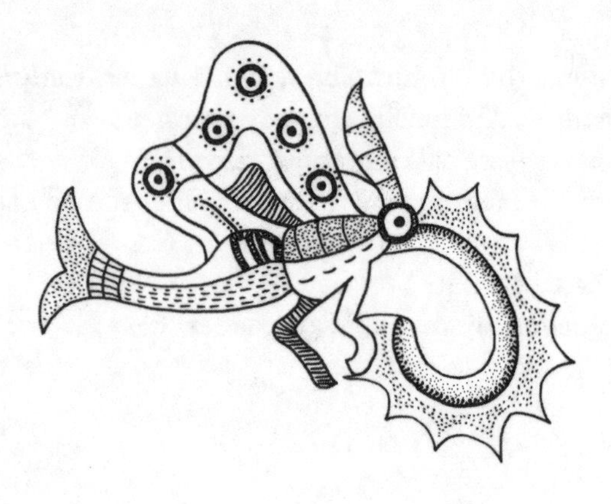

The Harrowing

I run my fingers through damp and sandy soil and listen to the sounds of the night. The canoes are pulled up on the beach, and I can hear waves slapping against the sterns. An endless blanket of stars gives the night sky a frosted look. The whitish band running across the heavens marks the Road of the Dead—the path taken by so many of my ancestors after their souls traveled to the western edge of the world and made the leap through the Seeing Hand and into the Sky World.

I wonder if I will ever follow in their footsteps, or if I even want to.

I reach up and rub my thin face, feeling the high cheekbones, the triangle of my nose, and point of my chin. I force myself to smile, and know that it makes my broad mouth into a rictus mindful of a death mask. Some call me a beautiful young woman. Who are they trying to fool?

For the moment, all that matters is my deep, burning anger. Call it an inferno between my souls. A hot, roaring, devouring kind of fire.

I stare out at the river, which is nothing more than an inky darkness in the night. I hear a fish splash, the croaking of a thousand frogs, and the whir of the night insects. Even through the pungent tang of the greasy puccoon-root mosquito repellent that I've slathered over my skin, I smell the musky scent of river, of willows, and cottonwoods along the bank.

I think of the Powers inherent to water—of the Tie Snakes who live in the river's depths, and Snapping Turtle, and the Underwater Panther. I think of the stories told by Albaamaha elders late at night. Of men who swam down into the depths and darkness and became Tie Snakes themselves.

Since the night I drank the nectar, I, too, have become a being of darkness. Ultimately, the nectar will be my weapon of revenge.

War Leader Strong Mussel barks a laugh—the sound of it as disturbing to me as the cracking of a wooden beam. I really hate that man. Him, and all the warriors that my father sent to "escort" me to my new home. To the husband I am promised to marry.

My father? He is White Water Moccasin of the Chief Clan, high minko, or supreme ruler, of the Sky Hand people. My mother is Evening Oak of the Raccoon Clan, who serves the people as high matron.

It is to be my "honor." Those are my mother and father's words. The verdict and order of my lineage and clan. Their ultimate betrayal after I came so close to escaping.

I still don't know how it went wrong. Just an accident of circumstance? Or Power inserting itself into my life?

Power can be such a capricious force, working for its own purposes. Changing lives. Playing with someone like me as if I were nothing but a toy dangled from a string. I'd made it. Escaped. Run away with young Straight Corn. We were free, taken in among the forest Albaamaha.

For those few months, we lived the rapture of our love, sharing laughter, smiles, hopes, and exploring our bodies. . . .

But I lose the thread of my thoughts. I need to concentrate on where I am and why. It's been twenty days now since leaving Split Sky City. I have been paddled up the Black Warrior River, carried across the portage and through the T'so lands, and down to the Tenasee River. From there my seemingly inexhaustible guards raced downriver to the Mother Water. After resting for a day at its confluence with the Father Water—and visiting with the passing Traders—we're heading up the great river.

This night we are camped below what are called the chains, a rocky constriction in the Father Water's channel. Immediately east and behind our small camp, a gray, moss-covered, sandstone bluff rises. Its base is choked with brush, its top forested with oak, maple, ash, and hickory trees.

Our camp is positioned on the sloping bank of the river—a narrow, sandy strip of low-terraced beaches left by the falling water lines. War Leader Strong Mussel has ordered my bed to be placed between the fire and the canoes, where it is illuminated by the crackling bonfire. The rest of the warriors surround me in a half circle, barring any chance of escape into the willows just up from the beach.

As if I could get away in the first place. Strong Mussel has tied a rawhide leash to my right ankle. He cleverly poured water onto the complicated knots, which caused them to shrink so tightly I'd need a couple of hands of time and the use of a pointed hardwood stick or a sliver of bone to work them loose. No fool, he checks my tether every night and again the next morning.

I could cut the strap with a sharp stone or a flake of bone, but they search the ground carefully before each camp. I never have less than three sets of eyes on me at any given time.

My people are the Sky Hand Moskogee. Masters of the raid and war. We are adept at taking and transporting desperate prisoners over long distances. Once upon a time, I took pride in that, having watched our victorious warriors returning from distant raids, parading their prisoners before them. Now I stare longingly at the darkness, wishing I was just beyond the fire's gleam. Out there, where I could vanish into the night and fade into nothingness.

My party of warriors might be called an "escort," and I might be the first daughter of White Water Moccasin, of the Chief Clan's ruling lineage. My uncle, who is mother's brother, or mosi, *might be the tishu minko, or second chief of the Sky Hand people. I might indeed be the second-most important woman in my people's world, but after what I have done, Father, Uncle, and Mother consider me a disgrace. A scandal to be dispensed with, eliminated, and forgotten. All of which means I* am *as desperate a prisoner as these veteran and blooded warriors have ever transported.*

I listen to an owl hooting up on the cliff, and the warriors tense, gazes shifting to the night. Owls are considered bad luck among my people. Especially when they are encountered by war parties. This, however, is a peaceful expedition. A fact signified by the White Arrow that Strong Mussel carries before him.

White is the color of peace and tranquility, of wisdom and restraint and harmony. None of which exists within my storming souls. I am red inside, the color of chaos, blood, conflict, and creation.

I am here because I fell in love with Straight Corn. They knew, of course. There were never any secrets in the high minko's palace. But they thought it a child's infatuation, as though I was enamored of a kind of sophisticated pet. The sort of girlish intrigue that would wane when I became a woman.

I'd passed my fifteenth summer when the cramps and bleeding started. Dutifully, they locked me away in the Women's House for the obligatory lectures on how to behave like a proper woman. I was told in detail how a woman's monthly discharge had to be restricted to the Women's House. That it would pollute a man's Power, sicken his souls, and contaminate his possessions. A boring and endless repetition of the things I'd grown up hearing. As if I hadn't had it pounded into me since I was a baby.

Then they'd given me my first woman's skirt with its carefully tied virgin's knot, fixed my hair, and paraded me out into public for my woman's feast. For two days my womanhood was celebrated: They dangled me before every high-ranking male in the territory as a potential wife. I was given the most lavish of gifts.

And then, the final night, as guests were leaving, and Uncle and Mother where slapping themselves on the back in celebration over the triumph, I sneaked out into the darkness, took Straight Corn by the hand, and we ran away together to start our new lives.

As I sit here by the river—surrounded by guards—and nurse the rage in my heart, I wonder where he is. Is he staring up at the same night sky? Is he, too, hearing a distant owl? Is he longing for me as much as I long for him?

I know they didn't catch him. I saw Fox Willow slip away before she was spotted. She would have warned the others, given them ample opportunity to ghost away into the forest before Uncle's warriors could be sent to comb the area.

Knowing how important Straight Corn is to the Albaamaha resistance, they'd do everything in their ability to keep him free. For that, at least, I can be thankful.

I may be promised in marriage to the Morning Star, but I am far from consigned to my fate. While I was in the forest, living with the Albaamaha and sharing Straight Corn's bed, I learned the ancient ways. Became an initiate into the ancient secrets of darkness and the dangerous arts.

For now I must bide my time. Strong Mussel understands intuitively. He knows I'm far from being defeated. Somewhere, some way, I will see my chance to get away. Can he and his warriors maintain their vigilance forever?

But eventually I will no longer be his concern. Once I become the Morning Star's wife, everything is going to change. The rage is going to burn free, and I will find my way back to Straight Corn. Assuming I can be clever enough and use the ancient arts to their fullest effect.

This one thing I swear on the blood of my ancestors: Straight Corn, I will find my way back to you no matter what the cost! And no one will stand in my way.

Willing the Power to rise within me, I close my eyes, find that place of strength deep in my core. I extend my arms to either side, stretching, feeling the slight breeze on my skin.

As I touch the Power, I send my call into the night. I feel them stirring, the strengthening of wings. Around me, the night stirs.

Yes, come to me! Bring the ancient Power.

I feel the first of them as they alight on my hands, forearms, and shoulders. Their wings caress my cheeks.

Why haven't I done this before?

A scream jerks me back to the now, and my eyes blink open.

More screams.

At first I can't make sense of the sight. The warriors are on their feet, arms flailing at a swarm of humming moths.

Is this my chance?

I get to my feet, take a step. Only to feel the leash pull tight.

Batting at the swarm of moths around us, Cloud Tassel—eyes wide with panic—nevertheless keeps hold of my tether.

The moths vanish into the night. But I smile. It will only be a matter of time.

One

Moths, fluttering in the night.

Swirling around her.

The silent beating of frantic wings felt instead of heard.

Teasing her skin.

Big moths. Their dancing passage caressed Clan Keeper Blue Heron's dreams throughout that night.

As if dusted by them, she came awake, her skin oddly dry and itching. She could still feel the soft puffs of their passage—as though the insects had fled but an instant before her eyes opened.

Morning light—gray and cool—filtered in from the narrow gaps where her thatch roof overhung the plastered bedroom walls.

She groaned. Images of blurred wings, of darting shapes, and the sweetly dangerous fragrance of narcotic-laced nectar lingered in the fringes of memory.

Pus and dung! What had possessed her? Moths, of all things? Granted, they were the sacred kind: humming moths. The big ones with yellow-and-black-striped abdomens. The kind that thrived in darkness and feasted on tobacco, datura, and nightshade—plants bursting with Spirit Power. Dangerous plants whose use granted visions and opened doors into the mirror realms of the Dead and the Underworld.

Blue Heron's heart beat with a sense of dread—as if the moths had borne tidings of some occult threat.

Shaken, she tossed her blanket to the side and sat up. Fitting her feet into woven-cord sandals, she reached across for her dress: a colorful thing decorated in chevron patterns of red, white, black, and yellow.

Getting control of herself, she attended to her toilet and ran a comb through her graying hair before knotting it into a bun and securing it with a copper pin that ended in an embossed plume.

What terrible thing is coming now?

Humming moths were creatures of the night. They hovered above datura blossoms, long tongues sucking the sweet nectar, dancing with Sister Datura's dulcet seduction. Feeding as they did on narcotic plants, it was said they carried messages to and fro between the disparate souls of the Dead.

Their larvae—large green caterpillars—greedily devoured the leaves of the deadly plants, seemingly immune to the toxins that would send a human being's souls drifting so far from their comatose body that they could never find their way back.

She stared up at the Four Winds carving behind her bed: the four-spiraled symbol of Cahokia's ruling clan. Across from her, brightly colored tapestries hung on the dividing wall. Below them were her intricately carved and inlaid storage boxes and baskets.

Blue Heron sighed—circling moths still clinging to the edges of her consciousness—and walked out into her palace's main room.

In the center of the mat-covered floor a cheery morning fire crackled and snapped sparks toward the high, thatch ceiling. Smooth Pebble—her cousin and political assistant—poked at the fire with a stick, rearranging coals under a ceramic pot. Smooth Pebble was berdache, a woman's soul born into a man's body. Well past the age of forty, her hair had started to gray and was worn in a bun held in place by a shell comb. Today she had dressed in a utilitarian gray skirt.

Dancing Sky, Blue Heron's new head of household, was dipping water from one of the jars that had been carried up from the creek. The woman—in her early fifties—had shared a long and checkered history with Blue Heron.

"Keeper? I take it you didn't sleep well?" Smooth Pebble asked as she took Blue Heron's measure. Rot it, the woman knew her too well.

"Nightmares," she muttered before sinking onto her litter where it rested atop its dais just behind the fire.

Smooth Pebble poured steaming black drink—a tea made from roasted yaupon holly leaves—into a cup and handed it to her before asking, "Hopefully it wasn't that accursed southern snake god."

Blue Heron smiled warily, then blew on her tea to cool it. They'd just avoided disaster—and who knew what kind of chaos—in the wake of a Mayan lord's arrival from distant Chichen Itza. He'd appeared in

Cahokia bearing a hideous snake god that had resided in a specially carved standard. She and Night Shadow Star had managed to destroy both the *kukul* and its human companion by the narrowest of margins.

"No snakes." She paused. "Humming moths."

Both Smooth Pebble and Dancing Sky studied her thoughtfully before Smooth Pebble asked, "You doing something with Spirit plants that I should know about?"

"I have enough nightmares just dealing with the plots, politics, assassins, and our beloved living god up on his mound."

At the mention of the living god, Dancing Sky made a face. She would remain a heretic, a disbeliever, until the day she died.

As humming moths and the Powers of the night preoccupied Blue Heron's thoughts, she fingered the scar on her throat where an assassin's knife had come within a whisker of ending her life.

"I don't have any idea why the creatures should have filled my dreams." She took another sip of tea.

"You are the Keeper of the Four Winds Clan," Dancing Sky replied. "Your family is tied to Power. It runs in your veins along with your blood."

Blue Heron smiled and stared into her tea. Power and insanity. The legacy of the Four Winds Clan.

"*Your line was always filled with madness,*" the old soul flier, Rides-the-Lightning, had told her once, "*It was made worse when Morning Star was reincarnated in Black Tail's body. The god's Power has carried down among his descendants in ways a human being's souls cannot contain.*"

The body that now hosted the living god had once belonged to her nephew, Chunkey Boy. His brother, Walking Smoke, had turned out to be an insane murderer. Blue Heron's niece, Night Shadow Star, ended up so possessed by Spirit Power that her souls spent half their time walking in the Underworld. And the youngest sister, Sun Wing, was a soul-broken woman who whispered to herself, broke out in tears, and rocked back and forth while she stared at nothingness through vacant eyes. So much for her brother's children.

As Blue Heron sipped her morning tea, she wondered. Power—the energy that infused Creation—permeated everything. Power might be likened to the Spiritual blood of existence. It flowed from the great two-headed eagle, *Hunga Ahuito*—who perched at the zenith of the domed sky—down through the descending levels of the Sky World, to the Earth, and then into the Underworld all the way to where Old-Woman-Who-Never-Dies sat beneath the World Tree's roots at the lowermost level of Creation.

And where do I fit in?

Having just popped into her head, the question startled her. She'd never given it much thought. Her world, her skills—as Cahokia's master spy—were in the tortuous mazes of human ambition, greed, passion, and desire. As the most feared woman in Cahokia, her tangled web of informants was second to none. While others spent their lives placating the Powers of Sky, Earth, and Underworld, she spent hers in the frantic quest to maintain her great city's peace and harmony. No matter how many heads she had to crack to do it.

The ways of Power—while she respected them—remained carefully removed to the sidelines of her life and concerns.

At least until humming moths infiltrated her dreams to leave her shaken and unnerved. A sign? Or just something she'd seen or overheard that stuck in her souls?

Moths or not, it was going to be a miserable day. Matrons and high chiefs from the Four Winds Houses that ruled districts across the great city were gathering. At the Four Winds Clan House they would assemble to pick a new clan matron, the supreme ruler for the entire Four Winds Clan.

Smooth Pebble—reading her thoughts—said, "The position has been left open since your sister Wind was appointed *tonka'tzi.* That was last spring. You know it has to be done."

Tonka'tzi, or the "Great Sky" was the titular head of state, the political leader of the great city, and subject only to the will of the Morning Star.

"Spit and blood, woman, don't I know it? It's just that the battle between the Houses to pick a new clan matron is going to be long and acrimonious—a miracle if it doesn't end in bloodshed and civil war."

She ran another swallow of yaupon over her tongue, enjoying the flavor, sensing the quickening of her blood as the tea hit her stomach.

Movement at the door interrupted her thoughts as String Runner appeared. In his early twenties, spare of frame, with a face like a wedge, he bowed low.

The sensation of unease returned with a passion. Phlegm and weak piss, if it wasn't one thing, it was another.

"Enter," she called, and the household went still as the lanky man crossed the great room and carefully dropped to his knees before the fire. His chin was so pointed she wondered if it would stick in the floor, but he only touched his forehead to the mat. Then he raised his head. His face was tattooed with the traditional pattern of the Surveyors' Society, done in lines and angles.

"String Runner," she greeted warily, "you're here early. Concerned about your missing Spirit Bundle?"

"Yes, Keeper. My master, High Line, is most unsettled. The Bundle is one of our most important possessions. To have it gone, who knows where, is not only disturbing, but dangerous."

She considered the deep-seated worry behind the young man's dark eyes. Not that she didn't have her own stake in the matter. The living god had sent his lop-jawed and scarred old war chief—a man called Five Fists—with a personal message that Morning Star would like the missing Bundle found and returned to the Surveyors' Society post haste.

One didn't disappoint the Morning Star. Not and remain healthy. Those who displeased the living god found themselves strapped into a wooden square on the Great Plaza while the crowd burned their naked bodies with fiery torches and cut little pieces of flesh from their bones.

"I am aware, String Runner. Believe me. All of my people are working on this."

"Hearing that relieves us, Clan Keeper. But it has been four days now. Surely there has been some word. Some clue." A flicker of panic glinted behind his eyes. "That anyone would desecrate our temple so? *Dare* to place hands on the Bundle, let alone remove it? It's just . . . well, unheard of. Not to mention the Power inherent in the Bundle. As it is, *when* it is restored, it will have to be purified. Ritually cleansed. The disruption that will cause . . ." He winced, unable to finish.

Blue Heron fingered the wattle of loose skin beneath her chin. "My agents have had their noses in every basket, box, and pack in the city. We've made some progress."

"You have?"

"Enough to determine that this wasn't just any theft. A dirt farmer didn't happen to wander into your temple, scratch under his arm pit, and pick up the nearest sacred bundle he happened upon. Had he, word would have gotten to us through the Earth Clans. This was a planned operation. Conducted by someone who knew exactly what they were after and how to get it. That being the case, it has narrowed the field of suspects considerably."

"Then, you know where it is?"

"We have an idea."

And by Piasa's swinging balls, if I'm wrong about this, it will mean my hide.

She told him, "One of my best people is attending to our most promising lead. Even as I speak."

"I would hope so. The Bundle can only be entrusted to someone of impeccable character. A pious person of outstanding virtue, celibacy, and restraint of bodily urges, a man without blemish. A reverent individual dedicated to circumspection and moral rectitude."

Blue Heron swallowed hard, hoping to hide her slight wince.

Two

The young slave girl belonged to a Quiz Quiz war leader named Sky Star. The Quiz Quiz were a people who lived far to the south along the Father Water, their Nation one of the many along the lower river. Seven Skull Shield considered them all to be barbarians.

The slave girl was no exception. She made the most peculiar and barbaric sounds, her throat swelling, eyes closed, as if it were all she could do to keep from crying out in ecstasy. The way she rocked her hips back and forth, Seven Skull Shield was half afraid she'd rip his shaft from its root. The bed frame beneath him creaked and strained in time to her wild gyrations.

Filling her lungs, she barely managed a half-strangled shriek as her body tensed, quivered, and pulsed. With one last shuddering breath, she collapsed onto his chest.

He lay on his back, blinking past her hair as he studied the soot-blackened poles that held up the thatch ceiling. The woman was panting on his chest as if she'd run her lungs out. He reached down and cupped her bare buttocks, thankful she couldn't see the relief on his face.

"First Woman take me," she whispered, voice heavy with southern accent. Not to mention that she was missing her front teeth. "I've never known thuch a fire of delight could burn through my body."

"Must be those southern men. Something about the heat. They just can't put enough stiff in their rods when it's all muggy, swampy, and sweaty all the time."

Her missing front teeth gave her a terrible lisp: "You make a thpell on me? Yeth?"

"Oh, no," Seven Skull Shield told her dismissively. "We do it this way all the time up here."

She raised up to look him in the eyes, her small pointed breasts tickling his chest. "I am yourth now. Forever. Let us go. I cannot thtay here. Not with him."

"He's your master. You belong to him. It's what a slave woman does."

She made a face, the grimace distorting the smudged tattoos on her cheeks. Her dark eyes gleamed in her wide face with its flat nose. Through her toothless lisp, she demanded, "Thteal me."

"You would turn me into a thief! Why did he bring you here?"

"I thpeak language." She gave a half shrug. "He need thomeone to tell him when priests not looking. Is better if that thomeone warm him bed, too, yeth?" She wiggled her hips suggestively.

"I'd say you're a pretty good bed warmer." He smacked her round buttocks. Considering the rest of her, they were her best attribute.

At that moment, a most vile stench rose to his nose. A smell that mingled rot, swamp gas, and liquefied feces all in one.

"Wath that?" the girl gasped, scrunching her nose, eyes squinting.

"Farts!" Seven Skull Shield snapped, reaching for a gourd container. He raised onto his other elbow, flinging the hollow gourd with all his might as a brindle-coated dog shot for the door and vanished outside.

"When did he sneak in?" Seven Skull Shield waved away the stench. "Caught the filthy beast chewing up a rotten duck carcass this morning. Knew I'd have to pay for it eventually."

"Why you keep thuch a vile dog?"

Seven Skull Shield grinned. "Let's just say I owe him."

She continued to study his eyes. "He kill you, you know?"

"Who? Farts? Just because of a few vile—"

"I mean *him.*" She tightened on his now limp shaft and jerked her head toward the temple next door. "For doing thith, Mathter kill me, too. We need to go. He be done with ritual . . . come thoon."

"I'm pretty hard to kill." Seven Skull Shield glanced around the room. It was small, containing only a couple of baskets and the bedding belonging to the Quiz Quiz chief. Dawn's pale light now streaked through the gaps around the door. Morning was coming. "But you're right. I need to go."

"Take me!" she almost cried out as he slipped from beneath her and felt around for his breechcloth. The frantic way she'd ripped it off and slung it to the side, it could be anywhere.

Seven Skull Shield narrowed an eye. "On one condition. This thing he took from the surveyors . . ."

"Is about tho big," she indicated by extending her arms. "And tho high."

"I need that."

She narrowed her eyes. "You came for that? Thath's why you take me to bed?"

"If you weren't you, I'd have never taken you to bed. You understand, don't you? You had to be just the way you are and no different. I wouldn't have had you any other way. If you hadn't been exactly yourself, you'd have been somebody else. And, well, you wouldn't have done what you just did."

He watched her eyes go vacant as she struggled to follow his meaning.

He gave her his most winning smile. Gods rot it, if she screamed, called out, the Quiz Quiz warriors would be pouring through that door in a flood. They were an unsympathetic lot, totally lacking in understanding, let alone a sense of humor. They'd no doubt take a dim view of him bedding their war chief's bed toy.

She fixed her gaze on his dangling manhood as she decided that whatever he'd said must have been complimentary. Then she gave him a gaping grin, which exposed where her owner had knocked out her front teeth.

"If I take you away from him, will you help me?" He finally found his breechcloth draped over the tip of a chunkey lance that had been braced against the wall.

"I help," she told him.

"Good. I need you to get dressed. Step out to the Avenue, and cry out in Quiz Quiz, 'I'm telling Morning Star what you've done!' "

"Thath's all?" she lisped.

"No. I need you to turn and run as soon as the first of Sky Star's warriors sees you. Run like the wind down the Avenue to the statues of the eagle guardians where they stand on either side. Turn right." He tapped her right arm. "This is your right. Just beyond the statues, you'll see a temple. Behind the temple is an altar. You understand altar?"

She nodded, worry building behind her eyes.

"Lift the wicker hatch in the back of the altar and climb inside. The Sky Star's warriors will run past. You wait there until I come get you. Not long. Maybe a couple of fingers of time."

"You promith?"

He gave her a wink. "You will be a free woman here in Cahokia. No more slavery. I give you my word." He pulled on his breechcloth, swirled his split-feather cloak around his shoulders, and nodded to the door. "The sooner you call and run, the sooner you're free."

She hesitated, and he could see her doubts swirling. "If you lie, I better off dead than go back wiss him."

She pulled on her plain brown skirt and—not daring to look back at him—hurried out the door.

Hot on her heels, Seven Skull Shield ducked around the small house and over to the rear of the larger council building. Farts was watching him warily, head down, ready to duck if Seven Skull Shield was going to throw anything more dangerous than an empty gourd.

Soft singing could be heard from inside the Council House. The building was round, domed, maybe ten paces in diameter and as tall in the center. It stood atop a low rectangular mound no higher than Seven Skull Shield's knee. Streamers of smoke ghosted up from the smoke hole atop the rounded roof and trailed off to the east.

Seven Skull Shield shot Farts a look as the dog followed him around the building's curve. He extended his hand in the flat-palmed "stay" gesture. The big brindle dog dropped, giving him an attentive stare through its odd eyes: one blue, the other brown. According to the tale, Farts was a pack dog and hunting beast bred by a distant people who lived high in the shining western mountains.

Crouched down, Seven Skull Shield hid just out of sight of the east-facing doorway. Behind him rose the sprawl of River Mounds City—a closely packed collection of warehouses, palaces, temples, workshops, and residences. No more than a stone's throw to the Council House's north lay the Avenue of the Sun, Cahokia's mighty east-west thoroughfare.

And there the slave girl stopped, staring back uneasily. She spread her arms in the universal "now what?" sign.

Seven Skull Shield cupped his hands around his mouth and pantomimed shouting.

A flash of understanding supplanted the confusion in her face, and she cupped her own hands and began shrieking in some foreign language.

The Singing inside the Council House went silent; and Seven Skull Shield ducked back as two men emerged, took one look at the slave girl, and started forward. She continued to shriek away in her incomprehensible tongue, even as Seven Skull Shield gave an energetic wave of the arm, hoping to get her moving.

She seemed to understand, spun on a heel, and pelted away down the dawn-grayed avenue.

The two men shouted—an action which drew still more of their companions from inside. In a long line the Quiz Quiz warriors charged out after the fleeing woman. Weirdly tattooed southern barbarians, they wore their long hair in an odd topknot; restricted atop the scalp, it rose in a pom that fell in all directions. Fabric breechcloths were wrapped at their loins, and they'd greased their sun-blackened bodies so that they glistened in the morning light.

No sooner had the last charged off in the woman's wake than Seven Skull Shield allowed himself a satisfied grin. "By Morning Star's cock and balls, I'm good!"

He hurried to the doorway, and ducked inside. A fire crackled and snapped in the central hearth; its light illuminated the room. In the rear—atop an inverted basket that served as an altar—rested an opened box: a beautiful thing crafted from red cedar. Its sides had been artfully carved in relief to depict Horned Serpent with his widespread wings, while circling around the beast were intertwined Tie Snakes. Pearls, shell, and copper had been inlaid into the wood.

A large gray blanket had been draped over some sort of big, rounded object that rested on the floor between the fire pit and the altar. Seven Skull Shield was on the verge of kicking it when he saw the missing surveyors' Bundle directly behind the open box and basket.

The Bundle looked just the way the Keeper had described it: a long, cylindrical bag of finely woven cloth dyed in red, yellow, black, and blue. Seven Skull Shield plucked it up, feeling its contents. Supposedly the Bundle contained surveying instruments: levels, poles, lengths of knotted cord, and curving, flat sections of wood. Which seemed to be what he was feeling. About four hands in diameter, and half as tall as he was, the Bundle was lighter than Seven Skull Shield had anticipated. He stuffed it under his left arm and turned.

As he did, the mysterious blanket-covered form on the floor rose, the blanket falling back to expose a big man who'd been on his knees, forehead pressed to the dirt in prayer. He had painted his face yellow with an inverted black V over his mouth. Sky Star. The Quiz Quiz war chief. No doubt about it. The pom of hair rising over his head flipped back as he jerked his chin forward. Anger quickly replaced surprise as he fixed on the heavy cloth bag under Seven Skull Shield's arm.

Whatever Sky Star said was in Quiz Quiz—a language mostly incomprehensible to Seven Skull Shield's ears. The intonation, however, was universal in its challenge. In a liquid move, the muscular man reached into the open box, lifting out an ornate brown-flint dagger. The piece was intricately flaked and as long as the war chief's forearm—the sort of knife used in ritual executions and sacrificial bloodletting.

Seven Skull Shield swallowed hard. Got a glance into the box, seeing a stuffed hawk, eagle talons, the top half of a human skull, carved human arm bones, a collection of hairy scalps.

He instinctively recognized both the box and contents: *War Medicine!*

So that's what they'd been doing. A ceremony to offer thanks to the sacred Quiz Quiz War Medicine Bundle. A demonstration of their appreciation for its Spiritual help as they snuck away with one of Cahokia's most prized possessions.

And it had worked. Right up to the point that Seven Skull Shield had wheedled his way into War Chief Sky Star's bed to diddle his prized slave girl.

The Quiz Quiz—smile predatory—was now Singing. A war song no doubt that called upon his personal Spirit Power and medicine. Sky Star had dropped into a crouch, eyes bright with intent, the knife held low as he sidestepped around the War Medicine box. Supple muscle slid beneath the warrior's greased skin. He moved like a leashed panther, coiled, deadly.

"Oh, rot and bother," Seven Skull Shield muttered, clutching the surveyors' Bundle before him. The old joy was rising deep in his chest. The howl was building down in his throat.

But if he succumbed, allowed himself the primal joy of the fight . . . ?

He's going to kill you!

How, then, could he get out of . . .

It came to him in a blink. He distracted the Quiz Quiz with a grin and a ribald wink—and, as if it were a box of vipers, gave the War Medicine box a swift kick. As the box crashed into the Quiz Quiz, its contents scattered onto the packed clay floor.

For an instant Sky Star froze, eyes wide, expression one of horror and disbelief.

Seven Skull Shield had already launched himself, knocked the man flat. Then he was running, clearing the fire with a flying leap. No sooner was he out the door than he heard a wailing shriek of rage from behind.

"Dog! Let's run!" he called over his shoulder, catching a glance of his big-boned and ugly beast as it sprang off the low mound, ears flapping, gaping jaws wide.

Feet hammering the clay, Seven Skull Shield shot across the Avenue—still mostly vacant this early in the morning—and charged between the warehouses across the way.

The shrieks of pursuit, however, kept getting louder.

What in the name of Piasa's swinging balls was wrong with the guy? If Sky Star were any kind of superstitious foreign barbarian, he should have stopped to pick up the sacred War Medicine contents—should have been petrified at the extent of the pollution and profane disrespect shown his most holy of holies.

Instead, the fool was following hard on Seven Skull Shield's heels.

Which was a problem. As Seven Skull Shield liked to say, he was built for strength, not for speed.

If he had one advantage? He knew River City Mounds like no other man alive. Rounding the corner of a shell warehouse, he grabbed a latrine screen and pulled it down behind him. Next he toppled a drying rack, then snagged a pestle from its mortar and chucked it, one-handed, over his shoulder and into the path of the raging Quiz Quiz.

Farts seemed to be having the time of his life, bounding and leaping at Seven Skull Shield's side. Figured that the silly dog hadn't a clue as to the serious nature of their predicament.

Nor did the Surveyors' Bundle, with its awkward bulk, do him any favors. The thing had him half off balance.

He rounded a stone-grinder's workshop, expecting a clear avenue between the buildings, and barely managed to keep from flying full-tilt into a post wall. As it was, he got a hand out to take most of the impact.

In disbelief, he turned, finding his way blocked by the buildings on either side. Wall-trench buildings were made this way. The four walls were prefabricated, lashed together, and dropped whole into trenches excavated into the ground. Then they could be tied together upright, plastered, and the roof put on. Build a house in a day. Quick, easy construction.

But some pus-sucking idiot had left one in the way.

Even as Seven Skull Shield turned, the Quiz Quiz was upon him. Instinctively he raised the Surveyors' Bundle just as Sky Star thrust with his long blade. Slanting morning sunlight glittered in its glassy ripples as the blade pierced the heavy cloth bag.

Seven Skull Shield bulled his way forward, bellowing, "You *maggot* mouth!" Then, filling his lungs, he howled, trying to back-heel the foreign warrior. "Piece of walking *shit! Cut me?* Slice *me* up?"

The Quiz Quiz, like a dancer, skipped back, pulling his blade free. A clever smile played at the man's painted lips, eyes alight with the thrill of battle. Quick as a copperhead, he skipped, darted, and dodged in attack.

Again Seven Skull Shield caught the blade with the Bundle, this time rolling it in his hands. Chert was razor sharp, but brittle. The long blade snapped in half before the Quiz Quiz could pull it back.

"Now it's different." Seven Skull Shield tossed the Bundle to the side, spreading his arms. "Come on, you worthless, penis-breathing, *shit-nosed bag of puke!*"

He and the Quiz Quiz slammed together, but to Seven Skull Shield's dismay, his grip slipped on the man's greased skin. Like a fish through fumbling fingers, the Quiz Quiz slithered out of Seven Skull Shield's grasp, flipped, and threw Seven Skull Shield flat on his back.

Howling like a mad man, Seven Skull Shield desperately tried to bat the Quiz Quiz's hands away as they locked on his throat. As inexorably as drying rawhide, the warrior's grip tightened, shutting off Seven Skull Shield's air.

"Foul pus-licking . . ." the words choked into nothingness. Lungs heaving, Seven Skull Shield clawed for the Quiz Quiz's face, but the man kept ducking away.

A roaring—like the pounding rapids of a great river—filled Seven Skull Shield's hearing. A circle of darkness seemed to close in around his vision. His heart beat like a stone hammer in his chest, and panic replaced his rage.

The Quiz Quiz hissed in delight, a madness filling his excited black eyes. His grimace was now a grin that distorted the yellow-and-black face paint into a hideous mask.

This . . . is . . . the . . . end.

The words seemed to float between Seven Skull Shield's souls. Their hazy softness, like fluffy down feathers . . .

A flicker of brindle-splotched brown flashed across his narrowing gaze. He felt the impact. As if from a distance, he heard the Quiz Quiz scream.

And then the crushing grip was gone; great cool drafts of air were filling his lungs. His vision cleared, and he struggled up to see Farts, his wide jaws clamped around the Quiz Quiz's muscular shoulder. Farts never did anything with finesse, let alone growling. He sounded more like a wounded bobcat than a dog as he savaged the screaming warrior's shoulder.

For his part, the Quiz Quiz now found himself unable to get a good hold on the dog. Each time he got a grasp, the beast's loose skin seemed to melt right out of his fingers. And for his part, Farts was wiggling and thrashing, his tail like a whip in the air.

Never one to lose an opportunity, Seven Skull Shield shook his head to clear it, and leaped onto the sprawled Quiz Quiz.

"Now let's see how you like it, you *vomit-sucking puddle of piss!*"

Even as he got his fingers around the warrior's neck, he heard as well as felt the man's bones snapping under Farts' mighty jaws.

This time the scream was choked in the Quiz Quiz's throat. Bouncing his full weight up and down, Seven Skull Shield tightened his grip, watching the foreign warrior's eyes flicker back and forth, turn dull, and roll back in his head. Then the body went limp.

"Farts, that's enough," he gasped as he rolled back onto his butt. The dog reluctantly turned loose of the mangled shoulder, a question in his blue and brown eyes.

"I do believe he'd a killed me," Seven Skull Shield rasped as he rubbed his sore throat.

A voice intruded as it cried, "What in Morning Star's name is going on here?" A pause. "Is that you, Seven Skull Shield?"

He looked up, surprised by the crowd that had collected in the narrow passage between the buildings. He coughed. Fought the urge to throw up. The man standing with hands on hips in the front of the crowd was Bone Hook, a Trader in fish from down at the canoe landing.

Seven Skull Shield staggered to his feet. Kicked the Quiz Quiz, who was now gasping for breath. As he gulped for air, he rasped, "Someone tie this human bag of shit up good and tight. There's a couple of nice pieces of copper for anyone who will help carry him to the Keeper's palace."

"Figured that was you fighting back here. You woke up half the neighborhood." Bone Hook, thin-boned and skinny as he was, looked like he'd just gotten out of bed. His oily black hair was standing on end. "Nobody howls like you do when you fight. But I got to ask: 'Penis breathing, shit-nosed puke?' I mean, can't you do any better than that?"

Seven Skull Shield slapped the man on the shoulder as one of the cord makers bound the Quiz Quiz up tight. The war chief managed a limp shriek as his bloody and ruined shoulder was pulled back.

"Actually, I thought it was pretty good." Seven Skull Shield retrieved the Surveyors' Bundle from where it had been tossed. "By the way, you still looking for a wife? I know where there's a very supple young Quiz Quiz girl hiding under an altar."

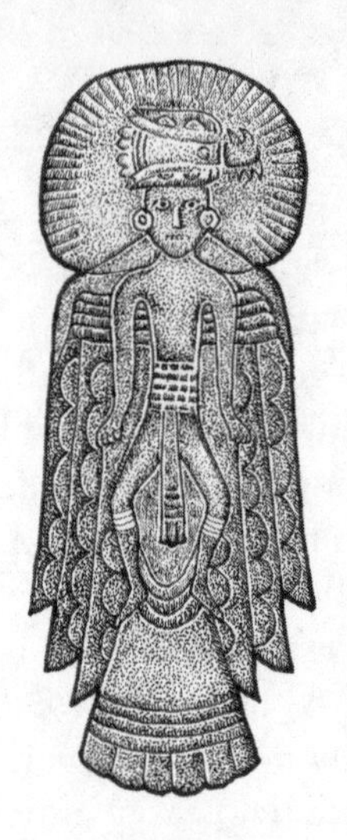

Three

The dreams had been terrifying. Afterimages—like shadows come to life—flickered through Night Shadow Star's memory when she snapped awake. Her heart was pounding as if she'd just run a hard day's distance from the Moon Mounds to her palace in the shadow of Morning Star's great mound.

And then she froze.

She wasn't alone in her bed. A warm body was pressed against hers; a man's soft breathing actually flicked strands of her long black hair where it lay across her chest.

Images of Thirteen Sacred Jaguar's body against hers triggered a terror that locked her muscles tight.

The man moved—went as tense as she—and hurriedly scrambled away. In the morning light, she recognized Fire Cat as he sat up from her bedding, his face pale. A look of panic glazed his eyes as he raised his hands defensively, fingers spread wide. "I'm sorry, Lady. I just . . . I didn't mean to fall asleep like that."

She drew a deep breath, remembering.

Yes, in the middle of the night. He'd awakened her from a particularly hideous nightmare where faceless women were chasing her through a distant conifer forest. As she had fled, the trees around her literally exploded in fire.

Fire Cat had appeared in her doorway, told her he would stand watch while she slept.

"It's all right," she told him, relief washing through her like a cool wave. "You did fine." A mere flicker of a smile crossed her lips. "Did I cry out again? Keep everyone awake?"

"No, Lady." He gave her a sheepish grin. "If you had, I wouldn't have been sleeping like a log. I'd have been awake. As I should have been. My apologies. It won't happen again."

She sat up, the blanket falling away, and pushed the thick wealth of her hair back over her shoulder. Gray morning light illuminated the carvings on her storage boxes and the patterns woven into the baskets where she kept her dresses. Her well pot stood atop its altar beyond the foot of the bed; and in a red-cedar cabinet she'd hung on her far wall rested the Tortoise Bundle.

Oh, I heard you. That was you tormenting my sleep.

Not that she didn't brew up enough nightmares of her own to fill her nights with panic, but the Tortoise Bundle kept sending fingers of Power to stroke her souls in the deep night.

"What do you want from me?" she couldn't help but cry.

"Lady?" Fire Cat asked, his expression wary.

She glanced at him, taking in the Red Wing Clan tattoos on his smooth face and strong cheeks. The muscles knotted around his full jaw. A red hunting shirt barely hid the corded strength in his arms and shoulders. By Piasa's misty breath, he was a handsome man. Tall and straight. His intelligent eyes were fixed levelly on hers.

"I was talking to the Tortoise Bundle."

As she said it, the tension faded from his taut body. A sign of the crystalline edge upon which they were both poised.

He glanced across the room to where the Bundle rested in its niche. "The nightmares are getting worse, Lady."

She reached up to rub her face, as if massaging it would restore some sense of the vitality that had gone missing from her life. "I am cursed, Fire Cat."

"You are chosen," he replied, as if that were all there was to it.

Her laughter came out as a bitter bark. "Look at me. Not even twenty. And what do I have to look back on?"

He glanced away, unwilling to answer, instead saying, "I'll see to your breakfast. Green Leaf should have the fire started and a stew warm."

Fire Cat started for the door, and she could see his slight limp, how he was still healing from the battle he'd fought against the hand-picked warriors Thirteen Sacred Jaguar had brought to Cahokia.

"Fire Cat?" she asked.

He turned, a deep and burning sorrow behind his eyes. "Yes, Lady?"

"If I were any other woman . . ."

A flicker of a smile tugged at his lips. "I understand, Lady. I really do."

Then he was gone.

Piasa had given her a choice. She could save her city, or Fire Cat.

And if I'd chosen him . . . ?

She drove it from her mind, climbing to her feet and opening one of her storage boxes in search of a skirt and cape.

As she dressed, she glanced at the Tortoise Bundle, looking so plain and dull in its scuffed, charred, and painted leather container. "I can't go on like this."

"*No, you can't,*" Piasa whispered.

In the corner of her eye she caught a flash of movement—a glimpse of yellow eyes, sleek gray hide, and rainbow wings. But when she stared full at the shadowed corner, he was gone.

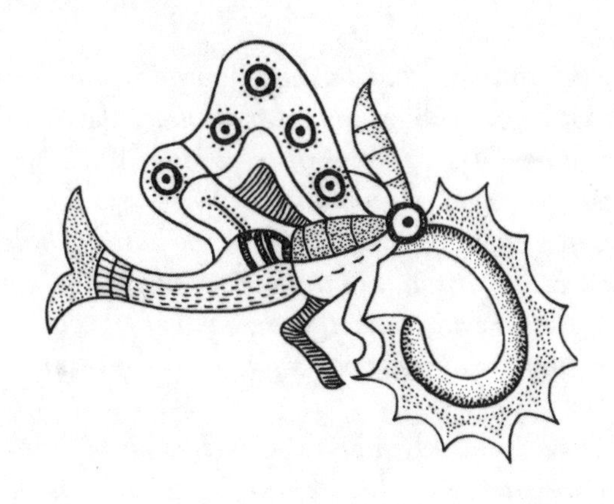

Into the Cauldron

I can tell that War Leader Strong Mussel suffers from a distinct feeling of unease as our small flotilla of canoes reaches its destination at Cahokia's bustling canoe landing. I can see it in the set of his jaw, the slight tightening around the corners of his eyes.

This is unusual. He's a man who unquestioningly believes in his own ability and personal Power. Who has stated that he fears nothing. I've always thought that to be the case.

The Chah'taw caught him once. Hung him in a wooden square and tortured him for several days before Strong Mussel could escape. The scars left from that torture pucker and bunch on his skin. While the war leader might not fear death, pain, or privation, I think the vast thronging hordes at the Cahokian waterfront intimidate him in a different way: This is like being cast loose in a churning and murky water—adrift where we cannot see the currents, threats, and dangers. A chaotic sea where we do not understand the rules or expectations.

I share his anxiety. I had heard—we all had—but never believed the stories about Cahokia. The political emissaries and priests who visited the Sky Hand had been explicit enough over the years. And it wasn't as if the notion of Morning Star being reincarnated into a human body wasn't credible—but the stories of the size and scope of Cahokia? Well, we imagined something a little bigger than Split Sky City. And now? To see River City Mounds, the incredible numbers of canoes and people thronging the landing, let alone the soaring heights of Evening Star Town across the river where it dominates the western bluff? Could humans really build such a place?

Hard enough just to think that this many people could be gathered in one locale! Had we not passed the teeming towns along the Tenasee, the Mother Water, and those crowding the banks of the Father Water south of Cahokia, a person might think that all of humanity crowded into this one spot.

For once, I am speechless as I try to take in the bustling landing. As hard as I work to demonstrate my disdain in front of Strong Mussel and his little band of warriors, my eyes are wide, and I know my expression is pinched. I can't stop from twisting my long braid into a tight knot—a trait I'm heir to when I'm overwhelmed.

The warriors, too, are clearly taken aback. It is visible in their darting eyes, in the slack set of their faces. They have no clue what to make of this place.

Well, good. Let them worry. They are getting no sympathy from me.

Even more discouraging, they have preened and painted themselves, dressed in their finest, each having called upon his personal medicine to make a grand impression upon our arrival. After all, they're the picked delegation of the lords of the south, of High Minko White Water Moccasin and Matron Evening Oak of Split Sky City. But as our canoe slides up onto the beach, no one so much as glances sideways at us. To the warriors' chagrin, we are ignored. Insignificant.

In the front of the canoe, Strong Mussel—decked out in his finery—holds the symbolic White Arrow before him. Painted in white, fletched with snowy egret feathers, the arrow symbolizes our arrival in peace. Among the Moskogee peoples it indicates the solemnity and importance of an emissary's mission.

No one gives Strong Mussel a second glance as they hurry on about their business.

I find this amusing. None of my captors had relished the "honor" of escorting their chief's despicable daughter to her fated marriage. Bringing me here meant several moons of time away from home, family, wives, and friends. The perils of distant travel, and no chance for the booty or fame that came with a raid.

The order was "Deliver the girl and come home."

Out of Strong Mussel's hearing, I'd heard a couple of the warriors mutter, "Assuming the Morning Star doesn't figure out he's being duped and kill us all."

They have such a high opinion of me.

For a long moment after Strong Mussel's canoe runs up on the beach, we just sit there like dolts. The other two canoes accompanying us have landed to either side.

"Who comes?" a skinny little man in a dirty breechcloth asks as he walks by. His question is in Trade pidgin accompanied by hand signs.

Strong Mussel replies the same way. "Her name is Whispering Dawn. Her father is White Water Moccasin, high minko of the Sky Hand Moskogee and ruler of Split Sky City. She is to marry the Morning Star."

The man shoots me a knowing glance, his thin face tattooed in designs I have never seen. Then he dismisses me with a shrug, saying, "Of course." And with no more ado, he walks off.

I blink. I know Strong Mussel does, too.

I was sent as a gift from the most powerful minko in the south to become the living god's bride! And the idiot just walks away?

"Who are these people?" Strong Mussel whispers to himself. Then, as if shaking himself awake, he steps out of the canoe. Shifting the White Arrow, he reaches down to offer me his hand.

"Shocking, don't you think?" I ask. "No one cares who you are." I stare around at all the canoes, hundreds of them, no . . . thousands. They line the shores or are paddled across the river to the landing below where Evening Star Town perches on its high bluff.

And the people! I see every style of dress imaginable. Their hair is done up, cut, braided, coiffed, and pinned in a bewildering array that defies description. The tattoos on their faces and arms are in alien patterns I've never seen. They crowd the landing, laughing, hawking Trade goods. Some perch on inverted canoes as they converse, others pack goods up the slope to the fantastic collection of thatch-roofed warehouses, temples, palaces, and ramadas. They could be a line of ants bent beneath their burdens. Dogs and children are everywhere. Someone plays flute music, and I hear a drum thumping in time. The air is filled with a cacophony of calls, laughter, and hawkers asking to Trade for food or trinkets.

"Hey, you!" Strong Mussel calls in Trade pidgin to a fellow standing beside a ramada. "We are Split Sky warriors. Which of these palaces up on the levy belongs to the Morning Star?"

The man plucks up a sack and hurries down to us. He looks Strong Mussel up and down as if he were a side of venison and says, "These are River House lands. Ruled by High Chief War Duck. Morning Star House is over east. Follow the Avenue of the Sun." He glances up at the sky. "You hurry, you might make it before sunset."

"Sunset?" Strong Mussel asks incredulously. "How far?"

"A half day's walk. A couple of hands' time if you run," the man tells Strong Mussel. Then he reaches into his sack, declaring, "I just happened to have a statue of Old-Woman-Who-Never-Dies! Carved of native Cahokian wood, by the finest of artisans. Blessed by the Morning Star himself. Consecrated in First Woman's temple by Matron Wind before she became the tonka'tzi. *Very rare."*

He sizes up Strong Mussel's ornamentation. "I could part with one for that fine swan-feather headdress you're wearing."

I gasp, swiveling my head in anticipation of Strong Mussel's explosion and the idiot Trader's imminent bloody demise. The war leader just stares wide-eyed, expression confused, as if he doesn't understand what he's heard.

Finally, through clamped jaws, he pinches out, "These are war *honors! Conferred upon me by the high minko!"*

The Trader, smiling happily, lifts the little statue to the light. The image depicts First Woman—called Old-Woman-Who-Never-Dies here in the north and among the Father Water Nations. She is sitting with her legs together, arms on her knees, her round head looking amused with a slight smile.

I make my plan. The moment Strong Mussel leaps upon the fool and starts beating the brains out of his skull, I'll take off running. Surely I can escape into this maze of people, hide, and easily elude my over-eager guard. They'll be distracted by the crowd as they rush to see the murder. I tense my muscles in anticipation of my chance.

"War Leader?" Cloud Tassel reads Strong Mussel's expression, steps up beside his superior, and places a hand on his arm. "We do not know the ways here. For all we know, in Cahokia swan-feather splays are Traded like shell beads."

The Trader, having quickly determined his error, backs a couple of steps away, bowing low and touching his forehead. "My apologies, my lord. I had no intention of causing offense."

The statue vanishes into the bag, to be replaced by a hand-sized relief carving of Morning Star, mace in hand, his forked-eyed face lifted, eagle wings spreading from his arms.

"This, my good foreign lords, is a one-of-a-kind creation. The image of Morning Star as his body-soul rose to the heavens at the end of the Beginning Times. Very Rare. Carved by one of the master carvers of Cahokia, in the shadow of the Morning Star's great temple in—"

"Be gone!*" Strong Mussel almost bellows, thrusting out a muscular arm and pointing.*

In the meantime I have sidled a couple of steps to the right. Checking my escape route from the corner of my eye, I figure I can charge off at an angle. If I can get around the ramada where an old woman is Trading bread loaves, I can dash across a fishing net where its owners were laying it out to fold up.

I just need to get to those buildings up the slope atop the levee. If they are as densely packed as the roofs indicate, I might be able to—

"Don't even think it." I jump when Cloud Tassel growls in my ear. How has he sneaked so close?

I shoot him a "who? me?" look of absolute innocence.

The Trader is scurrying away, shouting over his shoulder in a language I've never heard before.

Cloud Tassel, one eye on me, asks, "What next, my leader?"

I see the confusion in Strong Mussel's eyes. This is nothing like he expected. Here he is not a renowned war leader, but a stranger among a throng of strangers. Not the high minko's representative, but an unknown in the midst of countless vassals from distant Nations. He hasn't a clue about what to do next. People don't even notice the White Arrow that would garner instant attention anywhere in the Moskogee world, or among its enemies.

I laugh at the man's discomfiture. "Gather the things," I order, and point. "That creature said that the road to the Morning Star House, whatever that is, is up there. Let's get this over with."

"What's your sudden hurry?" Strong Mussel demands, suspicion replacing confusion.

"The sooner you've 'gifted' me to this Morning Star, the sooner I'm rid of your ugly faces. Or doesn't that make sense to you?"

I give him my sweetest smile and blink my eyes as if to beguile him.

In return, he glares his disdain, declaring, "It makes all the sense in the world, you disgusting little—" He bites off the rest, unable to say the words to a noble-born, no matter how much he hates me.

"Pack up!" he snaps at the warriors.

Within a couple of breaths, we're headed up the slope and through the throngs of people.

For the first time, I begin to fear the immensity of Cahokia. But with so many strangers, this will be an easy place in which to disappear.

Four

The Four Winds Clan House was an imposing structure. Situated west of Morning Star's great mound, and on the north side of the Avenue of the Sun, it dominated the southwest corner of the Four Winds Plaza. Each of the Houses maintained a local clan house in their own territory. They served as common ground where members of the Four Winds Clan could reside and meet. But this one—literally in the shadow of Morning Star's Great Mound—was the most prestigious. The seat of Four Winds authority and might.

To its great hall had been summoned the matrons from every House in Cahokia. Today they would begin the process of choosing a new clan matron to fill the seat vacated when Blue Heron's sister Wind became the *tonka'tzi*: the Great Sky, secular ruler of all Cahokia.

"I'd rather stick my hand into a basket full of water moccasins than go through this," Blue Heron muttered under her breath.

Dancing Sky, hearing, appeared amused. "Ah, the web you Four Winds weave. As if you didn't have enough enemies, you turn on each other."

"It's the matron's job to keep us from doing that very thing. The Houses may rule their districts, but the matron keeps them under control. With all the chaos let loose by the Itza's arrival, we've let it go for too long."

Dancing Sky gave her a bland smile before saying, "You know they've all been jockeying for position behind your back. Proposing marriages, spreading lies and subtle innuendo, hosting feasts, pageants, games, and exhibitions to promote their wealth and authority. Oh, sure, they present a benevolent public front, but behind it a ferment of intrigue, sabotage, threats, and accusations have nearly brought the Houses to war."

A situation that Blue Heron had barely managed to keep a step ahead of. "That would please you to no end, wouldn't it?"

Dancing Sky shrugged. "I am no fan of the Four Winds Clan, Keeper. For whatever reason, Power brought me down and destroyed everything I was. But I'm still Red Wing, and I've given you my word that I will serve you. Just know that you are walking into a hornet's nest."

Blue Heron nodded, studying her new housekeeper through narrowed eyes. That was the thing about the Red Wing. They valued their honor more than life itself.

"A hornet's nest indeed. But for the occasional tip sent my way from Evening Star House, even my network of informants wouldn't have been sufficient to keep this pot from boiling over. Thank the Spirits for that little dwarf of Columella's. His spies are almost as good as my own."

"Flat Stone Pipe," Dancing Sky said, placing the man. "I wonder what she sees in him? Columella used to be your worst enemy."

"Given recent events Columella and I have cobbled together a sort of alliance that benefits both sides." Blue Heron smiled. "We circle each other like two she-cougars, but we've actually come to like each other."

"You'd better hurry. They're over there. Waiting."

Blue Heron could almost feel the growing hostility radiating all the way from the Clan House where it stood diagonally across the Four Winds Plaza from her palace.

The plaza was reserved for the Four Winds Clan only, and boasted the second finest stickball and chunkey courts in the world after the Morning Star's. Here Dances and clan assemblies were held, as were feasts, weddings, and funerals.

Though she would have preferred to walk, the propriety of appearance dictated otherwise. As the Keeper, she didn't dare arrive on foot, or a moment too early.

She checked her appearance one last time in her polished copper mirror. Dancing Sky had painted her face in horizontal stripes of red and white. The pattern was unusual for a council session such as this, red being the color of disharmony, blood, and war, while white denoted wisdom and peace.

Let the rest of them chew on that for all the good it would do them.

Her hair was pulled into a severe bun at the back of her head and pinned with a dashing splay of white egret feathers imported from the south. She wore a vivid yellow-and-green cloak made of parakeet feathers. A fine dogbane-textile skirt hung at her waist and was embroidered with the Four Winds Clan spiral pattern. In her hand she carried her copper-clad staff of office.

"How do I look?"

Dancing Sky made a face. "All striped like that? I think you look confused."

Blue Heron shot the gray-haired woman a warning look. The Red Wing might be a captive and slave—but somehow her souls hadn't quite caught up to the reality of her new circumstances.

As Blue Heron was trying to decide what to do about it, Smooth Pebble interceded, saying, "I think they will get the point. At least, the smart ones will."

Which was exactly what Blue Heron had wanted to hear. Yes, this business of picking a new matron was important, but wisdom had to temper passion. If the House matrons allowed the red passion of emotion and self-interest to overwhelm the white of wisdom, they could precipitate disaster.

"How am I doing on time?"

"Late. I have your litter ready at the foot of the stairs," Dancing Sky called, having gone to the doorway to check.

The Red Wing's daughters, White Rain and Soft Moon, scrambled out of the way where they were leeching acorns as Blue Heron grabbed up her copper-clad staff of office and started across the floor.

White Rain was in her mid twenties, attractive and long limbed, with a delicately formed face. Soft Moon, though shorter, was all curves, full breasted, with a tiny waist and wide hips; she had just turned twenty. Men paid them way too much attention. After the defeat of Red Wing Town, the murder of their husbands and children, and subsequent slavery, the women didn't show much interest in returning.

"Wish me luck," Blue Heron growled. "I'm going to need it."

She stepped out onto her porch, staring across the avenue that separated her mound-top palace from Morning Star's great earthen pyramid. On the high palisade that surrounded the Morning Star's peak-roofed temple she could see a lone figure in one of the bastions. Sunlight glinted on polished copper as it illuminated the figure's headpiece. She couldn't distinguish features across the distance, but it could only be the Morning Star.

He seemed to be watching her, head cocked, feathered cloak shifting with the breeze.

Blue Heron walked forward to stand between the two carved Eagle guardian posts that dominated the head of her stairs. She met the Morning Star's distant gaze and bowed. Touched her forehead in acknowledgment and respect.

The Morning Star inclined his head slightly, but made no other response.

Spit and blood, why is he watching me?

A shiver ran down her back. One never knew with the Morning Star. More than once her life had hung by a thread, depending on his whim. In the living god's eyes, everyone was expendable—human life as transitory and ephemeral as the shadow cast by a passing cloud.

Inhuman.

But then, he was, after all, a reincarnated Spirit. A being not of this world, but of the Beginning Times. A spiritual essence called down from the ethereal realm to bring peace amidst a world of squabbling human beings. Given that, perhaps he saw people for what they really were.

She started down the staircase of squared logs set into the mound side, to where her litter waited on the beaten avenue. Smooth Pebble followed, and the litter bearers bowed in respect.

"To the Four Winds Clan House," Blue Heron ordered as she seated herself in the hide-padded chair.

Lifting the poles, her bearers swung her around and started southeast across the Four Winds Plaza. Quite a crowd had gathered at the chunkey courts. As her porters made their way around it, Blue Heron could see Fire Cat. His nearly naked body gleamed from a sheen of perspiration. Still-healing scars traced angry red lines over his skin as he ran forward, bent, and bowled his disc-shaped chunkey stone down the packed-clay court. Shifting his lance in midstride, his right arm went back, then flashed overhand as he cast his lance in pursuit of the fleeing stone.

The crowd whistled and cheered.

Sunlight glinted from the lance as it arced toward the fleeing target. The stone slowed, wobbled, and flopped on its side; an instant later the sharpened point of the lance embedded itself in the smooth clay no more than a couple of hands away.

More cheering from the crowd.

Blue Heron smiled with a deep satisfaction. After the capture of Red Wing Town, the heretic war chief, Fire Cat, had been brought to Cahokia—specifically so Night Shadow Star could torture him to death. Retaliation for the murder of her husband, Makes Three. Instead she'd cut Fire Cat's half-dead body down from the square, bound him to her service as a slave, and somehow saved Cahokia and herself.

"Interesting relationship they have," Blue Heron mused under her breath as she watched Fire Cat jog down the chunkey court to recover his lance and stone. In public both Night Shadow Star and Fire Cat maintained that they were implacable enemies forced together only by the machinations of Spirit Power. To Blue Heron's notion it was a miracle that two people who loved each other as much as they appeared to could even maintain such an illusion, let alone refuse to admit it to themselves.

Whatever the original cause of their association, somehow Fire Cat's epic chunkey skills, and Night Shadow Star's spooky Underworld ties, had saved the city from coming apart at the seams during the recent tenure of the Mayan lord. Night Shadow Star had ended up the richest woman in Cahokia as a consequence.

The irony wasn't subtle.

Blue Heron should have been on her way to the Four Winds Clan House to confirm Night Shadow Star as the new clan matron. She'd been groomed for the position since she was a girl. Had shown remarkable aptitude right up until her husband, Makes Three, had taken a Cahokian army north to defeat the Red Wing. When word of his death and the destruction of his army had come filtering down the river, Night Shadow Star had disintegrated into a grieving wreck. She'd surrendered herself to the narcotic embrace of Sister Datura, sending her dream-self to the Underworld in search of her dead husband's souls. In that dark underwater labyrinth—so she claimed—the Underwater Panther had seized her and devoured her. Made her into his creature: a woman of darkness and death.

To the Four Winds Clan, Night Shadow Star was now a sort of pariah. They were a Sky Clan whose Power, Spirit, and essence came from the celestial realms of *Hunga Ahuito.* Of the Sun, Moon, Stars, Clouds, Thunder, and Rain. Of the sacred birds including Eagle, Falcon, Hawk, and Heron.

Blue Heron pulled on the loose skin under her chin and frowned at the crowd at the base of the Four Winds Clan mound. They parted and made way for her arrival at the foot of the stairs leading up to the palace.

The clutter of litters, bearers, attendants, advisors, and observers shuffled, shoved, and shouted at each other in the process. But move they did. No one wanted to incite the Keeper's ire.

Blue Heron—conscious of the theater she was creating—sat for a moment after her litter had been lowered, a thoughtful frown on her face, eyes distant. The crowd went silent, as if waiting for some demonstration.

She rose to her feet, refusing to so much as glance at them. Attention on the stairs, she climbed in a slow and stately manner, her shining copper staff before her. Taking her time not only projected authority, it ensured she wasn't panting like a ragged dog when she reached the top. But the whispering crowd needn't know that.

"Ah, the games we play," she muttered as she reached the head of the stairs. Bowing her head, she touched her chin in respect as she passed between the two Eagle guardian posts. Immaculately carved, painted, and poised to strike, the Eagles glared at her through eyes of inset shell with black stone pupils.

The walkway to the veranda was lined with lower-status and younger relatives of the participants: sons, daughters, cousins, and nieces. For reasons of family politics, they had come in support of their House or lineage—or just to say they'd been present when the new clan matron was chosen.

As she passed, she heard the ripple of whispers run through them, "Look! It's Keeper Blue Heron!"

She kept her expression neutral, but let her eyes dart suspiciously from face to face—and was satisfied to see them cringe or quickly look away. Life was good when you still commanded respect.

Higher-status attendees crowded the veranda. Mostly older, these were siblings of the matrons and chiefs who waited inside. Blue Heron knew most of them by name—often because they were either old enemies, or allies, or both at the same time. These men and women were the real strength behind the Houses, the clan's people who did the work of running the districts, supervising the harvests, construction, work levies, and redistribution of food and goods. The ones who ensured the Earth clans maintained discipline, order, and peace among the always-volatile dirt farmers.

And, of course, it was among these individuals that the plots, schemes, and trouble were hatched. Their petty jealousies, ambitions, grievances, and feuds fueled the fires that kept Cahokia's cauldron at a slow boil. These were the people Blue Heron was tasked with keeping in line.

That she had done so was evident in the thinly veiled hostility, and oftentimes the outright anger, with which they viewed her approach. Oh, they tried to hide it with forced smiles and nods, but were she to ask, each could name a friend or relative that Blue Heron had contrived to exile to the colonies, or disgrace, or discredit, or even—on rare occasions—assassinate.

As they called out greetings, she nodded, acknowledging them by name and returning their pleasantries, making sure she paid attention to each, adding some platitude to which they replied with equal insincerity.

Then she stepped inside the doorway where a young woman announced, "Clan Keeper Blue Heron of the Morning Star House."

The din of conversation died down as the House matrons and high chiefs swiveled her direction.

"Hello, Green Chunkey," she greeted the corpulent high chief of Horned Serpent House. He gave her a smile, the fading serpent tattoos on his cheeks barely covered with a forked-eye motif in white paint.

"Keeper, good to see you on this auspicious day." He touched his chin with a fingertip, as if in the barest of acknowledgment.

Beside him stood Robin Wing, his sister and the Horned Serpent House clan matron. Unlike her brother, her long face and tall, thin body almost looked emaciated. She'd had a hard life, bearing seven children by a Deer Clan chief, all of whom miraculously had survived to adulthood.

"Good to see you, Keeper." Robin Wing gave her a wistful smile. "Should be an interesting couple of days."

"Should indeed," Blue Heron replied before moving on to High Chief War Duck, who ruled River House and its bustling port. He was a big man, thick-framed. What she'd call meaty. Over the course of his forty years, war and sport had left him with a scarred left cheek, a missing right eye, and a furtive if amused manner.

"Good to see you, Keeper," he told her, and pasted a smile across his square-jawed face.

"Keeping an eye on the Trade at the canoe landing, are you?"

"Of course. And forwarding a share of what my agents take from the chunkey courts to the Morning Star's warehouses. But then, you'd know all about that." He paused. "Haven't seen that Red Wing back recently. Saw him play a couple of times on my chunkey courts. He caused quite a stir, didn't he?"

"Night Shadow Star's servant has had enough to do just healing up from his combat with the Itza. I'll give him your regards when I see him next."

"Please do. Tell him he is welcome on my courts any time. Oh, and next time I see Crazy Frog, I shall give him your fondest regards," he added graciously.

Of course he knew she was dealing with Crazy Frog. An inveterate chunkey fanatic, gambler, and scoundrel, Crazy Frog had a finger in most of the illicit behavior on the waterfront. River City Mounds, after all, was the buzzing economic hive of Cahokia, situated as it was on the levee overlooking the canoe landing. At times a thousand canoes a day landed there, disgorging Trade from the saltwater gulf in the south clear up to the distant frozen north. From the far Shining Mountains in the west, and all the way to the eastern ocean. The place was a hive of Trade, manufacturing, gaming, entertainment, graft, and industry.

But it was Matron Round Pot—War Duck's younger sister and House matron—who was the brains behind keeping the froth that was River Mounds from foaming over. War Duck might have kept his one eye on the goings-on, but Round Pot quietly brokered the deals between the societies, workshops, temples, and warehouses. If anyone could be said to be the master of the compromise, it was Round Pot. War Duck, to his credit, was smart enough to follow her advice.

Now the woman—still in her late thirties—turned to Blue Heron, inclining her head respectfully. Like her brother, she was tall, thin, and graceful. The long black hair that she wore in an unfashionable braid hung down to her knees in the back. But for the oversized square jaw and flat nose she shared with her brother, she would have been an uncommonly beautiful woman.

"Keeper," she greeted. "Good to see you in health."

"And you, Matron. I hope your husband and children are well."

"Grass Seed has them downriver for the time being. It is my belief that all young people should learn the art of Trade. In addition, they need to see the southern Nations for themselves. Meet the chiefs. Learn something of the people they will eventually have to deal with."

"A wise policy." She paused. "Think you can find a compromise in this?" Blue Heron tilted her head to indicate the others.

Round Pot's dark eyes glistened. "Of course, Keeper. Dig deep enough and mutual interest can be found. If things become contentious, you might see the wisdom of suggesting that someone with the ability to broker deals take the matron's chair."

"Indeed." Figured that she'd offer herself. But then each of the House matrons was no doubt envisioning herself being seated in the matron's chair.

"Keeper." High Chief Wolverine interrupted her thoughts as he strode over and bowed at the waist; the move made his muscular body tense. Wolverine ruled North Star House and the district around Serpent Woman Town north of the oxbow lakes. Now he gave her a crooked smile, and amusement danced behind his hard brown eyes as he straightened. His face and arms were a weblike tangle of white scars from his years of trapping eagles, holding them by the legs, and plucking out feathers before releasing the birds back into the sky.

"Haven't heard from you recently. How are things in Serpent Woman Town?"

"Nice and quiet, Keeper. Just the way we like it. We've enjoyed a sense of relief since Spotted Wrist captured Red Wing Town. The fear has always been that if the Red Wing and their barbarian allies sneaked down the river, they'd attack us first hoping to gain a base to use against the Morning Star. The defeat of the Red Wing and the pacification of the north has removed any such notions among the barbarians."

"I'm glad the Morning Star's warriors have finally banished that worry. But sometimes I envy your location up north. The lakes provide a bit of buffer between your House and the rest of Cahokia."

"And sometimes that distance can be an impediment," Wolverine's sister, Matron Slender Fox, remarked as she stepped up beside him. Her long fingers tapped lightly on her pointed chin. She studied Blue Heron through languid brown eyes, a faint smile on her lips. As clan matron, she was known to be vindictive, often playing favorites. It was said that her husband—Cut Weasel of the Panther Clan—had given up on his attempt to keep other men out of her bed. Rumor had it that he stayed married to her only as a matter of status for his clan—and because on those occasions when she did call him to her bed, her performance made up for his humiliation.

Had Blue Heron her choice in the matter, she would rather have had Slender Fox's younger sister, Ripe Woman, as House matron. Ripe Woman was remarkably pragmatic and didn't let an itch in her sheath overload any vestige of good sense.

"Ready for me to become clan matron, Keeper?" Slender Fox asked in a saucy voice. " 'Bout time someone came down and put these southern Houses in order."

"I've heard your name being floated for the position. The decision will be thoroughly discussed. Though you'll need a bit of luck, I suspect."

"Too bad about Night Shadow Star, isn't it?" Slender Fox's expression had turned thoughtful. "Hard to think that someone who was so adept and gifted as a girl could choose such a disappointing change of direction as a woman. Must be difficult to stomach for those close to her."

Long practice kept Blue Heron from grinding her teeth. Not that she had that many left to grind. "Her palace still sits—literally—at the Morning Star's right hand. A circumstance apparently agreeable to both of them. Far be it from me to judge what Power does to people."

"No," Slender Fox said softly. "You just judge what people do to people."

A familiar voice called, "Rot and pus, Slender Fox! You never have had the sense Power gave a rock. Baiting the Keeper is like tapping a rattlesnake on the snout with a stick. Eventually you'll get bitten."

Matron Columella elbowed Slender Fox to the side, a finger jabbing at the woman's delicately shaped nose. "I still owe you for the time you lured Red Sturgeon into your bed. The poor man couldn't manage a stiff penis for months afterward. Said you shamed him."

Slender Fox shrugged. "He's *your* husband. Thought he might like to slip into a real woman's . . . Well, I can imagine what he's been dealing with all these years. No wonder you like *little* men. I hear Red Sturgeon's vanished off into the west somewhere."

Columella's eyes were thinning, her jaw going tight. Wolverine took his sister by the shoulder, easing her away and saying, "I think we should offer our respects to High Chief War Duck. He's been good to some of our nephews who think they have a future playing chunkey."

Even as he artfully sought to remove Slender Fox, the woman shot Columella a saucy wink.

Blue Heron placed a restraining hand on Columella's elbow as she started after her. "It's not worth it. That camp bitch hasn't a chance at the matron's chair. Doesn't matter what deals she's brokered with the other Houses. Between us . . . Well, enough said."

"Doesn't she *think*? Doesn't she *understand*?" Columella took a calming breath, her high breasts rising. She had piled her thick black hair atop the back of her head and secured it with a single feather-shaped copper pin. For a woman closing in on forty, she remained attractive and had kept her figure. In preparing for the council she had painted her face with the left side white, the right in red, as if she, too, worried how the meeting would proceed.

"You well know that she not only thinks, but understands. Charming opponents has never been Slender Fox's strength," Blue Heron told her. "She says and does what she does to mislead. To cause people to underestimate her. Then she finds a way around them, seeking to render them impotent in the process."

"Yes, yes, Flat Stone Pipe tells me the same. It's just that she infuriates me."

Blue Heron shot her a sidelong glance, lowering her voice. "I've heard nothing from Evening Star House. No strident voices calling for you to be clan matron. I thought—given Flat Stone Pipe's network of informers—that you'd have your rivals sorted out and made the subject of scandal and rumor by now."

Columella's calculating stare mixed with a slight shake of the head. "Walking Smoke dealt us too hard a blow. I barely kept Evening Star House together as it was. Might not have without your help. We're too weak. And then there's the matter of a debt we owe you. My children would be dead but for you and your thief. Now is not my time."

"So . . . who will you support?"

Columella's slight smile had an ironic turn. "Why . . . whoever offers me the best deal."

"*Tonka'tzi* Wind of the Morning Star House!" the woman at the door announced with enthusiasm.

Blue Heron bowed with the rest as they touched their foreheads in respect for the Great Sky. Wind stepped ceremoniously through the door.

Dressed to the hilt for the occasion, Wind barely nodded to the others as she strode past the fire and into the rear of the room. There, a dais had been raised and a litter placed atop it.

Tonka'tzi Wind seated herself, the copper-clad staff of office in her hands. Taking her time, she looked around the room. "Welcome matrons and high chiefs. Today we begin the important task of appointing a new clan matron. The best of us. To take up leadership of the Four Winds Clan, its lineages, and holdings."

She clapped her hands, voice raising. "Let us prepare ourselves. Bring the sacred pipe and the prepared black drink."

"It's going to be a long day," Blue Heron whispered from the corner of her mouth.

"As if Power were waiting on our every move and could care who we pick," Columella shot back in a murmur.

That was when Blue Heron noticed that Five Fists, the Morning Star's war chief, sat in the shadows beside the door. The man wasn't even Four Winds Clan and shouldn't have been allowed admittance in the first place. So, if he was here . . . ?

A bitter inevitability washed through her.

What was the Morning Star's game? And why was he interested in the deliberations?

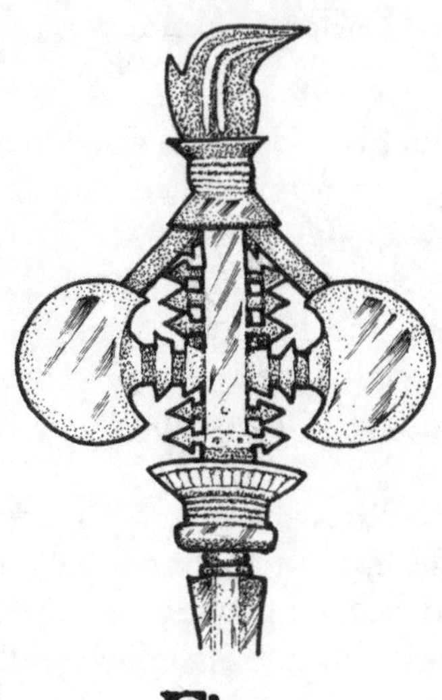

Five

She spread her firm thighs as wide as she could, and at the sight my shaft hardens like wood," Seven Skull Shield sang with gusto. *"With hands that are soft, she gives it a squeeze, which hammers my heart, and weakens my knees."*

He took a deep breath, belting out, *"My balls turn to jelly as I leap on her belly, then I slide it inside, for a magical ride."*

From across the yard, a voice sharp with disgust cried, "By Horned Serpent's crystal eyes, *will you shut up!*"

At the interruption, Seven Skull Shield looked across the small garden plot toward the weaver's workshop on the other side of Wooden Doll's ramada. The old woman who leaned around the corner of the structure might have been in her fifties, with a face wrinkled like an over-dried plum.

"What's the matter, don't you like good music?"

"I've heard dying geese that sounded better than that squalling. And yes, that foul woman sells her body, and yes, I enjoyed a good coupling in my younger days. But that don't mean I want *to hear about it!* Now shut up, or I'll have the local Hawk Clan chief send his warriors to *shut* you up! He knows me. Don't think he doesn't."

She was shaking her fist in anger, wild strands of gray hair floating about her head.

Seven Skull Shield looked down at Farts. "She knows the Hawk Clan chief in charge of this district. We quiver in terror."

Farts cocked his head, his floppy ears at the best attention they could muster. His blue and brown eyes watched with absolute concentration.

"I drove it in tight, much to my delight."

"Baa!" The crone reached down, straightened, and with all her might pitched a moldy squash rind in Seven Skull Shield's direction. From the feeble throw, she wasn't exactly going to make the opposing team tremble in a stickball match. Odd-shaped and curled as the rind was, it flew wide.

As if shot from a bow, Farts charged off to intercept it. Snatching the dried rind out of the air, he trotted back to Seven Skull Shield, flopped down on his belly, and began chewing the noxious thing into pieces. Pus and muck, the beast was going to have really hideous gas later in the day.

"Her eyes they went wide. In surprise she cried, 'No man ever filled me so fully inside!' "

The split-plank door opened to Wooden Doll's large house. A rather portly fellow—from somewhere down south if Seven Skull Shield was any judge of facial tattoos—gave him a disgusted look. As the man stepped out, he double-checked his breechcloth to make sure everything was tucked in. Reassured, he hurried off in the opposite direction from the weaver's.

"As I swirled it around, and she made a cooing sound. She arched her back. She purred. And I swear she quacked!"

Wooden Doll appeared in her doorway, wearing only a fine fabric skirt that clung to her hips. She leaned against the wall, a muscular calf extended. Crossing her arms under her full breasts, she cocked her head and sent long black hair spilling down her back. Through half-lidded eyes she studied him. As always, just the sight of her caused Seven Skull Shield's heart to do flip-flops.

"I swear"—he rose and lifted the box he'd been sitting on—"I thought that southerner was going to take all day. Funny thing, just this morning I was talking to a woman about how that muggy climate down there just wilts a man's—"

"He's a Pacaha subchief," she told him somewhat crossly. "I did my best to keep him relaxed, but your caterwauling beyond my door just put the poor man's nerves on edge."

"How'd you know it was me?"

Expression flat, she barely raised an eyebrow.

"Well, all right. Not just everyone has the rich tone of voice, let alone the finely rendered lyrics that seem to be Power's special gift."

He stopped in front of her. At his side Farts was panting, bits of moldy squash rind dotting his lolling tongue.

She glanced at the box. "That's a fine piece of work. Important?"

"Quiz Quiz War Medicine Bundle. *The* War Medicine."

Her eyes widened as she stepped back. "Seriously?"

"Yep."

"How'd you get it?"

"From the Quiz Quiz war chief."

She immediately looked over his shoulder as if expecting the Quiz Quiz to appear from between the buildings, blood and rage in his eyes, anxious to murder anyone who had the gall to steal his people's sacred medicine box.

"And where is this Quiz Quiz?"

"At Crazy Frog's. Waiting to be carried to the Keeper's where Blue Heron will doubtlessly ensure his few remaining days are most interesting and painful. The fool was sent here to steal one of the surveyors' sacred measuring Bundles." He jammed a thumb into his chest. "I got it back."

She gave a slight nod, lips quirking. "Why bring me the War Medicine box?" Her expression began to strain. "Oh, no. You wouldn't. Are you *insane*? You know the kind of Power invested in a thing like that?" She paused. "*Male* Power. Not the sort of thing a *woman* wants in her house."

"I think I broke it. The Power, I mean. When I kicked the box over and scattered all the sacred bits and bones and stuff on the floor. It sure didn't feel Powerful when I scooped up the pieces and tossed them back in the box."

"Even assuming you did, what do you want *me* to do with it?"

"Keep it for me. I want to see what happens. See, the Quiz Quiz sent the War Medicine to ensure that Sky Star—he's the war chief they picked—succeeded in stealing the Surveyors' Bundle. But I sort of disrupted their victory ceremony, got the Bundle back, captured Sky Star, and lifted the Quiz Quiz War Medicine. Which leaves me curious."

"You? Curious? Why does that worry me?" She made a face.

"So what are the Quiz Quiz going to do? Consider the War Medicine lost? Send a delegation to ask for it back? If they do, that's a lot of lost face and a public admission that they are really nothing more than a bunch of petty thieves. Which brings us to the next alternative: Will they try to quietly steal it back? But how can you steal it if you don't know where it is? Or, third, will they send an emissary to offer a ransom?"

"You still haven't said why you want to leave it with me?"

"As of this moment, only two people know where the medicine box is: you and me."

"I suppose you could stuff it back in storage in the hut out back. Pile blankets and robes on top of it." She shot him a furtive glance. "What if they never come looking for it? Make a new War Medicine in the meantime?"

"Eventually you Trade it off to the highest bidder. Pacaha, Quigualtam, Casqui, Caddo—there's a slew of Nations down south who'd bid a bundle for the Quiz Quiz's old War Medicine. You'll be rich."

"I'm already rich. What do you get out of it?"

He gave her his best grin. "Why don't we step inside, close the door behind us, and you drop that skirt while I try to figure out what I want in return?"

She blinked—as if to clear her thoughts—shook her head, and sighed. "I thought you had to get your captured Quiz Quiz to the Keeper?"

He glanced up at the sun. "I've got a little over a hand of time before Crazy Frog's people will be ready to move him."

"Skull, you absolutely amaze me." She reached out and took him by the hand. Slamming the door in Farts' face, she pulled the tie loose that let her skirt drop before he was halfway to her bed.

Six

The squadron second at the front of Night Shadow Star's guard called, "Make way! Make way for Lady Night Shadow Star!" as her litter was carried down the avenue along the western side of the Great Plaza.

Dressed in a wood-and-leather cuirass, a hardened leather helmet on his head, copper-bitted war club in hand, Fire Cat strode along immediately behind his lady's porters, guarding her back.

As they proceeded along the plaza's margins, it was as if a wave of silence rolled along with them. People who had been chatting, playing flutes, thumping drums, or cheering the stickball game in progress on the plaza's beaten grass went silent. They turned, watching in awe as Night Shadow Star's party passed, some pointing, others whispering to their companions.

Fire Cat—having been one of the most renowned war chiefs in the north as well as a Red Wing noble—was used to being the center of attention. And Night Shadow Star, sister to the Morning Star, the *tonka'tzi*'s niece, was no less a spectacle. She had, after all, been married to the Itza lord known as Thirteen Sacred Jaguar, and claimed to be possessed by Piasa's Spirit.

It left Fire Cat with a sour sensation in his gut that he'd created his own notoriety by winning one of the most contentious chunkey matches in Cahokian history. He had bet his life against that of a Natchez Little Sun. Not only had Fire Cat won by a point, but when he'd beheaded the Natchez chief, he'd won an incredible fortune that had been wagered on the game. Then he'd gone on to kill Thirteen Sacred Jaguar's dreaded Itza warriors in individual combat—a feat from which he was still healing.

Things just go from complicated to ever more complex.

The thought wedged itself in between his souls as he shot wary glances at the throngs of people they passed. Traders and hawkers had come from all around Cahokia's outlying areas—many having left home long before dawn to carry their goods to the Great Plaza in time to get a prime location.

Some displayed their wares on spread blankets; others had small stalls or ramadas beneath which tables had been placed. Every item under Cahokia's sun could be found: bread, soups, and baked fish; bundles of wood, planks, shocks of thatch, and beams; shell, wood, and ceramic beads; raw copper nuggets; wooden statuary; ceramic pots, bowls, and vessels; sacks of corn, beans, and squash; bows, arrows, paddles; marine and freshwater shells; chert hoes, nodules of chert and quartzite; textiles of all weaves and colors; feathers from the far south; furs from the far north, and every other conceivable thing.

Even the stickball game had slowed to a stop, the players panting as trickles of sweat ran down their hot skin. The look in their eyes was sobering, awe-filled, faces awash with wonder.

"Cahokia!" one of the stickball players shouted, raising his fist in salute.

"Cahokia! Cahokia! Cahokia!" the rest of the players began to chant, only to have the crowd take it up.

In her litter, Night Shadow Star sat up straighter; her head was regal given the way her long black hair was pinned with a polished copper headpiece. She turned, her gaze taking in the players. Then, raising her muscular arm, she knotted her fist and cried, *"Cahokia!"*

The crowd burst into cheers.

Where he marched behind, Fire Cat allowed himself a slight smile. The city hadn't been this unified since old Black Tail first bilked the people into believing he was the Morning Star incarnate. And even then there had been doubters.

It wouldn't last. Even as the crowds shouted, the Four Winds Clan leaders were locked head-to-head in a battle of wits and backstabbing while they sought to agree on a new clan matron. As in all of politics, there would be winners and losers, the latter smarting and vowing to wreak havoc on those who had thwarted their ambitions.

"Make way!" the squadron second continued to call as they rounded the plaza's southwestern corner and turned east. After passing the tall, conical Earth Clans burial mound, the escorting warriors cleared away the crowd that had gathered before Rides-the-Lightning's high temple.

Night Shadow Star's porters lowered her litter, stepping back to allow Fire Cat to offer her his hand. Not that she needed help getting to her feet, but it was one of the few times he was allowed to touch her.

As she rose, she met his eyes, smiling, as if in conspiratorial understanding. She was a tall woman, full-busted, muscular from her addiction to stickball, and supple. In defiance of her clan, she'd painted a three-forked design around her eyes to denote her allegiance to her Underworld master. A black skirt embroidered with interlaced white Tie Snakes hung from her waist, and she'd tied a cardinal-and-bunting feather cloak at her throat.

"Lady? Are you all right?" He could see the worry behind her dark eyes. In her other hand she carried the sack-wrapped Bundle.

"I'll know soon, won't I, Red Wing?" And with that she lifted her chin and turned to the long stairway that led up to Rides-the-Lightning's temple.

Fire Cat took a final quick look, seeing the people who now gathered to watch from behind the score of warriors. They kept calling out greetings and questions, and some were whistling.

Fire Cat placed his sandaled feet on the steps and trotted up after Night Shadow Star.

At the top he nodded respectfully to the two-headed Eagle guardian posts meant to invoke *Hunga Ahuito*'s Power and protection.

The temple that covered the mound's flat top was large, its walls plastered and painted, the bottom half red, the top white. A high-peaked thatch roof shot up like a wedge, its ridge pole adorned with carvings of Raccoon, Spider, and Buzzard, the couriers of souls to the Afterlife.

At the door stood the ancient Earth Clan's shaman called Rides-the-Lightning: a Spirit elder known to send his souls out of body and into the Land of the Dead in search of the lost and forlorn. The old soul flier stood with his back bent, limbs withered. Face, arms, chest, and stomach, his skin was a mass of wrinkles. Long-faded tattoos defied identification. Fleshy and round, the man's nose suggested a mushroom stuck to his face. The wispy thin hair on his head was the same white as his opaque and blind eyes.

Behind him stood four of his acolytes—all younger men in their forties and fifties. In any other company they would have looked old themselves, but in contrast to Rides-the-Lightning they appeared positively youthful.

"Lady Night Shadow Star," he greeted with a slight, toothless lisp. "What brings you to my door?"

"I would speak with you, Elder. Hear your counsel."

"Ah, enter. I have black drink ready." He turned, leading the way from long familiarity.

Following at Night Shadow Star's back, Fire Cat stepped into the warm interior. As he did, one of the priests closed the carved plank door, shutting out the light.

A fire crackled and snapped in the large central hearth, and as Fire Cat's eyes adjusted, he could see the intricately carved sleeping benches along the walls. In the rear hung a remarkable carving of the Morning Star in the Beginning Times; it depicted the hero as he carried his father's head away from the fabled Underworld courts where the giants once played chunkey.

Net bags filled with herbs and Power plants dangled from the willow-staves and soot-stained rafters. On the walls above the benches, masks had been hung depicting Spirit Wolf, Bear, Falcon, Ivory-billed Woodpecker, Antlered Deer, Buffalo Above, and Panther. They seemed to stare at Fire Cat through their hollow black eyes, as though judging the value of his souls.

The space beneath the sleeping benches was crammed tight with carved wooden boxes, intricately woven baskets, folded fabrics, and large engraved ceramic pots.

A shiver ran across Fire Cat's shoulders. The place reeked of barely contained Power, and he wasn't sure that Night Shadow Star wasn't feeling something in response. She held the leather sack with the Tortoise Bundle farther and farther from her body, as though the sack contained something increasingly hot and dangerous.

Rides-the-Lightning seated himself on a wooden box to one side of the fire and gestured to the mat-covered floor.

Night Shadow Star carefully seated herself, taking special care of the Bundle. Fire Cat dropped to a crouch behind her, wary eyes on the priests as they retreated to the corners of the room. A young boy carefully dipped sacred black drink from a steaming pot behind the fire. He offered it first to Rides-the-Lightning, who drank, and then passed the large shell cup to Night Shadow Star.

After she had chugged down a goodly portion, she handed the cup to Fire Cat. He placed the rim to his lips and drained the last of the black drink, surprised that she'd included him.

Through it all Rides-the-Lightning sat motionless, his white-blind eyes fixed on a distance only his souls could see.

As Fire Cat handed the empty cup to the youth, the old soul flier said, "I had hoped you would come to see me. The Tortoise Bundle is a

Powerful being, is it not? I've barely had a night's peace since Lichen gave it to you."

"The voices, the images, peculiar visions . . . They jumble in my head the moment I close my eyes. Strange places. Sometimes desolate and rocky. Other times jagged high mountains. Fields of snow and odd-looking people." She shook her head. "Why are you not sleeping, Elder?"

"I can hear the racket all the way over here, girl. Whisperings, laughter, warnings called out. Threats and pleas. And those visions? They're memories. Things the Bundle and its keepers have seen. No wonder Piasa is irritated—the Bundle is getting in his way."

"But they are both tied to the Underworld. To Old-Woman-Who-Never-Dies. Her Power."

A faint smile exposed his pink gums. "Does Evening Star House not feud with Horned Serpent House? Or River House with North Star House? Yet they are all Four Winds Clan."

"But . . ."

"Lady, Bundles are beings. They live their own lives, with their own personalities. Have their own Power. Bundles are collections of diverse and unique objects, each with its own character, that create a greater personality. A concentration of Spiritual essences that interact in a way that serves some particular purpose. A way of modifying, and to some extent controlling, the Spiritual world around us."

Fire Cat noticed the tightening at the corners of Night Shadow Star's lips before she said, "I *know* that, Elder."

"Ah, but do you *understand* that which you claim to know? For example, did you know that one of the reasons the Tortoise Bundle is upset is because it needs to be fed?"

Fire Cat glanced down at the sack in which the Bundle now rested. Somehow he'd never considered the ritual care of a Bundle to be "feeding."

"I gave it its own place of honor, a shelf opposite my well pot." Night Shadow Star, too, was now fixed on the sack.

"Have you smoked it in sweetgrass and sage? Offered it corn or meat? Treated it as if it were alive? Like a valued companion?"

"I've shown it great respect."

Rides-the-Lightning said dryly, "For that, at least, it is thankful."

"All right, I will do better." She placed hands to the sides of her head, eyes pinched closed. "If it will just let me sleep!"

"The Bundle *and* Piasa," Fire Cat interjected. When Rides-the-Lightning turned sightless eyes on him, he added, "She cries out to Piasa in her dreams as well. It's as though he's torturing her."

"I don't see him as much," she said. "The flickers at the edge of my vision, his whispering in my ear. It's changed. I can feel the hostility. As if I've done something wrong. And I haven't! I've done everything Piasa has ever asked of me. Defeated Walking Smoke . . . destroyed the Itza!"

"He's jealous," Rides-the-Lightning told her.

"Jealous?" Fire Cat asked. "But he's a . . ."

"Of course, young warrior." A knowing smile bent the old shaman's thin brown lips. "To have devoured Lady Night Shadow Star's souls and made them his own is one of his greatest achievements. He controls the most Powerful woman in Cahokia. And now, suddenly, a dying priestess shoves the Tortoise Bundle into her hands? A Powerful interloper who vies for the lady's affection and attention?"

"Blessed Spirits, she's caught between them?" Fire Cat wondered, concerned gaze turning to Night Shadow Star. She looked pale, oddly frail.

"I didn't ask for this," she whispered.

"No," Rides-the-Lightning responded, "and I'm afraid I have more unsettling news. Just sitting here, I've been listening to the Tortoise Bundle. It's not sure that it likes you."

"What does that mean?" Fire Cat asked.

"This is just the beginning." Rides-the-Lightning's opaque white eyes might have been fixed on a distant place as he said, "To be caught between two Spirit Powers that don't get along is bad enough, but if one of them decides it really doesn't like you? Well, warrior, it will torture you in insidious ways that will drive you to madness and a terrible death."

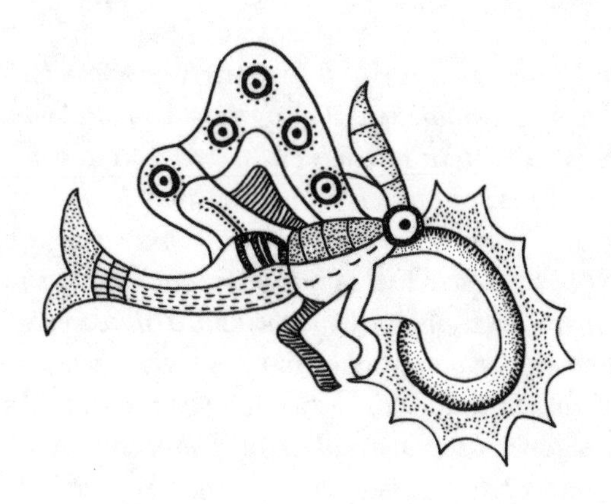

Two Sticks

I'm still dazed by Cahokia. By its vastness. We have been walking since midday, and not making very good time. The Avenue of the Sun is full of marvels, things we can't help but stop and stare at. It's not just the temples, but the exquisite guardian posts that mark the edge of River Mounds City. We're constantly scurrying out of the way as gangs of men shouldering great logs come barreling down the Avenue. Then there are the stone carriers, muscular men bearing litters piled with sandstone slabs, or harder boiling stones of granite, schist, or cobbles I can't identify. Then come lines of people bent under burden baskets filled with corn, maygrass seed, goosefoot, and little barley. And others packing smoked carcasses of deer, turkey, and dried fish.

When we finally make it to Black Tail's tomb, we file off and stare at the huge earthen monument where the first host of the living god was buried. It's a ridge-like mound with a large, ornate charnel house at its base. People throng around the bottom of the mound, praying, offering flowers and painted sticks topped with feathers. Here and there are bowls filled with food that have been left for the hero's sustenance in the afterworld.

"Do you believe this?" I ask cautiously.

Cloud Tassel sucks on his lips, then shakes his head. "I wouldn't have. But to see so many people worshipping a man so long dead? And look at the size of that mound! Just for one man?"

"Not just a man," a voice says in passable Moskogee.

I turn and see a fellow—perhaps in his late thirties—with Albaamaha tattoos. He has his hair pinned back with wooden skewers. A simple breechcloth is wound around his lean hips, and a coarsely woven cloak hangs over his muscular shoulders. I would describe his face as bold. A wicked scar runs down the left cheek. The man's nose is like a wedge, and what look like Albaamaha Dogbane Clan tattoos line his forehead and cheeks.

He steps forward, a grim smile on his lips, something impenetrable behind his hard eyes. "This is Black Tail's tomb," he continues. "Built in honor of the man who first surrendered his body for the reincarnated god."

He gestures toward the tomb. "Not only was the miracle performed right here, on this spot, but when Black Tail's body finally gave out, it was on this same soil that the Morning Star's essence was called into Chunkey Boy's body, ensuring the living god's continued presence here among men." A pause. "That huge mound holds the bodies of more than a hundred young women, noble-born prisoners, and captives. All sacrificed as payment in blood for the miracle of the Morning Star's resurrection."

"So," I ask, "do you believe he's really the Morning Star of legend? Recalled to earth and given a human body?"

"Since I first came to Cahokia, Lady, I have seen many miracles. This whole place, all of it, had you come here two generations ago, would have been a no-man's land. You would have found the various towns racked with war as Gizis, Jenos, Tharon, Petaga, and Black Tail fought among themselves. Then the Four Winds requickened the Morning Star's Spirit in Black Tail's body. In the wake of the miracle, peace was made. A peace which has lasted for two generations.

"The Four Winds Clan was given domination, and the Morning Star decreed that old Cahokia be flattened, leveled, and surveyors brought in to make the city a reflection of the Sky World itself. This they did, using measurements based either on eleven or twenty-two times the sacred length of measure. The angles were precisely calculated against the movements of the sacred moon. Everything was aligned to the maximums and minimums in the moon's eighteen-point-six-year cycle across the sky. A recreation of the cosmos. A living map upon which the movement of moon, stars, sun, and heavens can be plotted and followed."

"Sounds a bit presumptuous." Strong Mussel fingers the White Arrow.

The Albaamaha's answering smile is almost condescending as he says, "No more so than Split Sky City, War Leader. It, too, is laid out as a reflection of the Moskogee world. Or so I am told."

"Who are you?" Strong Mussel demands. "Name your clan and tell me your business here."

"I am called Two Sticks, Chikosi. *Of the Dogbane Clan. My business here is my own." He raises his hand, expression hardening. "And you are far from Split Sky City at a place holy to the Morning Star and the Four Winds Clan. Do not allow your arrogance to lead you into a mistake that would get you, and your friends here, hung in a Cahokian square."*

At the term Chikosi, even I bristle. Derogatory, it means "auntie's people."

"You know what we do to mouthy Albaamaha?" Strong Mussel takes a step forward.

Two Sticks inclines his head toward a couple of Cahokian warriors who lounge before the charnel house. "They have no doubt noted that I've been most courteous and done nothing to offer you offense. While you might easily dispose of them, should they step over to see what the ruckus is about, it will be difficult to extricate yourselves and flee. Dressed as you are, you will find it impossible to disappear into the crowds. And whatever your mission is, it certainly would be disrupted."

It pleases something deep down inside me as I watch Strong Mussel literally vibrate with anger. I have never liked the war leader, and I do have a certain tolerance for Albaamaha, being married to one. I decide to give Two Sticks the benefit of the doubt. Even if he called me a Chikosi.

"Morning Star's peace be upon you," Two Sticks says, flicking his fingers at his chin in a mockery of the Cahokian gesture of respect.

I raise my hand to wave goodbye. That's when he catches a glimpse of the tattoo. The one on the back of my hand. I see startled recognition, and he pauses, frowning as he studies me.

Could he know? It is an Albaamaha design, of course. But I don't see a similar tattoo on his hand to indicate he is an initiate.

"Go on." Strong Mussel waves him away. "Go bother someone else."

Two Sticks' black eyes are in a stew. "What is your purpose with the young lady?"

"She is to be wed to the Morning Star," Cloud Tassel barks. "Not that it is any concern of yours."

I can see the fermenting thoughts behind Two Sticks' eyes. "You asked my business here, War Leader? I came originally as a Trader. I have stayed on over the years, performing services as a means of Trade. Sometimes it is translation, other times I provide information, and I do odd jobs. I also act as a guide and interpreter for parties such as yours."

"We don't need a guide or interpreter." Strong Mussel lifts the White Arrow as if it explains everything.

"Ah, of course." Two Sticks inclines his head indulgently. "To whom will you present your White Arrow?"

"To the Morning Star himself."

"No, you won't. When you arrive at foot of the Morning Star's mound tomorrow, you will find a crowd waiting to see if they can obtain an audience with the Morning Star. You will be but one of hundreds. If you are lucky, one of the young men will recognize the importance of the White Arrow, and he will send someone to find someone who can speak Moskogee to ask the nature of your visit. He will then carry that message to the tonka'tzi. *Who, for the time being,*

is buried in talks with the other Four Winds Houses to name a new clan matron. So it might take a couple more days before she finds the time to receive you."

"But this is Whispering Dawn! Daughter of High Minko White Water Moccasin and Matron Evening Oak! Offered as a bride! To marry *the Morning Star!"*

I am wondering if Strong Mussel is going to burst his throat, so tense are his muscles. The veins are standing out like ropes from the side of his neck.

"Have you any idea how many women have been married to the Morning Star? They number in the tens. Did you send a messenger in advance to give Tonka'tzi Wind notice of your impending arrival?"

"No. I carry the White Arrow!"

Two Sticks twitches his lips, amusement writ large on his scarred face. "My inclination is to leave you to your own devices and derive my amusement from afar. However, I find myself in need of Trade these days. Seems I made a bad wager on a most important chunkey game a while back. And though I don't particularly like working for—"

"We can take care of ourselves, Albaamaha." Strong Mussel asserts.

"Can you?" Two Sticks looks up at the western sky, where the sun is hanging low. "Where are you sleeping tonight? Just figuring to throw out on the Great Plaza? Or alongside the road? You may have parched corn in those packs the warriors are carrying, but where are you going to find water to soak it? What are you going to use for firewood to cook it? And what if it takes you two weeks to get an audience with the tonka'tzi, *let alone with the Morning Star?"*

Strong Mussel looks suspicious. "Why do you care?"

"Actually, I don't. But for the contents of one of those wedding boxes your warriors are carrying, I can get the girl delivered to the Morning Star in a couple of days at the longest."

"Those are gifts *in those boxes. For the Morning Star!"*

"I know what you're thinking. Why should you believe some footloose Albaamaha who probably has a score to settle with the Chikosi? So I'll tell you what. Let me take care of you tonight, and you can wander over to the Morning Star's mound in the morning and learn firsthand that I'm right. Then we'll dicker out a deal that's fair to both parties."

"How far is it to the Morning Star's palace?"

"It will take you another three hands' time to get there. But we're not going that far. For the price of a shell necklace I can get you lodging in a Duck Clan Council House for the night. It will include firewood, water, and the security of knowing that all of your packs will be present when you wake up in the morning."

"You mean someone would take our packs?" Cloud Tassel asks uneasily. "They are our *property."*

"And if you should be sleeping, and someone were to pick one up and walk away with it, that pack would become their *property. Welcome to Cahokia," Two Sticks tells him with a crooked smile.*

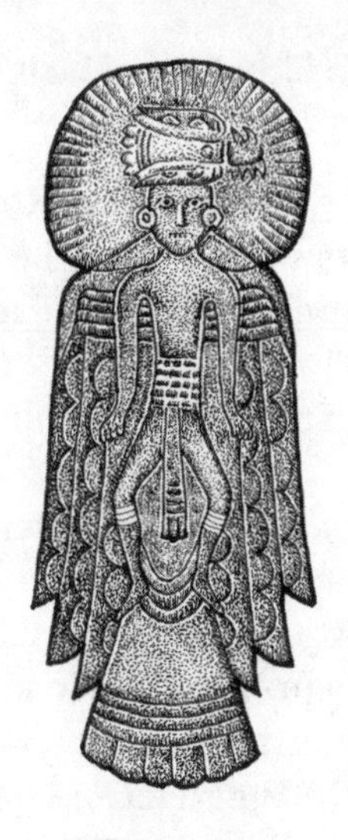

Seven

Foul, bickering, vile, two-legged vermin!" Blue Heron growled under her breath as she rode across the midnight-dark Four Winds Plaza. Her porters were moving slowly, taking their time, feeling their way. For some reason it wasn't considered healthy to trip and wreck, thereby tossing the Clan Keeper face-first into the dirt.

That sent a spear of morbid amusement through her.

"That bad?" Smooth Pebble asked from where she followed behind Blue Heron's litter.

"I'd rather deal with scorpions. They display their stingers right up front. When it comes to treachery, the little beasts could learn a lot from Four Winds clan matrons and high chiefs. It would be about backstabbing and character assassination, graft, and intrigue!"

"Was there any progress?"

"Sure. Each house has pushed its own matron to step into Wind's old chair. And after a solid day of arguing their positions, they've convinced themselves that they—and only they—are fit for leadership."

"Any alliances between them?"

"Just me and Columella." Blue Heron fingered the scar on her throat as she stared up at the cloud-black night sky. A slight breeze from the east carried the scent of smoke, latrines, and the musky, damp-and-earthy odors of marsh, mud, and water. "She will back whomever Wind and I decide to support. As a result, I've been particularly solicitous to seek her advice."

"How is that going over with the other Houses?"

"When we talk, the looks we get from the others are filled with acid, bile, evil, and lots of loathing distaste. At least among those who are kindly disposed toward us."

"And who has Morning Star House nominated for clan matron?"

"Corn Otter."

"I see." Smooth Pebble paused. "Makes sense I guess. She's the oldest daughter born of Corn Tassel, Red Warrior's second wife. Which makes her a half-sister to Night Shadow Star and Chunkey Boy."

"From the tone in your voice, you don't sound impressed."

"She's just . . ."

"Not matronly material?" Blue Heron chuckled. "I know. She lacks the devious streak necessary. The woman is just too pleasant and trusting. Doesn't think five moves ahead, let alone have that instinct to go for the throat."

"Then why nominate her?" Smooth Pebble sounded confused.

"So that we can deeply and regretfully dismiss her from the running the first time we have to make a compromise. Corn Tassel walks away knowing we fought for her first daughter. Then we nominate Light Woman, Corn Tassel's youngest daughter from Red Warrior's loins, and we offer her up for consideration."

Catching on, Smooth Pebble said, "But you're figuring on sacrificing her, too?"

"Of course. I like the girl, but sometimes she's just too petty."

"What about the third wife, Left Trout? Are you going to put up any of her daughters?"

"Depends. We might. But by that time, we're hoping that we will have enough allies to pitch Sacred Spoon."

"Your cousin? Why her?"

Blue Heron narrowed her eyes as her porters rounded the base of her mound. "She's gifted. Clever and canny. She has a good eye for reading people, is moderately attractive, and has the wits to know when to keep her mouth shut."

"If you want attractive, why not go for her younger sister, Rising Flame?"

"Because I want a matron, not a dark-eyed conspiratorial vixen with a roving eye for men to bed and a reputation for entanglements that, so far, have narrowly avoided disaster."

Blue Heron made a face as her porters lowered her litter at the bottom of her stairs. "Besides, she despises me."

"My, I touched a nerve, didn't I?"

"Oh, hush, berdache. Give me a hand up."

As Smooth Pebble raised her to her feet, Blue Heron rubbed her face, her entire body warm with that numb exhaustion that presaged sleep. Step by step she climbed her stairs, then touched her forehead as she passed the guardian posts and plodded to her front door.

She nodded to her guards and barely noticed the bundled shape on her porch—too dark to make out the details. Looked like someone awkwardly sleeping on the planks. Dancing Sky would tell her if it was important. She stepped inside, the interior of her palace illuminated by the crackling central fire. The familiar wall hangings, the statues, intricately woven textiles, and art hanging from her walls felt warm and comforting after her trying day.

Blessed gods, home!

Now, if she could just stumble back and throw herself in her bed. . . .

"You look like pestle-pounded dog shit," a familiar voice noted from her right.

She stopped, wobbled on her feet, and turned. "It's the middle of the night, thief. What are you doing here?"

Seven Skull Shield was leaned back on one of the sleeping benches, one muscle-thick thigh pulled up, a bowl of corn stew in his lap. And yes, that vile mongrel dog of his was sitting on the bench next to him. The big beast had its odd bi-colored eyes fixed on the bowl in Seven Skull Shield's lap; twin streamers of drool were soaking into one of the fine buffalo-wool blankets upon which the beast and its master perched.

"Came to make a delivery." Seven Skull Shield waggled the horn spoon in his scarred right hand. "You know, this is absolutely excellent. Dancing Sky has put just the right hint of sassafras and mint in with some of that wild rice from up north."

"Gods, all I want to do is sleep. Take your delivery and go away."

Seven Skull Shield shrugged, expression bland. He turned his attention to the dog and remarked, "Well, all right. Guess we could let the Quiz Quiz go. That Surveyors' Bundle now, if the Quiz Quiz were willing to go to such lengths to steal it, there's no telling what we could get for it in Trade at the canoe landing." He paused, thoughtful. "And if I offered it to Crazy Frog, with his connections, I could probably afford—"

"You *have* the Surveyors' Bundle?" His words finally penetrated her fog of exhaustion.

"Well, not for long, especially if it's as valuable as I think it is. And there's no telling what the Surveyors' Society might give to get it back now that you don't want it."

She placed a hand to her weary brow, trying to massage thought back into her feather-filled head. "Why do you do this to me?"

He gave her a grin and winked. "Because no one else would dare to,

Keeper." He jerked a thumb toward the recess under the bench. "The Bundle's the long cloth-wrapped thing you see there. It's got a lot of sticks and arcs and cords and things that they use to lay out angles and measure distances. Just wood and fiber. No telling why they make such a fuss about it."

"Because, you fool, according to the stories, the Tunica engineers who laid out Cahokia brought that Bundle from way down on the Great Western River. They, in turn, supposedly received the Bundle from the moon. Yes, the one in the sky. According to their story, Moon sent them the Bundle so they could lay out their towns and temples in line with the lunar maximums and minimums. The Tunica came to Cahokia upon learning of the Morning Star's reincarnation. They taught our surveyors, and the Bundle became enshrined as their most sacred and precious possession."

Seven Skull Shield craned his neck to stare at the cloth-wrapped object behind his feet. "From the moon, you say?"

"No. So *they* say. But who am I to question?" She shook her head to clear it. "Stop distracting me. Where did you get it?"

"From a Quiz Quiz war leader. He's all bundled up out front. A little worse for wear. Some of Crazy Frog's people carried him over here from River Mounds. Crazy Frog would like you to think kindly of him. No charge."

Rotted gods. That meant she was even more in debt to Crazy Frog. If she had to owe a favor to a miscreant, why couldn't it be to one she could hang in a square without threat of retribution?

"And does this Quiz Quiz have a name?"

"Sky Star. He's supposedly some sort of war chief."

"Pus and blood." She knew who he was. First in line to step into the high chair at Quiz Quiz. The current high chief's firstborn and favorite son. Recently known for kicking the stuffings out of the Pacaha and taking a chunk of their territory east of the river.

"You know that he stole the Bundle? For a fact?"

"Well, his servant girl said he did. And after she lured his warriors away, I caught him praying under a blanket in front of the Bundle. And when I took the Bundle, he chased me to get it back. Then we had . . . um, what you'd call an altercation before witnesses. So, yeah, I think he's in it up past his bruised and broken nose. I figured him for the square. That's why his arms and legs are mostly still attached."

She closed her eyes, sighed, and rubbed her temples harder. Phlegm and spit, this was going to cause trouble. On one hand, the surveyors were going to be in a whirl-tailed rage because their Bundle was not only stolen, but defiled. They would demand the culprit be punished to the fullest extent. Hung in a square to be burned, cut, and slowly dismembered.

On the other hand, the Quiz Quiz weren't going to take the slow torture and death of one of their favorite sons with any kind of sympathetic understanding.

"I'll have him delivered to the Surveyors' Society in the morning. They can treat him as they will. If we're lucky, this is something he cooked up without the high chief knowing about it."

She saw Seven Skull Shield's eyes shift uncomfortably—a trait she'd have missed had she not known him so well. "And why don't you think that's the case?"

"Trust me, he didn't do this on his own. He'll probably admit it in the square. And there's the rest of his jolly little band of Quiz Quiz warriors still running around out there. They hadn't paddled away from the canoe landing as of when I left River Mounds. Surely they had to have seen Sky Star being carried away."

"Then I guess it is what it is." She turned. "Smooth Pebble. I know it's the middle of the night, but let's do this now. Find Squadron First War Claw. Have him take the Surveyors' Bundle and that stealing war chief. Roust the guard for an escort in case those pesky Quiz Quiz are lurking around the Surveyors' Society House. Once you deliver the Bundle and the thieving culprit into *their* hands, it's their problem to deal with."

"Yes, Keeper." Smooth Pebble reached down and dragged the long, awkward Bundle out. Even as she did—giving Seven Skull Shield a dismissive shake of the head—she couldn't hide the quirk of amusement.

After she left, Blue Heron shot Seven Skull Shield a critical glance. "You hiding something?"

"No. Did you have a good time selecting a new Four Winds clan matron?"

"Is that supposed to be a joke?"

"Go to bed, Keeper. You're asleep on your feet."

"For once, thief, I can agree with you."

"Well, just for propriety's sake, I'll keep it to myself, I promise."

"And if that dog pisses on the floor . . ."

"Yes, yes, Farts and I know. He'll be headed for the stew pot."

Trouble with the Quiz Quiz? On top of the machinations of the matron selection? What else could go wrong?

Why does Seven Skull Shield look so satisfied with himself? He's hiding something.

She shoved it out of her mind as she wearily plodded toward the wondrous sanctuary of her bed.

Eight

With all his might, Fire Cat swung the copper-bitted war ax. His muscles had warmed and loosened, and the stiffness in his left leg continued to fade as the days went by. Scars—still angry and red—traced patterns over his right elbow, made a crosshatched design along the ribs on his left side and hip, and left an angry red groove in his left thigh. Reminders left by the deadly, obsidian-edged war clubs the Mayans called *macuahuitl.*

He took a breath, leaping, feeling the pull in his healing leg. Yes, he was getting it back. Day by day his skill improved. Soon now, he would be as he was: sharp, deadly, balanced, and strong of wind. Leap, thrust, parry, cut. He practiced with the ax as though in an intricate dance.

He restricted his activity to the narrow mound-top yard in front of Night Shadow Star's palace, but his daily practice drew a crowd. They gathered on the avenue that separated the base of her mound from the Morning Star's. In silence they would watch, catching glimpses of him as he swung, lunged, darted, and ducked in the shadow of Piasa and Horned Serpent's guardian posts.

He, a man who hated Cahokia—despised its rulers—had somehow become the city's most renowned warrior. People placed flowers at the base of Night Shadow Star's mound as a token of their respect for his prowess.

This was the very ground he'd fought upon. The place where he'd defeated the Itza warriors, one by one, until bleeding and staggering, he'd been able to claim their carved snake standard. Called the *kukul,* it had contained the deadly War Serpent's Spirit.

As if it were yesterday, he could remember Night Shadow Star's eerie voice whispering from the Spirit World; yet he'd heard her so clearly. Warning him. Coaching him, during those last desperate moments of his battle with Red Copal.

The Tortoise Bundle had allowed that—forged the link between Night Shadow Star's souls in the Spirit World and the combat he'd waged here atop this mound.

And now, that same Bundle had taken hold of her, was slowly tearing her apart. Just as Piasa, her Underworld lord, was pulling her the other way.

Spirit Power was always a tricky business, those who belonged to it little more than gaming pieces to be cast in its service.

Panting, sweat beginning to trickle down his hide, Fire Cat sought to unleash his rage and anger. They'd smoked the Tortoise Bundle according to Rides-the-Lightning's instructions. They had left it offerings of milled corn, sage, tobacco, and yaupon.

It had helped. Night Shadow Star had slept the night through. Though not peacefully. While she hadn't moaned and cried out, she'd nevertheless tossed and turned.

And between dozing, he'd watched over her, as he'd done since she'd cut him down from the square that cold and rainy night last spring. As he'd sworn he would do until his last dying breath.

Finally exhausted, staggering and clumsy, he stopped, propped his hands on his knees, and sucked full breaths as his body trembled from the workout.

"Come," a voice called. "I have tea."

He blinked, wiped the beading sweat from his brow, and saw Night Shadow Star where she'd seated herself on the veranda step. In the morning sunlight, her midnight hair gleamed with a bluish tint. She'd parted it in the middle and left it to hang down her back in a wave. A red-and-white fabric cloak hung at her shoulders, and she wore a blue skirt.

Loose-limbed, he walked over and dropped beside her, still panting.

"You're looking pretty good out there." She handed him the straight-handled cup with its winter-solstice design: a cross, circle, and extension to the southeast.

"I'm still not completely recovered."

"I'm not sure either of us will recover fully. Pus and rot, Fire Cat, what more can Power take from us? We're like the ball in a stickball game: As soon as we think we're flying one direction, we get flung another." She paused. "And it always comes at some terrible cost."

He sipped his tea. "Great things never come without pain, risk, and sacrifice. Take this morning. I would fight another half dozen Itza just to sit here in the sun and enjoy your company."

A smile flickered and died as she fingered her own cup and stared into her tea. "Do you ever miss your wives and children?"

"All the time."

"I'm sorry they were killed. If I could go back, I'd—"

"Lady, we live between the balance of red and white, rage and wisdom, war and peace. Red Wing Town was at war with Cahokia. We destroyed three of the Morning Star's armies before Spotted Wrist achieved his impossible victory."

He shrugged. "You know the stories of the Beginning Times as well as I do. It's the way the world became the world. Order forever in conflict with chaos."

She stared sightlessly across at the Morning Star's mound. "But there's so much needless pain. My husband . . . your wives and children."

"Perhaps they are the lucky ones. Gone to the Land of the Dead to live among the ancestors." He gave her a smile. "Pain is the price for rebirth. I think it's all been directed, that Piasa picked us because of all the people in the world, we were the best suited for the coming struggles."

She shot him a worried look. "I find nothing reassuring in those words."

"Oh? You're Chunkey Boy's sister—one of the most prominent women in Cahokia. Look around you. This whole city is dedicated to the sky, oriented to the rising of the moon at its minimum. The surveyors are called with their posts, levels, and strings to ensure each building is oriented correctly. The Great Observatory, the position of the mounds and temples—all are laid out with precise standard units of measure to chart constellations, to reflect the path of the moon, sun, and stars through the sky."

He lifted an eyebrow. "And now, here you are, Piasa's creature, possessed by his essence, a symbol of Underworld, smack in the middle of a city dedicated to the moon and the sun."

"Reconciliation of opposites?"

"Balance."

"And why did Piasa insist that I cut you down from the square that night?"

"So that I could drag you out of the river after you defeated Walking Smoke. So that I could pull you back from the Underworld when you go soul traveling." He grinned. "And someone had to kill that bunch of irritating Itza warriors and win you a fortune at chunkey."

"Rot take it, but you almost make sense." She ran her thumbs down the sides of her cup. "But what about the Tortoise Bundle? It's a complication, an obstacle to Piasa."

Fire Cat squinted up at the sun. "It was an ally of necessity. The Bundle was the key to defeating the Itza. But like you said, it's a complication. Its keeper was dying, and now it is here."

He paused. "Think of it like a high chief's mistress being brought into his palace. She's disrupting the order of things, upsetting the wives and children, making her own seductive demands, and everyone is now uncomfortable."

She laughed at that. "You know that firsthand? Brought one of your mistresses into your palace up in Red Wing Town, did you?"

"No. It's an unfortunate failing of mine that I have always dedicated myself to the women to whom I have been bound." He sighed. "I'll leave bed hopping to the thief."

"I want my new 'mistress' out of my house."

"Then we would have to find her a new keeper. Have any ideas?"

Night Shadow Star—looking disturbed—slowly shook her head. "No. And Fire Cat, from the standpoint of politics, there's another problem. The Tortoise Bundle is a symbol to the Earth Clans. Years ago Black Tail tried to have Lichen hunted down and the Bundle destroyed. Somehow they both survived. Now it has come to me. Do we want it going back to one of the Earth Clans, where it can become a rallying point for rebellion?"

"The Red Wing in me says yes." He chuckled at the stiffening of her body. "But for your sake and the city's, I think not." He paused. "Leave it with Rides-the-Lightning?"

"If he wanted it, he would have said something. He's ancient and could die at any time. Then who would get it? One of his priests, but which one? And could we trust him?"

Fire Cat took another drink of tea, running the fingers of his other hand down the smooth handle of his war ax. "Nor can you just blithely hand it over to one of the Four Winds Houses. Just behind us—on the other side of the plaza—they're locked in verbal combat to choose the new matron. It will change the dynamic of Power for whichever House gains possession of it."

"I just want it out of my head. It's bad enough with Piasa whispering in my ear all the time."

"Which brings up the final concern: It has to be the right someone. A person the Bundle respects and accepts as its keeper."

In a dry voice, she quipped, "In other words, you're saying it won't be as easy as standing on the Great Staircase and broadcasting to the crowds in the plaza that we need a new keeper?"

"Probably not," he agreed, equally as dry.

A rapping of sandaled feet heralded a messenger charging up her stairs who warily touched his forehead in respect to the Piasa and Horned Serpent guardian posts.

Night Shadow Star and Fire Cat stood as the youth then prostrated himself before them, crying, "Lady Night Shadow Star! The Morning Star requests your immediate presence in his palace. He would discuss a matter of state. May I inform him that you are on your way?"

"Inform the Morning Star that I shall attend him as soon as I have dressed. You may go."

Fire Cat watched the young man rise, his staff of office in hand as he retreated and scurried down the stairs.

"And there," Fire Cat reminded, "is another wrinkle. If you'll recall, the charming Chunkey Boy was desperate to get his hands on the Tortoise Bundle. Lichen avoided losing it to him by the narrowest of chances."

"Chunkey Boy died when the Morning Star took over his body. You remain a heretic, don't you?"

He ignored her barbed defense of Chunkey Boy's fraud, adding, "If he so much as suspects we're looking for a new keeper, he'll ensure the Tortoise Bundle winds up in his hands."

Nine

Seven Skull Shield tossed a ripe plum into his mouth, delighted by the taste as the juices spurted over his tongue. It was coming up on equinox after all, and forest fruits and berries were ripening. As they did, people in the outlying villages scrambled to pluck the first fruits and raced to get them to Cahokia before their competition. Trade was always more lucrative before the novelty of seasonal firsts wore off.

He and Farts had strolled out on their early-morning walk, crossed below the Morning Star's mound on the Avenue of the Sun, and headed east. The air felt heavy, cool to the point of raising gooseflesh. He sniffed, catching the pungent scent of smoke from the morning fires.

He'd been tantalized by the baskets of plums displayed by two young men—barely more than boys—who'd laid them out on a blanket beside the plaza. Even though dawn had been no more than a gray haze in the east, the youngsters were already prepared. Other Traders were just arriving and setting up.

The boys were blinking, looking around owlishly, obviously amazed at having managed to claim such a perfect location for their Trade, the spot being on the plaza's northeast corner right next to the Avenue of the Sun.

Seven Skull Shield had offered them a whelk-shell columella that he'd lifted from the Keeper's cache—one imported from the distant gulf coast—in Trade for a basket of plums.

The look in their eyes had been magical, as if all the wealth of the world had just been dropped in their laps. And well it might have been. As the offspring of poor dirt farmers out in the hinterlands, they might have only seen one or two such prizes in all of their years—and those would have been hanging as a pendant around some passing noble's neck.

Sometimes it was the little things. For the rest of their lives those two boys would remember the morning on the Great Plaza when a stranger Traded a basket of plums for wealth worthy of the Morning Star himself. The only thing better would have been to see the look on their parents' faces when they showed up at home with the piece.

"Life has its upsides, doesn't it, Farts?" he asked the raw-boned dog pacing at his side. Farts looked up with his odd eyes and gave a couple of swinging swipes of his tail in reply.

As Seven Skull Shield proceeded down the Avenue of the Sun, he popped plums one by one into his mouth. By the time he and Farts finally circled back to the Keeper's he knew that Dancing Sky would have breakfast ready. Probably boiled hominy seasoned with turkey meat and black walnuts. Just the thing to top off a belly full of plums.

A small crowd of early-morning pedestrians had gathered before the Surveyors' Society House where it fronted the avenue.

"What do you think?" Seven Skull Shield asked Farts as he led the way. Elbowing through the spectators he noticed that a square had been raised, and within it, had been tied a human. The wretch's wrists and ankles were bound to each corner, and though his head hung, the savaged shoulder dispelled any doubt of his identity.

"It appears that the Surveyors' Society took poorly to the theft of their surveying instruments," he noted to Farts.

Some of the people shot wary glances his way.

"Seven Skull Shield?" a fellow to his right asked curiously.

"As my mother's only child, that's me," he said easily. As he turned to face the man, Seven Skull Shield dropped into a slight crouch, flexing his knees, back, and arms. Given what he called his "colorful" style of living—not to mention his predilection for seducing married women—a significant number of his chance meetings with people weren't always amicable.

He blinked in the dawn, ready for the attack, but couldn't place the man's face. "Do I know you?"

The fellow was grinning, teeth white in the morning gloom. He was a big man, thick through the shoulders, his hair up in a common bun and pinned in place with wooden skewers. The tattoos on his cheeks were indistinct but reminiscent of the Panther Clan design. A deerhide cape hung down from his shoulders, and a long hunting shirt, belted at the waist, dropped down to his knees.

He had a square face, the nose mashed flat and skewed to the right from having once been badly broken. The eyes were wide-set beneath a jutting and scarred brow. That Seven Skull Shield didn't recognize him seemed hilarious to the man.

"You have the advantage of me, friend," Seven Skull Shield said easily, still ready for any sudden and bellicose moves. At his side, Farts had picked up on his unease, head down, the hair on his back rising.

"I *always* have the advantage of you. Slow as you are, thick-witted, and clumsy. Why, if it hadn't been for me, you'd have starved to death before your tenth birthday! But for me interceding on your poor behalf, you'd still be waiting to bed your first woman! Not to mention that they'd have hung you in a square by the time you were twelve if I hadn't kept your sorry arse—"

"Winder!" Seven Skull Shield cried as he launched himself at the man, clasped him in a bear hug, and tightened as if to squeeze the breath out of him.

"'Bout time, you worthless bit of maggot bait!" Winder pounded his back, laughing like a fiend.

Farts barked and leaped, tail thrashing, as he shared Seven Skull Shield's apparent delight. The other spectators edged back from the wheeling and back-heeling pair as they hugged each other and half wrestled across the avenue. Unable to control himself, Farts made a flying leap that knocked them sideways, scattering the last of the crowd.

Staggering for balance, Seven Skull Shield finally pushed away, laughing. He even had a few plums left in the now-crushed basket. He grinned and studied his old friend. "Where have you been?"

"Up and down the rivers, you stump-shafted and pathetic turd. Following the Trade."

"Farts! Down! He's a friend." Seven Skull Shield waved at the big dog to decease his frantic barking. Wisely, everyone else had either fled or was giving them a wide berth. Only the dejected figure of the Quiz Quiz hanging in the square remained unimpressed.

"What's it been?" Winder asked. "Nine years? Ten?"

"Definitely ten," Seven Skull Shield told him. "It was just before the last lunar maximum celebration. Old Four Steps had put together a canoe full of Trade for the south. Thought he'd try to get all the way to the gulf coast, remember?"

Winder's knob of a head tilted quizzically. "So, did it work out? You still with her?"

"Sometimes," Seven Skull Shield managed a shrug.

"Hard to think you chose a woman over me. Over the river. You loved the Trade. Loved the life. I'd never seen you happier than when you were riding the current, or the look in your eyes when we'd put in at some distant canoe landing. And there'd be this sense of awe as you looked around at the people, the buildings, at how they dressed and talked. You were a natural."

"I remember."

Winder studied him in the growing light, dark eyes pensive under the shelf of scarred brow. "So, was she worth it? You gave up a lot for her. Lost waif of an orphan as you were, no clan, home, no prospects . . . The river and Trade were your way out. The chance to become a rich man, earn some respect."

A hollow sensation formed under Seven Skull Shield's breastbone. "I've wondered. More than once. Asked myself if I should have gone with you that day." He waved it away. "Never saw you again after that, so the answer didn't really matter, did it?"

Winder spread his arms wide. "Well? Here I am! Happy and healthy! Some people call me the River Fox. I'm quick to take to the paddle, first to find that bit of Trade that will set fire to the desires among the Chitimacha, or to trick a Caddo into Trading the skin off his bones for a trinket. I tell you, Skull, Power favors me."

Skull. He called me Skull.

The realization rocked him slightly, harkening back to those days so long ago.

"What's the matter?" Winder asked.

"Nothing. Only two people on earth call me Skull."

He narrowed his eyes. "Me. And . . . her?"

Seven Skull Shield nodded his head, looking down at Farts, who was staring up at him through curious eyes, as if wondering at his master's unusual tone of voice. "You would, too, if you could talk, huh, Farts?"

The dog wagged his tail.

"What are you doing with your life these days? Married? Children?" Winder laughed and thumped a muscle-hard thigh with a fist. "By the Tie Snakes! Imagine that! *You,* as a father?"

"No wife." He grinned evilly. "Any children—and by rights there are more than a few—are being raised by men who don't know they're mine."

"Now that's my man." Winder grinned. "Me? Let's see. I'm up to fourteen now. Wives, that is. Trade being what it is, especially on the lower river, a man's got to marry into a people and clan. Makes it a lot easier on me, I tell you. I've got a roof and a bed waiting for me from one end of the world to another. Sometimes it's a stretch between homes, and most of them are matrilineal, so I don't make a scene if I find her belly swollen six months into a child when I haven't seen her for a year and half."

"Different ways for different Nations," Seven Skull Shield agreed. "Pus and blood, Winder. I've missed you. To see you again, it really is a wonder. There's so much to tell, to ask, to get caught up on." He gestured his excitement. "What brings you here at this time of day?"

"A job."

"Bit far from the river, aren't you? Or are you looking for some special bit of Trade? Though anything you might find on the Great Plaza is usually available at the canoe landing."

"I don't just Trade items, Skull." A sly smile bent Winder's lips. "I also Trade services." He jerked a thumb. "I was sent to find a man. Turns out he's here."

Seven Skull Shield followed the direction the thumb was pointing. "The Quiz Quiz?"

"He's not just any old Quiz Quiz, my friend. He's a very special Quiz Quiz."

"I know. He's Sky Star, a high-and-mighty war chief."

The light was good enough that Seven Skull Shield was able to read Winder's surprise. "Now, how do you know that?"

"I put him here. He stole something from the Surveyors' Society. I got it back for them."

It might have been years, but the expression on Winder's face when he was thinking hard hadn't changed a lick. Finally, he said, "You know, hanging the high chief of Quiz Quiz's son is going to have repercussions. Maybe the Surveyors' Society might want to reconsider before things get a whole lot worse."

"You here to cut him down? Is that what they hired you for? If you are, old friend, I'm going to tell you now: *Don't!* This goes a whole lot higher than the Surveyors' Society."

"How high?"

"Up to the Keeper, *Tonka'tzi* Wind, and probably the Morning Star. Especially if the surveyors don't get to salve their wounded pride and get some retribution for having to spiritually cleanse and appease their Bundle."

"By Piasa's swinging shaft, this couldn't get any worse, could it?" Winder made a face and shot an uneasy glance at the hanging Quiz Quiz. In the soft light, the war chief's wounds could plainly be seen now. Not just the mauled and broken shoulder, but places where the surveyors had beaten him and sliced off bits of skin. The man's genitals were painfully swollen from having been beaten.

"Yes, it could," Seven Skull Shield stepped close, placing a hand on his friend's shoulder. "You are the best friend I've ever had. You kept me alive back then. You and me, we go back to the beginning. I'd give my life for you. So, you have to tell me, Winder. What's your interest in all this?"

"A couple of Sky Star's warriors looked me up on the canoe landing. Said the war leader had been beaten up and kidnapped. Two of them had seen him being carried down one of the avenues to a Trader's house. Some clanless scoundrel called Crazy Frog. One went to get the rest, and the other one was waiting, watching. Then some Cahokians came out of the yard and chased him away. By the time the rest returned, Sky Star was gone. They asked me to find him."

"Just find him?"

"Just find him."

Seven Skull Shield sighed. "Here's what you do. You go back to the plaza, find a place in the sun, and watch the Morning Star play his morning chunkey game. Then watch the day's stickball games. Deer Clan from down in Horned Serpent Town is playing that shin-kicking Fish Clan team from west of Evening Star Town. People have been waiting for more than a moon to see this. Should be one bloody match-up."

He reached into his pouch, producing another whelk columella. "Trade this for the finest meal you can find, and feast. On me. Then watch the evening stickball game. You and me, we'll meet up at dusk in front of Night Shadow Star's palace, find a quiet place, and smoke, and talk, and catch up on each other's lives. We'll laugh. Tell jokes. Remember the old times. And tomorrow, you make your way slowly back to the canoe landing at River Mounds and tell the Quiz Quiz that you couldn't find Sky Star."

Winder had pursed his lips, eyes on the columella as Seven Skull Shield talked. For long moments, he ran his thumb down the polished spiral of shell. "What if my honor demands that I tell them?"

"There are times for honor, Winder. And there are times for good sense. Look around you. Everything you see—the Plaza, the avenues, the buildings, the mounds, the whole stinking city—was laid out by the surveyors. All of it measured by the fifty-pace cord and located by the strings and arcs in their sacred Bundle. Sky Star *stole* that selfsame Bundle. Like taking the thing that made this whole city. *Don't* get in the middle of this."

"What's your interest in all this, Skull? What do *you* of all people care? Why are you even involved? I mean, aren't you just another of the nameless bits of human . . . ?"

Winder glanced away, unable to finish.

"I was. Maybe part of me still is. But I'm no more the man I once was than you are. I can understand your obligation to the Quiz Quiz who hired you. I don't want to see you end up in a square. I've been there. It's no fun."

"You look pretty good for being hung in a square."

"It's a long story involving Natchez, Maya Itza lords, and treachery. I'll tell you tonight."

Winder's expression had gone back to thinking. Then, slowly, he nodded. "If it were anyone but you . . ."

"Thanks. That's a load off my soul." Seven Skull Shield grinned and offered the basket. "Here. Want a plum?"

Ten

It might have been the feeding, smoking, and ritual shown the Tortoise Bundle; or perhaps the Bundle had overheard—or somehow understood—her conversation with Fire Cat that morning. Whatever the reason, since then the Bundle had been mostly quiet in Night Shadow Star's mind.

In the resulting peace, she'd caught the usual glimpses of Piasa. The flickers at the corner of her eye. The shifting in the shadows. What terrible irony was it that the presence of the Spirit Beast—which usually terrified her—could ever be considered a relief?

The southern breeze teased her skirt, batting it against her long legs as she climbed the last length of the Great Staircase. It tried to flip the spoonbill-feather cloak she'd draped on her shoulders and tugged at the intricately carved bone pins she'd used to secure her hair. She hadn't painted her face, nor dressed particularly well; she did not want to appear vain just for a simple conference.

Fire Cat tramped up the stairs behind her, the barest trace of a limp in his left leg. Whenever she went to see the Morning Star, Fire Cat insisted that he don his full armor, that he appear in the living god's presence decked out in battle regalia. Partly—she assumed—it was because doing so irritated Five Fists right down to the man's bones. The broken-jawed old war leader was head of the Morning Star's security and cringed at the close presence of the armed heretic to the living god. And partly because her captive Red Wing heretic stubbornly clung to the belief that the Morning Star was a role played by a conniving Chunkey Boy.

That Fire Cat remained a heretic bothered her at some deep and fundamental level, but if that was the only aspect of their relationship that annoyed her, she could live with it.

"*And what if he's right?*" Piasa's subtle whisper caressed her ear.

"Right?" she asked, face quizzical. "What do you know, Lord? Why would you plant that doubt?"

"*Testing.*" Piasa's sibilant response might have been a trick of the wind.

She shook her head, refusing to be baited. If the Morning Star was nothing more than a role Chunkey Boy was playing with such finesse . . . ?

A series of memories rose up from the depths of her souls. Things that—were Morning Star not the living god—would be too unthinkable to endure. How he had called her to his room after the resurrection, leading her to his bed . . .

"Pus and rot, beast! Why do you do this to me?"

Faint laughter floated away on the wind.

"Lady?" Fire Cat asked. Normally he let her conversations with Piasa go unchallenged.

"My lord enjoys his little games." As if it were a game.

"Is it a warning?"

"Just goading. Probably that jealousy Rides-the-Lightning mentioned." She shot a glance off to the side, wondering if the beast would react, but nothing moved in the air around her.

Reaching the top of the Great Staircase, she nodded as the two warriors guarding the high gate bowed and touched their foreheads.

Before entering the palisade that ringed the mound top, she took a moment, letting her gaze travel across the great city.

The air was filled with a smoky haze—the result of thousands of fires burning across the far-flung metropolis. Cooking, firing pottery, heat-treating flint, sintering shell, drying fish and meat, disposing of refuse—the fires of Cahokia never ceased.

Her eye followed the Avenue of the Sun west, past the Four Winds Plaza and the Clan House, beyond the Great Observatory, all the way to Black Tail's burial mound, where the avenue bent off to the southwest.

In the distance, at the end of the urban sprawl, she could just make out the high palaces and Spirit poles of River Mounds City. The thickly packed structures masked the Father Water itself, but on the river's far bluff she could faintly distinguish the outlines of Evening Star Town.

To the south, at the foot of Morning Star's mound, stretched the Great Plaza with its renowned chunkey courts, World Tree Pole, and stickball fields. The Avenue of the Moon ran south from the Great Plaza, paralleling the side of Rides-the-Lightning's mound, and continuing on its elevated causeway down to the Serpent Mound. Then it angled to the south-southwest past marshes, farms, and fields until it ended at Horned Serpent Town. She studied the distance where it lay hidden in the smoky mist.

To the east, the Avenue of the Sun continued past temples, charnel houses, and mounds, and climbed through a cut excavated into the eastern bluffs. Passing beneath two mounds that guarded the headlands, it extended a half-day's run beyond her view to the Moon Mound—the great lunar observatory out in the treeless Great Prairie. There the road turned southeast along the lunar maximum line and could be followed all the way to the distant Mother Water River.

All of this was built on the miracle of the resurrected Morning Star. How could Piasa hint that it was founded upon a hoax? Even in jest?

Fire Cat was watching her ever so attentively. While he couldn't have a clue as to her thoughts, he read her unease with an uncanny eye.

Pus and sputum, how had anyone—let alone this one-time enemy—come to know her so well?

He raised an eyebrow suggestively, which caused her to laugh and say, "Come on, Red Wing. Let's go see what complexity the Morning Star wants to throw in our path this time."

She led the way through the gate. In the courtyard before the palace stood the towering red-cedar post, its sides carved to illustrate stories of the Morning Star's exploits in the Beginning Times. The lowest engraving showed his birth, along with that of his twin brother Thrown-Away Boy, the Wild One. It depicted his chunkey game with the Giants; his resurrection of his father's head; the ascent into the sky; and his metamorphosis into Bird Man. Or it once had before lightning strikes had traced their burn patterns down the mighty pole.

She touched it reverently as she passed. Beyond it—rising against the sky—stood the Morning Star's palace with its towering thatched wedge of a roof. The high ridge pole was topped with carvings of *Hunga Ahuito*. Workers hanging from ropes were retying bundles of thatch in preparation for winter. No other building in the world was savaged by as much wind and storm. Maintenance was a constant.

People sat, slouched, or stood in knots, waiting for their chance to have an audience with the living god. Off to one side stood a Duck Clan man with two beautiful daughters. They looked excited and expectant, having been decked out in their finest dress. They kept flashing smiles, fidgeting, undoubtedly having been chosen to share the Morning Star's bed. Not only was the honor sought by each of the Earth Clans, but the women would be considered doubly blessed if they conceived, and their value in marriage would increase twofold.

As Night Shadow Star led the way, a murmur rippled through the crowd, all eyes going to her and Fire Cat. As if on order, the people dropped to their knees, bowing and touching their foreheads as she and Fire Cat passed.

As *Tonka'tzi* Red Warrior's daughter, she'd grown up with the honors of rank, but with the defeat of the Itza had come a subtle change. What had been a grudging respect was now an awed reverence that left her discomfited.

Nor was it just her. They treated Fire Cat with the same zeal. His status as her oath-bound servant just added to his allure as a hero.

The warriors guarding the palace doors bowed low before stepping to the side. Out of whimsy, she reached out and ran her fingers across the masterful relief carved into the doors. The images depicted the Morning Star—eagle wings spreading from his arms, face displaying the two-forked eye design, a stunning copper headdress atop his skull. A turkey-tail mace was raised in one hand. The other held a broken chunkey lance.

Inside, the great room was illuminated by a large central fire. Once a year, during the Busk, it was extinguished and rekindled by the Morning Star, from whence embers were carried to reignite the fires of Cahokia.

The opulence and décor had lost their luster for her. The sleeping benches were indeed carved masterpieces; the copper, wood, textile, and effigy hangings gracing the walls had been so well rendered as to be alive. A wealth of copper, lace, fur, shell, and precious stones and statuary lurked in every cranny.

Along the west wall were the recorders, messengers, and advisors from the various societies. A handful of warriors in full battle dress stood opposite them along the east wall, no more than a step behind Five Fists. The gnarled old warrior stiffened at the sight of Fire Cat, irked as she knew he'd be that the armed Red Wing heretic was once again in proximity to the living god. No love was lost between the two.

In the place of honor behind the fire rose a dais. Atop the clay and wooden construction rested the Morning Star's stunning litter. Cougar hides draped the carved wooden frame. And there the living god sat, leaned forward, chin propped on a knee. As always, he was dressed immaculately in a white apron; a stunning turkey winter-feather cloak was thrown over his shoulders. Face painted white, his eyes were surrounded by black-forked designs. A polished split-cloud-design copper headpiece held his tightly wound hair bun in place.

Night Shadow Star didn't hesitate but walked past the fire and into his forbidden and inviolate personal space.

A gasp went up, as it always did. She had violated sacred ground where no one was allowed to pass without the Morning Star's express invitation. Night Shadow Star, however, strode forward as his equal—an affront only she had ever been allowed to get away with.

She kept her expression composed as Five Fists doggedly started forward, his broken-jawed expression more grim than ever. Behind her, Fire Cat had pivoted and dropped into a defensive posture, war ax at the ready.

With a wave of his hand, Morning Star gestured the fuming Five Fists back.

Night Shadow Star stopped a pace short of his dais. Looking into his painted face, she smiled and inclined her head. "Great Lord, what did you wish to discuss?"

She might have detected ferment behind his eyes, a tightening of the jaws, but then his placid calm returned. "I was surprised to learn that you were not involved in the choice of the new matron."

"I am sure the Houses will make every effort to choose the right person to replace Matron Wind."

"After recent events, I assume you know that none would oppose you?" He paused, as if considering. "Though, perhaps, as the voting comes to an impasse, you might appear at the last moment as a means of solving what seems a deadlock?"

She chuckled softly. "The Four Winds Clan is a Sky clan. As you well know, I serve a different master these days. One steeped in Underworld Power. To most in the Four Winds Clan I am unsettling at best, an unnerving disappointment to many, and for some, a pariah."

"Then you will not offer yourself? No matter what?"

"No."

At that juncture, a woman stepped out of his personal quarters in the rear, and keeping her distance, walked wide around the eastern perimeter along the wall benches.

Morning Star glanced her way as the woman slowed, a questioning tilt to her head. She was immaculately dressed, the fine features of her face painted in black and white. Thick raven hair tumbled down her back.

Night Shadow Star recognized her cousin, Rising Flame. The woman regarded her thoughtfully, something smoldering and triumphant behind her eyes.

The Morning Star's slight inclination of the head—as if a nod of assent—brought a smile to Rising Flame's quick features. She grinned to herself as she continued on her way. Something about her walk, the sensual sway of the hips, the manner in which she flipped her thick hair back, reeked of sexuality.

It wouldn't be the first time Morning Star had been bedding one of the elite women in the Four Winds Clan. Night Shadow Star fought back the unsavory memory of another time. Of convincing herself that her brother was dead. That it was the living god who—

"You serve your master well." The Morning Star's sibilant words interrupted her thoughts. "Your refusal is the Four Winds Clan's great loss."

She heard Piasa hiss in delight as she reordered her priorities, then asked, "Who do you suppose they will choose?"

"I wonder?" He studied her carefully, as if searching for some betrayal of expression.

Then, as if disappointed, he said, "Are you familiar with Split Sky City?"

"Muskogean. On the Black Warrior River. Down south of the bend of the Tenasee River. The ones who call themselves the Sky Hand moved into Albaamaha territory and are building their city. The Albaamaha resent the fact that their homelands have been seized, and Sky Hand warriors are there to insist the Albaamaha chiefs supply the men and women conscripted to do the hard work."

"Has your lord mentioned any of this? Any word from Old-Woman-Who-Never-Dies and the Underworld?"

She crossed her arms under her breasts, cocking her head. "No. What do *you* hear from the Sky World?"

He hesitated, which immediately caused her concern. The Morning Star always played a deep game. No question, no matter how seemingly innocent, was as facile as it seemed.

"Just once, Lord, you might tell me right out what concerns you," she added, "instead of the layers of subterfuge which always seem to cloak our relations. I might better anticipate and deal with the threat if I understood its nature."

A flicker of smile crossed his lips. "Moths are creatures of the night. One normally thinks of them as beings of the Sky World. Inoffensive for the most part. But some serve a more sinister Power, one that feeds on darkness and deadly nectar.

"In the Dream, I felt the moths, almost silent as they whirred through the air around me. Giant moths. Terrible things. You know the kind. Those that feast on nightshade, datura, and tobacco flowers. But these were so much bigger. When I reached out, they landed on my hand, clinging to my fingers. When their tongues lashed out, they began sucking the life out of my flesh. I could feel it draining away with each pulse of their abdomens."

He seemed to lose his train of thought, eyes fixed vacantly on her breasts, emphasized as they were by her crossed arms.

He's the living god, not my brother, she reminded herself. Nevertheless, uncomfortable images flickered to life. Again her memories went back to that day after the Morning Star's resurrection into Chunkey Boy's body. Of how he'd called her to the palace, how he had declared himself to be the living god and said that her brother was dead as he led her to his bed.

It wasn't incest!

It had been sex with a living god. Not her brother.

The incest had come later, at Walking Smoke's hands.

A terrible day.

One so traumatic she'd forced it from her souls.

Refused to believe.

. . . Until Piasa and Horned Serpent dragged it out from the hidden recesses down between her souls. Made her remember as she hovered on the verge of death in the Underworld's watery labyrinths.

The faintest quiver of his lips made her wonder if he was reading her mind.

"So you called me here to discuss a Dream where giant humming moths were drinking your blood?" she asked coldly, a shiver of unease running down her spine.

"Something is coming," he told her, having once again shifted his attention from her breasts to her eyes. "Ask your lord if it comes from the Underworld."

"*Most interesting,*" Piasa whispered in her ear. "*Darkness, flowers, and nectar—all deadly—brought together.*"

"Yours?" she asked softly.

"*Someone else's. An ancient Power rekindled to no purpose you would call good.*"

"Witchcraft, then?" she asked warily, searching for Piasa at the edge of her vision. But her lord gave no hint of his whereabouts.

Morning Star had watched her interchange, the faintest hint of distaste on his lips.

She took a deep breath. "My lord suggests that it is old Power. As he says, 'rekindled to no good purpose.' "

Morning Star's eyes thinned in his painted face, and he nodded slightly as he thought. "The purpose of the Dream becomes clear. We are warned."

"Should I care if terrible oversized fluttering insects suck your blood and devour your flesh? *You* are *not* my master."

Another gasp went up around the room.

His smile was a fleeting thing. "You and I share an understanding, Night Shadow Star. Twice now, we have aligned to save our city and world. In the night, something dangerous comes."

"*Yes,*" Piasa whispered from behind her ear. "*And it frightens him.*"

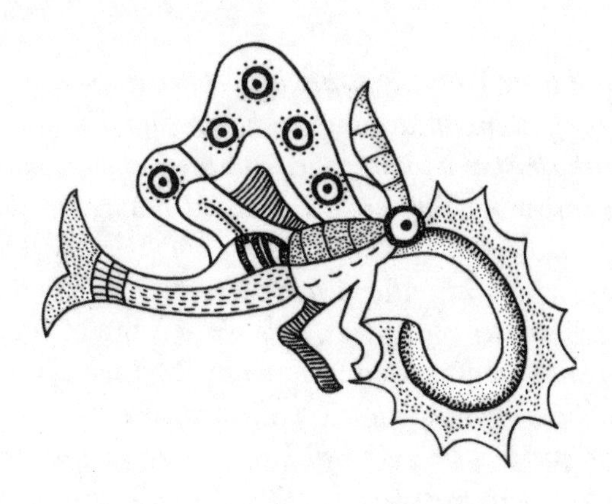

A Swirling of Chance

Two Sticks proved as good as his word. The Duck Clan Council House where he put us up is an earth-covered dome perhaps eight paces across and twice a man's height under the smoke hole in the center. Kind of tight quarters for twenty warriors and me, as well as the packs. They put me clear in the back, farthest from the door. To have escaped in the night I would have had to pick my way across all those sleeping warriors. And, once again, I have that cured-leather leash tied to my ankle.

The knot isn't as tight, but if I sit up and start picking at it, Cloud Tassel or Strong Mussel will feel it.

Not that I am so sure about running away anymore. I mean, I have to, don't I? The man I love is waiting for me somewhere back in the forests east of Split Sky City. And the last thing I want is to be married off to whatever kind of "thing" the Morning Star is.

A living god?

A mythological Spirit from the Beginning Times?

One that changed bodies every time he wore one out?

How does that *work?*

And the last thing I want is for him to jam himself inside me after some "wedding" ceremony.

The only man I've ever shared my body with is Straight Corn. I want to keep it that way. Part of that comes from my Sky Hand upbringing. Unlike so many Moskogee people, the Sky Hand—like the Four Winds Clan—are patrilineal. That means descent is traced through the father's line. A man wants to know that he truly sired his heir. Our women are noted for being chaste and circumspect in our dealings with men, unlike those saucy Chah'taw who'll slip off to the bushes with anyone. But then, they're matrilineal. Doesn't matter who the father is. Any child conceived belongs to the mother's clan. Makes them a great deal more reckless about who they'll lift their skirts for.

But I'm losing my point. After what we've seen of Cahokia, I'm not sure that running off is such a good idea. This place is huge! *We traveled for* half a day *from the canoe landing, and it's been through solid city! Constant buildings, temples, charnel houses, closely packed dwellings with crowded garden plots, and people everywhere. We still haven't arrived at the Morning Star's palace—though we've at least seen it in the distance.*

It was right at dusk. The sun shining red in the west bathed the great black mound in orange light. Where they stuck up above the clay-coated palisade, the high-peaked roof with its statues and the soaring Spirit pole were visible. The place was ablaze in the sunset.

We stood in awe.

It looked worthy of a god's house, all right, but I don't want to be one of his wives. And I sure don't want to be any part of Cahokia, with its smell of garbage, rotting feces, urine, and clouds of flies and mosquitoes.

This place stinks. I mean really stinks. Filled with as many people as Cahokia is, how could it not? Throngs of human beings, foreign and strange, not all of whom wash each day, and every dwelling and Council House has a latrine—usually an old pit screened by a wicker partition. In addition we passed a lot of gaping borrow pits where they've excavated earth for mounds. Water has seeped in to create scummy ponds that people use to discard basket-loads of trash. At times the smell, and the flies and the clouds of mosquitoes, really are overpowering.

Everything about this place scares me—right down to the way people look at me as if I'm nothing more than a mild curiosity, surrounded as I am by my garishly dressed warriors.

I've been a lot of things in my life—exalted, pampered, hunted, despised, and shunned—but never inconsequential. It's a sobering experience.

These thoughts are in my head as the first voices carry from outside the Council House. Looking up through the smoke hole, I see that the stars are fading. Dawn is here.

I use my foot to kick Strong Mussel. "Hey! War Leader. It's morning. Why don't you prove your worth by leading me to the latrine."

He comes awake like a warrior should: crisp and alert.

"Take her," he tells Cloud Tassel.

The squadron second pulls himself into a sitting position, blinks—not as quick to his senses—and yawns. Grabbing up my leash, he gestures. "After you, Lady."

I get to kick my way across the floor, rudely waking warriors as I make my way to the door. Call me petty. It's a tiny bit of payback given what they've put me through.

Two Sticks has slept just outside, back to the wall, his cloak pulled tightly around his shoulders. Given the morning chill as we step outside, it had to have been uncomfortable. Inside, with a smoldering fire and packed with bodies, the temperature had been quite nice.

I lead the way, my leash flopping, to the latrine out back. It consists of an odiferous hole in the ground. Inside the cool air has left the swarms of flies dormant, so I can squat with my backside unmolested by the beasts.

When I am escorted back to the doorway, Two Sticks is in conference with Strong Mussel. The war leader is nodding his head to something the Albaamaha is telling him.

"Let's eat!" Strong Mussel declares. "And get packed."

The warriors leap to their tasks, and within a finger's time last night's corn gruel is reheated and venison jerky is passed around.

Before the sun peeks above the crowded rooftops bordering the Avenue of the Sun, we are on the way again. This early in the morning the great thoroughfare isn't nearly as crowded, and we join a scattered procession of people headed east. They carry packs on their backs, or litters piled with bread, pottery, textiles, or other goods.

"They are all headed to the Great Plaza," Two Sticks explains. "Some have been walking most of the night. They hope to arrive early enough to get a good location near the plaza. They want to have their wares displayed long before the first chunkey game."

"Is there a special ceremony today? Some celebration that brings them all in?"

Two Sticks gives me a condescending look. "No, Lady. It's like this every day. On ceremonial days like equinox? They come a week early, and it's all a person can do to get within a bow-shot of the plaza. Tens of thousands flock to see the Morning Star and the ceremonies. And there are games. Stickball. Chunkey. Races. You should have seen it when the Red Wing played the Natchez Little Sun a couple of moons back." He makes a face. "Who would have thought a slave could play like that? Cost me a fortune."

"What happened?" Cloud Tassel asks.

"You've heard about the Mayan lord? The one who traveled here from distant Chichen Itza?"

"Yes, something," Strong Mussel responds.

"The Natchez came here as escorts for the Itza lord. The Natchez leader, a man they call the Little Sun, had beaten the Red Wing at chunkey before. Sent him home naked and humiliated. I'm not sure what happened after that. I know the Red Wing was sent away, that he played some games in River City. Then, as if spit out of the empty sky, he's back at the Great Plaza, challenging the Little Sun to play for his life.

"The Little Sun was very, very good. People were speculating that he might even be able to beat the Morning Star. That's how good he was."

"But the Red Wing won?"

"Can you imagine? A disgraced slave!" Two Sticks waves his hands with passion. "The whole city bet against him. I bet against him. You should have seen the pile of wealth. And then he wins! Cuts the head right off the Little Sun's body."

"He's the same slave who beat the Itza warriors in single combat?" Cloud Tassel asks.

"And captured their snake god," Two Sticks agrees. "The whole city went wild. And within a day, the Itza hangs *himself. Nothing has been the same since."*

As we walk, I keep watching the Morning Star's palace as it looms ever higher in the sky before us. The great black pyramid mound upon which it sits is inky in shadow; atop the highest level, the palace's high roof seems to cut the sky. The towering Spirit pole is like a spear thrust into the morning. A lower level extends out on the south like a terrace, facing the plaza. This is the walled Council House—the place where Cahokia's ruling class meet and entertain foreign embassies and conduct the city's business.

Two Sticks informs us that to finally be received up there, we have to go see some lower functionary for approval. This really has Strong Mussel fuming and muttering under his breath about "ignorant, arrogant, over-stuffed foreigners." As he does he fingers the White Arrow and glares sidelong at Two Sticks, wondering if he is being played for a fool.

Around us the buildings are grander, packed closer together, and we arrive at an open space dominated by a great circle of posts, behind one of which cluster a group of priests. I can't see what they're doing exactly—something with sticks and strings that sight along the shadows cast by the poles.

"The Great Observatory," Two Sticks explains. "These are the Sky Priests who serve both the Day Society and Night Society under the watchful eye of the Sky Flier, their oldest shaman. The Day Society measures the movement of the sun across the sky; the Night Society plots the movements of the moon and stars."

We are all in awe. Of course the Moskogee chart the skies. Our greatest shamans study these things intently, but to see the huge circle of posts, watch the priests with their strings, it becomes real to me.

"Ahead on the left is the Four Winds Clan House where the new matron is being chosen," Two Sticks explains as we approach an incredibly ornate palace atop a flat-topped mound.

A crowd has already gathered around its base, where a profusion of litters have been placed and porters crouch, talking and laughing. In the front, the area before the stairs is jammed with well-dressed young people. More crowd the yard before the palace and cluster around the incredible carvings of the Cahokian two-headed eagle atop the stairs.

"The elite of the Four Winds Clan," Two Sticks tells us. "And the reason we have to hurry. Our destination is there." He points northeast across the plaza with its World Tree pole, stickball grounds, and chunkey courts. "That's the Keeper's palace."

The mound-top building he points out sits in the shadow of the Morning Star's great pyramid. Another high-roofed, plastered palace fronted with eagle guardian posts.

"Cut across the plaza?" Strong Mussel asks.

"It's the Four Winds Plaza. Their sacred turf. We go around."

"Quite a chunkey game," Cloud Tassel notes, and indicates where a throng of people are already gathered at the closest chunkey court. Even through the crowd I can tell that only one man is using the court.

"That, my friends, is Fire Cat. The Red Wing. Bound in service to Lady Night Shadow Star. He's the one who saved Cahokia from the Itza lord." He made a face. "And cost me a fortune."

"Is he better than the Morning Star?" Strong Mussel wonders.

I see the man bowl his stone and cast his lance after it. As he charges down the court, the rest of the action is obscured by the people crowding around. A cheer goes up. Must have been a good cast.

Two Sticks makes a dismissive gesture. "They've never played each other. The Red Wing is a known heretic. Word is that he still believes the Morning Star is nothing more than Chunkey Boy playing at being a god. Some say that if he played, and lost, the Morning Star would take his head. Others say that Night Shadow Star prohibits him in order to avoid the upset if he should beat the Morning Star."

It is sobering to make our way around Night Shadow Star's ornate palace high atop its mound. At the top of the stairs, beautifully carved statues of Piasa and Horned Serpent rise against the morning sky and stare down on us with malignant eyes. They send a shiver down my spine, given my familiarity with the Powers of the night and Underworld.

Reflexively I rub the tattoo on the back of my right hand.

The guardians might be alive, each watching me pass below like defenseless prey beneath the gaping jaws of ruthless hunters. It is like being trapped. Hemmed in with Night Shadow Star's mound on one side, the Morning Star's on the other. I feel *the guardians' Power—and for the briefest of instants think I hear them whispering to me.*

Then we are past, and on my right I can look up the slanting side of the Morning Star's earthen pyramid to the high palace above. The wall that surrounds the palace blocks the view, but I see a single man standing atop it, looking down. What seems to be polished copper gleams on his head.

"Feeling nervous?" Cloud Tassel asks Strong Mussel.

"I can believe that a god lives there," the war leader whispers, so low that only Cloud Tassel and I can hear.

We pass a series of society houses on our left and stop before the palace that lies directly across from the great mound's northwest corner. Warriors stand guard at the bottom of the stairs, where a litter waits. The porters squat on their haunches and watch our approach with mild interest, as if they see parties of Moskogee warriors dressed in finery march up all the time.

Two Sticks steps up to the oldest of the warriors and bows low, touching his forehead with his fingers. He speaks in respectful Cahokian. The guard looks us over, casually notes the White Arrow that Strong Mussel holds so prominently before him, and nods his head in assent.

"Stay here," Two Sticks orders, and then he sprints up the stairs, pausing only long enough at the top to pay obeisance to the two eagle statues that stare down at us with angry yellow eyes.

"Why are we waiting on an Albaamaha Trader?" Strong Mussel wonders. "I carry the White Arrow. I should be the one going up there to meet with this Keeper."

The two Cahokian guards, each wearing armor, watch us through arrogant and wary eyes. They have strung bows strapped across their bodies and quivers full of what are undoubtedly war arrows on their backs.

"You could just let me go," I suggest. "You've delivered me to Cahokia. You can go back and report success to my father. You're already heroes."

I just get disgusted looks in return.

Two Sticks appears at the top of the stairs with a gray-haired, rather muscular woman. She's dressed in a functional wrap pinned above the left shoulder. White shell necklaces wink in the morning light where they are wound tight around her throat.

"War Leader, you and the girl may come up," Two Sticks calls.

"Untie my leash," I suggest.

"And have you take off at a run and embarrass us? Absolutely not," Strong Mussel says through a growl. "Up the stairs, girl. And remember that I'm right behind you."

I climb the squared timbers where they're set into the earthen ramp. At the top I'm shocked by the incredible detail carved into the guardian eagle statues. The feathers are so well rendered the great eagles could be alive. Instinctively I touch my forehead as I pass.

Then I turn my eyes upon the palace before me. Several people wait on the veranda, including a muscular man in his late twenties; he wears nothing but a hunting shirt and rope belt hung with a couple of pouches. A big-jawed, ungainly looking brindle dog watches him with odd blue and brown eyes as the man spoons up soup from a gourd bowl.

The man's tattoos are smudged, almost unrecognizable, and the lascivious look he gives me makes me want to throw something at him. He grins as if he's visualizing running his hands over my breasts and spreading my legs.

I feel my face flush, and then we pass inside. What should be relief drowns in awe. The first thing a person notices are the walls, hung with spectacular textiles woven into pictures and geometric patterns. The rear is covered with a meticulous carving of the Four Winds design. Shields, copper images, a couple of human skulls, and wooden reliefs sculpted by experts and painted by masters are everywhere.

The sleeping benches—while imminently functional—are artwork, each piece carved by an expert. The furs and woven blankets are lush and neatly folded. And in the space beneath the benches I can see gleaming, burnished pottery and phenomenal basketry. Inlaid and polished wooden storage boxes abound.

Two Sticks drops to his knees before the fire, bowing his head all the way down to the woven-cane matting.

I stop behind him, refusing to bow. I am, after all, the high minko's oldest daughter. Strong Mussel, however, falls to his knees as if he's in the presence of the highest and mightiest of nobles. But what does he know? He's only a war leader.

The object of all the flurry sits across from us on the other side of the fire: An older woman—perhaps in her fifties—studies me as she uses a shell comb on her graying hair. She sits on a raised dais covered with panther hides. I can see what look like star-burst tattoos on her cheeks. A beautiful parakeet-feather cloak is draped over her shoulders, and she wears a soft dogbane fabric skirt dyed midnight black with oyster-shell beads sewn to the front.

She has a high forehead and evaluates me though quick dark eyes. I can't tell what she thinks of my refusal to bow.

Two Sticks rattles off some greeting in Cahokian.

The woman glances at the White Arrow, quickly assesses Strong Mussel, and then takes in my ankle leash. She says something in Cahokian, as if it's an offhand observation.

To my surprise, it is the servant woman—who I now realize is a berdache—who says in passable Moskogee, "The Keeper would know the purpose of your arrival in Cahokia."

Strong Mussel raises his head. "We come as the representatives of High Minko White Water Moccasin, of the Chief Clan, of the Sky Hand Moskogee. This woman is his daughter, born of High Matron Evening Oak of the Raccoon Clan. Her name is Whispering Dawn, and she is offered in marriage—along with gifts—to the Morning Star as a sign of the high minko's fond regard, and in hopes of establishing stronger ties with the living god."

All of this is duly translated to the Keeper as Strong Mussel speaks. A slight smile bends the old woman's lips; as she lifts her chin I see a thin white scar across her throat.

As the Keeper replies, the berdache translates, "Why did you send no advance courier to warn us of your arrival? We could have prepared a place and reception for you."

Strong Mussel blinks foolishly. "We carry the White Arrow."

The Keeper smiles and nods, saying, "Yes, we understand and respect the value your people place in it. Our apologies for your reception. Are you here to establish an embassy?"

"Excuse me?" Strong Mussel is clearly out of his element.

I take over. "She asks if we are here to establish a permanent presence in Cahokia, War Leader." I use a soft voice, that of a superior to a subordinate. "Answer yes so you don't sound like an idiot and embarrass us all."

"Yes, Keeper," Strong Mussel says through a tight throat.

My heart leaps. Here is a way out, if I can just steer my stupid, head-bashing captor into something he is entirely unprepared for.

The old woman studies us through implacable eyes that I cannot read. Though I really don't like her, I keep my expression bland. All I need to do is buy time until I can make my escape.

Eleven

Clan Keeper Blue Heron studied the young woman across the fire from her, who stared back through calculating and rebellious dark eyes—obviously self-possessed even if she barely looked old enough to be considered a woman.

That she had refused to kneel, that she carried herself like a noble, and that she remained uncowed enough to keep her wits indicated that she was indeed High Minko White Water Moccasin's daughter.

As if I didn't have enough to bother me today.

"Two Sticks," she asked the kneeling Albaamaha, "you're sure they don't have any of our language?"

"Most assured, Keeper. The Chikosi are an arrogant people, considering themselves in all ways superior to others. They can converse with the other Moskogee speakers because the languages are related. But they won't even bother to learn T'so, even though they share a border with the Yuchi."

She studied the war leader, who looked uncertainly at her, the White Arrow held erect before him as though it were a sacred relic that would shield him from any unpleasantry.

"What is your take on this, old friend?"

Two Sticks said, "Keeper, the girl is an unwilling participant. They treat her like a war captive. Hence the leash on her ankle. My guess is that she's unruly, did something that offended her family, and was sent here to marry the Morning Star as punishment."

"Any idea what she did to deserve this?"

"No, Keeper. They haven't given me the opportunity to be alone with her to ferret out the whole story." Two Sticks gave her a slight smile. "But the girl treats me with uncommon courtesy given that she's the high minko's daughter."

"Find out for me, if you would." To Smooth Pebble, she said, "The Tunica embassy is empty for the time being. House them there until the *tonka'tzi* can receive them properly. And please explain that their unexpected arrival and the current constraints of our own politics dictate a delay in properly receiving High Minko White Water Moccasin's daughter. That we sincerely value his offer of friendship, the forthcoming marriage, and the importance of establishing close and long-lasting relations with the Sky Hand Moskogee."

Smooth Pebble had been translating as Blue Heron spoke. The girl's eyes had flashed triumphantly, while the war leader barely hid his growing dismay.

He started to complain, only to have Whispering Dawn silence him with a word and gesture.

Most interesting. He wants to cut and run, and she's playing for time.

"Clever girl," Blue Heron whispered under her breath. To Two Sticks, she said, "You've always provided me with worthwhile information, old friend. I am appointing you as my liaison to Lady Whispering Dawn. Find out what you can about why she's really here, and what she intends to do."

"Of course, Keeper." Two Sticks touched his forehead with his fingers.

"Smooth Pebble, please be sure that the war leader understands that Two Sticks is to be given every courtesy as my agent vis-à-vis communications in advance of the wedding."

"What are you thinking?" Smooth Pebble asked.

Blue Heron pulled at her wattle. "The Sky Hand are building an ambitious new Nation south of the Tenasee. Most of what we know of them is through Traders. My suspicion is that *Tonka'tzi* Wind would appreciate the chance to talk with young Whispering Dawn, here. Eventually some of our colonies might end up as potential sources of conflict with the Sky Hand. A smart policy is to understand what sort of people we'd be dealing with."

"Keeper?" Two Sticks said respectfully, "Given the way they watch her, I'd say the girl is going to run the first chance she gets."

"Please see that she doesn't," Blue Heron told him. "Ask Seven Skull Shield if he'd mind helping you keep an eye on her just in case."

"Yes, Keeper." Two Sticks touched his forehead again and stood.

Blue Heron made the Traders' universal "that is all" sign with her hands. She watched as Smooth Pebble led the way out, followed by the girl and her war leader, and finally Two Sticks.

"Interesting," she noted as Dancing Sky walked up with the Keeper's paint palette and grease paints.

"Red and white again today, Keeper?"

"No, let's go for yellow and black. Colors for birth and death. Better suits my mood for dealing with those backstabbing miscreants."

Dancing Sky indicated the departed Sky Hand and her party. "You ask me, she's going to be trouble."

"That little slip of a thing? She's barely more than a child."

"I'll remind you that you said that when the time comes."

But Blue Heron's mind had already moved on to the serpents' nest of intra-clan politics next on her schedule. God's rot it, choosing a matron shouldn't be this complicated.

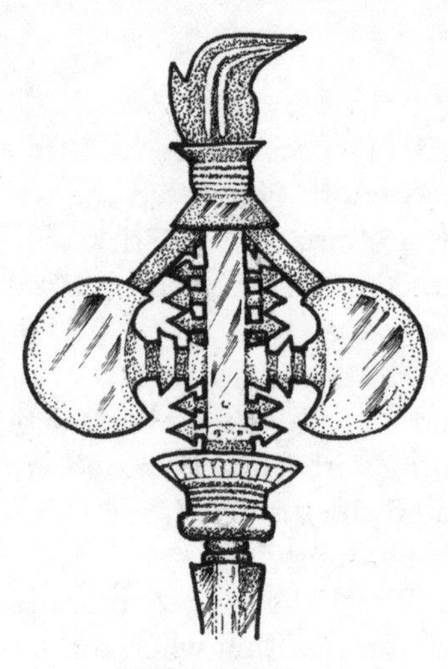

Twelve

The young Chikosi woman was worth a second look. As Seven Skull Shield followed along behind Smooth Pebble, Two Sticks, and the Sky Hand party, he watched her, admired the sway of her hips and the smooth lines of her back. A thick mane of inky black hair had been tightly braided and hung down past her rump. Her shoulders were just right for propping a man's hands on as he looked into her eyes.

And, to his complete delight, she'd given him the sort of disgusted and dismissive look a smart woman would give a maggot-infested loaf of moldy bread.

In other words, a challenge.

"Keeper wants you to help me keep an eye on the Chikosi," Two Sticks had told him as they were leaving the Keeper's.

At Smooth Pebble's nod of assent, he'd slurped down the last of his sunflower-seed soup, let Farts lick the spoon and gourd bowl clean, and collected his pouches before ambling along in their wake.

The way led south along the western margins of the Great Plaza, passing the *tonka'tzi*'s Palace, the various society houses, charnel houses, and temples that lined the plaza down to its southwest corner. Then the way led due west from the great Earth Clans' burial mound, past embassies, dwellings, and cramped gardens, to a well-appointed and spacious dwelling a bow-shot to the east.

"The Tunica aren't using this?" Seven Skull Shield asked Two Sticks as they came to a stop before the looming building.

"Civil War down in Tunica country. The White Heron Moiety town was captured by the Red Staff alliance. The White Herons recalled their embassy until things are sorted out."

"Too bad," Seven Skull Shield mused as he inspected the buildings. Perhaps five paces in length by four wide, the main structure was of trench-wall construction dug down a half body's length into the ground. After construction was complete, the excavated dirt had been piled halfway up the walls for insulation, making the interior warm in winter and cool in summer. The steeply pitched thatched roof looked in need of repair, and the Tunica had drawn some kind of birds on the walls that Seven Skull Shield thought might have been anhingas given the specimens he'd seen Traders carry up from the south.

A dome-structured council house sat to the right with a sweat lodge immediately behind. To the left stood a recently reroofed ramada, complete with a log mortar and pestle out front.

Two Sticks was explaining things as the overdressed Chikosi crowded around with their bundles, packs, and ornate gift chests. To Seven Skull Shield's eyes, the Moskogee looked anything but reassured. The two lead warriors—including the one who clutched the White Arrow like he wanted to strangle it—were glancing around with nervous eyes.

And the girl? Well, she just took in her surroundings with a scheming expression on her pretty young face.

Ambling over to the domicile doorway, Seven Skull Shield looked inside. A squared-off log had been set vertically in the floor to act as a stepping post leading down to the hard-packed subterranean floor. As his eyes adjusted he could see that the wall benches were in good shape and wide enough for two people to sleep side by side. A collection of pots—probably not worth the bother to transport back to Tunica—had been left behind. The central fire pit needed cleaning out. A pile of dried corncobs for the fire were stacked in the corner.

Two Sticks followed him in, stepping down to the floor. The Albaamaha Trader looked around as the Chikosi cautiously stepped down, muttering among themselves as they took in their new home.

Seven Skull Shield waited for a gap in the line and climbed up and out to make room. The girl was standing to one side, arms crossed under her pointed breasts, one foot forward.

As he ambled over, Seven Skull Shield read the distaste in her eyes. In Traders' sign language, he asked, "Why the guards?"

Her hands quickly formed her reply. "Perhaps they are to protect me from leering men who think with their shafts instead of their heads. Why do you care?"

"And the leash?" he signed, before pointing to the strap tied to her ankle.

She just scowled in return, her expression promising violence.

"If you ran, where would you go?" he signed as he ignored her glaring hostility.

Thoughts raced behind her dark eyes, as if deciding how much to tell him. Her hands and fingers began to fly. "I would go home. Back to my husband. A man could make a small fortune in Trade in return for getting me back to Albaamaha country. My husband's clan would be most grateful."

She made the gesture for "but!" and her eyes narrowed. "When I find that man he will be an honorable warrior. Not a leering camp dog like you."

Seven Skull Shield grinned down at Farts. "She thinks I'm a camp dog. Wonder what that makes you?" Signing back, he said, "When I find such a man, I'll let you know."

He gave her a wink and turned to Two Sticks, asking, "Now, why would a pretty young thing like this leave her husband and be brought all this way to marry the Morning Star?"

"My guess is that she disgraced her family. The Chikosi are prickly that way. Arrogant, stuck up, priggish—"

The girl barked something in Moskogee which made Two Stick's fight a smile. "She doesn't know your language, but she knows the word Chikosi. Sky Hand—even disgraced daughters—don't like the word. This one is proud."

Seven Skull Shield gave her another ribald wink, which brought a flash of angry color to her cheeks. "She thinks I'm a scoundrel."

"You *are* a scoundrel."

"Well, you're a spy."

"We both work for the Keeper. We're both spies," Two Sticks countered. Then he chuckled. "So what do you think?"

"The girl's going to run first chance she gets."

"But not yet," Two Sticks decided. "Back at the Keeper's the notion of starting an embassy was her idea. War Leader Strong Mussel was taken by surprise. Delivering the girl to the Morning Star's bed isn't working out quite like he anticipated. The warriors are grumbling, wanting nothing more than to get back to their canoes, shove them out on the river, and head home."

Sharp-eyed as always, Seven Skull Shield noticed that Two Sticks kept glancing at the tattoo on the back of the girl's right hand. It looked like some kind of stylized moth, recognizable only because of a long curling proboscis and spotted wings.

"What is that tattoo?"

"On her hand? Local design back home." Two Sticks shrugged. "More of an affectation, really. Just art."

He's not telling me everything.

Which was curious, since he and Two Sticks both served the Keeper.

So, what game is Two Sticks playing?

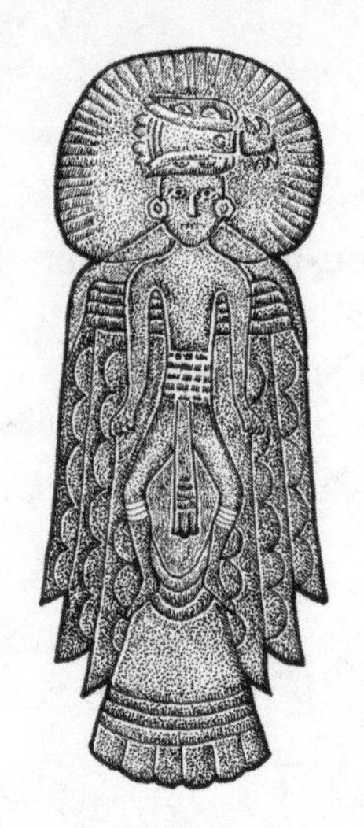

Thirteen

What's the latest?" Blue Heron asked Columella after prayers were offered, black drink was brewed, the pipe smoked, and the afternoon break was called. She nodded a brief recognition as Slender Fox walked past and headed for the Clan House door.

The rest of the delegates looked irritated and hostile—on the verge of violence. For the last two days, messengers had been shuttling back and forth, some of whom Blue Heron's spies had been able to shadow. Deals were being brokered.

Columella raised an eyebrow as she watched Slender Fox's exit. "Outside of the she-bitch getting her sheath greased last night?"

Word was that Slender Fox had slipped into War Duck's bed sometime in the middle of the night. And sure enough, that morning he had come out in support of her nomination to the matron's chair. Apparently his announcement came as a complete surprise to Round Pot, who had pretty well sewn up Horned Serpent House's support after Robin Wing had been voted down by a mere two votes.

Through deft maneuvering Round Pot had built enough consensus during the talks that even Columella had been speaking in her favor. Blue Heron herself wasn't sure that having her on the matron's chair would be such a bad idea.

The betrayal had—for all intents and purposes—cut the legs out from under Round Pot. The expression on the woman's face had been painful to see: half anger, half disbelief, and totally humiliated. Since her brother's declaration, she'd sat stiffly, expression cast in stone, eyes focused somewhere beyond the room in a future that boded no good for her brother.

Columella laid a hand on Blue Heron's shoulder. "You know what this means, don't you?"

Blue Heron glanced over to where Wolverine had War Duck off to the side. The high chief of North Star House was smiling as he talked in low tones to his counterpart from River Mounds; one hand gestured intimately. No doubt Wolverine was sweetening whatever deal Slender Fox had sensually whispered while she used her sheath to milk away the last of War Duck's resistance.

"I sure do. Morning Star House now has Round Pot's vote. Anything to thwart Slender Fox and North Star House. From a three-way tie, we're now at a two-way deadlock. Evening Star House, Morning Star House, and Round Pot against War Duck, Horned Serpent, and North Star Houses."

Columella's eyes narrowed to slits. "All you need is Robin Wing's support, and it's over. She has no love for Morning Star House, it's true, but she may have even less for Slender Fox and her pernicious ways." She paused. "Did you have a countermove in mind?"

Blue Heron nodded, lowering her voice. "If I withdraw Light Woman's nomination, would you nominate Sacred Spoon?"

Columella hesitated, confused. "She's not even Red Warrior's . . . Oh, I see." A subtle smile played at her lips. "My, you are indeed clever, aren't you? She's far enough removed from your brother's lineage to still the critics' claims of dynastic privilege, but still a close cousin."

"And a very competent woman. Balanced. Thoughtful. She doesn't play favorites, but will act for the good of the city and clan."

Columella studied Blue Heron for a moment, as if trying to scry out what hidden motive she was concealing.

"Oh, stop that! Not everything I do is a superbly calculated trick. I actually believe she's the best person for the job."

Columella casually mentioned, "You know my son, Panther Call, is fifteen this year. He needs a wife. Sacred Spoon has a daughter who will become a woman soon."

"White Frond. Sacred Spoon's oldest daughter." Blue Heron arched an eyebrow. It was an audacious request on Columella's part. But then, the matron had never been anyone's fool—except where her dead brother had been involved. "I'll have to talk to Sacred Spoon. She's no doubt made other plans for the girl. But if I can talk her into it, it works for me."

Columella smiled her satisfaction. "Then, perhaps, while you finalize my son's wedding to your cousin's daughter, I'll go have a little chat with Robin Wing and see just what, exactly, Evening Star House could provide her in return for a vote for Sacred Spoon."

Blue Heron sighed with relief. "We might be able to wrap the whole thing up by this afternoon. You know, woman, there are times when I'm so glad the Morning Star didn't hang you up to die in a square after that nasty business with Walking Smoke."

"I know," Columella replied airily, "since, as I recall, you were going to be hung in the square right next to mine. Figured I'd never get a good night's sleep out there with you moaning and screaming all night."

Blue Heron pointed a suggestive finger at her friend. "Let's just get this done. I want to be home in time for supper tonight."

But it didn't work that way. It was late, long after dark, when her litter bearers carried her up her staircase and deposited her on her veranda.

As she stood and waved them away, a shadow emerged from the darkness. "Keeper?"

"Oh, it's you, thief." She smiled bitterly, the last of the arguments from the Clan House still echoing inside her skull.

"We might have a problem."

"With that Moskogee girl?"

"No. I ran into an old friend this morning. He had an interest in that Quiz Quiz that stole the Bundle. I was supposed to meet him earlier tonight, but he didn't show up."

"Pus and blood, the last thing I want to hear about is that Quiz Quiz! He's hung in a square, isn't he?"

"Yes, but—"

"Then forget it! It's the Surveyors' problem."

"I think Winder is going—"

"I'm not listening to this." She clapped her hands to her ears and bulled her way through the door. "I'm going straight to bed, and if you don't want to find yourself hanging in a square beside that accursed Quiz Quiz, you'll drop it now, thief. I told you to keep track of that Moskogee girl, so please, just do so!"

And to her immense satisfaction, Seven Skull Shield nodded, shrugged his thick shoulders, and left her to her bed and nightmares.

Fourteen

With a coarsely woven cloth, Fire Cat wiped the sweat from his face and took stock of his performance. He had been smooth on his launch, fluid in the bowling of his black stone, and had shifted the lance from his left to right hands with complete economy. But something in the timing of his stride and the release of his lance had been out of step.

As he sucked at his lips and stared down the chunkey court, he wondered if it wasn't time to return to River Mounds City again and play a couple dozen matches under Crazy Frog's watchful eye.

Who'd think it? The key to keeping the edge in chunkey comes not from propitiating Power and the gods, but from playing under a gambler's keen eye.

He glanced past the crowd of observers lining the chunkey court to where the throng of hangers-on waited at the Four Winds Clan House. Bless Piasa's hanging balls, Fire Cat was thankful that Night Shadow Star wasn't involved in that mess, or he'd be there, guarding her back.

And she had enough problems to deal with as it was, given her entanglements in the Spirit World.

He made a clucking sound to express his worry as he collected his stone, lance, and cape. Then he waved at the people who'd gathered to watch his practice, turned, and started for Night Shadow Star's palace.

"Red Wing?" one called. "Any chance you'll play the Morning Star?"

"Is it true that Lady Night Shadow Star forbids it?" called another.

"When will you play for the public again?" yet another demanded.

"Yes! Play an opponent again," came an almost desperate cry from still another.

"I serve at my lady's pleasure," he called back. "I wish you all a fine day."

He ignored their entreaties, pasting an inoffensive smile on his lips as he plodded the short distance to Night Shadow Star's clay-capped black mound, its sides packed and smooth. He couldn't help but note the crowd paralleling his direction on the Avenue of the Sun, pointing, watching with reverent or excited eyes, but not daring to set foot into the forbidden Four Winds Plaza.

Why can't they just leave me alone?

Of all the repercussions because of his actions on Night Shadow Star's behalf in their battle against the Itza lord and his Natchez allies, the last thing he would have feared was celebrity. Now, up past his eyebrows in it, he absolutely hated the adulation. This was nothing like he'd known as a lauded war chief, or as a Red Wing noble. This was *worship* by strangers, and it upset him down to the core of his souls.

Glancing up at the Morning Star's high palace, he thought for the first time that he actually had something in common with Chunkey Boy—a suffocating loss of privacy and self.

He hurried along the north side of Night Shadow Star's mound, wishing he could run to escape the fans who'd followed him from the court, but unwilling to demean himself so.

And as he approached the avenue another crowd—this time of Earth Clan folk, commoners, and dirt farmers—formed to greet him.

"When are you going to play the Morning Star?" a Duck Clan warrior asked. "Do you think you could beat him?"

"Yes, we want a match," another—Deer Clan from his apron—insisted.

"I'd bet my life on you," a woman shouted from the back.

"I serve at the will and pleasure of my lady," Fire Cat repeated as he waved them back. "Let me pass, please."

For the most part they stepped back, beaming delight. A couple of them, however, pressed forward, reaching out, some brushing fingers on his arms as he passed. A little boy ran up, slapped a hand on Fire Cat's lance, and giggled as he darted back to his proud father.

"Hey!" a young woman called, brazenly matching step with him, reaching for his arm. "What are you doing tonight? You need company? I'd give you a shell necklace."

"What?" Fire Cat demanded, shying away as she tried to press herself against him. He'd reached the guards now, thankful that they were hurrying forward, shooing people out of the way.

She was maybe twenty, muscled like a stickball player, with high breasts and a well-defined stomach. A skirt hung low on round hips, and she struck a suggestive pose, one leg forward. A gleam of anticipation shone in her eyes as she flipped back thick black hair.

"Tonight!" she called. "You come get me at the foot of the stairs. I'll put a squeeze on your shaft that you'll never forget!"

"Go on! Get back!" Squadron First War Claw growled, pushing the woman to one side.

As if to leave no doubt about her intent, she pulled up her skirt to expose her womanhood, then undulated her hips suggestively.

"Pus and blood." Fire Cat started up the steps.

"Oh yes," War Claw growled behind him. "She's been down there waiting. Says she's between moons. That a man's seed will take. That she wants you to sire her child."

Fire Cat bowed his respects to the Piasa and Horned Serpent guardian posts at the top of the stairs and slowed, glancing at the squadron first. "Why are you here? I doubt it's to keep me from being mauled by some desperate woman."

War Claw chuckled. "That one down there, from the looks of her, could have any man she wanted. Offered myself, I did. Said she wanted you, and only you, to plant a child in her." The squadron leader waved it away. "Must be a tough job, satisfying all those swooning women. Better you than me. But no, I'm here because of her."

Fire Cat followed War Claw's pointing finger. A woman knelt on the veranda, knees together, back bent, arms tucked close. Wild black hair spilled down to hide her face.

Fire Cat walked cautiously forward. War Claw wasn't just any squadron first, but commander of the Morning Star Squadron, the elite force of warriors who guarded not only the Morning Star himself, but the high-ranking Four Winds Clan nobles who lived around the Great Plaza.

Fire Cat dropped to a knee on the veranda and took in the fine texture of the woman's skirt, her beaded cloak. "Lady?"

"Hear the whispers?" a weak voice asked. "She's calling, you know. Hear . . . Oh, yes . . . yes . . . yes . . . Father of Waters flows so rich . . ."

Fire Cat reached down, lifting the woman's head and parting her hair. She blinked, eyes staring vacantly. It took a moment for him to recognize her thin face. "Sun Wing?"

A quiver of a smile died as her lips began to soundlessly recite. A frown deepened in her forehead.

Like all of Red Warrior's offspring, she was an attractive woman, her features so like Night Shadow Star's. Her gaze flickered from side to side, and she seemed to pause in a half-formed thought. "He who loves is lost and gone," she whispered. "Render of the fair heart's song . . ."

"Lady Sun Wing!" Fire Cat gave her shoulders a shake. "What's wrong? How can I help you?"

"Crazy, you know," War Claw muttered from the corner of his mouth. "Hasn't stirred from that house the Morning Star put her in until today. She just busted out the door and started across the plaza like a woman with a purpose. People were everywhere. Six Fletching was in charge. Didn't want to make a scene by picking her up and hauling her back. The gossips have enough to wag their tongues about. So he sent a runner for me and followed along to keep her out of trouble, and she came here. Climbed up the stairs, and stopped right where she is."

"Did she say anything? Call for Night Shadow Star?"

"No. Just hunched down here spouting this nonsense. When I got here, I asked for Lady Night Shadow Star, but Winter Leaf said the lady couldn't be disturbed."

"Sometimes Winter Leaf doesn't have the sense the Creator gave a rock. Help me. Let's get her inside."

Fire Cat laid his chunkey gear to the side and got an arm under Sun Wing's arm, lifting her as War Claw took her other arm. Sun Wing's lips curled into a slight smile, her eyes half-lidded as she walked along complacently. "Feathers colored, the dead are laid . . . logs across and dirt is made. . . ."

"You ever heard this before?" War Claw asked as they guided Sun Wing inside and Fire Cat led the way across the floor to one of the wall benches in the back of the room.

Winter Leaf stood from where she was weaving on a loom and stared in dismay. "You're bringing her in?"

"She's Night Shadow Star's sister," Fire Cat growled. "What were you going to do? Leave her out there on the veranda babbling to herself?"

"But the Lady—"

"Is she Spirit traveling?"

"No, just sleeping. It's so odd," Winter Leaf said. "It's the first time in days. When I went in and called out that Sun Wing was here, Night Shadow Star didn't even stir. Knowing that she hasn't had a good night's sleep, I figured she needed it more than she needed to visit with her sister."

Fire Cat straightened, carefully inspecting Sun Wing. The woman seemed completely indifferent to her surroundings, eyes focused someplace beyond this world, lips moving as she mouthed odd words.

War Claw led him to the side, voice low. "You know what happened to her? Why she's the way she is?"

Fire Cat nodded. "I was there, remember? Didn't get more than a glance at Sun Wing. She was sprawled naked on the floor, screaming in a pool of blood. Severed pieces of her sister were scattered around. Like a nightmare come to life. Night Shadow Star told me that when she walked into the room Walking Smoke had Sun Wing hanging upside down, a knife to her neck. Sun Wing came that close to having her throat slit."

Fire Cat shrugged. "That kind of terror? Do anyone's souls survive such a thing intact?"

War Claw took a deep breath. "Rides-the-Lightning was supposed to call her souls back. Return them to her body. He did the best he could, but wasn't sure he'd succeeded after the four days were up. Then Sun Wing was placed in that house over on the other side of the plaza. Since then, she's just eaten, drank, slept, and kept to herself. Sometimes she just sits on her sleeping bench and holds herself as she rocks back and forth all day long."

Fire Cat fingered his chin. "But she picks today to suddenly run to Night Shadow Star's and kneel on the porch?"

War Claw gave another of his enigmatic shrugs. "What do you want to do with her?"

"Let her sit for the moment. I need to check on Night Shadow Star."

Fire Cat took a moment to retrieve his chunkey stone and lance and stow them before he stepped into Night Shadow Star's personal quarters. She lay on her side, her hair a dark swirl on her bedding. Her face was tranquil, her breathing deep and regular. This time her bedding wasn't wadded and disheveled where she'd been thrashing, tossing, and turning.

Fire Cat could almost feel the peaceful depth of her sleep.

He frowned, turned, and walked to the Tortoise Bundle where it rested on its special shelf. The scuffed leather cover seemed innocuous for once. "Just this once, let her sleep. That's not asking too much, is it?"

But the Bundle remained mute.

Fire Cat made a face and returned to the great room. War Claw was fingering his chin, narrowed eyes on Sun Wing. "What does the Lady Night Shadow Star say, Red Wing?"

"Winter Leaf was right. She's sleeping like she hasn't in two moons, and I'm not waking her." He gestured to Sun Wing. "For the moment she's not hurting anything. When Night Shadow Star awakens, we'll see what she wants to do. In the meantime, leave her guards here. We'll feed them and see to their needs until it's time to take Sun Wing back home."

War Claw lifted a skeptical eyebrow. "You sure you don't want me to take Lady Sun Wing back now? I mean, with your lady sound asleep and not much else happening, you could send Winter Leaf off on some errand or another."

"And why would I do that? You're not making any sense."

An impish smile bent War Claw's normally humorless lips. "And on my way out I'll send up that slippery-sheathed vixen waiting below so that you can . . . um, fulfill her needs."

Fire Cat chuckled. "On second thought, Squadron First, I'd rather you called up another two tens of warriors in ranks to guarantee Lady Sun Wing's safety—and to ensure that saucy minx down there doesn't creep in the back way. 'Cause if she does, I'm running and leaving you to whatever fate the Spirits decree."

Meanwhile, on the bench, Sun Wing's mumbling voice could be heard, chanting, "Born of Sun. One is slayed. Here, by the long trail, his corpse is laid. . . ."

"What *is* that?" War Claw asked.

"Nothing I've ever heard." But it sent a shiver down Fire Cat's back.

Fifteen

"Do you think this is going to work?" Sacred Spoon asked as she stared around the crowded Four Winds Clan House. Most of another day had been spent in arguments, accusations, and recriminations. The final vote would be coming soon. The participants seemed to anticipate it.

"I think so." Blue Heron glanced over to the side of the room where Slender Fox and Wolverine stood in council with their brother Sliding Ice and younger sister Ripe Woman. War Duck, with Green Chunkey at his side, stood at the fore of their united block of votes for River Mounds and Horned Serpent Town.

To her cousin, Blue Heron added, "Slender Fox thinks she's got it. Robin Wing will be the kicker. Columella's deal with her was that we'd withdraw Light Woman's nomination."

"And how did Light Woman take that?" Sacred Spoon shot a look at where her cousin stood in the rear.

Light Woman's falcon-feather cloak was thrown back in concession to the stifling heat—too many bodies packed in the room. The expression on the woman's face wouldn't have been more bitter had she just been slapped.

"Not well." Blue Heron fingered her chin. "If you win this, I would suggest some efforts be directed at soothing her hurt. For the moment she's just seen the matron's chair slip away, but when it sinks in that it was you or Slender Fox, she won't necessarily like it, but she'll accept it."

From her litter chair on the dais behind the fire, *Tonka'tzi* Wind called out, "A final vote is in order. I'm about to call it. Are there any other statements?"

Blue Heron stepped forward to the speaker's position before the fire and raised her hands high. "Morning Star House has heard the objections raised by High Chief War Duck and High Chief Green Chunkey against Light Woman. While Morning Star House believes it has the votes necessary to force the issue and place Light Woman on the matron's chair, it is our considered opinion that doing so would sow such discord that the harmony of the Four Winds Clan might be irreparably rent asunder."

She took a moment to stare around the room. "In concession, and as a gesture of Morning Star House's goodwill, we withdraw Light Woman for consideration as clan matron."

On Slender Fox's side of the room every expression was stunned, as if they were clubbed fish.

Good! Blue Heron thought to herself. *Caught them by surprise.*

"Does Morning Star House offer another to stand for the matron's chair?" Wind demanded.

"We do not," Blue Heron announced. "At this time, relations are so strained that any woman put forward by Morning Star House, no matter how qualified, will be rejected outright by North Star, River Mounds, and Horned Serpent Houses."

She saw a gloating satisfaction fill Slender Fox's catty face. The cunning sheath thought she'd won.

"Are there nominations from any of the other Houses?" Wind asked, her slitted eyes on Blue Heron as she stepped back. That the *tonka'tzi* didn't know the plan—thought Blue Heron was giving up—actually brought a quiver of pleasure to Blue Heron's breast.

Columella stepped forward, raising her arms. "Evening Star House offers Lady Sacred Spoon of Slick Rock's lineage, daughter of Chief Takes Blood and Eel Woman of the Panther Clan."

"She's Morning Star House!" Slender Fox cried.

"What of it?" Columella shot back, then turned her attention to the surprised Wind. "Evening House offers Sacred Spoon as a compromise, given that the Keeper—in the best interest of the clan—has withdrawn Light Woman. The complaint has been that authority was concentrated in Black Tail's lineages. Slick Rock served as *tonka'tzi* during Cahokia's formative years. Slick Rock's daughter Swan Tail held the position of clan matron before this council voted it to Wind. Now that Wind has vacated the chair, Evening Star House sees no problem returning the matron's chair to Swan Wing's niece, Sacred Spoon."

Columella stepped back amidst a rising murmur of speculation.

Tension rose in the crowded room.

"Does anyone else support Sacred Spoon as possible clan matron?" Wind demanded, her face like a frozen mask.

Robin Wing and Round Pot both stepped forward, calling, "We do," in unison.

From where she stood in the crowd, Columella shouted, "Call the vote, *Tonka'tzi*. Let us elect Sacred Spoon as clan matron!"

Hisses and barely stifled curses came from Slender Fox's side. Green Chunkey had a thoughtful look on his face as he considered his suddenly rebellious sister. War Duck looked fit to be tied, staring daggers at Round Pot. In her turn, she studiously ignored her brother, expression stoic. So much for River Mounds' vaunted unity and compromise.

That's going to be an interesting relationship from here on out, Blue Heron thought.

Wind cleared her throat, announcing, "Very well. If there are no other comments, I will call the vote."

"There are other comments," Five Fists called from the rear. He marched forward, almost shoving his way through the crowd. In his wake came Sacred Spoon's younger sister, Rising Flame. In her early twenties, she was a tall, muscular stickball player with a raven-dark wealth of thick hair piled high on her head and pinned with a copper headpiece. She had painted her face white with black forked-eye designs that mimicked the Morning Star's. A brilliantly colored cloak of painted bunting feathers hung from her shoulders, and a short white skirt was tied at her narrow waist to emphasize her hips and long legs.

Five Fists strode to a stop at the speaker's position. Rising Flame positioned herself beside him, a curious smile on her face, eyes narrowed in what looked like satisfaction.

Wind had straightened, her copper-clad staff of office in hand. "War Leader Five Fists, you have no standing here. As a member of an Earth Clan and a—"

"I come as escort for Lady Rising Flame," Five Fists announced, and paused as he looked around the room, eyes like hot black coals. A faint amusement could be seen in his lop-jawed face. "I speak for the Morning Star. Or would you deny him a voice in the Four Winds Clan?"

Wind had a perplexed look—taken aback as she was. Not even as *tonka'tzi* would she dare deny the Morning Star.

Before she could formulate a response, Five Fists turned, searching the faces around him. "Would any of you? Go on. Speak up! Who among you would deny the Morning Star a voice in your council?"

Blue Heron's heart began to beat harder. What scheme was this?

Why on earth would the Morning Star insert himself into the Four Winds council? And more to the point, who in their right minds would stand against him?

Five Fists—as he'd known from the start—heard no dissent. Which was when he stepped back, leaving Rising Flame alone before the fire.

"What's she doing?" Sacred Spoon demanded, starting forward.

Blue Heron reached out, clamping fingers on the woman's upper arm. "Don't even think it. If this is what I think it is, it's all over."

Rising Flame lifted her chin, staring haughtily into Wind's eyes, and said, "I offer myself as clan matron. I am Rising Flame, of Slick Rock's lineage, Morning Star House, daughter of Takes Blood and Eel Woman, and the chosen of the Morning Star."

She paused for effect, looking around the room with challenging eyes and repeating, "The *chosen* of the Morning Star."

"As a woman of the Four Winds Clan you have the right to offer yourself." Wind took a deep breath, a look of futility on her face. "Is there anyone else who supports Rising Flame for clan matron?"

For a long moment, no one moved. Five Fists began to grin, a growing gleam in his eyes as he fixed on War Duck and raised a suggestive eyebrow.

The high chief of River Mounds stepped up beside Rising Flame and chuckled humorlessly to himself before he said, "I withdraw my support of Slender Fox and place it behind Rising Flame."

He was but the first of many.

"Just what is happening here?" Columella asked as she slipped up beside Blue Heron and Sacred Spoon.

"The vote on Rising Flame's ascent to the matron's chair just became a formality," Blue Heron said woodenly.

"Why is Morning Star interfering?" Sacred Spoon demanded through a forced exhale.

"That," Blue Heron told her, "is the real question."

To Begin the Dance

The day I arrived at the Tunica embassy, I decided if I was going to take control of my destiny, I must assert myself. I am the high minko's daughter, after all. I may not have wanted it, but this is what I've been trained for: to be a leader.

If I was not to be treated like a bit of chattel—a mere trophy female captured on a raid and given away like some prize—I had better start acting like a lady of noble birth.

I started by pointing to a sleeping bench in the center of the back wall closest to the fire and stated, "That's mine. You will have the warriors place my bedding there."

Then I looked at Strong Mussel, ordering, "Come with me, War Leader."

I climbed up out of the house and surveyed was my new domain. To the east the skyline was dominated by conical burial mounds and high temples atop earthen pyramids. Through a break in the houses to the north I saw the tonka'tzi*'s remarkable palace with its statuary and soaring Spirit poles, and beyond it, the Morning Star's great mound and sky-scraping home.*

Strong Mussel followed me out, still holding my despicable leash. I said, "Oh, hand it over. I'm not running today. I give you my word on the honor of the Chief Clan. On my ancestor's bones."

He looked skeptically at me. His lips quivered as though arguing with himself; then he handed the leash over. I wrapped it around my wrist.

I checked the council house, finding it pretty much the same as the one we'd slept in. The sweat lodge behind it was a low dome big enough for six people to scrunch themselves inside. I was pleased to see a pile of stones and the fire pit outside for heating them.

In the distance, I hear a great shout. Someone is beating on a pot drum. Sounds like some sort of celebration.

I walk over to the dwelling and seat myself in the sun, back against the wall. "Two Sticks," I call. "Would you be kind enough to come and explain some things to me?"

The Albaamaha is talking in a low voice to that despicable hulking Cahokian. They both come, the Cahokian's remarkably ugly dog following along behind in a loose-limbed gait.

Two Sticks drops to his haunches, the Cahokian doing the same, much to my dismay.

Strong Mussel still stands, fidgeting, holding the White Arrow as if for reassurance. He looks like a man whose canoe has been spun around and around by a whirlpool until he has no idea which direction he was headed.

I say, "The war leader, here, hasn't bothered to ask, but we need to know: What's happening here? Why are we being shuttled around from one subordinate to another?"

Two Sticks studies me thoughtfully. "We just heard. While you were inspecting your new home, the Four Winds Clan has chosen a new clan matron. Some things, at least, will slowly return to normal. Including your reception as a visiting dignitary." As he talked, he signed for the despicable Cahokian's benefit.

"So that I have it straight, the Four Winds Clan rules Cahokia. The Earth Clans, under them, actually administer the separate areas of the city?"

"That is correct. Each Earth Clan district in turn is composed of separate villages filled with immigrants. They all have their own languages, temples, council houses, and plazas with their crude chunkey courts, surrounded by dwellings and farmsteads. These people are called the dirt farmers, and come from all over the world. They moved here to share the miracle of the Morning Star's resurrection into a human body."

"Do you believe that, Two Sticks?"

He shrugs. "How else do you explain the miracle of this giant city, Lady? The important thing is that all of these people . . . they believe it."

In the distance, another great shout can be heard.

Two Sticks tells me, "They celebrate the election of a woman called Rising Flame of the Morning Star House. Within the quarter moon there will probably be games. I would expect your wedding to the Morning Star to be postponed until after the celebration."

I can tell Two Sticks is holding something back, his gaze pointedly avoiding Strong Mussel's. "War Leader?"

"Yes, Lady?"

"Take two men and a string of beads. We passed Traders with firewood

back by the tonka'tzi*'s palace. We will need wood for the cooking fires tonight. Corncobs won't make us stew."*

As his eyes fill with suspicion, I wave him away. "Oh, go on. I'm not running. I'm still surrounded by warriors, and Two Sticks will ensure that I'm still here when you get back. Go. That's an order."

Still he hesitates.

"By the World Tree's roots, War Leader, if your remaining warriors can't keep me here, they don't deserve to call themselves Sky Hand. Go get wood!"

He rises to his feet, pointing at Two Sticks. "She'd better be here."

The Albaamaha raises his hands in submission.

I watch the war leader open a box, remove some beads, and leave at a trot with Cloud Tassel on his heels.

When I look back at Two Sticks, a faint smile teases his lips. In a low voice, he notes, "My uncle had a tattoo like yours on his right hand. It's not the sort of thing I would expect to see on a Sky Hand high minko's daughter's hand. You are not what you seem, are you?"

I glance meaningfully at the disgusting Cahokian who is watching through half-lidded eyes. Two Sticks is no longer signing.

Catching my meaning, Two Sticks says, "He has none of your language. And he certainly knows nothing of the Sacred Moth Society or its rites. So why don't you tell me exactly what is going on?"

"I was banished because I defied my clan and ran away to marry the man I love. My husband is Albaamaha. Straight Corn, son of Wet Clay Woman, matron of the Reed Clan." I raise my chin defiantly. "I love *him. I'd rather live in the forest with the man I love than rule Split Sky City. That's why they sent me here. As punishment. And I am just waiting for the opportunity to escape back home to him."*

Two Sticks stares speculatively at me, as if wondering if he should believe me. Then he fixes on my tattoo. Thinks. Finally he says, "I wouldn't run if I were you."

"Why?"

"Because you should be smarter than that. Your husband, this Straight Corn, he is an initiate?"

"Yes."

"And his uncle? He would be Hanging Moss, of the Reed Clan?"

"Yes."

"As I remember, Hanging Moss was well known as a shaman. Was a figure of authority in the Sacred Moth Society."

"These days he cares for the Moth Bundle. He calls the prayers. Dances with the moths."

Two Sticks chuckles softly to himself. "Lady, you probably don't realize the opportunity that is being handed to you. Right here. In Cahokia. Stay. Endure the living god's bed if you must, and found your embassy among the Cahokians. Be all that your heritage says you can."

"I could not care less about Cahokia. That talk about an embassy was to buy time to escape. I want to be with my husband."

"Oh, don't worry. Surely Straight Corn was apprised of your fate. You ran off and married an Albaamaha. What a slap to the Chief Clan. Exile is too good for your transgressions. Your father would have made you an example to all. Especially Reed Clan. Your value to my people—especially as a Sacred Moth initiate—can't be overstated. My guess is that they're already halfway here." Two Sticks smiles. "And your husband is in the lead canoe, paddling harder than the rest to come find you."

For no longer than it takes to catch a breath, I am stunned. "Halfway here?"

My souls are wheeling with disbelief.

As he watches my increasing excitement, I can see a spreading satisfaction behind his eyes. "You are a very important young woman, Lady. I begin to see Power's plan for you."

"What plan?" My heart is beating in my chest like a pot drum. Straight Corn is coming here? How well I can imagine him in that lead canoe, can see the desperation on his face. The bunching at the corner of his wide jaw. His muscles are knotting under his smooth brown skin as he drives the paddle deep, each stroke propelling a sleek war canoe across the swirling brown water.

Two Strikes has a new intensity in his suddenly gleaming eyes. "Lady, Moth magic is old, dating back to the Beginning Times when the Albaamaha and Koasati peoples first emerged into this world from beneath the roots of the World Tree. According to the old stories, when the people emerged it was night. They looked up and saw the stars, and were afraid. An owl hooted. Some turned around and fled back down into the earth."

I take over the narrative, saying, "The rest were ready to follow when the Sacred Moth fluttered out of the night sky. Smelling sweetly of datura nectar and tobacco blossoms, Sacred Moth fluttered around them. Enchanted, the people were reassured, and they followed Sacred Moth to a tobacco field, and realized that they had reached a good place."

Two Sticks points a finger at me. "You are making the journey from your own Underworld and have arrived at Cahokia, your new world. You have just emerged, and are thinking of fleeing back to the past: your metaphorical Underworld. But just as the Sacred Moth brought my people to understanding in the Beginning Times, it now leads you."

"Leads me where?" I am having trouble following his line of thought.

"Don't you understand? You are the chosen one. The woman sent to bring the Power of the night here, to establish it at Cahokia."

I am astounded. First at the notion that Straight Corn would be on his way. Which, of course, I should have realized, knowing my husband. But second, that I, a lowly initiate, would be chosen by Sacred Moth for such an important purpose.

As if reading my uncertainty, Two Sticks uses a conspiratorial tone. "It is not happenstance that you are the high minko's daughter. You are the bridge, Lady. A Sky Hand noble, you married an Albaamaha. You dedicated yourself to the ways of the night and Sacred Moth. Learned the potions and secrets of the sacred plants. By its machinations, Power has sent you here to marry the Morning Star and establish the Sacred Moth Society in the heart of Cahokia."

For the moment, I am too taken aback to absorb the importance of what he is saying.

"But I don't want to marry the Morning Star."

Two Sticks shrugs. "The Sacred Moth could not care less what you want. You are walking the path of Power, Lady. It will use you as it wishes."

Sixteen

Rising Flame!" Blue Heron almost spat the words as she sat on one of the Council House daises to the right of Wind's elevated *tonka'tzi*'s seat. They had retreated to the Council House—Cahokia's center of government—where it stood on the jutting southern terrace of the Morning Star's great mound. Blue Heron tapped fingers on her chin as she stared up at the soot-stained poles that supported the gabled ceiling.

"Morning Star must have had a reason." Wind sat forward on her panther hides and pretended to study the copper-clad staff of office that she held. She absently ran her fingers over the embossed spirals that represented the World Tree. It was topped with feathers and had a circular shell piece engraved with a circle and cross on the bottom.

"What reason? You tell me?"

"Can't. For the life of me."

"Rising Flame is aptly named. She doesn't have the control, the experience. She's hot-blooded and volatile. Too emotional. And not only that . . ." Blue Heron made a face but couldn't continue.

"You can't stand her," Wind finished her thought as she pulled her copper headpiece off. She shook out her long gray hair before running fingers through it. "I can't stomach her either."

"Nor could her last husband. She's freshly divorced. And that's another problem. She's going to have half the men in Cahokia flocking to her door, Earth Clans and Four Winds alike, all trying to snare her into a marriage. Even if she had the cunning it takes to spar with the likes of

War Duck, Slender Fox, and Green Chunkey, how could she give them her full attention when an endless stream of men are filing through her door?"

Wind shook her head. "Let alone the fact that the woman has spent most of her life traveling. All that time among foreign peoples? Being corrupted by their morals and beliefs? Who is to know what crazy ideas she has about how things are done? I wonder if she isn't more Casqui than Cahokian."

Unable to let the thought go, Blue Heron pointed a finger and added, "Let alone the ones she drags off to her bed. She has a reputation for such doings. Nothing like Slender Fox, but still—"

"You know, Sister," Wind reminded, "I heard the same things said about you once upon a time." She paused. "Just making note, that's all."

Blue Heron lifted her lip in warning.

Wind ignored her and twirled her staff. "Morning Star must see something in her that we don't."

"I wonder if she's been spending time with him? I had my people watching her sister. Making sure Sacred Spoon wasn't hiding any surprises that would be sprung the moment we offered her for matron." She screwed up her lips. "And keeping even better track of Slender Fox and the rest who were going to vote against us. Should have had my agents concentrating on Rising Flame."

Wind's chuckle sounded oddly hollow. "Got to hand it to you, you played that masterfully. You even took me by surprise. But for the Morning Star's interference, we'd be celebrating Sacred Spoon's ascent to the chair."

"If I was so masterful, why's Rising Flame the clan matron and Sacred Spoon's not?"

Wind frowned at her staff. "I didn't know what to say when Five Fists bulled his way up to the speaker's spot and brought everything to a halt. There is no precedent. Nor has the question ever been asked: Does the Morning Star have a voice among the Four Winds Clan because he's in Chunkey Boy's body? Or is he essentially a clanless interloper?

"And more to the point"—Blue Heron used a bony finger for emphasis—"are you going to be the one to deny him? Tell him his agent can't speak? Hmm? Did you see anyone in that council willing to offer so much as a peep of opposition? I sure didn't."

"A minor point. Rising Flame is Four Winds. She had a right to offer herself." Wind waved it away. "But it is done. Over. My bet is that she's got her servants and household moving her possessions into my old personal quarters as we speak."

Though she couldn't see it through the Council House walls, Blue

Heron glanced up in the direction of the Morning Star's palace. Could almost feel him up there.

What is your game, Morning Star? Did you specifically want a spoiled youngster? An inexperienced hothead who has spent half of her life living among foreigners? Why? To keep us all at each other's throats?

Wind must have been sharing her thoughts, because the *tonka'tzi* was shaking her head, eyes vacant and lips quivering as if she were conversing with her souls.

"It's not going to be good," Blue Heron concluded.

"No, I suppose not."

She looked up as the thief came plodding into the room, his ugly, big-boned dog padding at his side. "Is there some problem you have with understanding?"

"How's that, Keeper?" He grinned, bobbing his head and tapping fingers to his forehead. "Greetings, *Tonka'tzi.* Must be a relief to have that pus-rotted council over. Word on the plaza is that it's Rising Flame. I've seen her around. Looks a bit, um . . ." He shrugged his reluctance to say more.

"Young?" Wind prompted, shooting him a disdainful look.

"Exactly!" Seven Skull Shield snapped his fingers. "Hardly heard of her before. Would have figured you'd have chosen an older, well, more seasoned woman."

Blue Heron read Wind's building irritation. To still her sister's coming explosion, she held out a hand, snapping, "We *would* have! She's the *Morning Star's* choice."

Seven Skull Shield's blocky face pursed in a knowing frown. "That puts an entirely different spin on the old chunkey stone, don't it?" He shot her a curious look. "You know why he'd choose Rising Flame instead of someone you wanted?"

"No." she snapped, then relented. "And it's irritating me to no end. Now, is there a reason you came charging in here after Smooth Pebble told you to keep out?"

"Is that what she was trying to tell me?" Seven Skull Shield glanced down at the dog. "Guess you were right, Farts. She really didn't want me coming in here."

"One of these days, thief," Wind almost growled, "you'll push us too far."

Again Blue Heron waved her sister down, demanding, "Do you have a death wish? Or did you just wander off this morning and leave your good sense asleep in some woman's bed? Why are you here?"

Seven Skull Shield gave her a sly smile. "Just a feeling, Keeper. It's that Chikosi girl. The one you wanted Two Sticks to keep track of."

"What about her?"

"Call it a crawly feeling down in my gut. She managed to send those over-feathered warriors off for firewood this morning, and she and Two Sticks had a long talk."

"And you came here just to tell me that?" Blue Heron muttered.

"Well, he was signing to start with. Translating so I knew everything that was being said." The thief looked pensive. "Then he quit once he had the girl to himself, waving me off. Which was fine. I watched him and girl get right serious. And then she got really, really excited."

He paused. "I don't make a fuss about it, but I like people to think I'm dumb."

"A skill at which you overly succeed." Wind narrowed her eyes.

"Thank you, Tonka'tzi!" Seven Skull Shield beamed. "You see, I got a smattering of languages from my days on the river that I don't let on about. And down at the landing, listening to all the languages, hearing words while Traders are signing? You just naturally pick up a few words of this and that."

"Does this have a point?" Wind demanded.

Seven Skull Shield ignored her. "Now, I don't really know Two Sticks. So I was playing stupid while he and the girl talked. The thing is, I caught just enough to get the gist of what they were saying. Turns out she's already married to an Albaamaha, and he's coming here."

"You interrupted us for this?" Wind asked, still irritated.

The thief tapped his fingertips together as he spoke. "Two Sticks is really excited about this guy's arrival, and it has something to do with that tattoo on her hand. Now just why a married woman—"

"Excuse me," Wind interrupted. "What in the name of Piasa's balls are we talking about? What woman? Why do we care if her husband is coming here? And what does a tattoo have to do with anything?"

Blue Heron gave Seven Skull Shield the "go ahead" nod.

"Well, *Tonka'tzi*, supposedly she's the Chikosi high minko's daughter from down at Split Sky City south of the bend of the Tenasee. She was sent here to marry the Morning Star. But now we find out she's already married."

"Why haven't I heard anything about this?"

Blue Heron told her, "Because they just showed up on my doorstep. You were orchestrating the matron's council and had more to worry about than some war chief with a White Arrow and an offer of marriage from another young woman. We do these things all the time." She turned back to Seven Skull Shield. "So, why did you want to bother me with this right now?"

"Like I said. A crawly feeling in my gut."

"Pus and spit," Wind muttered. "I've got way too good an imagination to think about what's crawling around in your gut, thief."

"Go on," Blue Heron told him.

He pulled out a scrap of hide onto which had been drawn an image. To Blue Heron's eyes it looked like a big moth in side view. "That's as close as I can come to the tattoo on the girl's hand. The one that Two Sticks fixed on."

"And who's this Two Sticks?" Wind asked.

"One of my spies. An Albaamaha. He keeps track of the Traders coming in from the Tenasee. His job is to pick up any news about events in the Chikosi and Choctaw country. Give me a heads-up if trouble's coming our way. Those people down there don't like each other. The girl said she was here to establish an embassy, marry the Morning Star, and institute better relations between Cahokia and the Sky Hand. But like I said, it was all pretty slipshod. No messenger arrived in advance to announce their approach. Just the war leader, with his White Arrow, at the head of a party of warriors, and the girl being led around on an ankle leash. The man might be something on the battlefield, but he didn't have a clue about diplomacy."

"The girl and Two Sticks didn't talk about embassies, Keeper." The thief kicked his mongrel dog back before it could lift its leg on her dais.

"Then what?"

"That's just it. That crawly feeling. I figured Two Sticks would tell me the meat of it. He's one of yours, right? But when I asked him about it, he said that the girl was excited about marrying the Morning Star, about sharing the miracle of the Beginning Times hero reincarnated into a human body. About how her father would be a good ally for Cahokia."

"But you said you only have a smattering of Moskogee?" Wind countered. "How do you know she didn't?"

Seven Skull Shield spread his hands wide. "Because I've got enough, *Tonka'tzi.* She's waiting for her Albaamaha husband to arrive, and there's something about a sacred society. And clans. And the fact that her father banished her for marrying the Albaamaha in the first place."

He paused. "That moth tattoo has something to do with it. But more to the point, why did Two Sticks lie?"

"Because she's already married?" Wind wondered. "Then why would her father send her here to marry the Morning Star?"

"Her father is a high minko. Maybe he declared the marriage ended. Nullified," Blue Heron suggested. "Wouldn't be the first time."

"Or it could be that the Chikosi high minko is dumping his daughter on the Morning Star and doesn't want him to know." Wind countered.

"Knowing that she's disgraced does sour the pot more than a little. 'Here, Morning Star, take this girl no one wants. Sure, she's spoiled goods, but what you don't know won't hurt you.' "

"And it explains why the war leader was so unprepared. I can imagine his orders: 'Deliver the girl to the Morning Star, and come right home.' "

"Are these people truly that clumsy?" Blue Heron wondered.

"Is she young and attractive?"

"Not a ravishing beauty, but attractive enough, supple, and endowed."

"Then Morning Star won't care. What's another marriage in the long list of wives foreign chiefs have sent him? The recorders will note it, the ceremony will be short and to the point, and he'll take her to his bed. An emissary and priests will be sent to Split Sky City. A couple of months later, if the Morning Star is tired of her, she'll be allowed to marry some Earth Clans man and be a minor celebrity. Especially if she's pregnant. End of the story."

"Ladies," Seven Skull Shield interrupted, waving his bit of hide. "If that's the case, why would Two Sticks lie? Albaamaha hate the Chikosi, right? What would Two Sticks care? Even if Whispering Dawn was married to a relative of his, he'd want to ensure that the lost husband didn't show up, calling 'Where's my wife?' Embarrassing the Morning Star could wind up with Two Sticks, the girl, and the errant husband all hanging in squares."

"Albaamaha do hate Chikosi," Wind mused. "Maybe Two Sticks is figuring that the girl and husband are expendable. If he waits, lets her marry Morning Star, then exposes the fraud? It would be a huge black eye for the Chikosi. The repercussions would make a laughingstock of the high minko. Would definitely destroy any chance for relations with Cahokia."

"But Two Sticks could do that without waiting for the husband. All he'd have to do is tell me that the Morning Star was being set up, that the high minko was playing him for a fool, and it'd be flying fur and feathers."

"It's got something to do with that tattoo," Seven Skull Shield insisted. "Figure out what that tattoo stands for, you'll have Two Sticks, the girl, and the high minko by the balls."

"Perhaps," Wind said thoughtfully. "Keeper, send a messenger to the Morning Star when you get the chance. Let him know. In the meantime, stall. Let this play out and see where it leads."

"You sure you want to go that route?" Blue Heron asked.

"It's just as easy to hang them in squares next week as it is today."

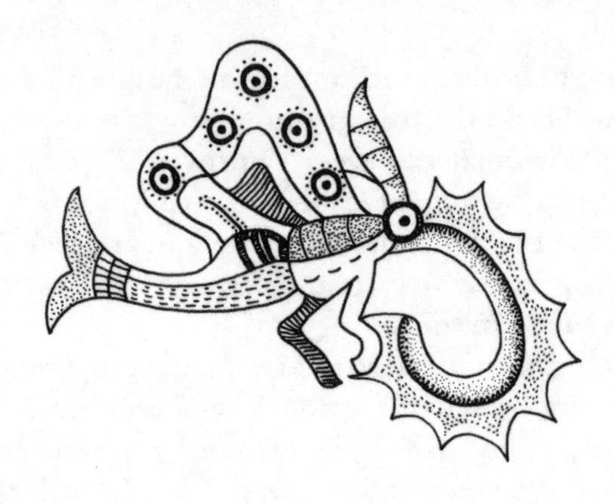

A Turn of Fate

Nothing was working as it should. Strong Mussel's plan had been to march up to the Morning Star, offer me as a bride, and quickly scoot back to his canoes and paddle home as fast as the current and strength of arms would carry him.

My plan was always to slip away before he had the chance to do that, vanish into the city, and make my way south to Straight Corn by whatever manner I could. Scary thought that, a young woman alone, traveling for days across half of the known world.

Love, however, is a strong motivator.

Then we arrived to find Cahokia bigger and more confusing than anyone could have imagined. My play for time has indeed worked. I have a nice small compound with a house, council building, and all the fixings of a minor noble.

Strong Mussel is fretting anxiously, waiting for a summons whereby he can deliver me to anyone who will take me to the Morning Star. That done, he can leave.

And as for me, I can't *escape. Not now. Not after what Two Sticks has told me. Sure, all the way up the river I dreamed that Straight Corn and his relatives would come and rescue me. You know, one of those impossible dreams. The kind you cling to because you don't have anything else. But I didn't really think it was a workable option. Strong Mussel and his warriors had a head start, and had made very good time on the rivers.*

I knew the reality. Even if Straight Corn had heard the same day I left, he would have had to organize canoes, stock up on provisions, Trade, and gather equipment. Then came the challenge of finding men willing to go. It meant leaving families at the beginning of harvest, collection of the nut crop now falling in the forest, and the fall hunting season for deer, turkey, squirrels, bear, and migrating waterfowl.

Assuming, of course, that his family thought enough of me to raise the pursuit. And you can bet I kept that worry locked in my head.

But the clincher hadn't really sunk in until Two Sticks brought up my tattoo. Of course I was important to the Albaamaha. I was *a high minko's daughter. I'd married one of their most eligible young men, and the Albaamaha were struggling for their very lives under Sky Hand domination.*

But most of all I was an initiate in the ancient arts of the night. I had begun my training in the ways of the darkness, had been instructed on the special Powers of the Sacred Moth. I might be only a novice, but I know some of the secrets of the society. And the society protects its own.

Of course they would be coming for me.

All I have to do is hope that in the turmoil of Cahokian politics, with the election of their new Four Winds Clan matron, I will be forgotten for long enough that Straight Corn can arrive, ferret out my location, and spirit me away some night before I am trundled off to the Morning Star's bed.

To that end, I am doing everything I can to allay Strong Mussel's fears. Which leaves me here, braiding hemp fibers into cordage as I sit in the afternoon sun and watch the hustle of Cahokia unfold around my "embassy."

We are somewhat off the main avenues, but the city reminds me of a hive. People walk through here constantly bearing bundles, packs, and loads of all kinds. They all speak in tongues I've never heard before and dress in the most outlandish manners. Every hair style imaginable—from completely shaved heads, to lopsided cuts, high-piled coiffures, intricate braids, and just leaving it to hang loose—can be seen within a single day's observation.

As I braid, I wonder how long it will take Straight Corn, assuming they are as driven as Strong Mussel's warriors and make the same time traveling. It might have taken a day or two for word of my fate to reach the forest Albaamaha. Another two or three days if the Reed Clan and Sacred Moth Society pushed for a rapid departure, ordering the best young men to drop what they were doing, pack, and hit the river north.

Ticking off the days on my fingers, I am shocked to realize that Straight Corn could arrive as early as the day after tomorrow.

I sit up as if slapped, souls racing.

How does my husband find me in the vast expanse of Cahokia?

The thought is frightening, and then I think like Straight Corn will upon arrival. I am supposed to be given in marriage to the Morning Star, so he will come here, to the Great Plaza and the Morning Star's mound. He will need to find a translator, and will start asking questions about the marriage. Has it occurred? If not, when is it planned? What day? Where is the bride quartered? How many guests have been invited to the ceremony and feast? Will there be the traditional chase? And so forth.

I frown and wonder if the Cahokians celebrate the chase like Moskogean peoples do. In it, the bride is expected to run and try to escape. For all I know, the Morning Star is a fat, windless fellow, and I'll be able to outsprint him. Among my people, any woman who can outrun a man can call the wedding off without any grounds for censure.

Given that the Morning Star has a reputation for being an outstanding chunkey player, this is probably wishful thinking bordering on the fantastical. On the other hand, I have barely begun to understand the depth of the Power Sacred Moth grants to his adherents.

In the meantime I'd better be pinning my hopes on something more realistic. Therefore, when we're finally summoned to the Morning Star's palace to present the marriage proposal, I shall ask for a half moon to prepare. After all, I am the high minko's daughter. I will need time to organize my wardrobe, to pray, to cleanse myself, fast, and follow the rituals. On the Morning Star's side, he will need to circulate the announcement, invite guests, orchestrate and plan a suitable feast, organize games, musicians, and dancers. And who knows what sort of preparations he himself must endure with prayers, offerings, sweat baths, purging, and purification?

He's supposed to be a living god. Maybe that means it will take even longer for him to prepare. I might have a full moon or more before the actual day. Plenty of time for Straight Corn to arrive and spirit me away.

Won't that be a slap in the face when Father finally learns about it?

I am chewing on these thoughts when a young man runs into the yard. He wears a spotless white apron on his hips; his cheeks are tattooed in a pattern I have come to recognize is the Panther Clan's symbol. A white-and-red-striped staff is clutched in one hand, and his hair is tied in a tight bun at the back of his head and stuck through with turkey feathers.

"Greetings," he calls in fluent Moskogee, though with a decidedly Casqui accent. "The Morning Star sends his best wishes. I am to escort you to his presence."

I shoot to my feet, the rest of the warriors rising, quizzical expressions on their faces. I must look just as dumbfounded.

"Right now?" I ask.

The messenger bends at the waist, touching his chin in a sign of respect. "Yes, Lady. I am to tell you that he has only learned of your arrival and regrets the delays that have no doubt inconvenienced you."

Strong Mussel comes bustling out of the dwelling where he has been taking a nap. He blinks in the sunlight, his hair disheveled. "Did I hear right? The Morning Star wishes to see us now?"

Again the messenger—much too polished to react to Strong Mussel's unkempt appearance—bows and touches his chin.

"But we have to dress!" the war leader cries. "Prepare!"

The messenger squints up at the sun, saying, "Then please do so." He smiles. "Now." Another smile. "I am to escort you."

"But it will take us—"

"Just do it," I tell him. "Hurry." To the messenger I say, "We will be ready as soon as we can. Surely you can understand the gravity of our mission. We will be delighted to begin deliberations today."

Something gleams behind his dark and liquid-looking eyes. He inclines his head and touches his chin.

I catch glimpses of him as we dress, paint our faces, and the warriors carefully fix their colorful feathers and jewelry. He is fidgeting, glancing uneasily up at the sun, clearly restless and unhappy at the delay.

Meanwhile, I don my second-best dress, comb out my hair and rebraid it. I loop a long clamshell necklace three times around my neck and, to make a point, daub my cheeks in black. Not exactly the color for a prospective bride.

Strong Mussel and Cloud Tassel scuttle about, shouting orders, looking out of sorts as they gather up the gift boxes and finally assemble the warriors.

I declare "We're ready" just as Strong Mussel sees my blackened cheeks. The color drains from his face, but I am already marching up to the messenger, ordering, "Let's go."

The messenger wheels, and I step out on his heels as Strong Mussel—clutching his White Arrow—slips close behind, whispering, "Lady? You can't go to this meeting with your face painted in black! What will the Morning Star think?"

"What's one form of death compared to another, War Leader?"

"But when your father hears—"

"It will no longer be his concern. We've kept the Morning Star waiting for too long as it is."

Knowing Strong Mussel can't see it, I allow myself a victorious smile.

We proceed along the Great Plaza's western avenue, our escort calling out as he raises his staff of office high. The people thronging the plaza margins ease back, making way for our passage. Out on the grass a spirited stickball game is in process. The thousand or so spectators call encouragement, howl disappointment, and scream in delight as their team makes a good play.

To the side of the thoroughfare are vendors offering every imaginable sort of Trade, from food to clothing to jewelry and art. The smells of cooked bread, fish, and turkey vie with the reek of unwashed humans and their waste, the prevalent smoke, and the damp scent of distant moisture. I am still not used to the mass of humanity.

People watch us pass with thoughtful eyes, interested, but not excessively so—as if this is just one of an endless number of processions.

Ahead of us the great mound looms. I feel a sense of growing dread as we round the corner onto the Avenue of the Sun and warriors step out to clear our way through the packed crowd at the base of the stairs.

People jostle to the side, casting a myriad of glances my way: some envious, others mildly irritated, and a few downright hostile, as if we're infringing on their access in some way or another.

We are led past the guards to the foot of the grand stairway. Guards stand to either side and touch their chins in recognition as we pass. Their armor consists of polished leather and wood, the feather splays on their shoulders giving the impression of fierceness. Beaded forelocks hang down over their noses from beneath buffed leather helmets.

"They look like showpieces," Cloud Tassel mutters uncomfortably, but I notice the tracing of scars on their arms where the skin isn't covered by wrist guards and feather bands. Something tells me that the Morning Star doesn't pick "showpieces" to guard the approaches to his high warren.

We start up the wide stairway, and the effect is sobering as my feet tread the squared logs set into the wide ramp. Ten people abreast could climb this. I've never set foot on anything so grand.

We pass through the Council House Gate at the top and into the council yard. The first thing I see is the towering central pole that dominates the courtyard. To the left stands the Council House and its ramada, where I expect to be received. A crowd of people congregate before the door, mostly women. I recognize the Keeper, formally dressed, where she stands amidst a group of older women. A tall, dark-haired beauty looks my way with haunting eyes.

Something about her makes me look away. Something dangerous. As if she is more than just a woman, and can send a chill down my spine with no more than a smile.

To the far right I see a small raised mound with another red cedar pole jutting from its top. Someone has told me that it marks the absolute center of the Cahokian world.

Instead of the Council House, we are led across the yard to the final stairway. Looking up, I feel small. Amazed. This might be a stairway to the sky, as it stretches up before me. An ascent into another world. I swallow hard, feeling my heart pound. The warriors accompanying me are also cowed, their eyes wide, breath coming short.

As we clear the height of the walls, I am ever more amazed. With each step we climb, I can see more and more of Cahokia. The great city stretches in all directions, broken only by areas of marsh and water. Atop the bluffs on the east, additional mounds and temples dot the skyline; the rooftops of dwellings and farmsteads crowd around them.

I look west and marvel at the stretch of city, seeing the Great Observatory, Black Tail's tomb, then the distant hazy silhouette of River City Mounds. Behind us the Great Plaza gives way to the Avenue of the Moon, which runs south on a raised causeway to more mounds, elevated temples and palaces, and what looks like clusters of farmsteads.

"By Horned Serpent's whiskers," Strong Mussel says breathlessly.

"If I didn't see, I wouldn't believe," Cloud Tassel agrees.

And still we climb, until we see Cahokia from the perspective of the two-headed eagle that dominates the soaring palace roof rising before us.

Two more guards touch their chins as we approach the walled gate. And then we are inside, the courtyard smaller, dominated by the tallest bald cypress post I have ever seen erected. I bend my head back to stare at its lightning-scarred heights, awed by the magnificent carvings that cover every surface.

Here, too, there are people: immaculately dressed and sporting remarkable face paint, iridescent feathers, cloaks of the finest quality, and remarkable headpieces. They watch us pass with a curious detachment, and I can feel the rising tension among my escorting warriors. They've never been treated with such apathy, or endured this feeling of inferiority.

Nor have I.

Blessed Ancestors, I've been foolish!

I was being arrogant and silly. I should have demanded *that we take more time, attend to dress and ornamentation. Compared to the finery surrounding us, we look like muddy quail in a flock of painted buntings.*

Idiot! Idiot! For just a moment, I can't stand myself. How stupid can I be? And it doesn't end with me. Father, in his ignorance, wanted to punish me. Thought he'd shoot two birds out of the sky with one arrow by sending me here and marrying me off to the Morning Star. Fool that he is, he couldn't comprehend Cahokia any more than I could. My paltry escort of a mere twenty warriors bears small gift boxes filled with shells, feathers, and textiles that are nothing *compared to the wealth and exotic finery I see draped on just these minor functionaries waiting in the courtyard!*

My mouth has gone dry. My heart hammers as we are led to the remarkable double doors carved with such artistry and detail that the image of the Morning Star depicted upon them might be alive.

Then we are inside, blinking our eyes, taken aback as they begin to adjust. I had thought the Keeper's palace to be the most opulent building I'd ever seen. It is nothing *compared to the Morning Star's palace. In the firelight I see the most incredible tapestries, colors that would seem to be the rainbow splashed on earth, beautiful ceramics, polished copper images of unimaginable wealth, the finest lace-work, shell and mica effigies, masterpieces carved from gleaming and waxed wood—it just boggles the mind.*

The walls here, too, are lined by functionaries. All but the recorders are dressed in the most outlandish finery. A big, fierce-looking warrior stands before the fire. He watches us approach with eyes that remind me of hot obsidian. His face is scarred and tattooed, but unbalanced. I realize that his jaw was so severely dislocated in the past that it sits irrevocably to one side. A simple falcon feather juts to the side from his hair bun, and his forelock is held in place by a single white shell bead. Nor is he dressed to perfection, but wears battle-scarred armor and holds a battered, stained, copper-bitted war ax.

All of which combine to make him even more impressive and threatening than the overdressed, perfectly polished warriors who stand in a uniform line against the eastern wall.

Our messenger brings us to a halt before the warrior, announcing us in Cahokian.

My eyes on the grizzled warrior, I don't notice the individual seated on the high dais behind the big central hearth. Only when he speaks do I look past and first see the living god.

So striking is he that I can indeed believe him more than mortal. The first thing that catches the eye is the facial paint: white with black forked-eye designs running down his cheeks. A black triangle, its point at the septum of his nose, runs down to cover his mouth. A fantastic two-headed-eagle headpiece rises from what looks like a Spirit Bundle atop his head. Shell maskettes that resemble human faces cover both ears. Thick layers of shell necklaces hang from his throat, and an immaculate white apron embroidered in black drops to a point between his knees. I can see scalp locks tied around the front.

So much for my fantasies about a wedding race. He is young, muscular, and looks every inch an athlete. It will take Powerful magic to beat him at anything. If he is truly a living god, I will have no hope.

He is watching me with hard, dark eyes. As I look into them I feel suddenly shaken, and a shiver runs through me. Unnerving.

I don't even notice that I've grabbed up my braid and am twisting it in my fingers.

"Welcome," Morning Star tells us in accented Moskogee. I recognize it as a Casqui dialect, which should not surprise me. They are the closest Moskogee-speaking Nation to Cahokia, and major Trading partners.

As if recovering from paralysis, Strong Mussel and the warriors drop to their knees, lowering their heads to the matting.

Somehow I successfully fight the urge. Though I am shaking, my stomach is knotting itself into a hard ache, and my mouth is dryer than sun-baked clay,

I lock my knees. I swallow hard, reminding myself that I am a high minko's daughter. Of the Chief Clan, of the Sky Hand people.

"Greetings, Morning Star," I manage to answer, though my voice is strained, and, I fear, squeaky.

"I understand that High Minko White Water Moccasin has sent you with an offer of marriage and that you wish to open an embassy from the Sky Hand so as to improve relations with Cahokia?"

I see rising interest behind his eyes, as he looks me up and down. His gaze rests too long on my hips, as if peering beneath my skirt, then rises to my breasts. Finally his eyes meet mine, and the effect is physical, as if my nerves are shocked.

Words won't come. To my immense embarrassment, I can only stand there, almost panting for air, my mouth agape.

"That is correct," Strong Mussel replies, having overcome enough of his awe to find voice.

"Then be welcome," Morning Star commands. He utters what sounds like an order, then follows it with, "I have ordered black drink and the sacred pipe. Let us drink and smoke, and I shall hear the request of High Minko White Water Moccasin."

He rises, stepping down from the raised panther-hide chair.

Fear sparks electric through my body, paralyzing me as he walks up. Cocks his head. A black eternity lies behind his eyes as he stares into mine.

I flinch as he reaches down. At his touch, I jump, as if stung. Then he raises my hand, and I almost shudder as his gaze fixes on the tattoo.

"Your father's goals are easily understood, Whispering Dawn. But what dreams and desires, I wonder, are driving you?"

I still cannot answer, even as a group of young men rush forward with steaming black drink and a great carved pipe.

"It's all right," Morning Star adds in a reassuring tone. "I wouldn't think of disappointing such a willing young woman. I have ordered a feast. And lest you fret that I might not be as anxious as you, we shall be married within the next hand of time."

He smiles. "Just as soon as the formalities are seen to."

It is all I can do to keep from breaking loose and running.

Seventeen

So, there goes the Sky Hand party?" the Keeper noted in surprise.

Night Shadow Star turned from where she stood before the Council House talking with Blue Heron and Wind. One of the Morning Star's messengers preceded a moderately dressed young woman with a black-painted face. She walked at the head of a small party of foreign warriors. All in all, she looked absolutely average, until she cast eyes on Night Shadow Star.

"*Ah, the Powers of darkness stir,*" Piasa whispered behind her right ear.

Even as Night Shadow Star's master spoke, the girl seemed to tear her gaze away, averting her eyes as though to avoid Night Shadow Star's. In a matter of heartbeats the party had crossed the plaza and were climbing the long stairs toward the Morning Star's high palace.

"Did you send for them?" Keeper Blue Heron pensively asked her sister.

Tonka'tzi Wind shook her head. "Pus and rot, no. I've had my hands full preparing for this accursed reception. Our panting camp bitch of a cousin sent me instructions. Can you believe it? Details of what food to have prepared, how much black drink, how she wanted to be seated, which attendants should be placed where. You'd think she was a bloody clan matron."

"She is," Blue Heron muttered in reminder.

"She is darkness," Night Shadow Star couldn't help but say as she watched the young woman climb in advance of her party.

"Snot and spit, she's just a cousin," Wind replied, attention on her fingers as she rubbed them to remove a soot stain.

"No. The Sky Hand. The Chikosi girl."

"What do you mean?" It was Blue Heron who fixed curious eyes on her.

"I'm not sure. Something Piasa just whispered to me."

"Told you," Blue Heron murmured softly to her sister, then turned her gaze to where the Chikosi party was nearing the top of the high stairs. "So, Wind, if you didn't send for her, it would appear that the Morning Star has taken matters into his own hands."

"What is this about?" Night Shadow Star asked, a curious unease inside as Piasa flickered at the corner of her vision.

"Not sure," Blue Heron growled. "She and her warriors just showed up. Said she wanted to establish a Chikosi embassy, and her father had sent her marry the Morning Star as a way to cement the alliance. I sent one of my spies to figure out what they were really after. The thief overheard that she's already married. To an Albaamaha. Thought Chikosi nobility hated the Albaamaha. And for some reason my spy refused to tell us that little fact."

"Darkness flows," Piasa whispered ominously.

"What does that mean?" Night Shadow Star asked absently as the Chikosi party vanished into the Morning Star's walled compound.

"Got me," Blue Heron said obliviously. "Probably some Chikosi internal squabble."

"Morning Star dances among the white blossoms of Dreams. Nectar rises with his blood. Who outsmarts whom?"

"Lord?" she asked with a frown. "I don't understand."

"Neither does the Morning Star."

"What?"

Like a snap of the fingers, the Spirit Beast vanished.

Night Shadow Star sighed. "Pus and blood, I hate it when he does that."

Both Wind and Blue Heron were watching her uneasily. And Fire Cat—who had been standing discreetly to one side—stepped forward, eyes wary, one hand resting on the war club hanging at his side.

"You seeing things again?" Blue Heron asked suspiciously. "Anything you'd like to warn us about?"

"That girl is going to be trouble."

"Like what?" Wind wanted to know—but at the moment, a runner burst through the Council Gate.

He trotted over, bearing one of the clan matron's staffs of office, and dropped to one knee to declare, "Clan Matron Rising Flame approaches."

"What now?" Blue Heron growled under her breath, then raised her voice as she said, "We thank the matron for apprising us of her approach. You may go."

The young man touched his forehead, whirled, and sprinted back for the door.

"Well," Wind said through an exhale, "we'd better take our places and get this over with." She turned, heading into the Council House to take her seat on the *tonka'tzi*'s dais.

A shift in the breeze brought the scent of boiling black drink from inside the Council House, along with the delicious odors of bison stew, hominy, and nut bread.

"Which means it's up to us to greet our overstuffed cousin. Let's go," Blue Heron said to Night Shadow Star as she led the way to the Council Gate.

Night Shadow Star followed to take a position beside her at the head of the stairs. Below them, the crowd thronged the Avenue of the Sun, leaving the plaza with its chunkey courts curiously empty, though a hard-fought contest was being waged on the stickball field just beyond the World Tree pole.

Rising Flame's contingent was readily apparent as it rounded the eastern flank of the great mound and headed for the base of the stairs. Fully four tens of warriors escorted the single litter, the advance ranks cutting through the crowd like a canoe through duckweed.

At the foot of the stairs, the procession stopped, and a decked-out squadron first gave Rising Flame a hand up once her litter was placed on the avenue.

"Who is that?" Night Shadow Star asked, unable to identify the squadron first across the distance.

"I think that is Tapping Wood, the one she just divorced. Fish Clan man, renowned war leader and squadron first. Dealt with that fractious Shawnee chief over east on the Mother Water a couple of years back."

The war leader touched his forehead in salute, and Rising Flame started up the steps as the crowd milled about and watched. It wasn't often that a new Four Winds Clan matron was chosen. Whistles, cheers, and jeers could be heard.

For her part, Rising Flame had dressed for the occasion, her thick black hair piled atop her head and pinned in place with eagle feathers. A remarkable lace cloak crocheted of delicately spun cottonwood down hung over her shoulders.

The textile skirt clinging to her hips was woven of the finest dogbane thread and dyed a deep, reddish purple. The front had been embroidered with the Four Winds spirals above, and chevrons below.

She had again chosen white facial paint with stylized forked-eye designs in black, invoking the Morning Star's favorite motif.

As Rising Flame approached at the head of her warriors, Night Shadow Star could make out the grim smile of satisfaction on her cousin's lips, see the sparkling triumph in her eyes. The pulse was pounding in the woman's neck, hinting at the joy that had to be bursting in her chest. From relative obscurity in the Morning Star House, Rising Flame was now thrust foremost into its ranks of authority and influence.

"Matron," Blue Heron greeted, and touched her forehead as Rising Flame stepped onto the platform.

"Keeper," Rising Flame answered with a slight nod of recognition.

Then she shot an expectant glance at Night Shadow Star, who replied, "Hello, Cousin."

"I am your matron."

"Of a sort. The Four Winds Clan exerts no influence over Piasa."

Rising Flame lowered her voice. "Oh, come now. This isn't petty jealousy, is it? If you wanted the position, you should have fought for it."

"I serve a different master," Night Shadow Star replied, meeting Rising Flame's calculating eyes. "My purpose in meeting you here, at this spot, is to ensure that you understand who and what I am from the outset."

"Is that a challenge, Cousin?" The corners of Rising Flame's lips had tightened.

"Consider it a warning," Night Shadow Star told her evenly, aware that Fire Cat had stepped up behind her and that Blue Heron was shooting her uneasy glances.

So, too, was Squadron First Tapping Wood. The warrior—in his mid thirties—stood on the stairs, dressed in finery, at the head of his small squad. The man looked particularly uneasy, as if thrust into a sloshing sea of unknowns. He kept shooting Fire Cat uneasy looks, as if sizing up a rival.

"Good!" Blue Heron cried with a clap of the hands. "Now that that's settled, if you would follow me, Matron, the *tonka'tzi* awaits."

Night Shadow Star gave her cousin a thin smile and spun on her heel, leading the way. Fire Cat stuck to her, marching at attention, one hand on his war club where it hung on his belt.

"Old enemy?" Fire Cat asked in a voice just loud enough for her to hear.

"The girl I once was treated her rather shabbily. I haven't always been the soft, inoffensive, and forgiving woman I am today."

From the corner of her eye she could see the crooked smile on his lips. Then he asked, "And the Fish Clan warrior?"

"Used to be her husband. She divorced him a couple of moons back. It must have been more amicable than was reported if he's backing her today."

"He looks grim and out of sorts."

"His reputation is as a military commander. The kind who likes to bash enemy heads in a hard fight. Political intrigue isn't his preferred method of relaxation."

"I'm with him there."

His muttered response amused her. Fire Cat's single-minded devotion to her had served her better politically than any amount of head-bashing. Right down to and including his fight with the Itza, which essentially liberated her from a fate worse than death.

As they approached the Council House door, the gathered nobles bowed, touching their foreheads.

Night Shadow Star was on the verge of stepping inside when Rising Flame called, "Wait. I would address the *tonka'tzi* and Keeper in private."

Now, that was a curiosity. Night Shadow Star turned, watching as Rising Flame separated herself from her retinue of warriors and marched up to the door.

"War Leader," the matron barked. "See that we are not interrupted."

"Yes, Matron!" Tapping Wood almost slapped himself in the forehead as he saluted.

"Keeper, if you would lead the way," Rising Flame said as she gestured. Blue Heron nodded and stepped inside, followed by Rising Flame.

Night Shadow Star took a step for the door, only to have Tapping Wood block her way.

"Lady, you will have to wait outside," Tapping Wood told her, his eyes communicating a deep unease.

Night Shadow Star smiled and held his gaze as she felt Piasa swell within her. She heard the Spirit Creature's voice as it spoke through her. "Do you wish to cross me, warrior?"

"N—No, Lady." He swallowed hard, pupils dilating and sweat breaking out on his upper lip.

"Then stand aside."

Almost trembling, Tapping Wood gulped and shuffled to one side, allowing her and Fire Cat to pass.

"I'd swear that is Piasa talking when you do that," Fire Cat mumbled.

"What makes you think it isn't, Red Wing?"

As they entered the room, Rising Flame was ordering, "Everyone out! All of you! Recorders, messengers, attendants—outside. I would speak to *Tonka'tzi* Wind in private.

Fire Cat shot Night Shadow Star a measuring glance as she made way for the exodus and strode up beside Rising Flame.

The matron gave her a disdainful glare, and said, "You are not needed here. Get out."

"Needed?" Night Shadow Star smiled, seeing the Piasa's shadow flicker in a darkened corner of the room. "No. Not yet."

"What is that supposed to mean?" the Keeper asked from where she had taken a position on Rising Flame's right. *Tonka'tzi* Wind sat regally on her dais, watching with an elevated eyebrow.

"Fingers of darkness and ancient Power are filtering through Cahokia. The Morning Star is gambling that we will all survive the test. But do continue." Night Shadow Star gestured for them to proceed.

"Gods, Niece, what do you know?" Wind demanded.

Night Shadow Star just smiled in reply.

"Are you *receiving* a new matron, or not?" Rising Flame's eyes flashed, her fist knotting. To Night Shadow Star, she darkly added, "And do not think for a moment that I have forgotten the things you did to me, how you and your brothers treated me."

"We will have time for that another day," Night Shadow Star whispered, images of a young Rising Flame in tears just behind her veil of memory.

Wind scowled at Night Shadow Star, then turned her eyes on Rising Flame. "Where is your retinue?"

"Outside." She stepped forward. "I will ask them in after we've clarified a few things. Then we can attend to the proper rituals and ceremony."

"Clarify what things?" Wind shifted on her seat to show her irritation.

Rising Flame walked up to the *tonka'tzi*'s dais. "You wanted my sister, Sacred Spoon. There is no secret about that. Everyone wants Sacred Spoon. She's always the favorite. The reasonable one. The one you can subtly influence with a well-thought-out argument. She's the one who compromises." Rising Flame shook her head. "The one you can control."

"Does this have a point?" the Keeper asked, a bitter twist to her lips.

"The point is that the Morning Star chose me." Rising Flame jabbed a hard finger into Blue Heron's sternum. "I am no soft lump of copper like my sister. I won't let you hammer me into whatever shape you desire for the moment. With my appointment, authority is once again returned to Slick Rock's lineage. And to a woman who knows her own mind. Just as the Morning Star wished."

"The way I heard it," Blue Heron said, "it wasn't your mind that had the Morning Star's attention."

Night Shadow Star watched Rising Flame's expression harden, the muscles in her cheeks flexing. "Do you not know *why* he stepped in, Keeper? Or are you really that dense?"

"Why? To meddle in Four Winds Clan business," Wind snapped, clearly disturbed by the interplay.

Rising Flame gave her a dismissive look. "Pus and blood, you really are that thick!"

"Thick?" Wind exploded. "You little arrogant sheath! I was matron while you were still sucking on Eel Woman's tit! Now, just because you've bled yourself into womanhood and you're Slick Rock's granddaughter, you think you're something special? If you hadn't been up there spreading for the Morning Star—"

Stop this!

The words hissed loudly in Night Shadow Star's left ear. She even glanced to that side, expecting to see Piasa crouching there, flicking his serpent tail back and forth like a whip.

"Enough!" Night Shadow Star shouted as she stepped up and pulled Rising Flame back far enough to insert herself between the woman and the furious *tonka'tzi.*

"Unhand me!" Rising Flame spat the words.

Night Shadow Star glared from woman to woman but kept her grip locked on Rising Flame's wrist. "Rising Flame *is* the clan matron. Duly elected. She *will* serve in that position."

"Niece?" Wind asked uncertainly. "You take her position?"

Night Shadow Star searched Rising Flame's hot eyes, saw the passion, and felt the racing pulse in her wrist. This was something more than Morning Star inserting himself in Four Winds Clan politics or just because Rising Flame had milked his shaft.

The rest is up to them, Piasa whispered in her ear.

At that, Night Shadow Star released the woman's wrist and told her aunts, "She is the matron. Deal with it."

Then, with Fire Cat following close on her heels, she turned and stalked from the room.

Eighteen

"What happened up there?" Fire Cat asked as he brought a steaming cup of mint tea to Night Shadow Star. She sat on her veranda step as evening fell over Cahokia. Equinox was coming, and with it the passage from summer to fall. The chill could be felt in the smoky and curiously still air.

Sound carried on the evening: the distant chopping of an ax, shouts between men on a work party, dogs barking, and the shrill cries of children playing. A collection of distant drums sent their rhythms into the darkening sky, and the lilting of a flute could be heard coming from one of the society houses immediately north of her palace mound.

Night Shadow Star was staring thoughtfully at the Council House, where its roof protruded above the protective wall.

"Morning Star always plays a deep game." She took the tea, barely sipped, and cupped it in her slender hands.

Fire Cat seated himself on the step beside her, letting his hands dangle as he propped his elbows on his knees. "Anytime he plays a deep game, Lady, it seems we're the ones who are at risk."

She smiled slightly, her face soft in the twilight. "You and I, Red Wing, are both playthings of Power. We may not live long, but in the short time until our deaths, it will be interesting."

He chuckled at that. "So I have noticed. Ever since the moment I saw you walk out of the rain that night. You had to be a Spirit. No human woman could be that beautiful."

"Is that what you thought? Then you were obviously delusional and barely in possession of your souls. I remember that night, too. Only I remember being naked, cold, and wet. Shivering down to my bones. And completely enraged that I had to spare your miserable life."

"You can always order me hung back in a square, Lady."

She looked sidelong at him, dark eyes large in her triangular face. A tease of a smile played at her lips; her hair was curled back, leaving shadows in the hollows of her cheeks.

"I will keep such an impossibility in mind, Red Wing. Though, given what we've been through, I can't imagine the sort of betrayal that could break my trust in you."

He took her hand, lifting it to his lips. "When I swore to serve you that night, I thought I was binding myself to First Woman. I could conceive of no higher honor than serving the goddess herself. Turns out I was wrong. Serving you has been an even higher honor. My body and souls are yours, Lady."

He saw her eyes close, saw the familiar tension in her lips, the rise of her shoulders as she drew a reassuring breath. She shifted her hand, grasping his and giving it a powerful squeeze.

"If we were in a different world, Red Wing . . ."

"But we're not, Lady. You serve your lord, and I serve you. Short as our lives may indeed be, we shall both continue to do our duties."

With a faint shake of her head, she asked, "How can you always remain so noble?"

"Because all I have left is my honor, my word . . . and you."

From behind the Council House wall across the way, the sound of a pot drum was followed by singing. "They're deep into the ritual now, Fire Cat. The Keeper and *tonka'tzi* are going to have their work cut out for them when it comes to building a relationship between themselves and Rising Flame."

"You think Morning Star did that to keep the Four Winds Clan at each other's throats?"

"Just the contrary. It may be that Rising Flame was the only choice that could have saved the Four Winds from murdering each other."

"You think?"

"We'll see, won't we?"

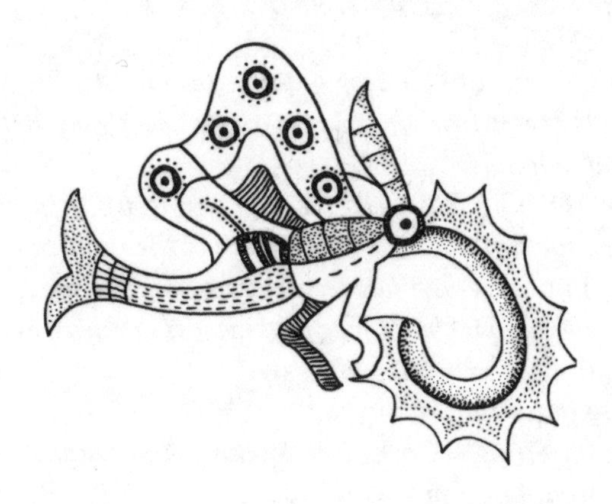

Shock

The muscles in my thighs are trembling, and I have a sick feeling in the pit of my stomach. I am standing side by side with the Morning Star, and he holds my hand as the bent-faced warrior wraps a beautiful yellow blanket around our shoulders.

I stare out at the room in a sort of daze. My blood, Powered by draughts of black drink, is surging in my veins. My skin tingles, draped as it now is in shell beads. A striking yellow cloak made of meadowlark breast feathers hangs from my shoulders. Colorful patterns have been painted on my arms, breasts, belly, and thighs. A feather headdress has been set upon my head, and my braid has been undone, my hair combed out, and left to fall in waves down my back.

This cannot be happening to me!

It's like a voice is screaming inside my skull.

Though my stomach is packed with food from the feast, I want to throw up. I can glance wistfully at the great double doors all I want, but between me and the freedom they represent are Strong Mussel's feasting warriors and a host of Morning Star's attendants. Were I to strip off my wedding raiment, leap the fire, and charge full-out, I would have no chance. Those doors might as well be halfway across the world for all the good it will do me.

To the right, a withered old soul flier—his face a mass of wrinkles—stares up at the roof with opaque white-blind eyes and sings some Cahokian blessing song. I haven't understood a word the old priest has said, but with each wheezing utterance, have felt my slim hold on hope slip away.

The old man pauses, takes a deep breath, and shouts, "Aho!"

The Cahokians cry "Aho!" *in unison, and a cheer goes up that is picked up by the Sky Hand warriors.*

"Come," the Morning Star tells me, tightening his grip on my hand. He turns, leading me toward the door in the back of the room.

I walk on legs that have no more feeling than stone; my frantic heart thumps against my breastbone. Tickles of fear and revulsion dance along my bones.

I am married!

I can't seem to grasp that reality.

When I married Straight Corn, it was with joy and anticipation. I couldn't wait to lay with him, wrap my arms around him, and invite him inside me.

Now I can't even manage to swallow, as if my throat has gone dry and my tongue is a hard knot.

I walk into the Morning Star's personal quarters as if in a daze, and barely register the lamps whose wicks float in hickory oil. The carvings, the shimmering of copper and shell inlay, and the fine fabrics—they all seem part of an incredible dream.

A small altar supports a remarkable paint palette and facial paints of all colors. A rack on the wall holds an array of headpieces of copper, feather, and fine furs. Resplendent feather and fur cloaks, maces, a remarkable composit sinew-backed bow and quiver, and other exotica clutter the tops of fantastically carved wooden boxes. To the side of the door, on a special display, are the Morning Star's famous copper lances and different colored chunkey stones.

Morning Star removes the blanket from our shoulders, folding it and laying it on one of the fantastically carved wooden boxes. Then he turns to me, placing his hands on my shoulders as he stares into my eyes. I tremble as I fall into his gaze, feel his Power. His face—white with black forked-eye designs—seems to expand. To fill the entire world.

His quick fingers untie the meadowlark cloak, and it slides down my back to the floor. Next he lifts the feather headdress from atop my head, taking a moment to run his fingers through my hair.

After that he removes the shell necklaces that were carefully draped around my neck during the ceremony. I am shivering as he loosens my skirt and lets it drift down my legs.

My jaws are locked, each hammering of my heart like a pestle pounding inside me.

And then I am lifted, laid upon the soft bedding. He carefully arranges my hair, as if to create a swirl on the soft bearhide robes.

I hear a cry, strangled deep in my throat, as I realize that he, too, is naked. When did that happen? Why don't I remember?

A moan dies inside me as he climbs onto the bed.

On his knees, he leans his head back and whispers a prayer. His arms are raised, palms up, as if in supplication. My gaze fixes on his erection, so hard and straight.

"Even if you have to endure the Morning Star's embrace . . ." *Two Sticks' words come floating out of my misty memory.*

Straight Corn is coming.

I am married!

He shifts to cover me. Somehow, I manage to spread my knees apart and expose myself. I bite my lip, expecting pain.

Instead, he sings softly to me, running fingertips down my forearms.

I blink, glance curiously at him, and he tells me, "We have no reason to rush, yes?"

I see reflected lamplight in his dark eyes. And he concludes, saying in accented Moskogee, "The night is filled with the beat of sacred wings."

Nineteen

Seven Skull Shield puffed out a frosty breath as dawn's pale luminescence spread along the eastern horizon. This time of year the Keeper's palace lay in the shadow of the Morning Star's mighty mound and high palace. Only in summer did it receive the sun's blessing as it rose above the eastern bluffs.

He kept his blanket clutched closely about his shoulders as he ambled down the Keeper's steps and onto the avenue. In his hand he clutched a gourd cup, and he sipped at the morning gruel that he'd dipped from Dancing Sky's cook pot at the central fire. The woman hadn't been paying attention. But then, there was a lot of that going around. The Keeper herself hadn't come home until late last night, and as usual, had been asleep on her feet. She hadn't even noticed that Seven Skull Shield and Farts had made themselves at home on one of the sleeping benches in the rear. This, too, would pass.

But until it did, Seven Skull Shield was delighted to enjoy the Keeper's largess, fine food, and warm palace.

Farts scratched anxiously at a flea and flopped down with a hollow thumping of bones as he watched Seven Skull Shield slurp his soupy breakfast.

Music carried on the morning air, flute and drums supporting male voices as they sang a song of greeting in one of the society houses just south of the Keeper's. A dog barked; he could hear the soft, repetitive thud as someone pounded corn in a log mortar. At this unwholesome early hour? And somewhere off to the north along the banks of Cahokia Creek an infant kept bawling.

"I should be going," he told Farts. "Probably ought to head back to the canoe landing. See if I can find out what happened to Winder."

He wagged his spoon at the dog, seeing a sharpening of the beast's brown and blue eyes. "It worries me. You see, Winder was my best friend. He and I, we didn't have family. We just lived in the shadows, sleeping where we could, stealing this and that, doing odd jobs for a meal. The two of us? We knew every backway through River Mounds City. Knew every loose section of wall where we could wiggle into a warehouse or workshop during the winter."

Farts uttered a half-whine of understanding. Or else he was asking for what was left of the hominy gruel in Seven Skull Shield's bowl.

On a hunch, Seven Skull Shield said, "Come on. Before we do that, let's go see how that Quiz Quiz is doing. Last I saw, he was looking pretty poorly, but hanging on."

And one thing was for sure, if Seven Skull Shield ever decided he was going to steal anything from the Surveyors' Society, he wasn't going to be foolish enough to hang around to conduct any silly ceremonies. No, indeed, given what he'd already watched them do to Sky Star, he'd have his butt planted in the first canoe out of the landing and headed downriver.

He rounded the corner of the Morning Star's mound and nodded to the guard. The warrior, looking cold and tired, didn't so much as narrow an eye in return. The usual collection of litters, porters, and runners huddled in little groups at the base of the Grand Staircase as they waited on the pleasure of masters who'd spent the night at the Morning Star's. Word was that they'd had another wedding up there last night.

Even in the twilight, youths were grading and smoothing the Morning Star's chunkey courts in preparation should the living god decide to play.

Traders and vendors were trickling in, setting up their wares around the Grand Plaza's peripheries. A few were already squabbling over space.

As the sky turned from indigo to violet and Cahokia seemed to appear out of the gloom, he made his way east past the great mound and stopped. Squinted.

Yes, that was the Surveyors' Society house on its low mound where it stood back from the Avenue of the Sun. The square where the Quiz Quiz had hung now stood empty.

So, had Sky Star's endurance flagged? Or had some passerby been overly enthusiastic with a knife or club? Maybe the Surveyors' Society had tired of his suffering and shown the dying man mercy?

Walking up to the square, Seven Skull Shield could see the dark stains on both the ground and bottom log: dried blood. Here and there were sticks with charred ends where people had used them to burn the captive. And there, too, were pieces of the ropes lying discarded on the ground. Okay, so they must have grown tired and killed the war leader before—

Seven Skull Shield frowned as Farts hitched his leg and peed on one of the support logs. He bent and picked up one of the short pieces, staring at the frayed ends. Obviously it had been cut with a rather dull edge, since it was partially frayed where it had been sawed at. Probably with a chert or quartzite blade.

Surveyors revered rope. It was, after all, one of the sacred implements of their society—the tool used for their precise measurements.

Farts was licking at the blood, and Seven Skull Shield kicked him away. It was hard to tell given the hard-packed earth, but it looked like Sky Star had been dragged out from the square before the marks vanished.

At that moment a man moved the society house door to one side, stepping out on the veranda. He glanced at the eastern horizon, yawned, and scratched his sides. Only then did he turn and glance Seven Skull Shield's way, taking in the empty square.

He started, then charged forward, leaping down from the waist-high mound and drawing to a stop, eyes wide as he stared at the square and demanded, "Where is he? Where is the Quiz Quiz?"

"You didn't take him down?"

The man rushed past Seven Skull Shield, staring up and down the avenue as the light turned pink on the horizon. "Someone has taken him!"

Seven Skull Shield winced, rubbed the back of his neck, and said, "Phlegm, pus, and piss. You go tell your people. I'll go tell the Keeper." He paused. "But first, you go check. Is the Surveyors' Bundle safe?"

At the mention, the man's eyes flew wide. Arms flailing, he charged back into the society house to emerge a moment later and call, "It's here!"

"Guard it! They might try for it again!"

With that Seven Skull Shield cursed, turned, and called, "Come on, beast." As he trotted headlong for the Keeper's he couldn't help but remember the look on Winder's face.

Tell me you had nothing to do with this.

Twenty

Clan Keeper Blue Heron watched Seven Skull Shield's broad back as he and his foul-smelling dog trotted out between the guardian posts and disappeared down the staircase. She could think of a great many ways to start a day that were better than being awakened to learn that a coveted prisoner had been taken from the Surveyors' Society square.

"It shouldn't be your problem," Dancing Sky said as she stepped up from behind and handed Blue Heron a cup of steaming sassafras tea.

"Don't those silly surveyors keep a guard out? Even Five Fists details a guard when the Morning Star has prisoners in the square. If just to keep a family member from sneaking in and hurrying the job along in the name of mercy." She tested the tea, found it too hot. "What's the matter with those people?"

"They live by their sticks and strings and arcs," Dancing Sky said with a shrug. "Maybe they've fallen so deeply into the study and computations that they've lost sight of reality."

"They did let the Quiz Quiz walk in and lift their most sacred Bundle. At least they didn't let that happen again."

Blue Heron thought back to the expression on Seven Skull Shield's face. The thief had been worried about the missing war leader. It was more than just the possibility that the Quiz Quiz might have held a grudge—something that would drive him to strike back at the thief who'd nabbed him. Whoever had cut Sky Star down and carried him off had rescued a man more dead than alive. A man incapable of seeking revenge himself.

No, this was something else, and it was not the first time Seven Skull Shield had been hiding something where the Quiz Quiz were involved.

As if I didn't have enough to worry about.

Like Rising Flame taking over the matron's duties. The pus-rotted gods alone knew how that was going to work out. And why had Night Shadow Star so firmly declared herself for Rising Flame?

That was Piasa's doing.

The realization sent a shiver down her spine. She should have recognized it the moment Night Shadow Star had stalked out of the Council House. The scary part was that both the Morning Star and Piasa apparently wanted Rising Flame as matron.

Why?

"Gods," she muttered to herself. "Why doesn't anything make sense anymore?"

Even as she said it, a messenger, his staff in hand, appeared at the staircase. He bowed before the guardian posts, trotted over to Blue Heron, and dropped to a knee, touching his forehead.

"Clan Keeper Blue Heron, Clan Matron Rising Flame requests your presence in the Four Winds Clan House to discuss security arrangements for the clan. The matron requests that you share breakfast in order to discuss the clan's business in a more relaxed circumstance. Formal dress is not required."

"Yes, yes. Now go." She waved the messenger away and scowled up at the brightening morning sky. "Piss and spit."

Dancing Sky watched the messenger's rapid escape. "Pity. I had the girls make a most wonderful hominy."

"How do you know it was wonderful?"

"The thief had second helpings."

"The thief would take second helpings of boiled water if he thought he was getting away with something."

She frowned again. "What are you getting away with, Seven Skull Shield?" She turned. "Dancing Sky, send word to Columella. Ask her if Flat Stone Pipe's spies can keep an eye on the thief."

"You suspect he's up to something?"

"He wouldn't be Seven Skull Shield if he wasn't."

Instead of using the litter, Blue Heron walked across the plaza to the Four Winds Clan House and hobbled up the stairs. She made her obeisance to the guardian posts and, to her surprise, was stopped at the door.

"Who comes?" the guard, a Fish Clan warrior, asked.

"You know cursed well who comes."

"Name?" He kept his eyes rigidly to the fore, face grim with the awesome responsibility that had been placed on his narrow shoulders.

"Tell Matron Rising Flame that the Keeper was here at her request. Then tell her that you refused me entry to my own clan's House. That next time she wants to talk to me, she can rotted well see me in my palace."

With that she whirled and started home.

She was halfway down the stairs when the guard called after her, "Clan Keeper! The matron will see you now!"

Blue Heron stopped short on the stairs, considered going on about her business, then turned back with a sigh. This time she was escorted directly into the large room, filled as it was with people—mostly those of Takes Blood's lineage who were reveling in the ascendance of their kinswoman to the leadership.

She strode past the central fire and took a position before where Rising Flame sat on a raised litter. The woman was dressed in a bright yellow skirt, copious shell necklaces hanging down between her breasts, and her hair had been pulled into a tight bun at the top of her head and pinned with a swan-feather splay.

She fixed irritated and gleaming eyes on Blue Heron. "Is there anything to report about the Four Winds Clan, Clan Keeper?"

"I have heard that we have a new matron." Blue Heron crossed her thin arms. "I am waiting to see if that is indeed the case."

"I'm surprised. You don't have a reputation for humor, Clan Keeper."

"And you don't have a reputation for good sense, Matron."

The room went silent, people staring.

"Would you care to elaborate on that, Clan Keeper? You know, you hold your position on the sufferance of the matron."

Blue Heron gave her a thin smile. "It is said that you don't think things through. For instance, had you attended meetings with the previous matron and *tonka'tzi* you would know that I don't generally give reports before an audience. If, however, you wish to conduct the clan's business in this fashion, be aware that your exiled brother Fire Light has sent a messenger all the way from distant Cofitachequi. He has been in contact with Green Chunkey and seeks to coerce Horned Serpent House to petition the Morning Star for a pardon at the Busk next summer. Fire Light's method of coercion is to remind Green Chunkey that he knows of the high chief's dalliance with your mother, Eel Woman, and the suspicion that—"

"Enough!"

"As you wish, Matron." Blue Heron turned on her heel and started for the door.

"Where are you going?"

"You said enough, Matron. The wording was plain: You have no wish to hear more."

"Are you doing this just to infuriate me?"

Blue Heron did an about-face, her gaze taking in the owl-eyed spectators. They were certainly getting their morning's entertainment. "I am doing this to get through your thick skull, Rising Flame. Not all of governing is about show and spectacle. Should you decide to employ yourself in the actual business of governing, we will talk. In private."

Rising Flame's face had gone brittle and red. "As of this moment, you are no longer Clan Keeper. Get out of here!"

Blue Heron sighed, nodded, and touched her head respectfully. "As you wish, Matron."

She left the room with a slight smile tugging at her lips and whispered, "Oh the storms of youth. Can't wait to see how you're going to deal with this one, you twitchy little bitch."

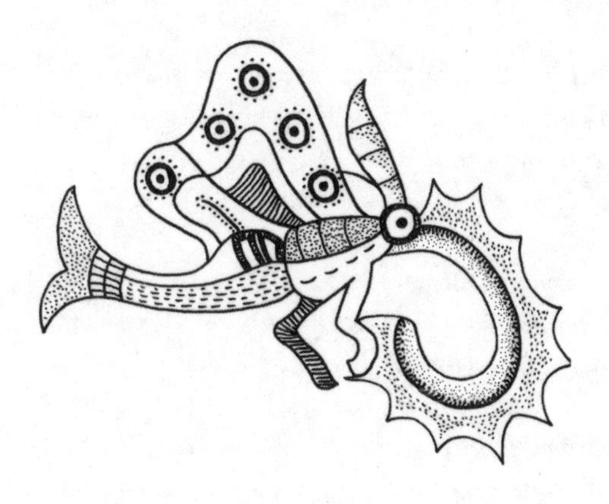

Awakening

It has been two days. I wonder who and what I have become. Everything inside me is confused, turned upside down, and at war with itself. As I lie on the Morning Star's bed and stare up at the high ceiling, I knot my hands on my chest and seek any strand of understanding that I can cling to. Anything that will bring me back to being me.

I swore *that I would simply lie there when he took me. Do my duty. I* promised myself *that I would not participate. That, though I had to share my body, I would not betray my love for Straight Corn. That inside, down in my souls, I would remain aloof.*

How then did the Morning Star seduce me into being the willing partner I have been for the last two days?

I can believe that he is indeed the living god. That he has used some incredible Power to make himself irresistible, to unleash such a rapture of sensations from my body. All of the Moskogee peoples have stories about Spirit Beings seducing young women. I'd always thought them rather quaint. A Tie Snake traveling through the forest happens on a young woman, and poof! Lays with her just like that. Usually producing a magical child in the process. The stories never made sense. If I—while walking through the forest—happen upon a magical snake, stone man, white buck, or whatever, the last thing I'm going to do in front of a terrifying Spirit Beast is fall on my back, pull up my skirt, and spread my legs.

But that is exactly what I've done with the Morning Star. He has made me part of the myth. And worse, I have not only panted for and craved the coupling, but enjoyed him.

He has treated me kindly, cherished me, made me laugh. But beneath it I can see the darkness, the danger, the terrible Power that lives behind his eyes. Like a moth to a flame I'm drawn . . .

I start, the effect as physical as a slap to the face.

Like a moth?

The words hammer inside my head.

Is this all his plan? Does the Morning Star know who I am? I stare at the tattoo on the back of my hand. If he is the hero from the Beginning Times, reincarnated in this young man's body, he knows that symbol, what it means.

At the same time, I am, of course, Whispering Dawn. Daughter of High Minko White Water Moccasin. My family is legendary for its strength and prowess, and I have proven myself courageous. I ran away. Married a man my family despised. I offered myself to the ancient magic, accepted the night nectar, and loosened my souls to fly and Dream with Sacred Moth.

*I begin to see my life through different eyes. It is as though I have been a blind child, pouting and petulant. Instead, everything that has happened to me—running away, falling in love with Straight Corn, learning the ancient ways, being captured, being brought here, and now this marriage to the Morning Star—*had *to happen this way. I have been chosen for great things. That is why I am lying here in the Morning Star's bed with a sexual afterglow.*

A feeling of awe washes through me, and I reach down and prod the tenderness in my right abdomen. It has been just about a half moon since my last flux. I am at the time of the moon when a man's seed has the best chance of catching.

Perhaps my sexual hunger is not all the Morning Star's magic, but some of my own traitorous body's doing?

I close my eyes, conjuring Straight Corn's face, seeing his shy smile, the gleam of love in his dark eyes. As the image of him forms, my heart aches.

"What are you doing, Whispering Dawn?" I ask myself. In that instant I feel a deep and burning shame.

And with it comes the realization that this might be the reenactment of a different story: that of the wife who betrays the husband she loves. That I might be the young woman who makes her commitment, then breaks it, dazzled and seduced away by a fickle Spirit Power—a living god in human form who unleashes waves of tingling ecstasy. In the end she is destroyed, abandoned both by Power and by the man she once loved, to become a pariah.

I clench my jaw and press my hands against the side of my head, as if by pressing, I can force understanding into my uncertain souls.

Where does the truth lie?

As if in answer, a humming moth descends from on high. I close my eyes as it hovers around my face. I revel in the patting air against my cheeks and nose. Feel its proboscis as it tastes my skin.

I feel the Power and know that I am chosen.

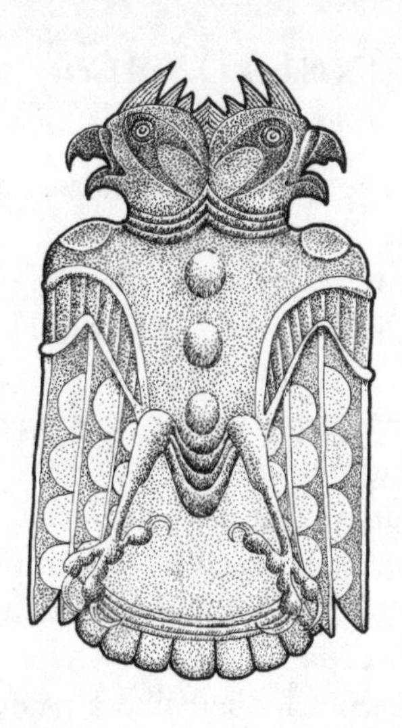

Twenty-one

Seven Skull Shield climbed up onto Crazy Frog's rickety platform and settled on the wooden bench beside the gambler. Crazy Frog might have been forty, though something about his age was hard to pin down. In fact everything about him was hard to pin down, given his average face, smudged tattoos, and unremarkable physique. He wore his hair in a bun with a plain wooden skewer through it. A coarsely woven hunting shirt covered his torso and was belted with a hemp-fiber rope.

Anywhere but up here atop this platform, Crazy Frog would have appeared so unremarkable as to be invisible. On his perch—the only one overlooking High Chief War Duck's River Mounds chunkey courts—Crazy Frog was as prominent as any man in the city.

He barely gave Seven Skull Shield a glance as he fixed on the two players occupying the long court before him. "This had better be very lucrative business. If you're just up here for a better view of the game, I'm going to have your legs broken."

Seven Skull Shield reached into his belt pouch and slapped a copper nugget the size of a hickory nut onto the bench where Crazy Frog kept his counter with its different-colored shell beads. The gambler used them to keep track of the scores.

With a quick sleight of hand, Crazy Frog palmed the nugget, asking, "What can I do for you?"

"To start with? Tell me who to bet on."

"I'd go for Skull Thrower. The one wearing black. He's three games up on Makes His Lance, the player in yellow."

If Crazy Frog knew anything, it was chunkey. He lived for the game, knew all the players, and better yet, who would win or lose. The other thing he knew was exactly what was going on in River Mounds City and the canoe landing. When it came to that, not even High Chief War Duck or Matron Round Pot had better sources.

Seven Skull Shield watched the two players crouch at the head of the court. Skull Thrower clutched his stone disc and charged forward, muscles bulging in his bare thighs. Makes His Lance was matching stride for stride, his lance balanced and raised.

Skull Thrower made what looked like a perfect release, bowling his stone with a looping underhand throw, the stone just kissing the packed clay as it shot forward like a thing alive.

In the next step, Skull Thrower had changed his lance to his right hand. Just as he and Makes His Lance reached the penalty line, they both launched their lances in a high arc.

Side by side, the lances cut through the still afternoon air; sunlight gleamed along their waxed and polished lengths as they curved toward the slowing stone.

Behind them, Skull Thrower and Makes His Lance called their encouragement to the flying lances. The crowds on either side of the courts were shouting, stomping, and clapping as they watched. As the stone wobbled and fell on its right side, Skull Thrower's lance thudded into the clay immediately to the right. Makes His Lance's shaft hit just beyond and to the left.

"Too close to call from here," Crazy Frog said with a grin.

The court judge trotted out with his knotted string and measured. Then, standing, he shouted, "Makes His Lance by a half a knot!"

The crowd erupted in screams of delight or outrage as the bets were called and the stakeholders surrendered wagered booty to the winners.

"You were saying about Skull Thrower?" Seven Skull Shield arched a suggestive eyebrow.

Crazy Frog gave him a sour look as he moved one of his beads from one column to another. "I liked you better when you were a faceless and nameless bit of walking dung. Now that you're a famous and prominent bit of walking dung, you've become insufferable. Did you come here for a reason?"

Seven Skull Shield hid a grin as he watched the two players collect their lances. Skull Thrower then picked up his stone, kissing it reverently.

"So, you remember the Quiz Quiz war leader?"

"Is he still with us? I figured he'd be screaming his voice box out while hanging in one of the Keeper's squares."

"The Surveyors' Society had him doing just that out in front of their society house. Built a square for him just special, the surveyors not being in the practice of torturing people as a general rule. And—novices as they are—it never occurred to them to leave a guard. Who'd steal a despicable criminal who'd had the gall to piss on the Surveyors' Society, right? Imagine their consternation when someone who didn't understand the magnitude of War Leader Sky Star's crime cut the dying Quiz Quiz down last night and carried the miscreant away."

"I'd say the Quiz Quiz has politically motivated friends."

"Indeed. Would it surprise you to learn that whoever did the deed has managed to raise the ire of not only the Surveyors' Society but also the high and mighty?"

Crazy Frog twitched his lips as he thought. Then said, "Next you are going to ask me to see if any of my people know if the rest of Sky Star's warriors are still around."

"You and I think a lot alike."

The gambler took a deep breath. "Is there any way I could persuade you to let this go?"

"Didn't I just explain that the Powers that be are irritated?"

Crazy Frog gave him a flat stare, stating, "You understand that this could turn into a real mess, don't you? It was bad enough that the Quiz Quiz sent their war leader to steal the Bundle. Twice as bad that he actually took it. And a whole lot worse that he got caught. And now, if his men took him down—thwarting the Morning Star's justice—they could *all* end up in the squares."

"And the whole Quiz Quiz Nation is going to go berserk," Seven Skull Shield finished. "They can't win, you know. In the end what can they do? Send an army north to punish us?"

"They'd be crushed before they reached the mouth of the Mother Water. And the second they sent their warriors north, the Pacaha or one of the other Nations down there would move on them."

Seven Skull Shield watched Makes His Lance and Skull Thrower take their positions, each leaning forward, concentrating on the court. It was Makes His Lance's turn to bowl, and the man cupped his white stone. They took their marks, launched, Makes His Lance bowled, and three steps later, both cast.

"Makes His Lance by two hands." Crazy Frog predicted, pausing to watch the lances as they curved through the air. Sunlight gleamed as they flew, and then they smacked into the smooth clay beside the stone.

"Good call," Seven Skull Shield told him. "You could do this for a living, you know?"

"Now there's an idea. Wonder why I've never thought of that on my own?" Crazy Frog moved his bead into another column.

"About the Quiz Quiz," Seven Skull Shield added. "We both know it's already a tricky situation. If bad goes to worse, their high chief will have to do something. He's got to, just to save face. But he can't act outright for the reasons we've already talked about."

"They'll send assassins," Crazy Frog predicted. "Some way of striking from the shadows."

"Unless I can stop it before it gets any worse. If you hear something, I'd take it as a favor if you'd contact me first."

"Don't want me grabbing the glory? Want to keep that for yourself so you can preen in front of old Blue Heron?"

Seven Skull Shield winced as Crazy Frog studied him through knowing brown eyes. "Let's just say I want to try and deal with this in a way that keeps as many people as possible out of the squares."

"You're hiding something."

"No, I'm not."

"So, what is it?" Crazy Frog shook his head in despair. "Don't tell me *you* had something to do with his escape."

"Pus and puke, do you think I'm *stupid*? Just trust me, all right? I need to deal with this in my own way."

Crazy Frog shook his head. "I swear on the Morning Star's balls, thief, whatever you're up to, you're more likely to end up in the Morning Star's square than that Quiz Quiz is."

"Do we have a deal?"

"Yes. For whatever good it's going to do you."

Twenty-two

I like what you've done to the place," Blue Heron told Columella. She looked around the Evening Star House palace and took in the new construction. Hard to believe that the last time she was here the entire palace had been in flames. Blood had been pooled in the matting, and body parts had been scattered across the floor.

Now that old palace was gone. Burned to ash. The mound upon which it stood had been covered with a new layer of earth. Columella had rebuilt the palace so recently the structure still looked new; the clay-plastered walls remained oddly bare of the usual Cahokian trappings. Overhead the ceiling poles were barely darkened by soot. The wood of the sleeping benches along the walls still smelled of sap.

The dividing wall in the rear that separated Columella's private quarters from the great room now consisted of a wattle-and-daub construction, but Columella had once had a magnificent weaving created from split cane hanging there.

On the other side of the fire, the Evening Star House matron reclined on her high dais. Columella wore a plain white dogbane-fiber skirt, had a modest split-feather cloak thrown over her shoulders, and for whatever reason, had allowed her hair to fall in a wave, its black threaded with occasional strands of white.

"It's barely a palace," Columella told her with a lopsided smile. "It will, however, keep us warm this winter. But now that we've drunk black drink, smoked the ritual greetings, and said the prayers, we can get to business. What do you need?"

Blue Heron slapped her thighs and grinned. "Is Flat Stone Pipe hiding in the cubby under your dais? I know it's hollow, and that he often secretes himself there and listens. If so, he can come out and relax. All that I need from you is your time, and to personally thank you for your support during the recent debacle in which Rising Flame was somehow made matron."

"Evening Star House had a debt to you, Keeper. I don't forget these things."

"I am Keeper no more." Blue Heron spread her hands in an airy gesture. "Which is another reason I am here. The longer I am gone, the faster things in Morning Star House will fall apart."

Evening Star straightened. "You are no longer Clan Keeper?"

"Been dismissed by the new matron."

Columella leaned back, fingers idly playing with the cougar fur on the hide covering her seat. Her expression was bemused. "I can't tell you the number of times I have wished to hear those very words."

"It is my delight that you get to hear them from my own lips, Matron."

"And what did Wind say?"

"I have no idea. Being relieved from any and all responsibilities, I figured it wasn't my place to inform the *tonka'tzi.* That would seem to be one of the clan matron's duties, don't you think?"

"Your sister is going to explode like wet clay in a too-hot fire. She'll be fit to chew stone. Nor would I put it past the Morning Star to vent his displeasure. You may not be liked, but you are effective. Any idea who the matron will name as your replacement?"

"None. Though she might choose her uncle, East Water. He's a well-respected warrior with connections among the Houses. Most consider him a no-nonsense military commander."

Columella tilted her head back and laughed. "East Water as Keeper? That is precious. The man has the guile and cunning of a floor mat. He isn't devious enough—not to mention he's as gullible as a strutting turkey in spring. And what about your spies? Will they report to him?"

"I doubt it." She grinned in satisfaction. "They are *my* spies. They trust me. Just as your spies trust Flat Stone Pipe. Where is he, by the way?"

"Keeping track of things, Keeper." She frowned. "Did you know your thief has Crazy Frog's people looking for the missing Quiz Quiz? And if he finds him, what then?"

Blue Heron caught herself reaching up to pull on the loose skin under chin. She really needed to break herself of that habit. "I suppose I shall have the Quiz Quiz's miserable carcass handed back to the Surveyors'

Society on my own. The time is coming when I may have need of favors."

"Bit late to start making friends, don't you think? You have a long-enough list of enemies to worry about as it is. And worse, you are no longer protected by your position."

Blue Heron chuckled in dry amusement. "It is a long list, isn't it? A fact I should be proud of given that—after all these years—I'm still here."

"And most of them, including a lot of my relatives, are not," Columella snapped, then relented. "You know that you'll be a target for retribution? All that protects you now is your family position. Not the assumed backing of the clan."

Blue Heron shrugged. "I may not have always made the right choices, and I admit to having made self-serving decisions, but I dedicated myself to keeping the peace. Hasn't been open bloodshed or vendettas between the Houses or the Earth Clans under my watch."

"Oh, I suppose that in your position, I would have done the same." Columella tapped her fingers. "And if you'd borne me any lasting ill will, you could have destroyed Evening Star House last spring."

Blue Heron pointed a gnarled finger. "The *tonka'tzi* and I wouldn't want anyone else in control on this side of the river. Yes, you've been a thorn in my shoe on occasion over the years, and your plotting to overthrow Morning Star House and supplant us has come closer to success than we've ever wanted to admit, but you've got sense and a long-term vision for the good of the city."

"Watch it. You are starting to sound maudlin." Columella struggled to hide a smile.

"I don't mean to." Blue Heron shrugged. "The events of last spring brought it all into focus. You are a much better ally than enemy. I would see your lineage and mine brought closer together. For Wind and myself, we'd be amenable to brokering marriages for all of your children. Strengthen the ties that way."

"We'll consider it." Columella told her with reserve. "But in the meantime, just what exactly is your plan? Somehow I can't see you letting the Clan Keeper's position slip through your fingers."

"Of course not. Just about now, I would imagine that things are getting a bit interesting for Rising Flame. Just enough time has passed that the Surveyors' Society has had time to communicate their outrage to the good matron. Not to mention that the high chiefs and matrons of the other Houses have all had a couple of days to stew on the outcome of the election. And then there are the delegations that have been put off while the Houses scrapped over the matron's position. By now their patience is exhausted. When my brother was the *tonka'tzi* he always shoved the excess off on Wind. She'll expect to do the same to Rising Flame. Who, of course, hasn't a clue."

"How long do you expect to let them stew?"

"Perhaps a week or so." She glanced around. "In the meantime I thought I'd take a look around Evening Star Town. See the sights. It's far enough away that I can't be snagged by Five Fists or War Claw, but close enough I can get back in half a day if something appalling happens."

"You are more than welcome to stay here in the palace, Keeper. In fact, it might be the safest and smartest place for you, given your current vulnerability and lack of protection."

"My most sincere thanks for your kind offer. However, I have already made arrangements at the Four Winds Clan House. Your cousin, who runs it, was most earnest in her assurances that my stay would be enjoyable."

"You sure that's a good idea? I'd call you a walking target for the moment."

"Not even Horned Serpent House could move on me this quickly. I'll be fine for a week or so, and by then I might even be Keeper again."

Columella shook her head. "Who would have ever thought I'd say it, but I look forward to your company this week. Flat Stone Pipe should be back tomorrow. You and he have so much in common."

"My pleasure." Blue Heron paused. "For now I will let you get back to your duties. You might, however, join me for breakfast at the Clan House tomorrow morning? Smoked paddlefish with fresh onion and beeweed seasoning is on the list."

"I'll indeed join you. It's been a while since I've checked on the Clan House. I wouldn't want Running Water to get sloppy."

"See you then."

Blue Heron was still smiling as she was carried out on her litter, her porters taking their time as she was borne down Columella's long staircase to the town plaza.

On the chunkey court, Columella's son Panther Call was practicing with his uncle, High Chief Burned Bone. As she was carried past, Blue Heron watched the young man bowl his stone and make a fair cast. He had potential.

South of the World Tree pole, a stickball game was being played by the renowned Deer Clan team. From the counters they were five ahead of their Fish Clan rivals.

When her litter was set down before the Four Winds Clan House, Blue Heron took her head porter's hand and was helped to her feet. Atop its mound, the Clan House with its guardian posts overlooked the plaza.

She waved her porter off as he offered his arm to help her climb the steps, adding, "I'll be fine. I'm just going to take a moment to watch the game."

"Yes, Keeper."

The appellation on the porter's part was pure reflex, she knew. She was still the Keeper in her own mind. Had been for so long she wasn't sure she could ever think of herself otherwise.

Stepping over, she joined the thin crowd and called out in dismay as bodies smashed together in midcourt. The clattering of racquets, the screams of men, and the hollow thumping of impacting bodies carried on the air.

Then a couple of Deer Clan players broke loose from the melee. A fleet-footed young man wearing a kirtle with a long flowing feather tail sprinted full-out for the goal. Just as he reached it, Fish Clan guards stopped his rush.

Undaunted, the youth reached back, putting all of his body behind the racquet as he launched the ball over the blockers' heads, and through the goal.

"Point!" the judge called.

A bellow of delight went up from the Deer Clan fans and players.

Blue Heron barely registered the two big men who had sidled up on either side of her.

She jerked when something pointed was jammed into her side.

"Don't make a sound, Keeper," the man on her right said softly. "If you do, your guts will be all over the ground."

"And by the time anyone figures out what's happened, we'll be long gone," the second told her, bending close.

"So we're just going to walk away like old friends," the first continued with deadly intent. "You be a good woman, and you won't get hurt. In fact, that's the last thing we want."

"Then . . . if not my death"—her heart was pounding—"what do you want?"

"We're looking for something. A prize possession that belongs to some friends of ours. Something that we think you have. That's all. If we can get it back, we'll call everything even all the way around."

"I don't have the foggiest idea what you're talking about!"

"Shhh. Don't make a fuss now. You ready? Let's walk. And remember, if you try anything? Shout out? Try and run. We'll either gut you, or knock your brains out, and be gone before you hit the ground."

"You're making a *big* mistake."

"Now, now, Keeper. It's just business. Trade, if you will. So let's go peacefully, and you won't be hurt."

She glanced up. Saw the look in the big man's eyes. He was pressing a long chert knife into the hollow under her right-side ribs.

The fellow's companion had a hand on his war club, holding it as if it were attached to his belt. They were river Traders from the look of them, well-muscled and sun-darkened. Neither had tattoos that were recognizable.

"Live or die. Right now. Make your decision."

Blue Heron—fear eating at her innards—nodded. "Let's go. I won't make a scene."

"Always heard you were a smart one."

She started walking, letting them direct the way south past the plaza and into the warren of temples, charnel and society houses, warehouses and farmsteads.

Casting a look back, she noticed that her porters had missed it all, talking and laughing as they waited by her litter.

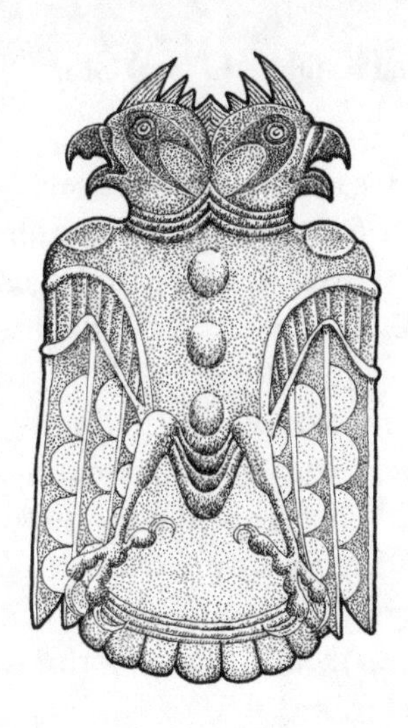

Twenty-three

Leave us!" *Tonka'tzi* Wind bellowed.

Like frightened mice and packrats, the messengers, recorders, lesser nobles, warriors, and priests scurried for the Council House door. The bravest ones cast quick and worried glances over their shoulders before they crammed themselves through the exit and out onto the Council House's enclosed plaza.

Oh yes, there would be talk aplenty tonight, wouldn't there?

Wind took a deep breath, as if the cool air could douse the hot rage in her chest. Her hands were trembling, and she sat bolt-upright in her litter atop the central dais in the Council House. Around her, the walls seemed to vibrate from outrage, or did she just imagine that?

Rising Flame, one defiant leg forward, arms crossed under her too-perfect young breasts, had her head back. Unabashed, she traded Wind stare for stare.

Wind exhaled slowly to buy time before she said something she couldn't take back. Those kind of things happened when she lost her temper—and this wasn't any ordinary, run-of-the-pack rage.

"You told Blue Heron she was no longer Keeper?" To her amazement, her voice held, though it sounded like ice.

"She did *not* show me the proper respect. I am the Four Winds clan matron. Not some lowly cousin to be abused."

"You are *an idiot*!" Wind couldn't stop herself. She rose from the litter, stepped down, and strode over to glare up into the young woman's eyes.

"Either that, or your head is as thick and senseless as a block of maple. Do you not understand? She's the spymaster! The one who has all the pieces. She *knows* each and every troublemaker in the city. Her people *trust* her. Not you. Not me. *Her.* There is a *reason* people call her the spider. She sits at the center of the web, can feel the tendrils when they get pulled from Serpent Woman Town, or when one of the Panther Clan chiefs up on the bluffs is about to start a war with a dirt farmer's community."

"No one is irreplaceable, Cousin. It's no different than if Blue Heron were to keel over of a suddenly stopped heart. Or fall down the Grand Staircase and break her neck. It's just a matter of putting someone the Morning Star approves of in her place. Whoever that is can hand out bribes as easily as Blue Heron did."

Wind closed her eyes. "Are you really that *simple*?"

"Simple? Do not patronize me. I know just as well as you that the Clan Keeper's position needs to be filled by someone who commands respect. A person for whom reputation and honesty is requisite. We need a leader who can inspire through leadership."

"Let me guess," Wind said dryly. "You're thinking of your Uncle East Water. War leader. Hero of the battle of the Wabash. Terror of the Shawnee."

Rising Flame blinked. "Well . . . obviously. If you came to the same conclusion so quickly, and without prompting, he is indeed the right man for the position."

"He is the *wrong* man for the position. He doesn't have the kind of coldly calculating character that it takes to be Keeper. And he's too damned honorable. He accepts people at their word. Doesn't know a lie from a promise. He's too—"

"Maybe *honesty* is what we need." Rising Flame's cheeks reddened with her own anger. "Blue Heron has a *thief* for a consort! She's doing business with every scoundrel on the waterfront. She's *subverting* young nobles, brokering deals with *slaves*."

"And who, *Cousin*, do you think knows the secrets? Or would you simply take Slender Fox at her word when you ask, 'Are you plotting against Morning Star House?' "

For a long moment they stared angrily into each other's eyes, Rising Flame refusing to answer, finally relenting, "Of course I wouldn't trust Slender Fox. Neither would Uncle."

Wind threw her arms up. "I can't believe I'm having this discussion."

"Me either. It's pointless. You are no long clan matron. I am. Picking the Clan Keeper is the Four Winds clan matron's responsibility. I've removed Blue Heron. It's done, and I will appoint someone else. I only came to tell you as a courtesy to the *tonka'tzi*."

"Get her back."

"Did you hear a single word I said?"

Wind shook her head. "You may be the head of the Four Winds Clan, but I am the *tonka'tzi*. If you cross me, you and I will go to war, and it will be arbitrated by the Morning Star."

"He hasn't always backed Blue Heron," Rising Flame reminded.

"Nor is he in the habit of backing stupid young matrons who precipitate a fight that will split the Four Winds Clan into factions and bring the city to instant chaos."

"And you—"

Rising Flame whirled as Master High Line, followed by String Runner, pushed his way through the door, declaring, "*Tonka'tzi*, this situation is intolerable."

High Line was a silver-haired elder—a tall, almost emaciated, sun-browned man made of ropy muscle on a bony body. His thin and curved nose literally hooked over his small brown mouth. A fire to match her own burned behind his black eyes.

"Master High Line," Wind said stiffly. "This is not the right moment to take up whatever—"

"Then I *will* take it up with the Morning Star. Where is the Keeper? My people have been to her palace and have been told that she's left the city."

"*What?*"

"Gone." High Line pushed his way up beside Rising Flame. "She is supposed to be *engaged* in finding the Quiz Quiz. I was to have reports daily. And worse, I am told by that Red Wing woman that Blue Heron is no longer the Keeper. Is that true?"

Wind said "No" at the same time Rising Flame said "Yes."

High Line blinked, then glanced back and forth uncertainly.

Wind chuckled, raising her hands and backing away. "All right, Clan Matron. There you go." To High Line she said, "Master Surveyor. Clan Matron Rising Flame will handle your problem from here on out. She has claimed responsibility."

"Good." High Line turned. "Where is the Quiz Quiz?"

"Who?" Rising Flame asked, her irritation visible in the knotting of her cheeks. "What Quiz Quiz?"

"The one from the square!" High Line thundered in rage.

"What square?" Rising Flame protested.

"The one who stole the Bundle!"

"Someone has stolen one of your Bundles?" Rising Flame slowly backed away, the first hint of uncertainty in her eyes.

At that juncture another messenger pushed into the room, a staff of office in his hands. He dropped to one knee before Wind and touched his forehead before declaring, "*Tonka'tzi*, it is my honor to inform you that War Leader Spotted Wrist is but a day's travel away upriver. He requests that an appropriate reception be granted to him and his warriors. I am to inform you of his arrival along with three squadrons, and request that the Four Winds Men's House be readied to receive him."

"Anything having to do with the Four Winds Men's House would be the province of the matron," Wind said coolly, pointing at Rising Flame. "I'm sure she will be happy to help you."

Next came a harried Albaamaha man with a scar on his face; he entered and prostrated himself before Wind. Looking up he said, "Great *Tonka'tzi,* I am so thankful for the opportunity to speak at last. I am to inform you of the arrival of a delegation from the Albaamaha Nation. We are aware of the Sky Hand Chikosi's request to establish an embassy in Cahokia. Therefore I have the honor of announcing the arrival of High Chief Hanging Moss and his nephew Straight Corn, of the Reed Clan, of the Albaamaha Nation, come to request an audience with the Morning Star and to engage in conversations preparatory to the establishment of an Albaamaha embassy."

Wind retreated to her dais and struggled to keep her expression under control as High Line and Spotted Wrist's messenger both besieged Rising Flame with questions and demands.

To the kneeling Albaamaha, Wind asked, "Have you a reference?"

The scar-faced man looked up, slightly mystified, and nodded. "I am of long-standing service to the Four Winds Clan. You need but ask the Keeper, great *Tonka'tzi.*"

"Ah, Clan Matron," Wind called. "Here is yet another one needing verification from the Keeper."

But Rising Flame could only glare back with eyes as piercing as bone stilettos.

Twenty-four

Fire Cat stepped out into the morning, his breath fogging. It wouldn't be long before the first frost. Purple light in the east cast the Morning Star's immense mound with its walls, World Tree poles, and soaring buildings as an inky black silhouette against the predawn sky.

He started to reset the plank door behind him when he noticed the young woman crouched in the dirt before the veranda. She huddled under a blanket, and as Fire Cat approached he could hear her whispering softly under breath, ". . . built a mountain out of dirt, raised on sweat and hurt . . ."

"Lady Sun Wing?"

She seemed not to hear him, eyes to the ground, shivering in the cold as she almost sang the words, ". . . Earth, hey Earth, from it spread. Raise the Underworld of the dead . . ."

Fire Cat reached down, placing his fingers against her cheek. The woman didn't seem to feel his touch. Her flesh was icy, and again the shivers racked her.

"How did you get away from War Claw?" Fire Cat wondered as he reached down and gathered the young woman into his arms. She tensed, a cry of pure terror in her throat.

"Shhh! You are safe, Lady. You are at Night Shadow Star's."

As she trembled and wept in his arms, he shouldered the door to one side and carried her in. With a sigh he lowered her by the fire's warmth, seeing her blink as she stared at the flames through glassy eyes. Her soft pink mouth hung slack, as though her souls were somewhere else.

Green Stick—who had been preparing a breakfast stew—shook his head. "She's back?"

"Why is she coming here?" Water Leaf asked as she and Clay String walked over from where they had been folding the bedding.

"I don't know," Fire Cat said thoughtfully as he rubbed the backs of his arms. "It's as if she's drawn."

He walked back to Night Shadow Star's room, leaning in to find her dressed and involved in the process of running a comb through her long and glossy hair.

"Lady? It's Sun Wing. I found her shivering out front and babbling in that odd voice of hers."

Night Shadow Star shot him a worried look, her expression pinched. "Gods. Just what I needed to hear." She blinked, looking exhausted. "I hardly slept a wink until sometime a couple of hands before dawn."

He glanced at the Tortoise Bundle where it rested in its niche. "I thought it had been quiet recently."

"Well, it's not now. I could hear it in my head for most the night. As if I didn't have enough Spirits whispering. Sometimes the voices are so clear; at others they sound like distant murmurings. And then there's Piasa flickering in and out at the edge of my vision."

She stood, set the comb to one side, and massaged her face. "All I need, on top of everything else, is to have to worry about Sun Wing."

Fire Cat carefully asked, "Maybe you are her only security? After all, it was you who saved her life."

"Accidentally. A half a heartbeat later and her blood would have been gushing into that pot they were holding her above."

"Nevertheless, she knows she'd be dead but for you. I suspect you are the only thing that keeps her nightmares from completely devouring her souls. I've heard the stories, Lady. They say she sits in that back room in her palace and screams when she isn't whimpering. Her souls are damaged. Insane."

"And what do you propose we do about it, Red Wing?" she snapped, then relented with an apologetic smile. "Sorry. Lack of sleep."

"Would it hurt if she stayed here for a couple of days? If you make her feel safe, perhaps just a respite, the chance to relax from her fear might give her enough pause to realize that Walking Smoke is dead."

"We hope."

"I wouldn't tell her that, Lady. But it might give her the chance to start healing."

"And what about the rest of the household?"

He gave her a grim smile. "They will happily acquiesce to whatever you decide. If they don't, I will, um . . . enhance their cooperation."

She chuckled, stepping up to him. He saw her start to lift her hands, as though she was going to place them on his chest. Catching herself, she stopped short and let them drop fretfully to her sides.

Her expression, however, remained warm. “Thank you, Fire Cat. I know she's nothing to you, and I realize her presence may create additional trouble for us, but maybe this will help.”

“She's your sister, Lady.”

He turned to go, but she reached out, laying a restraining hand on his arm. His skin tingled at her soft touch.

“Lady?”

She kept her eyes averted, though he could still see her blink, as if against tears. “I don't deserve you, you know.”

“Lady, I know no such thing.”

For a moment he battled with himself, wanting nothing more than to reach out and draw her to him. With the smallest effort he could pull her close, wrap her in his arms, and cradle her protectively against him. Perhaps ease some of her worry and distress.

Instead, he ground his teeth, tried to still his suddenly labored breathing, and carefully disengaged from her.

Once outside of her door, he stopped, took a deep breath, and composed himself.

Where she sat at the fire, Sun Wing was watching him with wide and knowing eyes. As if to him alone, she said, “The dark nectar is here. In the city, Red Wing. Only she can descend into the darkness and call him back to air, light, and sky.”

“What's she saying?” Green Stick asked, having turned back to his stew.

“Just ravings,” Winter Leaf replied from where she'd gone back to her folding.

“Doesn't matter,” Fire Cat told them. “Your lady has decided that Sun Wing will stay with us for a while. That perhaps we can allay her fears and madness long enough that the poor woman's souls will return to her body.”

Clay String made face, saying, “But Fire Cat, her souls have fled! What do we know—”

“It is *decided*.” Fire Cat pointed a hard finger. “I have told you our lady's word. That's an order.”

“We'll see to her comfort,” Green Stick agreed warily, though he clearly didn't like it.

“Down in the darkness, deep in the earth . . .” Sun Wing blinked at nothing. “That's where she has to go to save him.”

“Him? To whom do you refer, Lady?” Fire Cat dropped to a squat to stare into her vacuous eyes.

“The Morning Star . . . so close to death . . . ,” came her disjointed whisper.

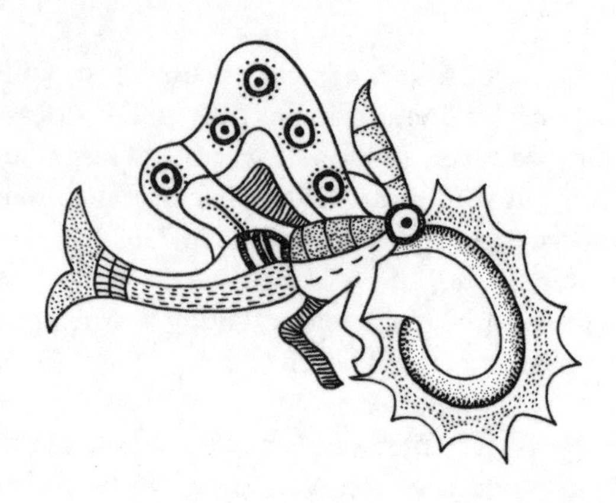

Epiphany

The sun is warm on my face as I sit in the courtyard, knees together as is proper for a Chief Clan lady of the Sky Hand. To occupy myself I ask for and receive a very fine shock of staves and pliant sumac strips. Since childhood, basketry has always soothed me, and while I am not nearly the master that some of the older women are, I have turned out some very nice pieces.

I build my base and establish my pattern, choosing a twill design. Once started, my hands fall into the routine as I cross one and skip two, to create a tight weave.

Once the mindless repetitive action of the hands is established, my mind can wander. My problem is that I don't know what I am supposed to do. How am I to undertake my great role? What does Power expect of me? How can I play my part when I can't figure out what the next step is?

So far I am enjoying being the Morning Star's wife. Yes, he has so many—most of them scattered around the city, visiting him when called upon to do so. And I already understand that, to date, I am something of a sensation, having been in his bed for so many days.

Nor is it a bad life. Just the contrary. I could spend hands of time just wandering about the palace, marveling at the artistry that has gone into the copper reliefs, the wooden carvings, textiles, and shell inlay. Any box I pull out is filled with marvels from the four corners of the world.

The Morning Star even let me try cacao from his diminishing stock—the most marvelous tasting and sweet drink I've ever savored. It was a gift from the Itza during their recent and tragic time in Cahokia.

And the food? Beyond compare.

I ate well in Split Sky City, but the kind of feasts cooked for the Morning Star are truly stunning. Some are spiced with achiote—another gift of the recently deceased Itza. Others are made with spices I've never heard of, like chilis, beeweed, and something called desert parsley traded from the distant Shining Mountains out west.

Just this morning I asked to accompany the Morning Star as he descended to the Great Plaza for one of his frequent chunkey games with a Four Winds noble, a high chief named War Duck.

I had a perfect spot where I could watch from the side of the court as the Morning Star—dressed in immaculate regalia—beat poor War Duck by eight points. Not that I couldn't have predicted. War Duck only has one eye. How could he have ever expected to come close to beating the living god? It's hard to judge distances with only one eye. Nevertheless, the man still bet his life on the game.

The upshot was that War Duck knelt and bent his head in defeat. To which deference, the Morning Star magnanimously granted him reprieve.

Even as he did, the Morning Star looked straight into my eyes, shooting me a saucy wink from behind his perfectly painted face with its white forked-eye pattern against a black background.

The effect is that we share a special relationship, a special intimacy that has taken me by complete surprise. To wit, I have no patience for the long periods when he is occupied by the various chiefs and society heads who have a claim on his time. Who would have guessed that being a resurrected god could be so draining and time-consuming?

But as soon as we step into his personal quarters, I am frantically tugging at the ties that hold his cape, almost jerking his headpiece off, and clawing at his apron. Can I really be my mother's daughter? Reared with the fine Sky Hand values of bodily restraint? It is as if I physically ache to impale myself on his ever-willing shaft. Nor is the result of doing so anything but the most delicious of ecstatic releases.

Were it not for that visit from the moth, I would assume that nothing could outweigh the miracle of my new situation. But I cannot forget the fluttering of wings against my face. Sacred Moth's Power was made manifest that night.

In the hand of time since I began to pursue this line of thought, I have woven a third of the basket. The World Tree pole is casting its shadow toward the palace door, indicating midday. And I am no closer to resolving my dilemma.

It is at that moment when Five Fists walks up with the Moskogee translator. I look up at the broken-faced war leader and see mild curiosity in his eyes. Through the translator, he says, "The tonka'tzi *requests that you come. She would have your words regarding an embassy from the Albaamaha."*

An embassy for the Albaamaha? What embassy? For a moment I wonder if the translator is missing something in the war leader's words, then shrug, laying my basketry to the side.

I stand and gesture that he lead forth.

I follow Five Fists through the palace gate and down the long stairs, again reveling at the incredible vista of city stretching in every direction. A brown haze hangs low, obscuring the horizon.

As we reach the council plaza, Five Fists leads me to the Council House itself. I enter with a sense of curiosity. It is here that most of the governance of Cahokia and its colonies takes place. The room is crowded with nobles. Recorders and messengers, with their staffs in hand, line the walls like beads on a string. Deer hides are laid out before the three daises in the rear. I see that the hides are maps. The tonka'tzi*—a woman named Wind—sits on a cougar-hide-covered litter atop the central dais.*

To her left is a young woman who I suspect is the new Four Winds Clan matron. She is attractive, not that much older than I am, perhaps in her early twenties. Her hair is done up in a splay of colorful feathers. As I enter she raises a speculative eyebrow, as if assessing me. I am dressed well, but not as spectacularly as either the tonka'tzi or the clan matron.

The knot of people clustered just this side of the maps turns toward me—and my heart stops.

In spite of the face paint, I recognize Hanging Moss, high chief of the Reed Clan, and head initiate of the Sacred Moth Society. He is the man who first offered me the holy nectar and sent my souls flying to the nether realms of the Spirit World. As his eyes meet mine, I see a twinkle of relief, and he bows his head in greeting.

To his left is Fighting Dog, the Reed Clan's war leader, a man whose head is sought by the Sky Hand. He is in his late forties, spare of frame, moderately muscled, with a narrow-boned face. He is a master of the ambush, a wily forest fox who has embarrassed my father's warriors time after time in the off-and-on-again conflict between the Sky Hand and Albaamaha.

To Hanging Moss's right is his sister, Wet Clay Woman, clan matron. To see her here is a real shock. She is the blood and bone of the Reed Clan—the heart of opposition to the Sky Hand's rule of the Black Warrior Valley. It seems inconceivable that she would leave her people to journey to this distant place.

And then Straight Corn elbows his way past his mother, a joyous smile breaking out on his lips. His large eyes are shining with relief, and I can see his throat working, as if he's almost suffocating with emotion.

I am on the verge of rushing forward and throwing myself into his arms when Hanging Moss gives me a hand sign: the tightening of the fist and twist of the wrist that signals caution. At the same time, in an almost hostile voice, he calls, "Do not *arrive at the wrong impression, Lady Whispering Dawn.*

We are not here to undercut your *Sky Hand embassy. We offer a truce, and only wish to establish communication with Cahokia."*

This is when I see Two Sticks standing off to the side, his lips pursed, expression that of a rabbit cowering under a single scraggly bush when too many hawks are circling in the sky.

Straight Corn mouths the word "Careful" and gives me a warning glance.

I stop short, wondering where the right path lies in all of this.

Think!

So if the Albaamaha have been talking to Two Sticks, they know everything about my time in Cahokia. That they know about the Sky Hand embassy is proof of that. I suffer a prickling of nerves. That also means that Straight Corn knows I've been married to the Morning Star—that I've been in his bed for the last week.

I feel my cheeks redden, and stiffen at the embarrassment and shame.

As if he reads my thoughts, Straight Corn gives me that soothing smile of reassurance that was one of the reasons I fell in love with him in the first place. He used to do that when I was being berated by my father or the matron. Or when I wasn't meeting the endless expectations other people had established for my behavior.

I find my voice. "What is your purpose here?"

"Balance, great lady," Hanging Moss says with an inoffensive resonance. "From the moment after the Creation when the Albaamaha emerged from the roots of the Tree of Life, we have sought balance and harmony. Our people have long desired to establish relations with the living god. Many talked about it, but few relished the notion of traveling so far, or knew what sort of reception a distant and pacifistic people such as ourselves might receive in great Cahokia. Nor did we know what stories the Morning Star and tonka'tzi *might have heard about us."*

He is playing to the Cahokians, of course.

"They are a just people, High Chief," I answer. "And though I am wed to the Morning Star, I have considered the problems between the Sky Hand and Albaamaha to be a local matter. Not the sort of thing the living god needed to concern himself with."

"Then you have no objection to the Albaamaha establishing an embassy in Cahokia, Lady?" the tonka'tzi asks through a translator.

I turn my attention to her, bowing my head ever so slightly and touching my chin in a greeting to an equal. "None whatsoever, Tonka'tzi. *Some of the Albaamaha clans have sworn fealty to the Sky Hand, and have subjugated themselves to our rule. The Reed Clan and several others have not. They remain an independent people. As such—though the Sky Hand might not like it—they have as much right to deal with Cahokia as any other free people."*

I can see the relief in Hanging Moss's eyes. Wet Clay Woman gives me a look that communicates that she could kiss me. Straight Corn is grinning, and Two Sticks has laced his hands together and is shaking them as if in self-congratulation.

During this interchange, my translator has been whispering into Five Fists' ear. Now the war leader asks, "Then I take it there will be no trouble between your peoples, Lady?"

I turn. "As soon as we are finished here, I will send a messenger to War Leader Strong Mussel, ordering him to behave and to keep the living god's peace."

I gesture to the Albaamaha. "The high chief and matron can speak for themselves."

Bowing low and touching his forehead, Hanging Moss says, "If anything, Tonka'tzi, *we are delighted to enjoy Cahokia's peace." He glances at me, an eyebrow lifted. "As part of our establishment of an embassy, we ask the lady if we might use the living god's peace to communicate directly with her. Face to face. This is neutral ground, removed from the hotheads and passions of our home territory. Matron Wet Clay Woman, here, is the leader of the Albaamaha resistance. Lady Whispering Dawn is the daughter of High Minko White Water Moccasin. Together they represent a potent path toward establishing a dialog between our two peoples." He pauses. "Is this acceptable, Lady?"*

I have sense enough to hesitate and frown as if considering. In the end I say, "I can see no harm. And you do understand that as the Morning Star's wife, I have certain obligations."

The smile on Hanging Moss's lips reeks of victory. "Of course, Lady." He bows and touches his forehead.

Straight Corn, however, has a tortured look on his face.

Well, don't fret, my husband. Now that you are here, it's only a matter of time before you and I are in that canoe, headed home.

I give the tonka'tzi *a gracious smile. Best not to play this too far lest I arouse suspicion. "Blessed* Tonka'tzi, *if you have no more need for me, I will leave you to work out the details with these Albaamaha."*

To Five Fists, I say, "When they are settled and ready, I assume you can have a litter and proper escort to see me to their embassy?"

He rocks his broken jaw, as if uneasy, and replies, "If the Morning Star so wills, Lady."

It is all I can do to keep from shooting Straight Corn a wink and a smile. But that will have to wait. For the moment I dare not risk even that. The slightest mistake could kill us all.

Twenty-five

So is this Two Sticks really one of Blue Heron's spies, or not?" *Tonka'tzi* Wind asked as she paced back and forth behind the fire in her large new palace. As with so many of Cahokia's key palaces, it too had been rebuilt in the wake of Walking Smoke's rampage. Larger than Red Warrior's old structure, the new palace was built atop a clean new cap of white clay that covered the old mound. The white color should have imparted wisdom and purity to those who occupied the place.

For the moment, all she could remember was that the mound had been consecrated by the blood of five Cahokian warriors who had been butchered by the Itza with their *macuahuitl* war clubs.

So much for peace and tranquility. That pretty much fit with her foul mood.

"All I can tell you"—Rising Flame sat in her own litter on the public side of the fire—"is that Smooth Pebble says that Two Sticks has often been at the Keeper's and has provided information. He was there with the Sky Hand delegation when Whispering Dawn was first presented."

"And then what?"

"No one knows."

Wind stopped, raised her hands, and clawed her fingers into fists, as if strangling the very air. "Something happened in the Council House today that we didn't understand."

"What?"

"I *don't* know. And that's what's driving me half insane. I can feel it."

She shot a look—cutting as an obsidian blade—at Rising Flame. "And there's still no word of Blue Heron?"

"I sent a runner to Evening Star Town. Someone said that they saw her there. That she was with Columella."

"So help me, Cousin, if we get through this . . ." She stared at her knotted fists, the knuckles gone white. "I have never felt so blind and dumb. It is like making decisions in the dark."

Rising Flame uttered a half-frustrated cry. "All *right*! Blue Heron can continue to serve as the Keeper. Of all the dung-licking idiocy, what have you people been thinking? You've got all of Cahokia's prestige and authority wrapped up between you, your sister, and your spooky niece. What happens if another assassin slips in during the night and cuts your throats? Have you thought of that? The whole city will be paralyzed."

"And I suppose you have the answer? So far, Cousin, you haven't exactly pinned my hair back with your outstanding acumen."

Rising Flame took a deep breath. "Being matron isn't quite what I expected."

Wind rubbed her eyes, feeling a headache coming on. "Oh? Well, perhaps you can throw another grand reception. Order a feast. Offer up a prize for the winner of a stickball tournament."

Wind heard the acid in her voice and winced, aware that her household staff were cowering in the corner. Rot take it, her emotions were getting the better of her.

Rising Flame, jaws clenched, was glaring through eyes that barely masked rage. The young woman took three tries opening her mouth then biting off the retort, before she finally stood, paced before the fire, and after a deep breath said, "Night Shadow Star was right. I *am* the clan matron. Her advice, perhaps through that vile Spirit Creature that whispers to her, was that we come to grips with that fact."

"Some grips!" Wind said through her own anger. "But it's not too late. If you can't—"

"*Blood and pus!* I made some mistakes. How did you do when you first stepped into the position? What? Oh . . . let me guess. You were perfect. Not a bobble, not a fault. Wisdom dripped from your every decision."

"Rot take you, no. It wasn't like that. Your grandmother, Evening Dove, offered counsel when I—"

"Ah! Yes! There it is. You had *help*!"

"You could have, too, if you hadn't driven Blue Heron away."

"If I'm to be matron, I've got to have respect. She *hates* me. Thinks I'm too young, that I'd fall on my back for the first man who walks past. As if *she,* of all women—given her history with men—has the right to judge."

Wind wheeled, pointing a finger. "You want to be a matron, then *be* a matron. You're sounding like a spit-licking and pouting child."

"At least I'm not an overdressed, arrogant—"

"*Tonka'tzi!*" A young man burst in the door, not bothering with the formalities. He barely looked to be out of his teens, was wearing only a breechcloth, his hair in a common bun. Sweat streaked down his face, bare chest, and legs. Clutched in his hand was an Evening Star House messenger's staff.

Gasping for air, he fell to the mat, crying out, "Matron Columella . . . sent me . . . Tell you . . . Keeper Blue Heron. She's vanished!"

Wind gaped, holding her breath. Felt the room spin. She forced herself to breathe, asking, "Vanished how?"

"She was to stay at the Four Winds Clan House in Evening Star Town. One moment . . . she was watching the stickball game. The next, she'd disappeared."

Wind fought off eerie fingers of panic. "You're sure? She didn't just decide to leave, maybe go somewhere else?"

"And leave her litter, *Tonka'tzi*?" The messenger looked up, desperation in his eyes. "My matron is scared, *Tonka'tzi.* She's sure something bad has happened. We are turning Evening Star Town upside down looking for her, and Flat Stone Pipe has his people asking questions, but so far there's nothing."

Wind settled bonelessly onto her litter; a feeling of futility robbed her of any coherent thought.

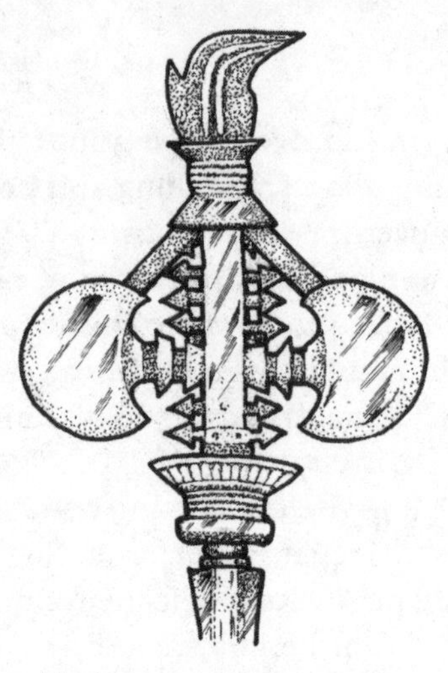

Twenty-six

Seven Skull Shield scratched the back of his head, hoping it wasn't lice that were causing the itch in his scalp. He hated lice—and the little beasts were everywhere in Cahokia. For the most part he could keep clear of them, especially if he was cautious about where he bedded down, and with whom.

The good thing about Cahokia was that it was essentially the Trading hub of the whole world, which meant insecticides—including puccoon from the southeast, red fir and pine sap from the eastern mountains, essence of high-mountain fir and larkspur mixed with gumweed from the western mountains, and other potions—were available to be rubbed into the hair. Various locally available noxious plants, including poison ivy, could be had to boil one's clothing in—you just had to stay upwind and not inhale any of the murderous fumes.

"I have to tell you"—Seven Skull Shield addressed his friend Black Swallow—"I never figured you for a domestic man. Let alone one so happily married."

He again glanced up at the fine new house in which he sat. It hadn't been standing for a whole moon yet, and still had that raw and new look where the vine bindings and split-bark ties held the roof together.

Black Swallow sat across the fire from him; a rather voluptuous young woman with a round face crouched at his side. She stirred the contents of a corrugated ceramic bowl that had its base planted deep in the coals. The whole house smelled of green wood, smoke, and the delicious odors of hominy, acorns, and hazelnuts, tempered by flakes of stewed turtle.

"I had to marry," Black Swallow said, holding up his mangled hands. "Hard to get the little things in life done with fingers like these."

Seven Skull Shield winced. "You know how much I regret the series of events that led to that happening. The Keeper didn't know me back then. Thought we were all a bunch of cutthroats. For all she knew at the time, one of us was *the* cutthroat, given the way people around her were being murdered right and left."

Black Swallow glanced sidelong at his young and nubile wife. Her name—in whatever barbaric language she spoke—was something like *A'na'na'ish'i'it'ah'hey.* Which is why Black Swallow cleverly called her "wife."

She smiled at her husband, eyes alight, and giggled. Then said something bubbly and full of stops in the back of her throat. An incomprehensible language Seven Skull Shield thought was spoken somewhere along the far western edge of the plains.

That was the thing about Cahokia. It had people from everywhere in the world. For a fact he knew that Black Swallow had bought the young woman from one of the Plains Skidi—distant relatives of the Caddo. Whatever the girl had expected—and Seven Skull Shield could certainly guess the grim nature of her past anticipations—she hadn't dreamed of being showered in beads, given a new house, fine clothing, warm bedding, plenty to eat, and a man who actually cherished her.

Given his service to the Keeper, Black Swallow had ended up a moderately wealthy man. He intimated that his healthy young wife reciprocated to his largess in her own creative and uninhibited ways. Fully aware of the charms of her body, Seven Skull Shield didn't need to strain his more than fertile imagination.

"You've done well," Seven Skull Shield admitted, and took a bowl of the stew "Wife" handed him. Raising it to his lips, he slurped, then pointed a finger at Farts, who was creeping closer on his belly. "Get back in the corner. You'll get yours later."

The big brindle dog yawned, stifling a muted cry, and retreated with a disconsolate look.

"Actually, I did do well, didn't I?" Black Swallow smiled his satisfaction. "I have Wife in my bed every night. You have that odiferous dog warming yours. Which, I'll have to admit, leaves you better off than I've ever seen you. But I've still got the better of the deal."

"So you say. Times get tough? I can always eat the dog." He smiled at Wife, happy that she had only a rudimentary understanding of

Cahokian. "Can't say but what people would frown if you whacked Wife, here, in the head and threw her in the stew pot."

Black Swallow gave him a thin and knowing smile. "Once upon a time, before I really got to know you, I'd have wondered if you were serious."

"Oh, I am. A falsehood has never passed these lips."

"Sure." A pause. "Neither has vomit, huh?"

"Are you being unnaturally thorny tonight? I thought we'd gotten past that bit of unpleasantry with your fingers. Especially after the Itza arrived."

"People down here in River Mounds still don't trust you, you know." Black Swallow cradled his brownware bowl in his crooked fingers. "If anything gives them pause in their skepticism, it's because Crazy Frog vouches for you."

"And Mother Otter thinks I'm some kind of walking slime."

"Which is the other reason people tolerate you. Given that Mother Otter thinks most of us are rabble, and she thinks you're worse than walking dung, you've gotta have something in common with the rest of us."

"I should express my appreciation for her kind service next time I see her."

"What? And ruin a perfectly good day if she's having one?"

Seven Skull Shield shot his friend a conspiratorial smile and took another gulp of the hominy. Wiping his lips, he added, "I don't get it. There are twenty-some Quiz Quiz warriors running around somewhere. Their big war canoe is still beached and under High Chief War Duck's watchful eye. Their war leader, Sky Star, is seriously hurting, with a crushed shoulder, numerous burns and cuts, and more dead than alive. It's not like they can just vanish. So . . . where are they?"

"That's a good question," Black Swallow agreed. "If it was just you bumbling around looking for them, I'd say they were camped in plain sight out in the middle of the Grand Plaza. But since Crazy Frog's people are looking for them, too? That means they really are hidden."

"I find things just fine, thank you. I caught the Quiz Quiz war leader the first time. Not my fault the stupid surveyors let him get stolen out of their square."

Black Swallow turned serious. "It means that whoever is hiding them fully understands the intensity of the hunt. I imagine that your Keeper is running spies in and out of her palace like termites in a hive. She's probably coordinating with every House in Cahokia, who, in turn, are whipping their Earth Clans chiefs to poke their noses into every basket and jar in the dirt farmer's communities."

"And Crazy Frog's people will be looking in all the dark and hidden places the Four Winds wouldn't think of."

Black Swallow paused over his hominy. "All of which means that while you're here eating my food, that Quiz Quiz war chief has been rounded up already and is headed back to hang in his square."

"I hope not. Means I won't have earned a nice warm robe-covered bed in the Keeper's palace." Seven Skull Shield gestured with his bowl. "Good as this is, you wouldn't believe the concoctions that Red Wing woman, Dancing Sky, cooks up. And while I will appreciate your floor tonight, sleeping on buffalo-wool mattresses agrees with my back."

Black Swallow blinked his eyes as if at an impossibility. "You poor abused wretch." Then his expression changed. "And does that excuse for a dog have to drool like that? The puddle building under his jaws is going to melt my floor."

Seven Skull Shield fished out another chunk of turtle meat and tossed it to the dog; Farts grabbed it out of the air, a curling streamer of drool spinning in the light.

"There. That will keep his leaking to a minimum."

"The thing looks half bear, if you ask me." Black Swallow took another swig of his hominy. "So what are you going to do if you find your Quiz Quiz? Pluck the wounded war chief from the midst of his twenty warriors?"

"Depends."

Black Swallow gave him the same skeptical look he'd give a lunatic.

Seven Skull Shield shrugged it off. "I'll send a runner for Blue Heron to order War Claw to come post-haste with warriors, and I'll hang around in the meantime to make sure the Quiz Quiz don't skip for the south before War Claw arrives."

"But if I, or one of my people, should find them first?"

Seven Skull Shield shrugged. "That's fine. Send your runner to the Keeper. I don't mind if you get all the credit."

"That makes you a most unusual man."

Seven Skull Shield grinned. "All these years and just now you figure that out?"

"Hey in there!" a voice called from beyond the door. "I'm looking for Seven Skull Shield."

Black Swallow arched an eyebrow, as if to ask, "You want to be found?"

Seven Skull Shield shrugged, laid his bowl to the side, and stood. He used the stepping post to climb up to the door and set it to the side before looking out into the gloomy evening. "Who's looking for Seven Skull Shield? Maybe I can get a message to him."

In the darkness he could just make out a fellow with long black hair hanging in a braid. A simple breechcloth with an apron hung at his waist, a poorly woven cape over his shoulders.

"I come from Crazy Frog. Tell the thief that the little man wants to see him. Right now. At the Evening Star palace."

"Why? What's wrong?"

"All I know is that something bad has happened to the Keeper. She's disappeared."

Twenty-seven

The room was small. Blue Heron figured it was no more than three paces wide by four long. She lay on her right side, arms bound behind her at the elbows by a short rope tethered to the hobbles that confined her ankles. They had at least thrown down a worn blanket to cushion her bones from the dirt.

Didn't matter. She hurt. Wasn't much feeling in her right arm, though she kept trying to shift and ease the circulation.

When she wasn't terrified, she was enraged.

A central hearth now smoldered; tendrils of smoke rose in the lazy air. From the angle of morning light slanting in the doorway, she could tell the building had been oriented toward the lunar maximum moonrise on the northeastern horizon. That fact was augmented by the carefully layered clay floor on which she lay: A compacted yellow silty clay had been carefully laid down. That it capped a layer of black clay could be seen where a wood rat had dug a hole behind one of the altar support posts on the back wall.

Moon temple. But which one? The entire city was oriented toward the lunar maximums and minimums. Each lineage, clan, ethnic group, society, collection of farmsteads, and even some families had their own small lunar temples. As a result there were thousands of them around Cahokia. Nor did they get a lot of attention during the nine-year period between the major lunar events. Some—depending upon the local tradition—were even left to the elements and then ritually refurbished and reconsecrated anticipatory to the ceremonies.

Listening, she could hear birds, the buzzing of flies, and the muted sounds of men talking. Somewhere not so far away, a dog barked and a young child squealed. Beyond that, she could hear only the soft rattle of cottonwood leaves and the breeze whispering in the moldy thatch overhead.

Sniffing, she smelled smoke, of course, but behind it was the wet odor of swampy low ground.

Hard to say where she might be, but it wasn't in a core urban area. This had to be in an outlying farmstead. The sort of place where she wasn't likely to be "discovered" by accident. Someplace isolated where the neighbors would *not* be talking about the old woman tied up in the lunar shrine.

She was considering this as a man darkened the doorway and stepped down into the room. She remembered him. The bigger of the men who'd taken her from the stickball game. One of the river Traders.

"How are you doing?" he asked, a slight nasal twang to his voice.

"I have to pee."

"Then go," he told her with a shrug. "I won't stop you."

"I'd like to use a pot, if you don't mind."

"Actually, I do. Our goal is to make you miserable enough that you will finally give in and tell us where the War Medicine is."

She blinked. "The what?"

"Don't play coy, Keeper. The War Medicine. Once we have that, we'll be gone."

She blinked as if it would clear her foggy thoughts, then smiled at the ludicrous position she was in. "Do you really think I, of all people, could get the War Medicine? The Men's Society wouldn't even let the *tonka'tzi* into the Men's House, let alone me. And, added to your problems, I'm no longer the Keeper. You kidnapped the wrong woman. Should have snagged up the new clan matron. Not that she could get you the War Medicine either, but she could appoint you a new Keeper to threaten, and you could go on about your business."

The big man dropped into a squat, muscular arms resting on the knotted cords of his thighs. He cocked his head. "You're really no longer the Keeper?"

"Matron Rising Flame—you've heard of her, right? She summarily dismissed me. Finished. Done. Can't make it more clear than that."

"So, I'm to believe that you can't help me. That I should just let you go?"

"That's pretty much it. I'd suggest you kidnap Five Fists or War Claw. They'd have a much better chance of slipping in and lifting the Four Winds War Medicine for you. Like I said—"

He reached out and slapped her hard on the face.

The sting of it brought tears to her eyes.

"I said, don't play coy."

Blue Heron worked her jaws, wishing for a drink of water as the sting faded. "Either you are an idiot, or you've got a huge hole in your understanding of how things are done in Cahokia. I *can't* get into the Men's House! I'm a *woman*. I'm not allowed."

"Do you take me for a fool?"

"I'm starting to." She flinched as he raised his hand again, but didn't strike.

"You know which War Medicine I'm talking about."

She slowly shook her head. "Now you've lost me. Whose War Medicine do you want me to get for you? And if not the Four Winds War Medicine, why come after me?"

He had his head cocked, eyes thoughtful. "I'm talking about the Quiz Quiz War Medicine. The wooden chest, the Bundle containing the Quiz Quiz war Power. They won't leave without it."

She struggled to understand. "You're working for the Quiz Quiz?"

"It's worth a fortune in Trade to me if I can get their war Bundle back. So far it's pretty much been a disaster for them. Sky Star's lucky to still be alive, but his days as a warrior are over. Though most of the scars and burns will heal, he'll never use his right arm again."

"So . . . you're telling me that the Quiz Quiz brought their War Medicine along to help them steal the Surveyors' Bundle?" She slowly put the pieces together. "Let me guess. After Seven Skull Shield captured the war leader, the Bundle disappeared?"

"It wasn't there when the warriors finally got back to the Council House. They thought perhaps Sky Star had taken it, but it wasn't with him when he was seen being carried to Crazy Frog's."

"Did you check with Crazy Frog?"

"After a roundabout fashion. We let him know that a reward was being offered for a box from down south. Since he had the Quiz Quiz war leader, it wouldn't have taken much to make the connection if he also had the War Medicine box and its contents."

"So Sky Star might not have had it with him when my people caught him?" she mused, enjoying the challenge of figuring it out even if her stomach was empty and her bladder too full. "Which means it was unattended for a time."

"Maybe."

"For how long?"

"Perhaps a half a hand of time? Maybe less."

She chuckled dryly. "If I know anything about War Medicine boxes, they're pretty things. All carved and decorated and inlaid with shell, copper, and precious stones. Anyone stumbling upon that kind of wealth, unattended, would have thought that all the Powers of Sky and Underworld had smiled upon them."

"What about your people? The ones who grabbed the war leader in the first place? This 'howling warrior' as the war leader calls him." He paused thoughtfully, his scarred brow scrunched, as if in thought. "Now, that wouldn't be Seven Skull Shield, would it?"

And the final piece fell into place. She pursed her lips, frowning. That night in her palace, he *had* been hiding something. Phlegm and snot!

She made a face. "Who?"

The river Trader studied her thoughtfully, his square face with its mashed nose oddly out of character for such cunning eyes. "Skull claimed responsibility for putting Sky Star in that square. He had a dog with him the day I saw him. A big dog. The kind whose jaws could have maimed a man's shoulder the way Sky Star's is now maimed." A pause. "He work for you?"

"We talking about that foot-loose thief that hangs around down at the waterfront?"

"The one who offered me a shell columella as a bribe to spend the day watching stickball games on the Grand Plaza? That's a lot of wealth. The sort he'd have if he'd been rewarded by the Keeper for having apprehended a Quiz Quiz war leader."

While Blue Heron bit her lip and tried to keep her face blank, the Trader rocked back, whispering, "My, my, Skull, you have gone up in the world."

"I haven't a clue as to what you're talking about."

He took a deep breath. "Well, Keeper, you'd better figure it out. And right quick. Which leaves me with an interesting dilemma."

"And what might that be?"

"If Skull's got the Quiz Quiz War Medicine, and that's the most likely supposition we can make, he's sitting on a potential fortune. He could trade it off to the Pacaha, the Quigualtam, the Casqui, or any of the southern Nations for a high chief's ransom."

The calculating eyes fixed on hers as he asked, "So, when I take the matter to Skull, what's he going to do? Surrender more wealth than he's ever seen in exchange for your sorry, worn-out carcass, or insist he's never heard of you?"

Blue Heron felt a tingle of fear lace its way through her. She'd always known the chances of dying in her bed of old age were slim, but she'd never figured it would be on the filthy floor of a dirt farmer's lunar temple.

Seven Skull Shield—if he really had the War Medicine—would Trade for her, wouldn't he?

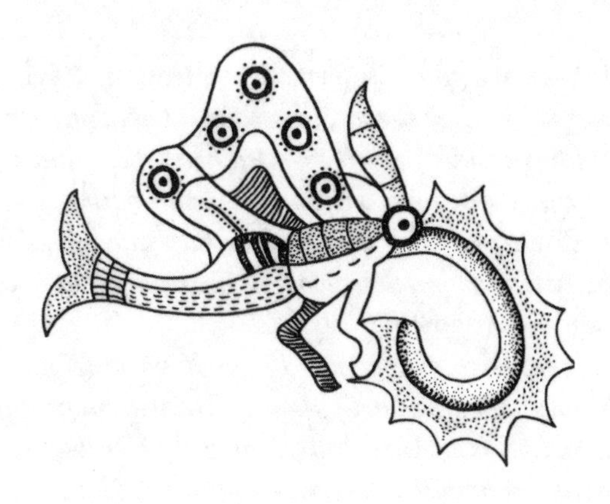

Anticipation

I am a high minko's daughter born of the Chief Clan. My mother is the Raccoon Clan matron. The blood of rulers runs in my veins. Why, therefore, do I feel like a foolish girl?

It has been but days.

It has been an eternity.

I have fretted and paced, made three baskets, and fought a continual battle with myself to maintain calm. A ruler should instinctively possess an internal calm—that patience and quality of soul to wait for things to come to fruition once a plan is in place.

Why am I bunched up on the inside, wanting nothing more than to bounce on my toes, throw my head back, and scream my pent-up anxiety to the palace ceiling?

"All things in their time," my father used to say.

Piss in a pot! I can't sit still for a finger of time, let alone compose my thoughts.

And worse, the Morning Star is watching me. He has been involved in discussions with some Four Winds war leader for most of the morning—a man who captured some city up in the north. I sat by the Morning Star's side during the welcoming feast, and then disengaged myself when the talk got down to business.

Sometimes it irks me not to understand their language. I could tell, however, that whatever the military venture entailed, it has all worked out successfully for the Cahokians. The great war leader was feasted, blessed, fawned over, and gifted with a remarkable parakeet-feather cloak before being dismissed with extra fanfare.

As I sit and fret, the Morning Star has just finished a ritual session with the new Four Winds Clan matron. She looked as uneasy as I feel. Something about the tension in her eyes, the way she sat, dressed in all of her finery. I'd say she acted like an imposter hiding inside a rainbow of feathers, shell, and exquisite fabric.

I have known the Morning Star for such a short time, but I could tell that he was somehow displeased with her, and slightly uneasy. Nor do I think that bodes well for the new matron. Displeasing the living god doesn't sound like a formula for a long and happy life.

Which sets my souls to quivering. I myself have seen the change in the Morning Star's eyes when he looks at me. Deeper, more intent. He cannot know that my husband is in Cahokia. That is impossible. And while I know that Five Fists was suspicious of my meeting in the Council House, he has to think it stems from the political situation back home. Why else would a Sky Hand chief's daughter brook a meeting with Albaamaha? The notion that I am on their side should be unthinkable.

Why, then, is the Morning Star giving me that look?

I could feel something different in the way he made love to me last night. A subtle coldness to the act, almost as if our joining were a sort of ritual. The impression I had—though the Spirits alone know where the notion came from—was of distance and inevitability. Was it because he knew that down in my souls I was making love to Straight Corn?

As I think this, a messenger bearing a stick is led into the palace to speak to Five Fists. I am vaguely aware of the tension as I anxiously rebraid my hair for the fifth time that morning.

Five Fists nods his head and walks toward me in that loose-limbed gait of his. He touches his forehead, saying, "Lady, the Albaamaha embassy requests your presence for a meeting to discuss the possibilities of a peace treaty between your peoples. I have been instructed by the Morning Star to provide an escort. He has granted you a hand of time with the Albaamaha, and a messenger to carry any instructions to your war leader, Strong Mussel. After which, your escort will deliver you safely back to the palace."

I somehow manage to act like a matron, nodding my head and keeping my voice level as I say, "Thank you, War Leader. I shall go and prepare myself."

Back in his personal quarters, I help myself to the Morning Star's collection of offerings, and it takes but moments to dress accordingly. Next I ask one of the Morning Star's servants to paint my face. I tell him to make my cheeks yellow with blue lines, and my forehead white.

When I am ready, and check out my finery, I walk imperiously to the great double doors. As I do I shoot a sidelong glance at the Morning Star. He is on his dais behind the fire, painted, primped, and resplendent. But even through the forked-eye design on his face, I can see how grim his expression is as he watches me. The sensation is almost electric as he meets my eyes.

He can't know. He just can't.

Twenty-eight

Night Shadow Star should have felt better, having had several nights of dreamless sleep. Instead of rested, her souls were oddly unsettled, her muscles heavy with fatigue. The voices had been plaguing her, hints of whispers in the air around her. She kept catching glimpses of Piasa, or sometimes odd flashes of light that danced across the darker corners of the room.

Phantoms. Visions that none of the others saw. Reflections of her personal Power. All reminders of the curse that kept her apart from normal people.

She wondered if it was madness—or just that she could hear past the boundaries that separated the world of people from the realm of Spirits.

At times the knowledge of how different she was drove her into fits of despair that turned so grim she toyed with the idea of just ending it all, freeing her souls to whatever fate the Powers of the Underworld decreed. Then, in contrast, she was possessed of such a lightness of soul that it seemed as if she could Dance the entirety of Creation. As if with each whirl of her body, the sun, moon, and stars spun in unison. Each beat of her feet upon the soil triggered the very heartbeat of existence. The blinding brilliance in her chest was the illumination of life itself.

And on days like today, where she balanced precariously between the extremes, the knowledge that those alternate conditions hovered just over the future's horizon both amused and terrified her.

If I could have any one wish, I would ask to be normal. Even if meant being a wife on a farmstead somewhere.

She pictured the life she would have: A nice trench-wall house with dirt-packed walls for insulation in winter, a stout ramada, and large storage cists full of corn, acorns, and hickory nuts would be hers. The house would be on well-drained and sandy soil. And it would have a view of the distant river. She would have three children: two boys and a girl. And at night, Fire Cat would return from the field . . .

Fire Cat?

She could see him so clearly: a satisfied glint in his eyes, that now-familiar smile molding his lips. Instead of a war ax, he'd have a long-handled hoe over his shoulder, its stone blade polished smooth by the soil.

The notion made her blink back to her senses. She sat in the rear of her palace atop the clay dais. On her lap, half forgotten, was one of her long-toothed combs. She'd been working the tangles from her hair preparatory to winding it into a bun and pinning it with a copper headpiece.

Around her, the household ran itself. Green Stick and Winter Leaf were talking quietly as they peeled pearl-sized onions for the stew. Clay String was gone for water. Sun Wing sat in the back next to Night Shadow Star's door, eyes vacant as she reflexively tied knots in a cord someone had given her. Once completely knotted, she picked them apart one by one, only to start reknotting it over again.

All of which was good. It beat Sun Wing's rocking, singing, and soft ranting about serpents, ice, and war.

The rest of the palace remained cluttered with every kind of pot, box, weapon, and container, not to mention stacks of fabrics, blankets, and robes—all winnings from Fire Cat's epic chunkey game with the Natchez Little Sun.

She had given away most of the largess, gifting it in grand ceremony to whomever walked by on the avenue below. Sacks of corn, little barley, maygrass, acorns, walnuts, and hickory nuts had been gifted to various communities of dirt farmers, and in a matter of a day, most of Cahokia's wealth was redistributed. An act for which people continued to sing her praises.

And Fire Cat's of course. He was the real hero.

The subject of her thoughts sat just outside the door in the afternoon light. He was sewing, repairing his armor, stitching the edge of his cuirass where the leather was separating. For the moment, she watched the muscles play in his arms, how his head was canted, the concentration in what she could see of his angled face, and how the light played on his tightly bound hair.

How odd that she'd imagined him as a farmer. A husband.

She found herself unsettled enough on those occasions when he slipped into her most erotic of dreams. His hard body would trigger a physical ecstasy so intense it would pop her awake in the night, gasping, her arms reaching up from her blankets to encircle him. Only to find lonely air.

She took a deep breath, closed her eyes, and fingered her comb. How much more impossible could her life be? Cursed by Power, hounded by visions and voices, and in love with a man she was forbidden to have, but who was bound to share her life.

"What did I do to deserve this?" she whispered under her breath.

Piasa didn't answer.

Then, in an attempt to stave off the descent into despair, she told herself, "Things are not that bad. I could still be married to Thirteen Sacred Jaguar, drugged, with his warriors sneaking in to rape me. Fire Cat could be dead on the chunkey field. My sister could have been sacrificed rather than just insanely mumbling to Spirits and knotting cords all day long while her souls roam. Or I could be Walking Smoke's captive."

Indeed, there were a lot of worse fates to contemplate than a full stomach, security, the wealthiest hoard of goods in Cahokia, an orderly palace, and Fire Cat, who at least offered companionship—even if he didn't share her bed.

She smiled to herself, resumed her combing, and set her hair in order. If balancing between Piasa and the Tortoise Bundle was the worst she'd have to deal with from this point forward, she'd be eternally grateful.

Even as she was entertaining this thought, a voice called, "Greetings! I come in search of Lady Night Shadow Star!"

She got to her feet as Fire Cat, out on her veranda, stood outlined against the light. Flipping her long hair back, she strode to the door, stepped out, and took a position beside the Red Wing.

Her souls froze. It had been a year since she'd seen the man last. As if but a moment past—rather than the long year—she remembered the charge she'd laid upon him: *"Kill them. Kill them all . . . and bring me their rotting heads!"*

A tremble ran through her as she heard Piasa laughing from somewhere behind her.

Steeling herself, she stepped forward, offering her hands to the big man. The first hint of gray now shaded his temples. The Four Winds tattoos on his cheeks were almost obscured by years of relentless sun, wind, and weather. The cunning glint in his dark eyes remained the same—as did the hard angle of both wide cheeks and strong jaw. Now a smile bent his thin lips as he grasped her hands in his.

Nothing had bowed his wide shoulders; the muscles in his arms and chest remained firm and hard, his belly rippled and flat. Paler skin contrasted with the tan and outlined where his armor usually conformed to his torso.

His hair was in a tight warrior's bun, pinned with simple wooden skewers. A bright red cloak of cardinal feathers draped his back, and at his waist an apron hung down from his breechcloth.

"Lady," he told her with a smile. "I am honored to see you again. You are as beautiful as ever. And word of your exploits has traveled far and wide, even to our distant ears."

She couldn't help but glance sidelong at Fire Cat, noting that he'd automatically tensed, expression wooden, back stiff as he took in the visitor's frame and bearing.

Spit and dung, what do I say?

Finally, she managed to stutter, "N-No more so than your exploits have been spoken of in Cahokia, War Leader."

"Just War Leader? I used to be a friend," he noted mildly, cuing to her unease. Then he glanced at Fire Cat, that old familiar quirk of amusement playing at his lips. "So, it is true. He stands at your side? A slave, they say."

Fire Cat had started to bristle, asking, "Lady? Who is this?"

"And so familiar!" The warrior released her hands, cocking his head as he inspected Fire Cat.

Night Shadow Star's heart had begun to race. "Fire Cat, this man is—"

"Spotted Wrist!" Fire Cat almost spat the words, his fists knotting, eyes narrowing to slits. Instinctively he rocked up on his toes, knees flexing.

"Stand down, Red Wing," she told him gently.

Spotted Wrist had watched Fire Cat's reaction as if it were high entertainment, and now raised his hands. "I come in peace, Lady. I seek only to pay my respects as an old friend, and to see if I can cage a cup of black drink and perhaps a bite or two of bread."

"We didn't know you were coming," she said weakly, off balance by the sudden pounding of her heart.

"I wasn't aware that I needed to send a messenger in advance. I would have thought word of my arrival would have long since been communicated to you."

"We've heard nothing. But then, with the new matron . . ."

"Ah, yes. I heard that you didn't even attend the choosing. Sounds like everything's in a slow boil of chaos. My apologies for just appearing out of the day. I could come back another time if it would be more convenient."

She made herself smile, dragging up old memories of the times he had shared her hearth, told stories until late into the night, and how he'd consoled her after word arrived of Makes Three's death. In many ways he almost had been more of a father, advisor, and confidant to her than Red Warrior had been. He remained the same man. That he'd taken Red Wing Town, destroyed the heretics, and pacified the north in the service of Cahokia and the Morning Star had been her earnest wish as well.

"Yes, yes, do come in." She reached out, taking his hand, smiling. "You are indeed welcome. Green Stick! Black drink and food for the war leader."

To Fire Cat she shot a pleading look. "He is my guest."

"Yes, Lady." Fire Cat said it through clenched jaws as he stood aside.

As she led Spotted Wrist inside, the war leader bent close, whispering, "Rather like having a rabid wolf on a leash, is he?"

"He's kept me alive, old friend."

She placed him at the fire and dropped down to take a seat beside him. Glancing back she was relieved to see that Fire Cat had remained at the door; he stood like a warrior at attention: head back, feet apart, hands clenched behind him, and his gaze on infinity.

She could only imagine the thoughts torturing his souls.

"So, I would hear it from your lips, Lady. What on earth possessed you to cut him down?"

"Piasa." She regarded Spotted Wrist thoughtfully, seeing the man she'd known for most of her life. Her father's best friend. "And yes, the Water Panther took my souls. I am his creature. I serve him and the Underworld."

The intensity of his study bothered her. Then he said, "You are different. Changed. Harder, dangerous, and cutting. Not at all the broken young woman I left behind."

"I may come across as all of those things, but obsidian has those same qualities. However, if you bend it, or drop it, like me it will snap and shatter into splinters."

"Perhaps." He gestured toward the door. "And the Red Wing? I sent him to you to torture to death after what he did to your first husband."

She paused, sniffed wryly. "Piasa ordered me to cut Fire Cat down from the square. Half dead as he was, he thought I was First Woman, appeared out of the rain and night to take his life soul to the Underworld. I hated the thought of cutting him down even more than I hated him. Barely restrained myself from killing him more than once. I came so close, and he begged me to do it."

"Why didn't you?"

"Piasa ordered me not to. In the end he was right. The Red Wing has saved my life over and over. Saved the city he says he detests." She smiled. "It's an interesting relationship."

The lines around Spotted Wrist's eyes tightened. "There are rumors. Does he serve you in the most intimate of ways?"

"No. As if it were anyone's business."

"It's not. I was just curious."

"What would you care . . . even if he did?"

"As you said, none of my business." But she could tell he was secretly pleased. "So first you defeated Walking Smoke, then managed to destroy the Itza and the Natchez who accompanied him. Heard you married that Mayan lord. What was that like?"

"A nightmare." She shook her head. "But what about you? You are the hero of the north. You did what three previous war leaders could not. You took Red Wing Town without the loss of a single man. What was it like, pacifying the north?"

"Taking the town wasn't that difficult. Getting three thousand men to travel that far that fast? That was the challenge. We had to outrun word of our coming. And, to be honest, Power was on our side. If we'd had to fight it out like my predecessors did, it would have been a much bloodier affair, and the north would still be in flames."

"But you took the town without a fight.'

"We were up and over the walls before they had a clue. The men were killed in their beds, the women and children rounded up and enslaved." He pointed a finger. "That, more than anything, made the forest tribes amenable to negotiating a peace. The Red Wing Clan had this reputation for ferocity and invincibility. That we could crush them so gave the barbarian tribes pause. I acted immediately, dealing with them one chief at a time. Since then it's just been a matter of keeping a lid on the pot, so to speak. Letting them get used to the idea that we're not going to hunt them down and murder them in their sleep unless they break the peace."

"Are you back for good?"

"I am." He took the cup of black drink that Green Stick handed him, offering it to the four directions, to sky, and to earth before sipping. "And I'd like to spend more time with you, if you wouldn't mind." He squinted into the rear. "Is that Sun Wing back by your door?"

"She seems to do better here. Curious, but when she's at peace, the Tortoise Bundle is as well." She took her own cup. "You've heard about that?"

"Word of your activities and achievements runs up and down the river faster than the migrating flocks of birds. I figured I'd find you installed as the Four Winds Clan matron. You were headed that way before your husband . . ." He didn't finish, but glanced suggestively toward Fire Cat.

"I cannot serve a Sky Clan when my Power comes from the Underworld." She, too, glanced at where Fire Cat remained at stiff attention. She'd seen him like this before, when she'd had to marry the Itza. "This is hard on him. Having you here."

Again that intent stare. "Lady, do you know what he did to your husband?"

She shook her head wistfully and dropped her voice below Fire Cat's hearing. "No. I heard enough of the stories from the survivors to guess how it went for him. But I value it that Fire Cat lied to me when he said Makes Three died well."

"You shouldn't use your husband's name. It can have—"

"I've seen Makes Three's souls in the Underworld, old friend. Having walked among the dead, I have latitude others don't."

"Then what of the here and now? I do hope that your Red Wing doesn't hold a grudge. Or would I be wise to appoint a full-time guard to accompany me?"

She laughed at that. "Fire Cat *does* hold a grudge. But if I ask him to swear on his honor to keep you safe, he will die before he'll break his word to me. The one thing more important to him than life is his honor."

"Are you so sure of that?"

"I am."

"How?"

"I am alive, Spotted Wrist." She arched a challenging eyebrow and sipped her black drink. "But for his impeccable honor, I would be long dead."

Spotted Wrist was watching Fire Cat through sloe-dark eyes, incalculable thoughts churning down in his souls. "What are your plans now, Lady?"

"To live a day at a time—to try and seek peace for my souls and find a way to balance the needs of Power. I no longer take such things for granted. Not after all that has happened to me."

"I could help with that."

She gave him a wry smile. "You always counseled me toward patience, enjoined me to behave better when I was a wild girl running with my rowdy brothers. A couple of times, you covered for some of my worst behavior when you shouldn't have. You were the friend I needed when Makes Three was killed, and led an army north to avenge him. Partly, I think, for me."

"A lot for you."

"All right, a lot for me. How are you going to help me now? Place yourself between Piasa and the Tortoise Bundle? Dance the delicate Dance that separates me from the Morning Star? Offer yourself as my shield against the vicissitudes of Cahokia's cutthroat politics and clan scheming?"

"I would," he said softly. "You are not the only one who has changed. I have, too. My lineage is descended from Red Night. Should some unforeseen woe befall Wolverine, I would be the logical choice for high chief of North Star House. White Phlox—despite being Wolverine's brother—could not succeed to the high chair if I, the Hero of the North, asked for it. After my meeting with the Morning Star this morning, I think I can ask for anything in Cahokia and be granted it."

"You have done him a remarkable service. Well he should."

He fixed his clever eyes on hers. "Yes, we have been friends for so long, and yes, I have sought to guide and befriend you when others would not. I stood by while you wept in defeat, laughed at your pranks, and watched your heart bleed with grief. But that was when you were a girl."

"And what am I now?"

"A woman. Perhaps the only one worthy of the Hero of the North. I didn't just come for the food and drink, or to catch up on the last year. I thought I would ascertain your situation and plans before I asked the Morning Star for permission to marry you."

Night Shadow Star's heart skipped; she closed her mouth lest she look foolish. "But, I . . ."

By the door, Fire Cat had gone so rigid he looked like his back would snap, his face a mask of agony.

"You needn't answer immediately." Spotted Wrist smiled. "Now, let's relax and talk gossip. I have so much to catch up on."

She could only stare.

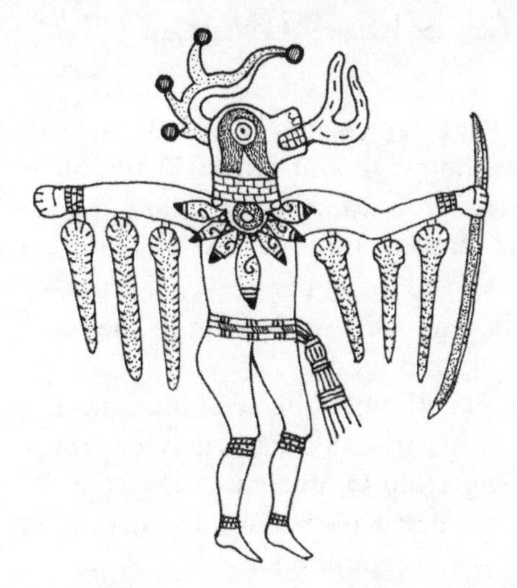

Twenty-nine

Sometimes dogs weren't very smart. To Seven Skull Shield's way of thinking, it was a trait the four-footed, tail-wagging beasts shared with most people. Take that very moment: Seven Skull Shield sat cross-legged before the crackling central fire in Columella's mound-top palace in Evening Star Town. A rich, greasy stew bubbled in the big, gray, corrugated pot set down deep in the coals. Tendrils of steam carried the stew's savory odor throughout the building.

Farts, ears pricked, eyes intent, crouched on his belly several paces away, his body literally quivering from excitement and expectation as he eyed Seven Skull Shield's bowl. Twin filaments of drool leaked from his jowls.

All that anticipation, and for what? A chance to gorge himself on the stew. And sure, it was made from a stock of mashed corn, little barley, maygrass seeds, wild plums, and squash, but the majority of the meat was . . . well, dog. As Seven Skull Shield constantly reminded his four-footed friend, dog was a common food in Cahokia. The carcasses of no less than three suckling pups had been tossed in to finish the recipe.

And there was Farts, apparently heedless of the fact that he was desperate to commit the foul act of cannibalism.

"Perhaps he hasn't a clue," Flat Stone Pipe noted where he sat to Seven Skull Shield's right, his own bowl in hand. He scooped out mouths full with a bison-horn spoon that he clutched in his small hand. And he could apparently read Seven Skull Shield's thoughts.

"I could tell by your expression, thief." The dwarf had an eyebrow lifted, his dark eyes knowing and amused. "Would you recognize the smell of human meat if you walked up and found it roasting on a spit?"

"Now, that, little man, I cannot tell. Seems to me that I might figure it out from the size and shape of the steaks."

"And if it were in chunks? Just floating in the broth? Perhaps sweetened with other spices and foods?"

"Now there I don't know." Seven Skull Shield gestured with his bowl. "But I think I'll see to it that Farts gets a couple of dried fish afterwards, since he's *not* getting so much as a lick of this."

"It wouldn't be the first time a dog's cleaned up the remains of his fellows, especially given as common as—"

"I have certain standards, little friend. Low as they may be."

Columella had been watching from the side of the room. She sat perched on one of the benches and helped her daughter Onion Flower as she worked on a fabric skirt. Now she called, "Did you come to eat, thief, or look for Blue Heron?"

"Are you absolutely sure she's missing?" Seven Skull Shield asked. "Sometimes that woman catches wind of something and, being the Keeper and all, takes off to deal with it."

"She's no longer the Keeper," Columella told him. "The new matron, Rising Flame, dismissed her."

Seven Skull Shield frowned in disbelief.

"Said Blue Heron didn't show enough respect." Flat Stone Pipe scooped up another spoonful of stew.

"Dripping pus and stinking blood," Seven Skull Shield growled, "what kind of nonsense is that? So . . . who's Keeper now?"

"Don't know," Flat Stone Pipe admitted. "My spies will send a runner the instant any choice is made."

"I told her," Columella said as she shifted the orange-dyed fabric so that Onion Flower could run a whipstitch along two edges. "Made no bones about it that she was as good as a walking target."

"So where did it happen? Who grabbed her?"

"My people have been asking around," Flat Stone Pipe told him. "As best we can discern from those who saw her last, she walked away from the stickball game with two men. Some thought they were either river Traders or loggers, given the muscles in their shoulders and arms."

"River Traders?" Seven Skull Shield mused, a feeling of dread building in his gut.

"One of the men may have had Panther Clan tattoos. The only other thing anyone remembered was that they were dressed well, which would argue against loggers."

"Any other word floating around?" Seven Skull Shield asked. "Like from someone who figured to take advantage of the Keeper's dismissal? Maybe settle a grudge?"

"That's half of Cahokia, thief." Columella inclined her head in a gesture that said he should know better.

"What have you heard about the Quiz Quiz?" Seven Skull Shield looked back and forth between them.

"Just what the Keeper . . . er, Blue Heron told me during her visit. That someone stole the man who stole the Surveyors' Bundle. She was expecting quite a storm as the new matron tried to deal with it."

"Winder," Seven Skull Shield said woodenly.

"What's a winder?" Flat Stone Pipe asked as he used walnut bread to sop up the last of his stew.

"Not a what, a who." Seven Skull Shield tipped his bowl up and drank the last of the dregs before he added, "Old friend of mine. A scoundrel like me. You'd like him, little man. When we were younger he took to the Trade. I ran into him out in front of the Surveyors' Society House. He told me he was working for the Quiz Quiz. Looking for the war leader."

"If he got the war leader back, why would he be interested in harassing Blue Heron? Let alone kidnapping her?" Columella wondered. "The smart thing would have been to toss what was left of their war leader in a canoe and break their backs racing the current back to Quiz Quiz. Taking the Keeper—even if it's for a payback—is like flicking a water moccasin on the nose. You're going to regret it."

Seven Skull Shield felt a sudden queasy understanding down in his gut. He had a feeling he knew what the Quiz Quiz were looking for.

But, did anyone else?

Flat Stone Pipe served Columella as head spy for a reason: He didn't miss much. Now the dwarf asked, "What are you thinking, thief? You know something?"

"Something I heard," Seven Skull Shield muttered. "Just a rumor. That they lost more than their war leader that day when I ran him to ground."

"Lost what?"

"Some sort of a box. Something they brought with them from Quiz Quiz."

Columella stared thoughtfully at the fabric in her lap. "Lots of boxes could have come with them. Why would they care about a box?"

"Because of what was in it," Flat Stone Pipe guessed, his intent gaze fixed on Seven Skull Shield. "What would you guess that was, thief?"

"Trade? Maybe for a bribe?" From long practice, he kept his face blank. It *had* to be that accursed War Medicine.

"Why would they stick their necks out—let alone poke the Cahokian wasps' nest—over a box of Trade?" Columella added from the side. "Call it a loss and run."

"Maybe it wasn't Trade." Seven Skull Shield set the bowl to one side, using the opportunity to point a hard finger at Farts as a distraction. "You stay right there, dog. You'll get yours later."

Farts answered with a tortured whine, as if he were starving and abused.

"It's something sacred," Flat Stone Pipe said. "Some Power charm, possession of the ancestors, a sacred artifact—something they can't leave behind."

"Why would they think Blue Heron would know where it was?" Columella asked.

Seven Skull Shield told her, "They know it was Blue Heron who orchestrated the snatch when I found Sky Star. They're going to figure that he had the box with him when I beat him up over in River Mounds City. That naturally I took the box to the Keeper. And now that they have the Keeper, they can Trade her for the box."

Flat Stone Pipe was watching him through narrowed eyes, which meant Seven Skull Shield had to be very, very careful. He kept his face as placid and calm as he could and truthfully said, "I can see what you're thinking. When the Quiz Quiz and I went at it in that narrow passage he didn't have any box with him. Just a long chipped-stone knife. It was just him, me, and Farts here. And by the time we were done, a whole pile of witnesses. Someone would have noticed a box."

"And you're sure the Keeper didn't send someone else after the box?" Flat Stone Pipe asked.

"I'm sure."

"Well," Columella asked, "what's going to happen when the Quiz Quiz finally figure out that Blue Heron doesn't have the box?"

"They'll kill her," Flat Stone Pipe mused, his thoughtful eyes still on Seven Skull Shield. "They're in too deep to let her go."

Seven Skull Shield stroked his chin. *Which means I've got to find her before that can happen. But how?*

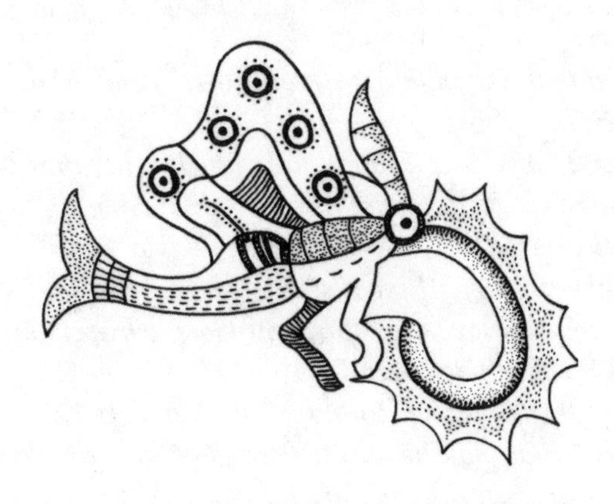

The Prize

Perhaps it is not fair. Nevertheless I cannot help but compare bedding the Morning Star to what I just shared with Straight Corn. I sigh and hold my Straight Corn close, feeling the man I love firmly in my arms. This is the boy who was my friend before he became my husband and lover.

I wonder what it means, sometimes, to have two husbands under two such different sets of values. Which marriage is more valid? Which should have primacy in my life?

"I hate sharing you with him." Straight Corn shifts his head, staring into my eyes. I can see the hurt and turmoil within him.

"There was nothing I could do. It all moved so fast. Once father's warriors had me, I barely had time to collect my wits before I was thrown into a canoe and brought here. And I sure didn't expect such a rapid marriage to the Morning Star."

I pause. "And it wasn't like I could turn around and run for it. Believe me. I really considered it. Wouldn't have made it past the palace doors before the warriors would have had me."

Spooned against Straight Corn's body as I am, I look up at the roof overhead. I can hear voices outside where my escorting warriors and the porters who carried my litter are waiting out front. They think I am discussing delicate peace terms.

Hanging Moss, Wet Clay Woman, and Fighting Dog had barely said hello before they ducked out the back way, exiting through a small doorway in the rear wall in order to leave us alone for a little connubial bliss. I'm delighted that they found a building with a back entrance. It might just save someone's life, depending on how things work out.

I know Straight Corn and I don't have much time, that they will be back soon, and we have to act as if we're really discussing diplomatic measures. Otherwise my escort will become suspicious. It is a foregone conclusion that they will report everything to Five Fists.

"I'm so glad you still love me," Straight Corn whispers into my ear. Then he sits up. "They will be back soon."

I reach for my skirt, pulling it up over my hips. As I do, the thought rolls around in my head that making love to Straight Corn is making love to a boy. That the act with him isn't the mature intimacy that categorizes the Morning Star's performance, let alone the intensity of my physical response.

The novice versus the master, my internal voice tells me.

I thank the Spirits that Straight Corn can't hear my thoughts.

He slips to the rear door, setting it to the side and reaching through to signal. Moments later Hanging Moss comes ducking in and climbs down to the floor. He is followed by Wet Clay Woman and finally Fighting Dog.

"Glad that you had a chance to get reacquainted," Hanging Moss says, giving me a wink. "Some of us remember the fires of young love."

I feel my face flush as Wet Clay Woman gives me a thoughtful nod and says, "You can always tell a fulfilled woman by the look in her eyes afterwards. Glad you married my boy, dear girl. You're good for him."

As everyone gets settled, I ask, "How soon can we escape from Cahokia? The back door is perfect. I can enter the front, and we can sneak right out the rear, then it's down the Avenue of the Sun to the canoe landing. Shove out onto the river, and we're home in two months."

Hanging Moss, Straight Corn, and Fighting Dog share glances. Wet Clay Woman stares down at her hands in her lap.

"What?" I ask, suddenly wary.

"We need you to do something for us first, Niece," Hanging Moss says. And as he does, he removes a small ceramic jar, its top sealed with wax. I have seen it before. On the night of my initiation into the Sacred Moth Society.

"You know what this is?" the old man asks.

"The sacred nectar," I reply. "The liquid that opens the doorway to the night. The Spirit drink that only humming moths can subsist on."

I have helped to harvest the tiny droplets from the insides of large white datura flowers. It is a painstaking job, and one that must be undertaken with the greatest of care.

"Will you help our people?" Straight Corn asks in his most earnest voice.

I see the pleading in his eyes, can almost hear the words he would say if the others were not present: "If our lovemaking meant as much to you as it did to me, you would do this."

"Of course I would," I answer. "Do you think now is the time for me to initiate the journey? Here? In the middle of the day? With an escort of warriors and porters just outside the door? It will be hours before my souls would be back in my body, and by then—"

"Not you," Wet Clay Woman tells me with a smile. "The Morning Star."

I blink, suddenly confused.

"And not just a drop on the tongue as you took in your initiation. But the whole bottle." Hanging Moss smiles and laces his fingers together around the bottle.

I feel my heart skip. "That much nectar? But that might send his souls forever into . . ." I can't finish the thought, remembering my own soul journey, filled as it was with terrors and delights. I remember flying with the moths . . . hearing the chiming songs of the Dead, drifting through the perfumed air above an endless sea of large, trumpet-shaped flowers. My souls were buoyed with darkness—a pulsing unity with the night.

"He is the living god, yes?" Hanging Moss asks kindly. "You will not kill a Spirit, Niece. You will, however, send him on a most extraordinary journey. His Power is tied to the second level of the Sky. Sacred Moth has its own Power. That of the night, flowers, and the ways of the Dead. Only you can send him on the journey. And upon his return, he will know who to thank for it."

"I don't understand."

Hanging Moss, in that mystical way of his, says, "Consider it a joining. A merging of Powers between Sky and Night. As you are only an initiate, I can't expect you to understand. That will come with time, and as you continue your study. But believe me, were you not a high minko's daughter, born of the Chief Clan, were you not a woman of great strength, commitment, and Power, Sacred Moth would never have asked this of you."

I am stunned, and somewhat humbled to think that such Power has chosen me.

Straight Corn leans forward, eyes gleaming. "Can you get the nectar into his drink? Maybe into his food? Some way so that he swallows the whole bottle?"

"It's sweet," I tell them, remembering my first faint taste. "They make sweets for him all the time. And I think I know a way."

Yes. I can do this.

It will be just before bed, a final treat before I insist on the manner of our lovemaking, which he encourages. What will it be like to be locked together as his souls are coaxed into the night and borne away on moth wings?

"You know how the sensations fade?" Uncle asks. "How you have those final thoughts before all is air, and night, and flight?"

"Yes."

"That's when you have to whisper to him," Straight Corn adds.

Wet Clay Woman follows up, saying, "Tell him your father, White Water Moccasin, sends his greetings, and that the Sky Hand hope he enjoys his journey."

This makes no sense. "But it's from the Albaamaha."

"We have our reasons," Uncle tells me, a placid smile on his face. "Trust us, Whispering Dawn. Trust Sacred Moth. Tell it to him, just like that, and as soon as the Morning Star's souls are aloft on the night, you hurry here. We'll be gone from Cahokia by morning."

"Headed home," Straight Corn assures me.

"You will have saved our people, saved your husband." Wet Clay Woman tells me.

"Yes, I can do this."

But I wonder why Fighting Dog is giving me such a satisfied look where he sits in the rear.

Thirty

Fire Cat sat on the edge of the veranda, his bare feet on the hard-packed clay of the mound top. Clay that had been soaked and consecrated with blood: both Itza and his own.

Around him the evening chill began to seep out of the darkening sky. He watched as the Morning Star's high palace faded in the reflected glow of the distant sunset.

It never stops, does it?

He placed a hand to his heart, feeling the rhythmic thumping as it beat within his chest. Inside, his guts felt as if they were serpents—alive and writhing as they twisted around each other in a sickening fashion.

Spotted Wrist. The man who had taken everything from him: family, heritage, town, people. Everything except his honor. Now, stripped down to that last claim on life, Fire Cat struggled to determine if even that was draining away.

I could kill him. No one would fault me. Not after what he's done to my family. The ancestors would demand it of me.

It would be his final act, of course. He would have to kill himself as soon as the deed was done. Save Night Shadow Star from giving him that look of despair and betrayal.

He heard her as she stepped out. Was acutely aware of her presence as she seated herself beside him.

"Black drink?" she asked, handing him a cup. "Freshly brewed. In a different pot from the one *he* drank out of."

Only she would think of that.

"I'm sorry," she said softly, and leaned her head back to stare up at the first flickering stars as they burned through the gloom. "His arrival was as much a shock to me as it was to you."

"Of course, Lady," he said, trying to keep his voice from sounding clipped.

"If we'd just had some time . . . some warning." She sipped her own drink. "Fire Cat, I need you to understand. He's an old friend. Perhaps more of a father than my father was."

"Interesting then that he'd want to marry you, the father-daughter taboo being what it is." This time he failed to keep the acid from his tone.

She bit off an exasperated sigh. "Blood and spit, what is it about men and marriage? What kind of fool would want me—of all women—for a wife?"

"Anyone with sense, Lady. You are the most Powerful woman in the Four Winds Clan. Beautiful. Young. As the war leader said, a worthy consort for any man climbing the ladder of success and authority." He paused. "Nor is it unusual in political marriages for an older, high-ranking man with prestige to marry a much younger woman he has watched grow into womanhood. Sometimes such girls are promised from birth."

"He has three Earth Clan wives up in Serpent Woman Town. They keep his household and manage eleven of his children. The four oldest are already married. Two are leading new colonies in the north. What does he figure? I'll relocate to Serpent Woman Town? Move into his palace and try to fit in as a fourth wife? Take orders from his older wives as Piasa and the Tortoise Bundle are filling my ears with their Spirit voices?"

"Lady, if the Morning Star orders—"

"I'll *not* marry him. It would be too odd, too . . ." She shrugged unable to find the words.

"You heard him. He said the Morning Star won't refuse him after his victories in the north." Fire Cat struggled to speak reasonably. "Chunkey Boy is your elder brother. Technically the head of your family. How can you refuse?"

"I'm not sure yet. I'll find a way."

He smiled grimly into the night, imagining the feel of a long chert blade as it was driven up under Spotted Wrist's breastbone and into his beating heart. Dead men no longer asked for young women to be their wives.

"Fire Cat, I have to ask you to do something."

"Of course, Lady."

"You must promise me that you will not seek vengeance. That no matter what, you will not harm him, nor cause him to be harmed."

"Lady?" he asked, wondering if her Powers had allowed her to anticipate his earlier thoughts.

"I would, in your position." A pause. "You are first and foremost a man of honor. You are no doubt thinking your ancestors demand it. That if you fail to act, it will reflect on you."

Scum and muck, she knew him too well.

"Lady, that man . . . What he cost me . . ."

She stiffened—the way she did when the Spirits were whispering in her ear—then relaxed. "Piasa is laughing. Amused no doubt by the way he plays us. By the twists and turns he throws in our way."

"Your master has a vile sense of humor."

"And I have a terrible apprehension down in my gut," she told him. "It would break my heart if you killed Spotted Wrist. More so if you murdered him to spare me from a marriage I don't want. Here is what you don't know: The things he did to you and your people . . . was at my request. I asked him to bring me your rotting heads in retaliation for what you did to Makes Three."

She clenched her fist, stiffening, before adding, "If you must have vengeance, take it out on me. I am more responsible for the brutality of his conquest than anyone."

He slowly shook his head. "I will never, ever, harm you."

"Not even by killing Spotted Wrist?"

His souls sang out in pain and disbelief as he whispered, "Not even then. I give you my word, Lady. He is safe from me."

She reached out, taking his hand in hers, squeezing it with such passion that it might be her last grasp on hope.

Consummation

I feel as if my body wants to explode. Everything inside me is running wild: fear, anticipation, excitement, panic, and hope all churning around like a boiling stew. He will know. How could he help but see it when he finally steps into the room?

I have only two of the hickory-oil lamps burning, keeping the illumination low. Perhaps, in the dim light, he won't see my anxiety. Maybe, when the time comes, I will manage to control my building terror and can make myself cool and collected as I hand him the blueberry juice I have prepared.

As I unbraid my hair and begin to comb it out, I go suddenly tense: This is my first attempt at seduction. I cannot make a mistake. I have to be in possession of my emotions. My expression must reveal nothing. I have to be irresistible.

But how? Believe me, Sky Hand women aren't trained in such things.

That knowledge does nothing to alleviate the electric tension that makes it difficult to even breathe. I close my eyes—wishing for my heart to stop its frantic pounding—and suck air into my lungs.

You are the daughter of the high minko! Your ancestors' blood runs in your veins. They were worthy. You come from them. Their Spirits were born into you. You can do this.

I feel my heart slow, the muscles of my chest loosening.

I am in this state—convinced of my own invincibility—when the Morning Star walks into the chamber, his feathers and flowing cape rustling. He looks radiant in his colors, with his remarkable headdress—this one a forward pro-

jecting curve into which miniature arrows have been driven. He is, indeed, the living god.

I am committed. Order myself to forget that part of me that is terrified. From here on out, what will be, will be. I am either dead, or alive.

My fingers do not tremble as I stand and reach out to unpin the gorgeous feather cape hanging from his shoulders.

"It has been a long day, husband," I tell him as I look him in the eyes. They are shadowed pools of midnight in the dim lamplight. I can feel his Power, his essence. It is like having the vast blue vault of the sky swelling in my breast.

I successfully untie his breechcloth and apron and let them fall. My breasts brush his chest as I reach up to unpin the polished copper headpiece with its Soul Bundle and eagle feathers. As I do, my nipples harden and send a thrill through me that he seems to share, for he inhales and tenses.

Then I step back, picturing myself through his eyes as I reach down and release my skirt. My breasts, belly, and thighs are accented by light and shadow, my hair spilling down in dark waves.

He steps close, wrapping me in his arms and presses himself against me. I sigh at the warmth in his body, clasp him to me, and run my fingers lightly over the rounded contours of muscle and bone.

His response is immediate. I bump my hips against his hardening shaft before I lean my head back and shoot him a delighted smile. "I have a treat for you."

"Blueberry juice?" he asks with a slight lift of an eyebrow.

"They told," I chide, even as my heart tingles with fear that he knows.

"Not much escapes me, wife," he tells me with a curious emphasis. His gaze pierces my soul.

For an instant, the fear struggles to escape; before it can, I break loose and hand him his nectar-laced cup. I place my own unadulterated juice to my lips, drinking it down.

Will he notice the difference in taste? I have emptied the entire little bottle into his cup. Just the way Hanging Moss instructed.

As he lifts it to his lips, his eyes are locked with mine. He hesitates . . . and time seems to stop. Lamplight flickers briefly in his dark eyes, and then he drinks with a slight smile on his lips.

"Most remarkable," he tells me. "Did you have anything else in mind?"

"I have been waiting all day for this," I tell him. "I want this night to be even more remarkable than ever before."

Placing my hands on his breasts, I shove him backward onto the bed. Then I leap onto him like a cougar onto a deer.

A fire burns loose inside me. I impale myself on his shaft; locking us together in a violent embrace. I become someone else, some thing *else. A creature possessed of a soul hunger. Nothing exists but this moment—as if the entire purpose of my existence is distilled down to this joining of loins. And it is savage.*

When it comes, the explosion in my sheath is like nothing I have ever experienced. The gasping cries are mine. I am consumed, devoured, and finally drained. Panting, I sprawl on top of him.

In the end I lift myself from his limp body and stare down into his slack face. His eyes are half closed, his mouth slack. His breathing is slow, and his arms have fallen to the sides.

"Morning Star? Husband?"

Nothing.

I pinch his shoulder.

No response.

Placing a hand to his sweat-damp breastbone, I feel the slow beat of his heart. His breath purls on my cheek when I lean close.

"That is a gift from High Minko White Water Moccasin and the Sky Hand." As if he could hear given the state he's in. But I promised Hanging Moss.

I roll off him, toss my hair back over my shoulder, and slowly catch my breath. I shiver as sweat dries on my flushed skin. I wonder if I will ever be the same again? And what sort of creature that was that took possession of my souls and body? That beast *couldn't have been me, could it?*

I am oddly weak as I climb to my feet and fish for my skirt. Carefully I dress, pick up the little nectar bottle, and then help myself to some of the more exotic items and stuff them into a sack. Lastly I take a fine buffalo-wool blanket and wrap it about my shoulders.

As I am ready to leave, I glance back at the Morning Star. I am not surprised to see the particularly large humming moth that hovers over his senseless mouth. The long proboscis is sucking desperately at the sweet trace of nectar on his lips.

Thirty-one

The sun beat down in warm yellow rays as Night Shadow Star reached out and parted the corn. At her feet, tangled vines of squash—heavy with fruit—wound across the ground. In amongst them bean plants flourished, pods heavy amid the green leaves.

Pushing the last of the cornstalks to the side, she stepped out into the yard and glanced over at her Spirit plant garden where datura flourished. The beautiful large white flowers contrasted brilliantly with the triangular-shaped dark green leaves. Behind it a stand of rattlesnake master plants gave way to nightshade. Off to the right her thick crop of tobacco had a lighter green color, the leaves wide, tall, and curled on the edges.

Have to water again, she thought, glancing up at the remarkable blue sky. Color. So much color. She loved the contrasts of garden and sky, her red soil, and the variegated greens of the vast forest that surrounded her little farmstead.

She turned and followed the path to her house—a snug trench-wall structure with a fresh new thatch roof. The walls were white-plastered and painted with spirals of yellow, purple, violet, crimson, and black. Even as she watched they seemed to glow, shift, expand, and contract. It hit her: The spirals were pulsing with life. As if in affirmation they began to shimmer and dance along the walls of the house.

For long moments she stood entranced, reached out with a hand until she almost touched the vibrant curls of light.

The bubbling laughter of children interrupted her enchantment as two little girls and a boy burst into the yard. Screams of delight broke from their lips as they chased each other in some sort of game of tag. The little boy, a chubby and brown-skinned imp with a thatch of black shaggy hair, was being ganged up on by his sisters. He dodged and darted, trying to keep from being "tagged" by his bigger sister. Just a glance at his face and she knew he was Fire Cat's son, just as the two little girls had her features.

Our children.

She placed a hand to her breast, smiling as the children ran and cavorted. Their laughter soothed her, brought a sense of peace and fulfillment to her anxious souls.

They're beautiful. We made them.

Which was what life was all about, wasn't it? Not the complications and endless conflicts of politics. Not the continual strife inherent to Power and its ceaseless struggle for balance. Not light against dark, wisdom against chaos, or white in conflict with red.

For one glimmering moment she understood that life was about perfect farms, laughing children, and that sense of fulfillment. Of being part of the continuum. Establishing one's place in the endless procession of being born, finding a mate, bearing young, and watching them grow as she herself aged. Just as her ancestors had done before, and her children and their children, and so on, would do.

"They're happy today, aren't they?" Fire Cat asked, coming up behind her.

She turned, greeting him with a smile. "It's a good day, husband."

His eyes were twinkling, the Red Wing tattoos on his cheeks radiant in the golden sunlight. She thought the lines of his face to be perfect, the humor in his smile, enchanting.

He bent to the side, lowering the turkey he carried to the ground. "Hunting was good today," he added, with a nod to the dead bird. "The children can use some of that boundless energy plucking it."

"Don't let them ruin the feathers," she told him. "I can split them to weave a new cloak in case winter ever comes."

"Of course." He stepped close, draping a strong arm over her shoulder and pulling her against him. She sighed, perfectly content with the warmth and love that seemed to leach from his firm muscle and bone into hers.

"Nuts are falling," he told her. "It will be a very good crop this year. Might have to dig another storage pit just to hold it all."

A colorful flock of buntings mixed with cardinals as they descended on the garden, apparently in search of insects. Odd to see so many, let alone flocking together.

"I couldn't be happier," she told him softly. The spirals continued to pulse and throb, the children to play, and Fire Cat folded her into a warm hug.

Just as her souls began to Sing with joy, the sky went black.

The air turned cold. Frigid.

She shivered, suddenly alone in the dark.

"What happened?" she cried out.

Around her, she could now feel the current as it moved slowly past, lifting her hair and floating it in streamers behind her. She stood in a narrow passage, the limestone on both sides dark and covered with roots. Her feet rested on soft mud, and filaments of moss flowed with the water.

Fear rose with the rapid pounding of her heart. She knew this place: the Underworld.

"Something's changed," Piasa told her as he appeared in a soft blue glow.

Night Shadow Star knotted her fists, tensing her shoulders. "I was so happy."

"An illusion. Another vision you spun for yourself." The fearsome Underwater Panther raised one of his yellow eagle's feet, raking the darkness with midnight talons. "This is the reality. What you have to look forward to. Your city, your palace, it's going to end now."

"Why?"

Piasa lifted his whiskered jowls into a snarl that exposed his curving canines, the pink cat's tongue curling. "He's been brought here. Into *my* realm. That stupid girl! Humans, you are all a plague. Of all the creatures of Creation, you are the only ones that insist on mucking around in Spirit Powers you *don't* understand. Do the bison? Do the deer? No. But give a human a vial of datura nectar, and she's creating havoc."

"I don't understand."

Piasa spread his wings. "Of course you don't. You've been using the Tortoise Bundle to Dream houses and gardens and children and a loving man, while a confused girl has been manipulated into precipitating disaster."

"Talk *straight*!"

"The Chikosi girl fed datura nectar to the Morning Star. Which drew Sacred Moth to drink his Spirit out of that wretched human body. And now Morning Star's been carried to the Underworld. Trapped here. In the darkness. Where he *doesn't* belong."

"The Morning Star has been eaten by a moth?" she asked, stifling a laugh.

In a lightning flash, Piasa grasped her in his taloned, crushing feet; the cougar's face thrust against hers. His breath—stinking of death and corruption—bathed her face. Deep in the yellow eyes, his black pupils were hot, sucking her souls into their searing depth.

"*He has to be freed.*" Piasa's voice cut through her like obsidian. "He is Sky World. His Power, here, is an infection. You've seen a wound fester? Burn hot and red in the flesh? Watched the pus swell and weep as it eats away at tissue? That's what will happen, woman: rot, and smell, and stink, and corruption, all sending its poison among the dead, sickening the Tree of Life, weakening Old-Woman-Who-Never-Dies."

He pushed her back, sent her staggering.

"That's what that little fool has done with her jar of datura nectar."

"You said a moth *ate* his Spirit?"

Piasa hissed, back arching, wings flared into bars of light as his rattlesnake tail whipped back and forth. "Sacred or not, a moth is still a moth. Just because Sacred Moth is filled with Power doesn't mean it has a brain in its head. It does what it does. Follows its nature. It is drawn to nectar, to drink. It can no more deny that instinct than can those moths that fly into flames."

"And a girl caused this?" Night Shadow Star asked weakly. Had she ever seen the Spirit Beast this enraged?

"The Albaamaha are a clever people, an old people, and Hanging Moss knew just how to bend an inexperienced and starry-eyed girl to his will." Piasa's smile wasn't pleasant. "He and Wet Clay Woman thought she'd be a way to strike at High Minko White Water Moccasin. Instead the Sky Hand sent her here, married her to a more important target."

"Why? Why would anyone do this?"

"So that the Sky Hand would get the blame for killing the Morning Star."

"Didn't the Morning Star know? Couldn't he see?"

"Of course," Piasa said simply. "Spirit Beings enjoy dancing with danger every bit as much as humans."

"So . . . how are you going to get the Morning Star back to the Sky World?"

"Me?" he asked, eyes narrowing with deadly intent.

"No!" she said, backing away. "I can't help you. I don't know anything about . . ."

Night Shadow Star blinked awake in her bed. Dark as her room was, it had to be the middle of the night. Her heart hammered against her breastbone; Piasa's foul breath still hung in her nostrils.

From across the room, the Tortoise Bundle was whispering, the voices issuing from it too low to understand.

She threw back her covers, feeling an electric tension in the air, as though lightning were about to strike. The blankets crackled, and her hair was floating from static. Every nerve in her body quivered.

She saw the dark shape in her doorway. A person, crouched.

"Fire Cat, is that you?"

Instead of Fire Cat's, a soft voice said, "Dream the big beasts to the stars, away. Their corpses bleach on dusty clay." A pause. "Change the land the People tread. Find a new way . . . or we'll all be dead."

"Sun Wing?"

Fire Cat's familiar shape appeared in the doorway behind Sun Wing's crouching form—a shadow against shadow, but she knew the way he moved.

"Lady?"

Night Shadow Star spun as her stomach tickled and went tight. Stumbling to her chamber pot, she barely had time to pull her hair back before she threw up.

As the spasms ceased, she felt Fire Cat's arms around her, asking, "Are you all right?"

"No. It's the Morning Star. We're in trouble. Bad trouble."

Thirty-two

The old weaver woman sat on a box just inside her front door and fingered the long whelk-shell columella that Seven Skull Shield had given her. On the looms to one side of the cramped and dark room hung half-finished weavings. Nothing fancy—just utilitarian everyday kinds of cloth, the sort that could be sewn into hunting shirts, working skirts, or capes.

Seven Skull Shield got a twisted sense of amusement out of the fact that the old woman despised him and Farts—and didn't particularly care for or trust Flat Stone Pipe either, believing as she did that dwarves were inherently dangerous concentrators of Spirit Power. Why else would they be so little?

But as bitter, sour, and unpleasant as the old woman might be, she'd nevertheless compromised all of her principles in return for a couple of skeins of buffalo-wool yarn and that long white columella Traded up from the gulf. One of the last of Seven Skull Shield's stock, to the old woman it represented a small fortune. And in return for it and the yarn, she'd allowed them access to the tight confines of her house—though she'd howled when Seven Skull Shield used a rock to hammer a short section of firewood through her clay-plastered wall to make a hole. Down at bench level, he'd driven another hole through the wattle-and-daub for Flat Stone Pipe to look out. Both allowed an excellent view of Wooden Doll's yard and ramada.

Now all that remained was to wait. A not-so-pleasant task given that the old woman's bedding smelled like it hadn't been washed in years, the room was cramped and dark, and in the limited time they'd been there, Farts had begun scratching as if an army of fleas had crept out from the cracked and battered ceramics and filthy fabrics stored under the bed.

The old woman just kept staring at them, eyes half-slitted as she murmured what sounded like curses under her breath. The entire time she kept running the columella through her wrinkled fingers. In an endless cycle, a wicked smile would fade into a frown before another eerie smile would take its place and the cycle repeated. Her wispy white hair seemed to float around her almost-bald head as the breeze drifted through the door behind her.

A faint stirring of the air wafted through the house and carried another whiff of the old woman's bedding to Seven Skull Shield's nose. He made a face.

So did Flat Stone Pipe who muttered, "I will remember this day. It's going to be right up at the top of my list of memories to forget." He leaned forward to peer out of the hole. "Still nothing but that litter and the bearers. How long do you think this will take?"

"Until Winder comes," Seven Skull Shield told him. "But he will come."

Flat Stone Pipe flopped around on the dirty blankets to sit with his back to the wall. "What makes you think he'll come here instead of sending a messenger to the Keeper's? That's the obvious place to deliver a message. And he could hire anyone at the canoe landing to carry it."

"This is Winder, little man." Seven Skull Shield reached down with a toe to scratch Farts where he lay just under the sleeping bench. The big dog uttered a squeaking yawn and tilted his head so that Seven Skull Shield's toe could find that itchy place just behind the right ear.

"As if that explains it all?" the dwarf asked.

"It does if you know Winder. He and I should have been dead a dozen times over. Some of the boys who ran with us were smarter, faster, or stronger. We made it, and they didn't." He shrugged. "Sure, some of it was just luck. Being in the wrong place at the wrong time. They went one way and got caught. We went the other and got away. But part of it was that Winder always thought past the obvious. Why take the first hiding place when the third or fourth—though taking more effort to find—would allow you sleep all night without keeping an eye open?"

"I see."

"So you have to think like Winder. Sending a message straight to the Keeper's might somehow be traced back to the source. So who would know how to get in touch with me without triggering any excitement?

Who would know how to deliver a message to my ears alone? Someone discreet. Trustworthy. And out of the loop and not to be suspected."

"Wooden Doll."

"Precisely. And not only that, sending the message through her is like a slap. It will be his way to say, 'Here. You chose her over me way back then. How did that work out for you?' "

Flat Stone Pipe stared up at him, eyes curious. "How did it?"

Seven Skull Shield craned his head around and stared through the hole at Wooden Doll's yard. The old male slave who had replaced Newe sat hunched before the door to dissuade interruptions to the proceedings inside. The porters waiting by the litter had surrendered to playing dice. And inside, behind that door, some strange man was . . . Well, never mind.

"Winder never understood," Seven Skull Shield admitted. "Maybe I didn't either. We were more than brothers. Bonded between souls. Each for the other. More than friends and boon companions. He expected me to go back south with him because that was our dream. We were going to make the impossible come true. We'd seen it, little man. Glimpsed the opportunity in potential Trade between the growing colonies and the older Nations. We obtained a big shallow draft vessel, rounded up the men to paddle it, and filled it with Cahokian wares for the Trade."

Seven Skull Shield smiled wistfully. "And then I stumbled upon Wooden Doll, this marvel of a woman married to a man who hadn't a clue of what a miracle he had in his bed.

"Did you know that you can fall into someone, like falling into a hole? That's what happened with Wooden Doll and me. We fell into each other and didn't come out for a couple of moons when we finally hit rock bottom."

"What went wrong?" Flat Stone Pipe asked.

"We were so busy being enchanted with each other that we forgot that I'm me and she's herself. Turned out that we were the sort of people that were the most compatible when we were passionately bedding each other rather than contemplatively living with each other. She put it best: I thrive on the uncertainty of the challenge, whereas she is satisfied to enjoy the spoils of success."

"I wish she'd chosen better neighbors," Flat Stone Pipe muttered as another breath of breeze blew the bed's stink up from below.

By the fire, the old woman hissed to herself and continued to finger the columella.

"I could pay her back," Seven Skull Shield said thoughtfully. "I could sing one of my songs."

"And I could pour the old woman's chamber pot over your head,"

Flat Stone Pipe shot back. "I've heard you sing. It's almost as wretched as that yowling you make when you fight. Either sound so appalling your old friend Winder—no doubt of man of tastes and refinement—would flee like a forest hare from a stew pot."

"You don't have a clue do you?"

"About what?"

"The sort of remarkable talent necessary to compose songs that touch the heart and get to the very meat of human existence in a hostile world. That I am so blessed by such ability is a true gift from Power. I have seen blooded warriors swoon, their squadron leaders moved to tears by my eloquence."

"I've seen them swoon and cry, too. They were tied in the squares and being tortured. Which, when you think about it, is about what your singing amounts to."

Seven Skull Shield snorted derisively through his nose. "I understand. You are not the first to utter such hateful sayings; I recognize your failing for what it is: pure unadulterated jealousy." He sighed. "Ah, the terrible burden Power has laid upon my weary shoulders."

"I can see why you have so few friends," Flat Stone Pipe told him as he bent to the peephole. "They've all either slit their wrists or banished themselves to the farthest colonies."

"As if you'd have any idea of—"

"Shhh!" Flat Stone Pipe, his eye to the hole, held up a small hand.

Seven Skull Shield pivoted on the bedding, stirring the smelly blankets in the process, and looked out his hole. Three men, two looking like dirt farmers, but with a curious oddity. And the third . . . ? Yes.

"That's Winder," Seven Skull Shield whispered as the muscular Trader walked up to the old slave at Wooden Doll's door.

They talked for a moment, the voices too low to hear, and the old man waved Winder back.

Seven Skull Shield's old friend took a careful look around, and for a couple of heartbeats stared hard at the old woman's house as if he were looking straight into Seven Skull Shield's eye. Then he stepped over to the ramada, nodded at the waiting porters, and took a seat with the two "dirt farmers." Seven Skull Shield had finally figured out that they were Quiz Quiz warriors in disguise.

"Very good, thief," Flat Stone Pipe whispered. "Looks like you cast your lance, and it hit the chunkey stone dead-on."

"Now, we wait, little man."

Winder, you're as clever as ever. But for this once, I'm a step ahead of you.

Thirty-three

Winder stood in the morning sunlight with his thick arms crossed and his back leaned against one of the ramada poles. He studied the woman's abode, seeing a larger than usual dwelling where it packed in among the buildings that cluttered River Mounds City. The walls were well plastered, the thatch roof in superb repair. A litter rested before the closed door; the porters tossed bone dice as they waited for their master.

An old man, a slave, kept station at the door and had been the one who told Winder he'd have to wait.

Two of the Quiz Quiz warriors who had accompanied him lounged to one side of the ramada. But for their facial tattoos, they didn't look much like Quiz Quiz anymore. It had been a fight, but a gasped order from the war leader had finally convinced them to take down their characteristic pom hairstyle, lay aside their regalia, and to don simple hemp-fiber hunting shirts.

The warrior called Red Stroke—despite the drab clothing—still looked like a lean, handsome, twenty-year-old heartthrob and ladykiller. Moccasin, at thirty, might have been one of the ugliest men Winder had ever seen: something about his short body and oddly proportioned, wide-mouthed, and squat face. Both warriors carried their weapons hidden in burlap sacks and, on Winder's orders, had coated their faces with a dusting of ash and grime, looking for all the world like dirt farmers instead of elite Quiz Quiz warriors.

They hated it, of course.

But so much had already gone so wrong. If Winder could save anything out of this, it would be worth a fortune. And the only hope Sky Star had left was Winder—and his knowledge of things Cahokian.

Winder had been Sky Star's guide to the Surveyors' Society House, had provided the distraction that allowed the war leader to sneak in and grab the Bundle. He had supervised and guided their retreat across the city, and had found what he thought was a safe haven for the Quiz Quiz—a place to wait out the storm as the Cahokians turned the city upside down in search of the stolen Bundle.

Who would have guessed? Seven Skull Shield—of all people—had sniffed out the Quiz Quiz. That Skull had interrupted one of the Quiz Quiz rituals, separated the war leader and the Bundle from his warriors, and somehow managed to subdue Sky Star? Unthinkable!

You aren't the same young man I left behind so many years ago, old friend.

It almost defied belief. Winder had been asking around. The gangly, awkward, not-too-smart but bull-strong youth he'd once known—and finally left behind to his foibles—was now a renowned thief, womanizer, and confidant of the Four Winds Clan elite. A sort of local hero and disappointment, all rolled into one.

"How did he do that?" Winder wondered to himself. It brought a faint smile of amusement to his lips. "Mud and fire, we had some times, didn't we?"

He and Skull, two half-starved, mostly desperate orphans, they'd lived by their wits. Survived. Learned the back ways and how to keep their bellies full—how to stay warm enough in winter and on the move in summer. Not that there hadn't been close calls, beatings, and the occasional painful comeuppance. Two of their friends had been caught and had their brains bashed out for theft. Another had ended up screaming his lungs out in a Deer Clan chief's square while his thin body was cut apart and fed to the dogs.

"But you and I made it," Winder whispered. He wondered what would have happened if Skull hadn't fallen in love. But then, that was Skull's eternal weakness: that insufferable and unflinching loyalty he had to people he cared for.

And Skull *had* cared for her.

With all of his poor, aching, young heart.

Cared enough that he'd given up on the river, the Trade, and the best friend he'd ever had.

A dog whined in the old weaver's house behind him, and he thought he heard someone whisper a command. This was followed by a barely audible argument. Winder turned, glancing back at the house, seeing where a couple of chunks of plaster had fallen from the wall and left holes. Life must have been hard for the old crone.

Winder turned his attention back to his target as a man stepped out of the woman's door, seated himself in the litter, and was lifted by his porters. A moment later, the old man guarding the door pointed to Winder and called, "She will see you now."

Winder grinned at the two warriors, giving them the "wait" sign, and ambled across the small yard to the ornate dwelling. He nodded to the old man and stepped inside, closing the door behind him.

The structure had been imposing from the outside, but inside it was even grander. Only the stack of wood beside the door looked ordinary. The floor matting was exquisitely woven, covered with softly-tanned bear and buffalo hides; the white-plastered walls almost gleamed where they could be seen behind the hanging tapestry, wooden carvings, and geometric designs. A fire in the center of the room not only illuminated, but provided a delightful warmth after the morning chill. In the back, an ornate and spacious bed jutted from the wall. A thick wealth of hides, blankets, and colorful fabric-covered pillows were piled atop it.

She stood behind the fire—a silky dogbane skirt clinging suggestively to her round hips, one leg defiantly forward. Her arms were crossed beneath full and round breasts, the dark nipples prominent. Glossy black hair fell in splendor down her back. Eyes tinted of soft night watched him curiously. She still had that face he remembered so well for its perfect proportions.

"Wooden Doll," he said wistfully, seeing her as Skull must have all those long years ago. She still reeked of a blatant female sexuality. "It's been a long time."

Her gaze sharpened with recognition. "A long time, indeed, Winder." A pause. "I think I like it."

"Like what?"

"The change. Last time I saw you, I thought you were too desperate. Everything was life or death, to be won now and at all costs. That frantic need for success has obviously been tempered by enough victories that you've finally become comfortable enough to have settled into yourself."

He laughed. "You always did have an eye for men and what they wanted." He glanced around. "You've done well. I see Trade from every corner of the world here." He stepped over, fingering one of the fabrics. "Mayan? I *am* impressed."

"A party of Itza were here this summer. No doubt you've heard."

"Indeed. I actually saw them when they were among the Natchez. They were being pretty stingy with Trade. That you ended up with a piece? You could Trade that for a fortune, you know."

"I do know." She stepped around the fire, studying him thoughtfully. "Speaking of Trade, what service can I provide you, Winder? Are you interested in my body, or the things I know? Given the way you're acting, I'd say the latter."

"Maybe both," he told her. "I have always wondered if what Skull gave up for you was worth the Trade."

"I'm not sure you could afford to find out. The Deer Clan chief who just left Traded three copper plates for last night's services. And that was just for the arts of my body."

Winder chuckled to himself. "Expensive, indeed. But perhaps for today I only need to get a message to my old friend, Skull. You do still see him, don't you?"

"On occasion. Most of his time is spent at the Keeper's these days. Or, if the rumors are true, the one-time Keeper's. You might want to check at her palace."

He gave her a victorious smile. "Actually, Blue Heron is no longer in her palace. She's enjoying . . . Well, let's say her present circumstances aren't as delightful and luxurious as her palace is reputed to be. You want to do Skull a favor? Tell him I've got the Keeper. If he wants to see her alive again, he'll have to Trade for her."

"You have abducted the Keeper? Are you mad?" She arched an eyebrow, lips quirked in amusement.

"No. Just providing a service to clients. As you yourself do. But perhaps in ways that aren't as memorable as those you no doubt have perfected."

"And what do you expect him to Trade for her?"

"He'll know. I'll send a message here, to you, tomorrow night, as to where and when we can Trade."

He watched her expression, saw the tightening behind her eyes as she said, "You were his best friend once. He loved you. It will break his heart if he has to go against you."

Winder glanced around, lifting his hands. "He loved you more than he did me, Doll. Yet here you are, a paid woman. Which leaves me to believe you broke his heart in ways I never could have."

Her expression pinched, fire behind her eyes. "*If* I see him. I'll deliver your message. No charge. For old time's sake. Now, *get out*!"

"You're still one of the most beautiful women in the world, Wooden Doll. Glad to see that you're using it to your advantage."

Then he touched his forehead in salute and turned to leave. He stopped at the door, glancing back. "Oh, and don't cross me. I'd hate for Skull to lose *both* of the women in his life."

Then he was outside, motioning to the warriors as he headed off between the buildings. To the old man, he said, "She's free again."

"You got the message to the woman?" Moccasin asked as he trotted up to match Winder's pace.

"The trap is set. As soon as my old friend shows up with the medicine box, we're out of here and headed home."

"What if they find the bodies?" Red Stroke asked.

"It's up to us to make sure they don't, isn't it?"

"And this woman?" Moccasin asked.

"We can't leave *any* loose ends that would implicate either the high chief or the war leader." He smiled sadly. "Which is a shame. She's such a beautiful woman."

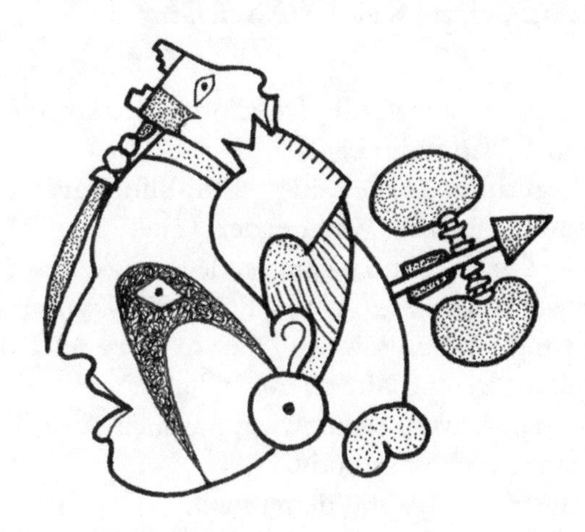

Thirty-four

Tonka'tzi Wind stood in the Morning Star's room, her back to the wall, a dull thumping of dread in her breast. Beside her, Five Fists blocked the Morning Star's doorway, and while his jaw might have been dislocated, he could still grind his teeth in fury and dismay. In the awful silence, Wind could hear them.

On the Morning Star's bed, old Rides-the-Lightning bent over the living god's supine body. Two priests stood—one on either side of the old soul flier—each bearing a bag of herbs, potions, and other divining objects. A deadly silence filled the room as Rides-the-Lightning shifted, bent his head close, and sniffed at the Morning Star's face, mouth, and then down his body to his genitals.

Finally he straightened. "His Spirit is in the Underworld. I can see its trace, like a trail of frosted white light in the darkness. He was carried away."

"Carried away?" Five Fists growled.

"By Sacred Moth," Rides-the-Lightning asserted. His priests reflexively stepped back, staring uneasily at each other.

"What sacred moth?" Wind asked.

"Old Power," Rides-the-Lightning answered. "Brought from the south. The Powers of the night and darkness, of the Spirit plants: tobacco, datura, jimson weed, and nightshade. Sacred Moth and his caterpillars. The only creatures that feed off the deadly essences of the plants . . . that's who has carried the living god's Spirit away from us."

Five Fists stepped forward, his expression strained. "Work your magic, Soul Flier. Bring him back."

Rides-the-Lightning turned his white-blind eyes toward the war leader. "Not so easy as that, War Leader. Like I said: This is old Power, filled with ancient ways, blind passages, dead ends, and clinging threads. Morning Star is a *Sky* Being. A very Powerful Sky Being. Do you need me to explain what kind of Power it takes to carry the living god into the Underworld, let alone bind him there?"

Both of the priests were swallowing hard, backing still farther from the Morning Star's comatose body.

"How was this done?" Wind demanded.

Rising Flame arrived and slipped past Five Fists' bulk and into the room. Wind held up a hand, stilling the matron, as she waited for Rides-the-Lightning's answer.

"Though the nectar, *Tonka'tzi*," Rides-the-Lightning said, sniffing at the air like a dog. "Wait." He turned his head slightly, still scenting, and seemingly followed his nose to a ceramic cup sitting on one of the intricately carved wooden chests.

Rides-the-Lightning carefully clasped the ceramic cup between thumb and forefinger, lifted it, sniffed again at the rim, and held it out. "Cloud Born? If you would be so kind. Do not touch this anywhere around the rim, but throw it in the great fire, please."

"Yes, master," one of the priests told him uneasily as he gingerly took the cup by the base and headed for the door.

Wind noticed that both Rising Flame and Five Fists scrambled to get out of the man's way.

"It was in the blueberry juice," Rides-the-Lightning told them. "A great deal of datura nectar along with the saps and juices rendered from the seeds."

Rising Flame was staring wide-eyed at the Morning Star's naked body. "I came as soon as I heard. What has happened?"

"Apparently the Morning Star's Spirit has been carried off to the Underworld," Wind told her. "But who did this?"

"The girl," Rides-the-Lightning told them. "His new young wife." Again he sniffed and followed his nose to a second cup. Lifting it, he inhaled along the rim. "More blueberry juice. Bearing her scent."

"Wouldn't he have called out as he felt the poison working on him?" Five Fists demanded. "Surely he had to have had some warning as the drink took effect."

Rides-the-Lightning gave them a toothless smile, his face wrinkling into a mass of lines. "She was most clever. Distracted him."

"We did hear a cry," Five Fists said warily, eyes narrowed as he studied the Morning Star's sprawled position. "A woman's voice in, um . . ."

"Ecstasy?" Rides-the-Lightning suggested when Five Fists hesitated. "From the odor of their combined excretions, I would call the coupling most energetic."

"You can smell that?" Rising Flame asked, shaking her head.

"Most assuredly, Matron."

The old war leader balled a fist and smacked it into his palm. "She went to visit the Albaamaha. To discuss keeping the peace between her Sky Hand delegation and the Albaamaha. Or that's the story."

Wind said, "That doesn't make sense. She was sent here by her father, High Minko White Water Moccasin, to marry the Morning Star. To establish relations between Cahokia and the Sky Hand. What do the Albaamaha have to do with it?"

Five Fists stroked his off-center chin. "She didn't have any nectar when she came here. Hardly had any possessions at all. The Albaamaha had to have given it to her yesterday. So are they part of White Water Moccasin's plot?"

"Plot?" Rising Flame asked, staring uncertainly at the Morning Star; then she glanced around, as if cataloging the room.

"It wouldn't be the first time a young person was sent as a gift in marriage, only to carry out an assassination," Five Fists told her. "And if you'll notice, Whispering Dawn is nowhere to be found. The guard at the gate said that a woman left in the middle of the night. If she isn't running for it, I don't know squash on a stalk when I see it."

"Some of the things are missing," Rising Flame said, pointing. "The buffalo blanket, a couple of copper plates, some statues. A whelk-shell cup."

Wind narrowed an eye. She'd heard that Rising Flame had been in the Morning Star's bed of late. Which made her ask, "War Leader, how many women has the Morning Star been with since he married the girl?"

"None, *Tonka'tzi*."

"That's a bit unusual, isn't it?"

"He seemed quite taken with her," Five Fists said. "As if somehow amused and entertained, even though she didn't speak a word of our language. But yes, it is unusual. He doesn't usually commit to just one woman for this long a period. In fact, some of the Earth Clan chiefs and immigrant leaders have started to complain, having daughters coming of age who seek the honor of sharing the Morning Star's bed."

"When a woman is sent in marriage, he usually marries them, spends a few nights, and sends them off to one of the regional palaces," Wind mused. "Treats it more like a ritual function. But amused and entertained, War Leader?"

Rides-the-Lightning inserted himself in the conversation, saying, "It is in our natures. We are drawn to Dance closest to the exotic flame that might burn us. Spirit Beings are no different; they are drawn to embrace that which might destroy them. Like weaving back and forth in time to a serpent, how many times can you caress it before getting bitten? And each time you do, and get away with it, the thrill becomes greater."

"You're saying *he knew*?" Wind gasped.

Rides-the-Lightning fixed his white eyes on hers. "Even living gods get bored with their existences, *Tonka'tzi*. Perhaps, like a moth, he is seeking a metamorphosis."

"But what do we do about this?" Rising Flame demanded, a look of near panic behind her eyes.

"Soul Flier?" Wind asked, watching the old shaman's expression tighten.

"I will see what can be done," he said, voice almost wistful. Then, to his priests: "Take me back to the temple. We must prepare."

"I'll send warriors to run the girl and those accursed Albaamaha down," Five Fists growled. "As soon as we have them, I'll clap her in a square, and she can contemplate the nature of her sins."

"I shall be curious as to how many you capture, War Leader," Rides-the-Lightning said as he started for the door. "And in the meantime, do nothing to the Morning Star. Though he appears dead, his body still lives. Though for how long," Rides-the-Lightning paused, "we cannot say."

Wind clamped her eyes closed. Spit and pus, if he died—especially from assassination—all chaos would break loose.

She turned, seeing Five Fists' look of disbelief and horror.

"What?"

"He told me!" Five Fists sounded half-strangled. "He ordered me *not* to punish her. How could he have known?"

She turned, staring at the Morning Star's somnolent body. *Was he really that desperate to die? And if so, why?*

"You may be under orders not to torture the girl, but War Leader, I am not!"

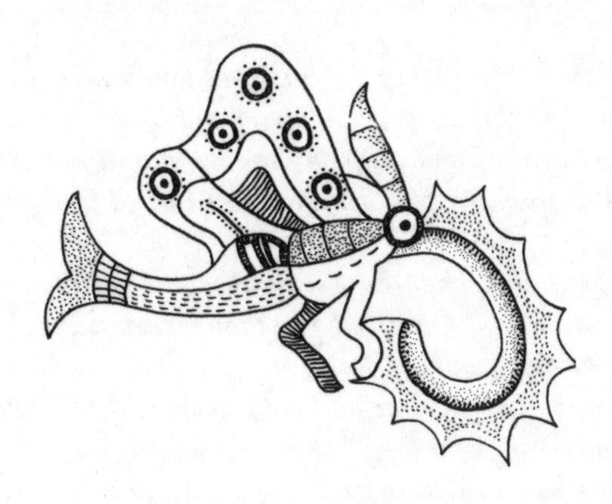

Lost

Morning has come. I have no idea where I am. I've been walking most of the night, and somehow I got turned around in the darkness. Why, of all nights, did this one have to be cloudy and blacker than a Tie Snake's pit?

Coming down from the Morning Star's Great Staircase, I turned right, west, trying to retrace the steps that my escort took to the small building that housed Straight Corn, Hanging Moss, and Wet Clay Woman. I remember they were somewhere just off the Avenue of the Sun, but not quite to Black Tail's tomb. I vaguely remember a charnel house on the north side of the road. It marked the place I needed to turn off.

The thing about charnel houses is that you don't need to see them to know they are there. The nose works just fine for identifying when you've arrived. I turned at the first scent of rotting human and stumbled around, tripping over things in the dark, being barked at by dogs, and bashing into ramadas and mortars.

Only to end up at the marshy edge of a creek.

So I tried to retrace my way, falling in holes, stepping in latrines. . . . It was a mess!

I recognized the Avenue of the Sun by the lighter color of the white sand that marked its way, and again, I turned west, only to encounter two charnel houses, side by side. Which wasn't right.

But how many had I passed while the porters carried me yesterday? I'd been so giddy over the notion that I'd be seeing Straight Corn, I hadn't been paying attention.

Somehow I lost the Avenue of the Sun and found myself fumbling around in the dark again, having to twist this way and that around farmsteads and gardens, and once again I ended up on the edge of mucky ground that tried to suck the moccasins from my feet. Every way I turned in the blackness, it just got worse.

Only by stopping, thinking, did I remember that the breeze had been puffing against my right cheek. Orienting myself so it caressed my left ear, I slogged my way back to harder ground.

"Where are you?" I kept calling out plaintively to the night while panic was kindled in my chest.

Time was everything. I had *to find my people, collect them, and we all had to make our escape to the canoe landing and be out of Cahokia by dawn.*

The panic got worse. I fled around in the night, panting and flailing my arms in front of me.

Getting ever more lost.

Getting ever more desperate.

Until the sun lightened the eastern horizon.

Having at least a direction, I plodded westward toward the river, picking my way through the buildings as they emerged from the night's pitch black.

And found myself here. At the edge of River Mounds City. I can recognize it by the huge guardian posts on either side of the avenue. As the overcast sky continues to gray, I can only stare back to the east, a keening in my souls, a physical sickness in my gut. I know Straight Corn and the people I love are back there, somewhere. I don't have a clue as to how to find them.

I hug both hands to my aching stomach, thinking I have killed them. By now that surly Five Fists has checked on the Morning Star. He will have noticed that the living god is lying naked atop the blankets. Alone. His new wife nowhere in sight.

He will have discovered senseless flesh.

Even as I think this, all of Cahokia is being alerted to find me. Warriors are being dispatched to capture Straight Corn and the rest of my family. Strong Mussel, Cloud Tassel, and the rest will be herded to the squares, protesting their innocence. Crying foul and betrayal.

I have failed everyone.

Most of all, myself.

Hungry, thirsty, and terrified, I follow a series of trails between the tightly packed houses. Tears of defeat are trickling down my cheeks. I am lost in the maze of buildings, but as long as I keep the dawn sky behind me, I'll hit the river.

Contemplating the fate of the people I love, I just want to die. My stomach spasms. I bend over and throw up.

Thirty-five

Fire Cat let a grim smile play across his face as he stared hard into Five Fists' gleaming black eyes. The old warrior's crooked face reflected rage and a deep-seated panic.

The Morning Star's palace was packed with people, all of them in a similar state of shock.

"Let us pass," Night Shadow Star ordered the grizzled war leader.

The old warrior continued to block their way to Chunkey Boy's personal quarters in the back of the palace. Around them the great hall was oddly quiet, somber, as nobles, recorders, and the usual press of servants and aides huddled along the walls and whispered to each other.

"The Morning Star is currently inconvenienced," Five Fists said stiffly. "The soul flier is attending to him."

"His Spirit is in the Underworld," she told him bluntly. "I need to speak to Rides-the-Lightning."

"You serve a different Power than my master, Lady. Perhaps you would know more about his condition, and how it came to be this way, than I would."

At the tone in Five Fists' voice, Fire Cat tightened his grip on his war club. He'd been waiting patiently for this moment. Sure, another ten warriors were clustered between him and the door, but it would be a pleasure to smack Five Fists' crooked face back straight, then whack it again to knock it out of alignment in the other direction.

"Let her pass," *Tonka'tzi* Wind called as she appeared in Chunkey Boy's doorway.

"But, *Tonka'tzi*. She's a servant of the Underworld. There's no telling what sort of trouble she might—"

"You're a fool," Night Shadow Star snapped. "Piasa doesn't want the Morning Star in the Underworld any more than the rest of us do. Now get out of my way, or I'll have the Red Wing move you."

"I order you to stand down, War Leader," Wind told Five Fists as she walked wearily up to the man. "Rides-the-Lightning has requested the lady's presence."

"It's not over between us," Five Fists whispered hotly as he stepped aside. Fire Cat glared into the old warrior's eyes as he followed Night Shadow Star and Wind to the rear.

People packed the inside of the Morning Star's opulent personal quarters: Rising Flame, Rides-the-Lightning, a bevy of well-known healers, several of the living god's attendants, Wind, and a couple of warriors who were apparently standing guard.

"Clear the room," Rides-the-Lightning called. "Lady Night Shadow Star and I must discuss things alone."

Fire Cat stepped aside as the others funneled out, most of them shooting him irritated glances.

"Lady?" he asked.

She raised a hand, flipping it to excuse him.

"Stay, Red Wing," Rides-the-Lightning said in his reedy voice.

"Soul Flier?" Night Shadow Star asked in surprise.

"The Red Wing must hear what I have to say."

She shot Fire Cat a curious glance, then stepped over to the bed, where Chunkey Boy lay flat on his back, arms to the side, a blanket covering him.

Fire Cat made a face, seeing his old enemy looking empty and vulnerable for the first time. The face paint had been wiped away, the man's hair fixed, and his eyes covered with a damp cloth.

He really didn't look like much without the regalia. Just an athletically muscled man in his twenties with pale and swollen lips.

"This is how you found him?" Night Shadow Star asked.

"No. He has been cared for." Rides-the-Lightning reached over, removing the cloth to check the vacant and half-lidded eyes. "His souls were carried away as he was coupling with the Sky Hand girl. That's how she distracted him."

Night Shadow Star surprised Fire Cat when she said, "I know when it happened. I was dreaming when Piasa carried my souls to the Underworld. Piasa is enraged and not a little frightened."

"I would guess he is," Rides-the-Lightning agreed. "The Morning Star is a Sky being. A Power out of place in the Underworld."

Fire Cat watched the unease in Night Shadow Star's face as she said, "Piasa referred to it as an infection, one that will sicken the entire world."

Rides-the-Lightning fixed his white eyes on Night Shadow Star, as if seeing into her souls. "The Morning Star's Spirit must be removed from the Underworld. You understand that, don't you?"

Her expression indicated distaste. "Somehow, Piasa thinks that I can bring him back." She gestured her confusion. "Why does he think it's up to me?"

"Because it is, Night Shadow Star." Rides-the-Lightning looked anything but happy. "This is beyond my Power. Many times I have gone into the Underworld in search of lost souls. That is a matter of following a trace, passing the guardians, and bringing back a fully human soul. This, however, is ancient magic. Southern magic. The Morning Star's Spirit has been bound in darkness by Sacred Moth. His Spirit is intoxicated with sacred nectar, and the two are in mortal combat. Sacred Moth seeks to devour Morning Star's essence, tainted as it is with nectar. To resolve such a conflict is beyond my abilities."

Night Shadow Star raised her hands in despair. "I have no training in such arts, Elder. I've barely survived my journeys to the Underworld as it is. You know how close I've come to losing my souls down there."

Fire Cat nodded, his pulse quickening. *Do not insist on this, old man. It's a miracle that she's still alive after the last time.*

The old man turned his blind gaze on Chunkey Boy. "His body is barely alive. Unless the Morning Star's essence is returned to the flesh within a matter of days, all is lost."

"So if Chunkey Boy dies"—Fire Cat narrowed skeptical eyes at the old man—"won't you just pick someone else and hold a resurrection? Isn't one imposter as good as another?"

Night Shadow Star shot him a look of disbelief.

Rides-the-Lightning uttered a soft laugh, sadly shaking his head. "Forever the heretic, Red Wing? Would that it were that simple."

As if Fire Cat's remark were the deciding factor, Night Shadow Star said, "What do I have to do, Elder?"

"Go after him."

"Lady?" Fire Cat asked, his anxiety rising. "The last time you took the datura—"

"You don't believe, Red Wing," she told him gently. "I do. It's not your decision." To Rides-the-Lightning she added, "I shall return to my palace, prepare the datura paste, and with luck . . . Why are you shaking your head?"

"This cannot be a soul journey, Lady. This time you must go in your physical body. Actually enter the Underworld in search of the Morning Star."

"*What?*" Fire Cat cried. "How? Dig a hole and bury her?"

Night Shadow Star ignored him, her attention fixed on Rides-the-Lightning. She'd gone pale, a near panic in her eyes, asking, "The cave?"

"That's right," the old man told her. "It's the only way."

"What cave?" Fire Cat demanded, his fear rising. "What's the only way?"

"The sacred caves," she told him, in a reed-hollow voice. "I have to descend into the depths to start my search for the Morning Star's Spirit."

"The sacred caves?" Fire Cat asked, having heard of them for most of his life. "The ones off to the west, a hard day's travel upriver from Evening Star Town?"

Rides-the-Lightning turned for the door, saying, "I shall have Five Fists issue the orders. Time is of the essence. How soon can you leave, Lady?"

Night Shadow Star's eyes were liquid with fear as she shot a worried look at her brother's limp body, and said, "As soon as I can dress for travel and collect the items I need."

Thirty-six

Blue Heron blinked awake, wondering whether she had heard something. Pain speared through her head as if a bitted ax was embedded in its crown. Each beat of her heart was accompanied by a throbbing agony. Had she actually fallen asleep . . . or simply lost consciousness?

What was it about that sound that had awakened her?

Maybe it was her imagination. How could a person hear when she hurt like this?

No, it had been a sound—a soft scuffling and rasping.

Mouse, maybe? Or a packrat?

I'd give my life for a drink of water.

Her tongue filled her mouth like a piece of dried leather. She couldn't swallow, could only gag, as she tried to stimulate saliva.

Her bruised cheek pressed against cold dirt, her left eye swollen closed. The length of her body—what she could feel of it—ached and throbbed. The rest felt of numb nothingness.

One of the Quiz Quiz had sneaked in last night just after dusk and started to beat her. He'd stuffed a cloth into her mouth and begun kicking with all his might. He had concentrated on her head and ribs, nothing held back as he smashed her time and time again.

By some bit of luck, the hollow thumps elicited with each impact had brought Winder. Then ensued a hot argument in Quiz Quiz as the burly Trader waved his arms, face a mask of fury.

In the end, the angry warrior had leaped onto the stepping post before vaulting out into the darkness. A string of what obviously were curses had marked his path.

"They blame you, you know," Winder had told her as he knelt down and squinted at the blood dripping from her nose. "It's your fault they had the Surveyors' Bundle, then lost it. That their war leader was captured and tortured. That the War Medicine was stolen."

She'd muffled a replay into the gag. The one he didn't bother to remove.

And then he'd climbed out and closed the door, lashing it tightly to seal her in. She had heard him barking orders, and two men, apparently guards, had been placed outside. Periodically she'd heard them talk, or shift, and once she caught the faint odor of tobacco despite her blood-clotted nostrils.

That had been hands of time ago.

Now Blue Heron wondered how long she'd been comatose. Wished she was that way again. Her head was in the kind of agony that felt like her skull was fractured into shards. If the kicks to her head had broken her souls loose to float away, if they'd escaped the pain and were already headed for the Land of the Dead . . . ?

Well, it would only be a matter of time before her heart stopped and the life soul faded from the broken husk of her body.

Everything hurt, especially breathing. How many of her ribs had the Quiz Quiz broken? Each time he'd kicked her, the blow had lofted her high enough that she'd bounced upon landing on the hard yellow clay.

When she inhaled, the odors of urine and feces mixed with the musky scent of damp soil and humid river air. The smell made her nauseous. Each time she'd had the dry heaves since the beating, the pain had left her wheezing, and nothing but bile had come up to coat the back of her gag.

Several times she'd heard the twitter of the blue herons as they winged south, and several times huge flocks of geese had passed over. Close to the river. She had to be.

She tried to shift, and groaned.

Pus and blood, why don't they just kill me?

In her fifty-some years, she had never been as ready for death.

She blinked, tried to open her puffy eye, and bent her head around just enough to see; the cracks around the roof were still night-black.

Again she heard the soft rasping.

Blinking in the darkness, she struggled to place the sound. She imagined it might have been that of a struggle: the soft thrashing of feet, followed by a choked rattle. But what could make that sort of—

A hollow clunk was followed by the whisper of wood on plaster. A square of lesser darkness appeared above where the door had been stealthily removed.

She sighed in weary defeat. The Quiz Quiz was back. He'd waited—bided his time, no doubt, until everyone was soundly asleep.

This time he'd kill her. Wouldn't be so bad. The pain would be gone; her souls were already floating, the room spinning and blurry.

Please, let it be quick!

A dark form blocked the rectangle of light that marked the door. She heard a stealthy foot feel around for the stepping post, and then the man lowered himself to the floor.

Blue Heron's heart raced.

Gods, so this is death.

It was one thing to intellectually embrace it; the souls, however, continued to panic and send fear burning through her battered muscles and bones.

She began to pant, laboring for air in spite of the lancing pain that made each expansion of her lungs agony.

That uncomfortable heat and prickle of fear-sweat traced patterns across her skin. The world seemed to fade.

"Shhh!" a voice cautioned from just over her head.

She tried to scream as a big hand clamped down over her mouth.

Please! Make it fast. Don't let it hurt!

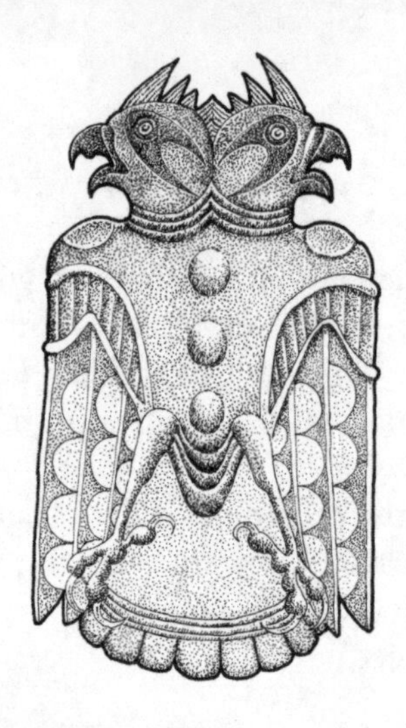

Thirty-seven

Tonka'tzi Wind propped her chin on her fist as she leaned forward and glared her displeasure at Rising Flame. She was perched atop her dais in the Council House—the room having been cleared at her order. Now the only sound in the great building was the periodic popping of logs in the central fire.

"So you've begun your stint as clan matron with disaster after disaster. You said you needed help; I'll give it. Reluctantly. Why? Because I don't have time to summon the clan leaders and ask for a recall vote to get rid of you. That means that you're all I've got in the current crisis. And because you were chosen by the Morning Star. Perhaps as his last request." A pause. "I have to assume he had a reason for choosing you, although figuring out what that might be completely escapes me at the moment."

Rising Flame glared back, a half-panicked desperation in her eyes. She'd gone pale, which accented the star tattoos on her hollow cheeks, and her full mouth was pinched.

She said, "I know you wanted Sacred Spoon. I've always been everyone's last choice, and I've hated them for it. You think my life's been easy, growing up in everyone else's shadow? Rising Flame? She's the daughter we don't know what to do with! Ship her out, send her off with the embassy. What do we care if she's shuttled back and forth among the River Nations? She's Morning Star House. And who knows? If she's paraded through far-off council meetings, maybe the barbarians will be duped into thinking we're taking them seriously!"

She snorted her derision. "Being born into Morning Star House is like being born into a pack of starving weasels. They'll all turn on you at a moment's notice."

She thrust out a slim forefinger. "I watched my brother Fire Light get himself exiled to the far east when he tried to buck Chunkey Boy. You wonder why there's bad blood between me and Blue Heron? It's because she played Sacred Spoon, my father Takes Blood, and my mother against each other. She was responsible for brokering my marriage to Tapping Wood. With *your* blessing, I might add. And yes, he might be a pretty good squadron leader for a Fish Clan man, but as a husband, he was an idiot."

"We all have our lives dictated by the needs of the clan. As matron, you'd better figure that out."

"Oh, believe me, I have." Rising Flame stepped forward, hands on hips, not more than a pace away. "Piss in a pot, Wind, if you and the rest of the matrons are so clever, cunning, and smart, why am I matron today instead of Sacred Spoon?"

"You wouldn't be, were it not for the Morning Star sending his—"

"Exactly!" Rising Flame crossed her arms in triumph. "Now do you begin to understand? If not, I could take a piece of charcoal and draw it all out on the floor for you."

Wind fumed under the young woman's knowing stare. As she did it soaked in that Rising Flame—young, without a benefactor, without a prayer to be taken seriously—had avoided the bitter infighting, the backstabbing, and treacherous deal-making required to collect enough faction-backed votes to win. While the Houses were obsessed with cutting each other's throats, Rising Flame had neatly circumvented each and every one of them. In the end, when the time was right, all it had taken was a word from Five Fists.

The realization was stunning, and Wind straightened, seeing the young woman clearly for the first time.

Rising Flame couldn't keep the satisfaction out of her voice. "That's right. Not only did I do it the easy way, but I'm the matron."

Wind grunted, both envious and irritated. "Yes, you're clever. Doesn't lessen the danger you're in or the mess you've made of it."

"How is it *my* mess? The Morning Star married the girl; I didn't."

"No, but you dismissed Blue Heron."

"And what difference could she and her spies have made?"

"Well, let's see, shall we?" Wind clapped her hands, calling, "Send in Smooth Pebble, if you would!"

She watched as the door was opened and the berdache was allowed in. Dressed in a skirt, and with a hemp cape hanging from her muscular shoulders, Smooth Pebble crossed the room and knelt, touching her forehead respectfully as she said, "Bless you, *Tonka'tzi.* Is there word on Blue Heron?"

"Rise, Smooth Pebble. No word, I'm afraid. The matron and I, however, have even greater pressing issues. The girl, Whispering Dawn, she was brought first to Blue Heron, isn't that right?"

"Yes, *Tonka'tzi.* One of her spies, an Albaamaha named Two Sticks, escorted the delegation to the Keeper's palace. The girl and her Sky Hand escort were seeking an audience with the Morning Star and, as they said at the time, to establish an embassy."

Wind saw the slight narrowing of Smooth Pebble's eyes. "Something about that bothered you?"

"It was the young Sky Hand woman. She was brought in wearing an ankle leash. Clearly a captive. But by the end of the session, she was giving the orders. Her squadron leader clearly had the matting pulled out from beneath him when she asked for permission to open an embassy. My suspicion was that he wanted nothing more than to deliver the girl and head for home."

"Like a man who knew he was delivering an assassin?" Rising Flame asked.

"No, Matron. More like a man who was anxious to be rid of an embarrassment and a problem. If you ask me, the girl wasn't sent here as a gift, but as a punishment."

"For what?"

"The thief reported that she was already married." Smooth Pebble shrugged. "To an Albaamaha."

"Which means?" Wind asked.

Rising Flame told her, "It means that the Sky Hand—especially the Chief Clan—despise the Albaamaha. They've conquered all but a handful of them."

Wind absently chewed on her knuckle as she tried to think it through. "Would have been nice to have known that little fact before we received that Albaamaha embassy, don't you think, Matron? Remember? The one that specifically asked to see Whispering Dawn?"

"Where is this Two Sticks now?" Rising Flame asked.

"I've no idea." Smooth Pebble spread her arms. "Since Blue Heron disappeared, well, most of her spies have been biding their time, unsure of their status, or if they're even needed anymore."

Wind closed her eyes. "That's a fine thing. Half of Cahokia's in a panic. There's no telling what the Houses are doing in the wake of the matron's council; the Morning Star's souls have fled, and his body barely clings to life; an assassin involved in either a Sky Hand or Albaamaha plot is on the loose; the Surveyors' Society is screaming at me for answers about the Quiz Quiz; my sister is abducted; and we're blind as gophers!"

At that moment, Five Fists burst into the room followed by a knot of warriors who half-dragged a young man. The war leader's crooked expression was darker than a thunder cloud, his hand on a war club. At a signal, his warriors tossed the young man to the floor as Smooth Pebble scurried out of the way. Wind recognized him as one of the Albaamaha who had accompanied the embassy.

"Got one of them," Five Fists declared, his scowling glare on the hunched young man on the floor. "He was hiding, keeping watch on that dwelling you assigned them to. Haven't found the others, and the place was empty. Cleaned out. The fire dead and cold."

Wind turned to the young man, perhaps no more than in his late teens. From his expression, he appeared terrified. "Where is the woman called Whispering Dawn?"

The young man blinked at her, wide-eyed.

"He has no Cahokian," Five Fists said. "We're waiting on a translator."

It was Smooth Pebble who stepped forward, bent down, and spoke to the youth. There followed an interchange in the sibilant Muskogean tongue.

Smooth Pebble looked up. "He says his name is Straight Corn, of the Reed Clan, of the forest Albaamaha. He came here to rescue his wife, Whispering Dawn. He says that the Sky Hand high minko, White Water Moccasin, sent his daughter here as punishment for marrying an Albaamaha. That White Water Moccasin wanted her to assassinate the Morning Star. He says that he and his relatives came only to stop the plot and get his wife back. That they have only love for the Morning Star."

The youth interrupted, speaking in a tumble of frantic words.

"He says that we should know that Whispering Dawn is innocent. That she was only doing what her father ordered her to. That the Cahokians should send an army to destroy the Sky Hand in punishment for their crimes."

More babble followed, the young man reaching out plaintively to Wind, eyes fixed on hers, rightly reading that she was the one in charge.

Smooth Pebble said, "He says that if you will pardon Whispering Dawn, that he, personally, as firstborn of the Reed Clan, will act as a guide for our army. He says he knows the back ways whereby we can attack Split Sky City and destroy the high minko and the Chikosi once and for all."

The stream of sibilant words continued, Smooth Pebble translating: "He says that we can keep Whispering Dawn as a hostage until White

Water Moccasin is captured. That of course the lying Chikosi will deny that he has murdered the Morning Star, but that we can ask Whispering Dawn who gave her the little jar of nectar. She will tell us it was her father."

"That's a lie," Five Fists muttered wryly. "I was there when the girl was dressed and married. She arrived with only the clothes she was wearing. I can tell you that no little ceramic jar was in her possession. She never saw her Sky Hand escort again after the wedding feast. They are still sitting, waiting, in that embassy Blue Heron appointed them to. I've had some of my people keeping an eye on them. If they were part of an assassination plot, they'd have slipped away in the night."

"Let's see how he responds to that," Smooth Pebble said, bending down. In a harsh voice, she barked out a string of Muskogean.

For long seconds, Straight Corn averted his eyes, a desperate look on his face. Then he clamped his eyes shut and bent his head forward until his forehead rested on the floor. His broken posture spoke with an eloquence unequaled by words.

Wind asked, "Smooth Pebble? Ask him why the Albaamaha wished the Morning Star dead? Ask him why we shouldn't send an army to exterminate them."

Smooth Pebble again resorted to the harsh tone.

"He says his people are innocent. It was not the Albaamaha, but his uncle and mother who thought up the plot. The two elders with whom you met in this very room. He says that Whispering Dawn is innocent. That the uncle put her up to it. Forced her to do it. That we should let her go and punish him."

"Where are the uncle and mother now?" Five Fists demanded.

"Gone," Smooth Pebble told him when she'd translated. "They left at dusk on the day he says the uncle gave Whispering Dawn the nectar. That they pressed Straight Corn to go with them, but that he loves his wife. That he stayed, hoping she would escape and they could flee together."

"Not very brave, is he?" Five Fists noted with disdain.

"He's trying to save the woman he loves," Rising Flame noted, a finger pressed to her lips.

"What about the Sky Hand embassy?" Wind asked. "Should we round them up, too?"

Five Fists grinned evilly. "That's a lot of squares to fill. That should come as a surprise to them."

"No." Rising Flame continued in her thoughtful pose. "Wouldn't it be better to just question them? Put a guard on them? Hold them in reserve?"

"For what purpose?" Wind asked. "Granted, it doesn't seem like they had a hand in this, but—"

"For leverage," Rising Flame broke in. "Whatever happens to the Morning Star will happen. His souls return, or they don't. He survives, or he dies. But the deed is done. And by the hand of the high minko's daughter. White Water Moccasin may be innocent of any involvement, but the act was committed by a member of his family. A woman he *sent* here."

Five Fists noted, "That makes him responsible as head of his lineage."

"Which means he *owes* us," Wind said, catching on. "Think about it, War Leader. We have colonies all up and down the Tenasee. The Matron's own brother, Fire Light, is building a colony in far-off Cofitachequi. At the same time, just south of the bend of the Tenasee, the Chikosi are rising in both military and political strength and influence. All that lies between them and our southeastern artery is the Tso Nation. Better if we have the Chikosi in our debt than outraged at us because we tortured their innocent warriors to death in revenge for a plot they didn't commission."

"Assuming they didn't," Five Fists countered.

"All the better," Rising Flame said as she studied the now-weeping youth on the floor. "We let them know that we are a just people, and that evidence points to the Reed Clan, and *only* the Reed Clan, of the Albaamaha. Then, if it turns out that the Sky Hand were indeed behind it, our outrage, and their obligation, is even greater. Meanwhile, it is circulated among the Albaamaha clans that we do not hold them responsible as a people—an act for which *they* in turn are grateful. To the Albaamaha, Cahokia is a just and understanding Nation, one to whom they, too, have an obligation."

Wind studied her cousin through slitted eyes. Masterfully done. And from an essential novice, no less.

"What of this thing?" Five Fists flicked his fingers at the groveling youth.

"He gets his very own square across the Avenue from the landing below the Great Staircase," Wind decided. "War Leader, be sure that he lasts a long time. Meanwhile, his uncle Hanging Moss, Wet Clay Woman, and that Albaamaha war chief need to be pursued. They have a lead on us, but four fast war canoes, with our strongest men to paddle in shifts, should overtake them before they reach the portage from the Tenasee into the Black Warrior River system."

"As you order, *Tonka'tzi.*" Five Fists indicated Straight Corn with a nod of the head, and his warriors stepped forward and lifted the stunned youth. Within heartbeats, they were gone.

"Good thinking, Matron. But it shouldn't have gotten this far," Wind mused.

Rising Flame watched her for a moment, lips pursed, then looked at Smooth Pebble. "No word from your master?"

"No, Matron." Smooth Pebble did nothing to hide the fact that she blamed Rising Flame for Blue Heron's situation.

"You had better hope that she hasn't come to harm," Wind said softly. "Because if I find out that your dismissing her caused her to suffer, I will destroy you."

Rising Flame shrugged. "If the Morning Star's Spirit doesn't return to Chunkey Boy's body, it matters not, *Tonka'tzi*. If the Morning Star's Spirit is trapped in the Underworld, no requickening and resurrection will ever be able to call the Spirit to another body. Ever. Cahokia will tear itself apart in days. Mass violence of a scale the earth has never seen. House turning on House, clan on clan, one dirt farmer community upon another, and family upon family."

"I don't want to live long enough to see such a thing."

"Oh, you won't," Rising Flame promised. "We are the ones responsible for the city. When it falls, they will come for us first."

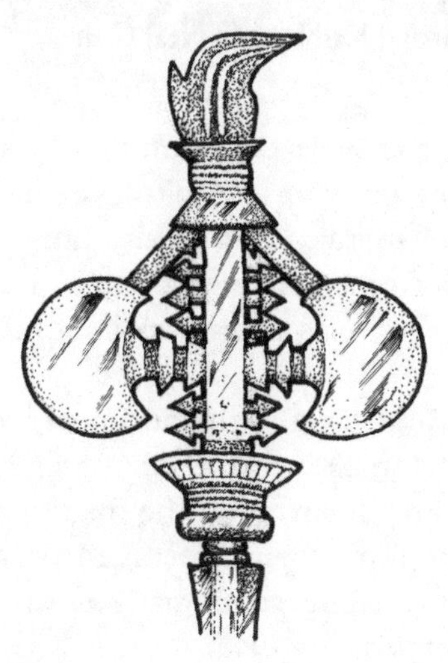

Thirty-eight

Seven Skull Shield carefully shifted his whimpering burden and heaved it over his right shoulder. Not so bad. But for the darkness, he could almost run.

As he eased out of the doorway, he could hear Farts' paws pattering on the hard clay, shishing through the beaten grass.

The two dark forms on either side of the door had a relaxed posture—that of a peaceful repose. And yes, they appeared perfectly comfortable with their backs leaned against the inclined soil that banked the little building's wall. And good thing they'd been there. Not even a flying standard could have marked the location with greater surety.

Seven Skull Shield resettled his load, heard a pained gasp, and started forward. The faintest of gray made a mere suggestion of a glow against the eastern horizon. Not much time.

Nevertheless, innate caution kept him from hurrying, and he let Farts take the lead. Dogs were better in the dark. Still, he'd had plenty of practice feeling his way with his feet.

Do it long enough and a person develops a sense for moving silently.

The web of tree branches barely stood out against the cloud-dark sky as he passed beneath the cottonwoods. They were old trees, protected and nourished for their cotton each spring when they went to seed. Once separated from the seed, the fine cotton-like fibers were spun into delicate thread and crocheted into remarkable and exquisite lace by Cahokian artisans.

Beneath the trees, the little community of four buildings crowded atop a truncated high spot where an old levee had been chopped away by the great river. The surrounding fields, clinging precariously to the edge of the swampy bottoms, had already been harvested.

The *see-ip, see-ip, see-ip* of a robin's call sounded from the darkness ahead.

Farts stopped short, head up in the darkness, ears pricked.

"Hey," Seven Skull Shield whispered under his breath. "We don't have all night." He used a toe to prod the dog forward again.

By following Farts' faint form he stayed on the trail as it wound through the weeds down to the sandy bank of the river.

Again the robin chirped.

"We're here," Seven Skull Shield called in response. Flat Stone Pipe sounded just like the bird.

"I was starting to worry."

"Oh, come on, little man, this is me we're talking about. Had a slight problem to solve. A really tough one."

"How's that?" Flat Stone Pipe's voice asked from the dark bow of a canoe.

"Well, it's hard for me"—he waded into the river and carefully placed his moaning burden in the canoe's middle—"to kill people quietly. It's all I can do to keep from howling, kicking, head-butting, and the like."

"Who'd you kill?" Flat Stone Pipe asked.

"Two Quiz Quiz guards. I figured we owed them anyway.

"How is she?"

Seven Skull Shield shook his head as he pushed the small dugout into the current and hopped into the stern.

"I don't know. She was tense as a board when I got to her. Then she just whimpered and went limp. Hasn't answered a single question. Hasn't even cursed me out for a fool, which really scares me. I figure we're barely in time as it is."

"And what do you think the Quiz Quiz are going to do when they wake up and find her missing?"

"Vendetta, my little friend. They have to hit back."

"I really wish you'd have let me go for some of our warriors."

"Since the last time we had this conversation have you figured out just how you were going to alert them, and still have us follow Winder?"

Seven Skull Shield heard a soft chuckle. "I suppose not, thief."

The dawn was now visible beyond the weeds that marked the high waterline on the river. "We'd better be making time; they're going to be finding my handiwork any moment now."

Grimly Seven Skull Shield drove his paddle into the river, sending them out into the thread of the current. He glanced at the limp bundle. *Come on, Keeper. Tell me you're still alive.*

But what was he going to do about Winder? What did he owe the man who once kept him alive?

He looked back toward the dark bank and knew his old friend would be coming for blood. This had gone from a mere theft to a matter of honor—one that could only end in yet more blood.

Thirty-nine

She's coming around."

The voice slipped into Blue Heron's shattered dreams. As it did, the deep-seated memory of a splitting headache surfaced into the real thing. She swallowed hard. It hurt.

Her mouth was dry, but through it she became aware of the most foul taste: dry bile, sour phlegm, and rancid pus all mixed together.

"Easy," a voice soothed.

Blue Heron managed to pry a dry and aching right eye open—the action painful as her lids dragged over her eyeball. The left barely opened, letting in a slit of light. Everything was blurry.

"Drink, now," the voice told her.

A cup rim was held to her lips, and she sipped at wonderful, cool water. Like an elixir it slipped down her throat and hit her stomach.

She gasped from relief, and whimpered at the spears of pain in her head and chest.

"Easy," the voice told her again. "We don't know how badly you're hurt. Some of the ribs may be broken, and you don't want to move rapidly lest they punch holes in your lungs."

Another voice said, "We've brewed some willow-bark tea mixed with datura. It will help with the pain."

"No datura," she said through a hoarse whisper. "Just the willow-bark tea."

"Of course," the voice agreed.

A warm, wet rag was placed to her eyes. A practiced hand carefully sponged them.

"That better?" the voice asked.

Blue Heron recognized it: Columella.

Blue Heron blinked her good eye, the blur swimming slowly into focus. Sort of. She knew this place: Columella's palace. The Evening Star House matron leaned over her.

"How'd I get here?"

"By canoe," the thief told her as he stepped up to stare over Columella's shoulder. "Figured I needed to get to you soonest, so Flat Stone Pipe and I set ourselves a trap."

"How was that? I was on a dirt floor. Moon temple. Somewhere by the river. Isolated."

"Figured all that out, did you?" Seven Skull Shield asked with a grin. "Well, we didn't have a farting clue. Still, if Winder was going to contact me, there was only one person he'd turn to."

Blue Heron frowned. "Who *is* he?"

She saw the wary tightening behind Seven Skull Shield's eyes. "Later," the thief told her. "What counts is that if he wanted to contact me, he'd go to Wooden Doll. Barely got there in time. Flat Stone Pipe and I hadn't been in that foul old woman's house for a half hand of time before Winder showed up with a couple of them Quiz Quiz."

"What old woman?" Blue Heron asked.

"Old bat that has a house bordering Wooden Doll's. A weaver. She's never really liked me, let alone my singing. But I grow on people once they really get to know me. And it didn't hurt that I gave her a goose-honking big shell to let me knock a hole in her back wall so we could watch Wooden Doll's door."

Seven Skull Shield's expression looked pained. "Can you imagine, Keeper? The old dried-up sheath thought Flat Stone Pipe and me were soul-sick with perversion! Twisted old wreck. After all the time I've spent waiting on Wooden Doll, she should have known I'm up for the doing and not the watching."

"Do you have a point, thief?" Blue Heron managed to whisper. Her souls were floating; it was so hard to concentrate.

He grinned. "You're getting better, Keeper. As long as you're irritated with me, you're healing."

"So . . . I take it Winder came?"

"He did." Seven Skull Shield seated himself on the side of her bed, hands clasped in his lap. "Flat Stone Pipe, Farts, and me, we followed him back to the canoe landing. He and his two Quiz Quiz paddled off north along the river's east bank.

"We stole a canoe and followed. Played like we were fishermen, casting nets, staying just far enough back to keep them in sight. Saw them make shore, and Farts and me sneaked in close just after dark."

"There were guards," Blue Heron whispered before she felt the cup placed to her lips again. She gulped the warm and bitter liquid, recognizing the bite of thickly brewed red willow bark and something else. Too late she realized it had to be datura. Curse them, the potion was going to ease her pain all right—and steal her wits in the process.

"The guards?" Seven Skull Shield grinned. "Now that was a problem. You think it's easy to strangle a man without he wakes up his companion sleeping no more than two paces away?"

She sighed, trying to place it all. "I don't remember. Just a hand coming out of the darkness."

"And you're not going to remember much for a while," Columella told her. "You've got one pupil bigger than the other one. What we could see of it, that is. That happens when your life soul gets knocked out of your head."

"You just kind of went limp and whimpery," Seven Skull Shield told her. "Made it real easy to carry you out of there."

"They wanted a War Medicine box," she said softly. "Said they wanted to Trade me for it. Didn't matter. They were going to kill me. Pay back for what the surveyors did to their war leader."

She saw Seven Skull Shield and Columella exchange glances.

"What?"

"Nothing you need to worry about." Columella said in an obvious lie. "For the moment you need to rest, drink red willow bark tea, and heal."

Even through the thief's grin, she could see his tension.

"Don't lie to me," she whispered. "What's really going on? Who is this Winder? What's this all about? They *stole* the Surveyors' Bundle. We got it back and captured the Quiz Quiz who did it. Of course we hung him in a square. What did he expect? That we'd just slap him on the back for profaning a Sacred Bundle, and wish him well on his journey back to Quiz Quiz?"

"Apparently the Quiz Quiz have other ideas, Keeper," Columella relented. "They wanted to pay you back, and now we've snatched you away from their vengeance. You know how the Nations are down south. This has become a matter of honor for them. A blood vendetta."

"That's insane! A group of Quiz Quiz against the might of Cahokia? When the Morning Star hears about this—"

"He's dead," Seven Skull Shield muttered.

Blue Heron—despite her groggy and numb souls—couldn't quite comprehend. "What do you mean, dead?"

Seven Skull Shield glanced uncertainly at Columella as he offhandedly said, "Or out of his body or some such nonsense. Something about that Sky Hand girl who came to marry him. Turned out she was an Albaamaha assassin."

A sudden spear of panic shot through her. "How's the city taking it?" Visions of riots, of burning buildings and people dead on the Great Plaza filled the eye of her souls.

"Relax," Columella insisted. "Flat Stone Pipe is keeping track of the situation and has runners wearing a rut in the Avenue of the Sun as the updates come in. Word is that the Morning Star's Spirit is in the Underworld and Night Shadow Star is going to get it back."

"She *what?*"

"It's under control," Seven Skull Shield told her, his expression obviously a lie. "And there's nothing you can do about it for the moment anyway. Whispering Dawn got the Morning Star to drink some kind of poisonous nectar."

"Knew that girl was up to no good. They catch her?"

"She's vanished."

"Bloody, dripping pus. What's Wind doing over there? Sleeping?" Spit and blood, could this get any worse?

Seven Skull Shield frowned seriously as he picked at his thumb. "Bet that new matron is figuring out right quick just what a job she walked into."

"And wishing she had Blue Heron back in the Keeper's position," Columella agreed.

"Keeper?" Seven Skull Shield asked. "Who beat you? Was it Winder?"

"No. One of the Quiz Quiz. Winder . . . stopped it. Got mad."

"Well . . ." The thief hesitated. "At least there's that."

"What does Flat Stone Pipe say?" Blue Heron would have made a face against the pain, but it hurt too much. Piss in a pot, her souls were wandering. So cursed hard to form a thought in her head.

"He's leading a party of warriors to the farmstead upriver where you were being held." Columella leaned back and braced her hands. "If Winder has the sense Power gave a rock, he'll have pulled out with the rest of the Quiz Quiz."

"Won't be much trouble to find him," Blue Heron said through a slow exhale to limit the pain in her ribs. A dreamy and floating sensation was filtering in at the edge of the pain.

"I wouldn't bet on that," the thief told her.

"Oh?" she mused as Sister Datura's gentle fingers lifted her away.

"You gotta understand, Keeper," the thief said from somewhere far away, "that if there's anyone in this city as smart as me, it's Winder."

Columella's distant voice asked, "And you think he's still a threat?"

Seven Skull Shield's voice faded as he said, "With Cahokia in chaos and no organized pursuit, he'll be figuring a way to kill the Keeper. And he'll do it if we're not . . ."

But she missed the rest, her souls buoyed and fluttering on Sister Datura's golden wings. She felt herself floating . . . floating . . . And then she was gone.

Forty

Across the wide Father Water—its roiling surface dotted with canoes—Winder could see Lady Columella's high palace were it rose above the clutter of buildings that surrounded Evening Star Town's plaza.

He stood on the levee's slight slope where it overlooked the southern end of the canoe landing. His field of view was hemmed on both sides by walls, as the buildings were packed tightly here, real estate being what it was in River Mounds City. A barely audible curse could be heard from the society house behind him.

Have to deal with that. Things were getting too dangerous just to lose it all on the chance that some passerby might recognize that one of Sky Star's people was speaking in Quiz Quiz. It could precipitate the final disaster of disasters in what was increasingly a desperate venture.

Knotting his fist, Winder watched the muscles bunch and slide under his deeply tanned forearm. The tendons stood out from his wrists, knuckles like white moons above his thick fingers. And even then he continued to tighten his grip until his hand cramped and shook with the effort.

If only that could be Seven Skull Shield's neck that he was squeezing the life out of. It *had* to be Seven Skull Shield. Who else could have slipped in, murdered two veteran warriors, and ghosted away with the old woman? Who else *would* have? Anyone else would have come with a war party—as happened no more than a finger's time after Winder managed to evacuate what was left of Sky Star's war party.

Fortunately the Quiz Quiz were indeed veterans. They knew how to lay low and vanish into the weeds as pursuit passed them by. The only surprise to Winder came with the recognition that the warriors who'd raided the cottonwood farmstead had been dispatched by Evening Star House. He'd recognized the designs on some of the squadron leaders' shields.

Evening Star House? If anything, he would have expected War Duck's River House warriors to be dispatched in pursuit. The high chief of River House could only be counted on for so much.

"Come on, think," Winder told himself.

"Think what?" Sky Star asked as he hobbled up next to Winder. The war leader was healing, his wounds having scabbed up enough to allow him to walk without tearing them open. His arm, however, remained in a sling. Whether the Quiz Quiz war leader considered it fortunate or not, the slashes in his cheeks had disfigured his tattoos beyond recognition, and his telltale pom of hair had been removed along with a round patch of scalp. The bare and blood-clotted skull was now covered by a soft fabric cap.

"I'm trying to figure out how they found us." Winder shot a speculative glance at the war leader. "They had to have someone watching the paid woman's. That's the only explanation. Better yet, it was Skull himself. Were it one of the old woman's spies, they would have gone straight to War Duck and ordered out a war party."

"Two of my warriors are dead!" Sky Star said through gritted teeth.

"They wouldn't have died if they hadn't been asleep," Winder replied angrily. "Nothing else explains how they could have been strangled so easily by one man. You ask me? Given the damage they've caused us, they got off easy."

"My remaining warriors don't like it that the bodies were sunk in the river. They should have been buried with respect on the—"

"Do *not* dare to lecture me about respect," Winder snapped, turning his hot gaze back toward Columella's distant palace. "War Leader, since I brought you here, *every* mistake has been a Quiz Quiz mistake. You let Skull trick you out of the Surveyors' Bundle. You lost the fight that got you captured and the War Medicine Bundle stolen. If you will remember, *I* cut you down from the square and got you back to your warriors. I kidnapped the old woman for you. Took her right out from under Columella's nose. It was *your* warrior who beat her half to death—and if there's a comeuppance for that, it's on *your* shoulders. And finally, it was *your* warriors who were supposed to be on guard and keep the old woman safe."

Winder let his arms slap futilely to his sides. "So now we're right back where we started. Without even the leverage to bargain for the War Medicine, and with the Four Winds Clan fully aware that their Keeper has been beaten bloody by a Quiz Quiz who held her captive."

"You were the one who was followed from the paid woman's," Sky Star retorted, his voice slightly slurred because of the missing teeth knocked out by the surveyors who'd tortured him.

"Maybe." Winder shrugged. "Among other reasons, it was against that possibility that I detailed those guards, which, if you will recall, *you* argued against."

Sky Star's eyes narrowed into an angry glint. "I should send you packing for your arrogant tone. It was *you* who were supposed to keep us from trouble in Cahokia."

Winder made a *tsk*ing sound with his lips. "Fine with me. Hand me my Trade, and I shall be gone with the current."

"We don't have the Bundle."

"You *had* the Bundle. You *lost* it." Winder looked around, indicating the closely packed buildings. "So, what are you going to do when I'm gone? What's your next move?"

Sky Star deflated like a punctured fish bladder. "You are right. Save us, Winder. Figure some way to get our War Medicine box back, and I shall give you all that I own. Otherwise all I have to look forward to is shame."

Winder felt crawly down in his guts. He should leave. Take the opportunity to cut his losses and move on. But Sky Star was a rich man, his lineage prominent among the Quiz Quiz.

If I can manage to salvage some semblance of success out of this incredible mess, I can name my price. I'll be the most famous Trader on the river.

As he turned his attention back to Evening Star Town and Columella's palace, his breast warmed with renewed anger.

Rot take you, Skull, you're the only thing standing between me and the greatest triumph of my life!

So, how did he pay his old friend back?

Striking at Wooden Doll would be the easiest. But she, apparently, wasn't nearly the weakness she'd once been for Skull. For all he knew, they barely spoke.

No, it was the Keeper now: Skull's pathway to respectability, prestige, and status. That's who he had to strike at—even if the old woman was locked away in the Evening Star House palace.

And the turmoil—if the rumors were true and the Morning Star was dying—might give him the freedom to do so. In fact, it might give him the opportunity to snatch an even greater prize than the Surveyors' Bundle during the ensuing chaos.

"War Leader? I think I have a plan."

"I would expect no less from you, Trader." Sky Star tried to smile, but it obviously hurt too much for his wounded lips.

Forty-one

Night Shadow Star walked out from the camp, which had been set up just outside of a small community. A mere collection of farmsteads and Trading booths, the place stood on a high terrace above the murky waters of the River of the Northwest. She heard Fire Cat as he walked out into the night behind her and took up a position a step back from her right shoulder.

It had taken two days to reach this point: a day to reach and assemble the flotilla of fifteen canoes at River Mounds City, and another to paddle up the Father Water to its confluence with the great River of the Northwest, then east to the sluggish tributary on the north bank commonly called Cave Creek, which marked the access to the uplands.

They had reached Cave Creek just at dusk, paddling along its channel until the heavy war canoes began to ground. One by one the warriors had carried the craft up onto the terraced flat below where the creek emerged from broken sandstone uplands. Here a small community of farmsteads catered to pilgrims, offering them food, items of Trade, and lodging.

Just beyond the little settlement, her escorting warriors had laid out a fortified camp, cooks immediately pitching in to build fires and unpack cooking pots, dried corn, and hickory oil to make stew.

War Leader War Claw had orchestrated the entire thing—not missing a beat in seeing to Night Shadow Star's comfort, even to the point of setting up a shelter for her.

Now, having eaten and ordered the guards to stand to, she had walked out to stare up at the irregular and forested hills that rose like a rumpled black mass in the night.

Crickets, night birds, and frogs chirped an irregular symphony, and wings hummed somewhere off to her left as she looked up at the starlit sky, its constellations pointing toward the North Star.

Cool air flowed down Cave Creek's valley, bathing her face and barely teasing her hair.

Stilling her souls, she could feel the Power. There. Just up past the mouth of the shallow valley. Voices whispered in the dark air around her, sibilant, mostly unintelligible—only the occasional word or phrase distinguishable. Phantoms of shadow flickered at the edge of her vision.

The Spirits were active this night. Faint laughter carried down from the stars above, issued from a hollow and nonhuman voice.

This was a holy place, ancient. Guarded by Power.

Tomorrow they would follow the pilgrims' trail up the valley to where the Cave Watchers' Society had their society house beside an ancient spring. Dedicated and small, the Watchers' Society subsisted on the offerings of those seeking the cave—and allowed only those who possessed the authority or Power required to enter the portal.

It was a journey not to be made lightly, for as one of the most sacred entrances to the Underworld, it was guarded by Horned Serpent himself, and Piasa was known to stalk its dark depths.

Some said the cave served as Old-Woman-Who-Never-Dies' vagina—the very route from which First Man had entered the world after Creation. That from here had come Corn Woman, who gave birth to the Hero Twins: the Morning Star and Thrown-Away Boy.

But more than that, it was up this portal that the Morning Star was said to have carried his father's head after defeating the Giants in that most deadly game of chunkey. According to legend, it was here—in this cave—that the Morning Star had brought his father, First Man, back to life.

She inhaled deeply of the night, smelling the dry scents of grass and early autumn forest carried down from the uplands.

"I can feel your worry," Fire Cat said from behind her.

"I was here once before. As a child. It was required of us. Part of our education as the heirs of the Morning Star House."

She tried to keep the tension from her voice.

"And?" Fire Cat asked softly.

"I was scared to death." She rubbed the backs of her arms, as if to fight goose bumps. "The priests tell terrible stories about the darkness; about Horned Serpent guarding the mouth of the cave; about the foolish people, the unworthy ones, who wander in without protection and are eaten by the monsters."

She laughed humorlessly. "After having been devoured by Piasa, that holds nowhere near the terror it once did. Ironic, isn't it? This place scared me down to my bones, and now I come back, a creature of the Underworld, a servant to one of its most terrifying lords."

"I've heard the stories." Fire Cat stepped close behind her shoulder, following her gaze toward the dark valley. "I never really thought I'd ever be here, in this place."

"What if I can't find him?"

"You will."

"What if I can't save him?"

"If Chunkey Boy's souls are in the Underworld, Piasa will lead you to them."

She smiled warily as an image tried to form out of the night, only to flicker into nothingness. The visions were worse than normal. What would it be like tomorrow, down in the darkness, once again in that place that had frightened her to the point of tears?

"Chunkey Boy? You still cannot believe, can you?"

"My beliefs do not matter. Whatever is required of me tomorrow, I shall stand behind you."

"Fire Cat?" She shook her head. "I should do this alone."

"I have sworn to—"

"You don't understand. I've *been there.* In that cave. This isn't a Spirit Dream. It's an opening to the Underworld. It is guarded by Horned Serpent . . . and believe me, he is not to be trifled with. Piasa prowls the darkness on his taloned feet. Images are drawn on the walls, and while at first they appear as drawings, they act as links to the Spirit itself. The drawing can be inhabited by Horned Serpent. One instant you perceive a picture of black on stone. The next it thickens, shifts, and molds itself around the Spirit Beast, giving the creature form and substance. Before you can scream you are in those terrible jaws."

She blinked, seeing the teeth, smelling Piasa's foul breath. "They close around your head in a flash; the teeth, like spikes, rip along your scalp."

Her hands were clenched. "It's the snapping and crushing of your skull that's the worst. You *feel* it and *hear* it as the bone breaks. Then the pain slices through your head. Blasting pillars of agony that sear through you like white fire . . ."

She fought for breath, the memory paralyzing, her heart pounding.

"I was chosen, Lady." His firm words poured through her trembling souls like a tonic. "It was Piasa, after all, who ordered you to cut me down that night. Later, I saw his blue haze in the river that day I pulled you back into this world. He let you talk to me while your souls were in the Underworld."

His tone turned wry. "No Underworld Spirit Beast will devour me as long as I am faithfully standing at your side. That, you see, is what determines if I am worthy or not."

At the courage in his voice, her panic receded. "It will not be like fighting Tula or Itza warriors. What I have to do, it will be in black darkness, surrounded by the souls of the Dead. There will be nothing for you to fight, Fire Cat. No physical enemies to slay."

"Then I shall be bored, Lady."

She turned then, studying his night-black face. "Have you no fear of what we're about to do?"

She could just make out his faint smile before he said, "Actually going *into* the Underworld? It frightens me to my bones, Lady. On the other hand, if I am devoured by a monster in the Underworld it will be a fate preferable to having to live in the same house where you are married to Spotted Wrist."

At the tone in his voice, the last of her fear drained away. Clasping him close, she laid her face in the angle of his neck and laughed away the last of her panic.

After all, if they survived this, Spotted Wrist would be waiting.

Yes, she could face anything with Fire Cat behind her.

Out in the darkness, Piasa chuckled maniacally.

Forty-two

On the high corner of Columella's palace mound, where it rose above Evening Star Town, Seven Skull Shield stood with his thumbs tucked into his rope belt. The heights gave him a good view of the wide river, the canoe landing, River Mounds City, Marsh Elder Lake, and the clustered buildings around the Avenue of the Sun as it made its way east toward the Morning Star's mound.

He wondered how Blue Heron was doing. She had taken a turn for the worse, her souls having fled her body. Perhaps the bruises and broken bones had been too much for her to bear for the time being. Just the sight of her wounds enraged him.

The man who had inflicted that hurt was out there. Somewhere. Hiding.

The entire city might have taken a pause, its termite-hive activity slowed to a crawl. The effect was as if the whole of it was holding its breath, waiting, unsure. Word of the Morning Star's state had spread to even the lowliest of dirt farmers. People by the thousands were flocking to the temples, making offerings to Old-Woman-Who-Never-Dies, or to the Morning Star himself. A sense of near-panic hung like a low cloud over the city.

Flat Stone Pipe's spies had been trickling in all day. Word was that thousands had gathered in the Great Plaza—heedless of the chunkey courts, blocking the avenues with their throngs, surrounding the great mound. They stood, faces lifted toward the high palace where the living god's human body lay at the edge of life.

Word had also come that Night Shadow Star had been dispatched to bring the Morning Star's Spirit back to Chunkey Boy's host body. However *that* worked.

Seven Skull Shield made a face. He had actually watched her flotilla of canoes as it pulled out from the canoe landing and paddled north. If the stories were true she was going to the resurrection cave—the place where legend said that the Morning Star had brought his father's head back to life in the Beginning Times. There Night Shadow Star would descend into the Underworld and bring the living god home.

"Best of luck with that, Lady," he whispered, sending a small prayer her way. Without a doubt, she was one of the spookiest people he'd ever known, but she'd stood up for him—and done it at a time when she shouldn't have had a thought in the world but for herself.

That kind of character deserved loyalty.

He narrowed an eye, returning his attention to the long sprawl of River Mounds City, where its buildings clustered atop the high ground along the old levee.

He couldn't get Blue Heron's battered face out of his thoughts. The facial bruises had mostly turned purple, as had her swollen-closed eye. The black-and-blue ribs, the scabs where ropes had cut into her wrists and ankles, and the wheezing that came with each of her labored breaths hung full and heavy in his souls.

Of course Flat Stone Pipe's warriors had found nothing when they raided the farmstead where Blue Heron had been held. Winder was much too quick for that.

"So where are you, old friend?" Seven Skull Shield carefully studied the city across the river. As his gaze searched, he pictured the warehouses, the narrow passages, the workshops, society houses, and temples. Where would Winder seek to hide?

During Walking Smoke's terror, the exiled lord had rented warehouses on both sides of the river to conceal his Tula warriors and captives. Even then the fiend had needed inside help from Columella's brother to get away with it. Did Winder have such an ally in War Duck's House?

"You think that's where they are hiding?" Flat Stone Pipe's voice surprised Seven Skull Shield.

He looked down to where the dwarf had appeared beside his right leg. "Good work, little man. You can move silently when you want to."

"When one's legs are as short as mine, one learns alternatives to running. Stealth and small stature seem to be amicable companions."

"How's the Keeper?"

"Still unconscious. My lady is worried. Blue Heron's souls should have returned to her by now. We've considered sending her to Rides-the-Lightning, but he's busy with the Morning Star."

"If she dies . . ." Seven Skull Shield knotted a fist as he studied the vista. Well, it would tear something apart deep down inside him. Hard to believe that she'd become so dear to him, as different as they were from each other.

The little man, too, was staring fixedly at River Mounds City's sinuous sprawl. "You think he's there?"

"I do." Seven Skull Shield rubbed his jaw. "Winder told me he'd become an influential Trader. Said he had wives all over on the southern rivers. He was obviously famous enough to be hired by the Quiz Quiz as the person to help pull off their most daring exploit. And he almost did it. Would have but for a chance remark that took me to a frustrated woman."

"I've seen you hung in a square, seen you emerge from fire and smoke and death. But I've never seen you look so grim," Flat Stone Pipe observed, and tilted his head to indicate the palace. "It's a wonder the beating didn't kill her outright."

Seven Skull Shield nodded and ground his jaws. "She said it wasn't Winder—that he stopped it. But what's bothersome is that he allowed it to happen in the first place."

The little man gave him a grin. "You care for her. Most don't."

"Let's just say that the Keeper is an acquired taste. Curious as it may seem, we actually see eye to eye on a lot of things."

"What about this Winder? You've been closemouthed about him."

"Think of him like my older brother. Always the smart one, the fast one. He took care of me the way an older brother does. Kept the other boys from ganging up on me. Made sure I had something to eat, even if it meant he went short. He was there to share his blanket when we were sleeping in the snow."

Seven Skull Shield smiled wistfully. "People don't think of orphans in Cahokia. Everything is clan, lineage, and family. With no one to speak for us, protect us, or feed us, we rely on each other." He paused. "Make our own rules, laws, and ways."

"It's a miracle you weren't whacked in the head."

"We were fair game, all right. Some of those we ran with met that very end. More than once it was just dumb luck that saved us. Had we been anywhere but Cahokia . . ."

He shook his head, remembering the times they'd careened through the back ways, running flat out from angry men with clubs. Theft—even of a few morsels of food—was a killing offense. But he and Winder, they'd known the holes, the gaps, and dark recesses where two desperate boys could dodge and hide.

"When River Mounds got too dangerous, we'd scurry over to Horned Serpent Town. As soon as the people there started to get wise, we'd slip up to Morning Star House and lift things from Traders around the Grand Plaza. When word began to circulate there, it was up to Serpent Woman Town. When that went bad we'd finagle a way to Evening Star Town, and by the time they started hunting us, we'd cage a ride back across the river to the canoe landing and start all over."

He couldn't help but grin. "Winder really was the sharp one. It was his idea to paint different clan markings on our cheeks after a successful robbery. Taught me how to change my hair. You should have seen the sparkle in his eyes when we'd lift a nice piece, or the feeling of victory when we passed ourselves off as people we weren't."

"Best of friends?"

"Inseparable." Seven Skull Shield chuckled at the memory. "He and I shared our souls, our hopes, our dreams. I remember how his face would light up as he talked about the grand things we would do. We were both going to be chiefs, marry beautiful women, found our own clans."

Seven Skull Shield paused. "Funny thing is, he actually succeeded. Became a rich Trader. A man with a lot of wives scattered across the Nations, which is as good as founding his clan. He's wealthy, respected."

And what have I become?

A sensation of loneliness grew in his breast. Nothing had really changed for him, had it? He was still a man without family—a homeless vagabond drifting from bed to bed.

In those days, he and Winder were family. Each was willing to sacrifice himself for the other. "How did we lose ourselves?" he asked the wind.

A vision of Wooden Doll's smile, of her warm body as she extended her arms to enfold him in a hug, filled the eye of his souls.

I fell in love.

Again he saw that last day as Winder's canoe pushed out from the shore. Winder stood in the bow, shouting across the years, *"You sure she's worth it?"*

What would have been different if, at the last moment, Seven Skull Shield had called, *"Wait! I'm going with you!"*

Instead he'd waved, feeling as if his heart were breaking. After watching Winder's canoe disappear downriver, he'd walked back to the dwelling he'd vowed to share with Wooden Doll. There, in those walls, "forever" had lasted less than a moon.

"I can sense your melancholy, thief." Flat Stone Pipe reached out to slap Seven Skull Shield on the thigh. "Time changes people. . . . Alliances shift."

"He's my best friend, little man."

"Look at me, thief."

Seven Skull Shield glanced down to see the dwarf's earnest expression as the little man said, "He might *have been* your best friend. A man like a brother to you. Once. You also told me that you met him in front of the Surveyors' Society House . . . that you explained to him that the Quiz Quiz was not to be touched." A pause. "And he freed the captive despite that."

"It was his obligation."

"Would he have acted in such a contrary manner to your interests when you were youths? Ah, I can see the answer in your eyes. He would not. And had the roles been reversed? If *he* had asked *you* not to interfere with his business, would you have gone ahead and disregarded his wishes?"

"No."

"Then do not blame yourself, Seven Skull Shield. He is no longer worthy of your friendship. A true friend is someone who will do for you what you, in turn, would do for them."

"Perhaps. Doesn't make it any easier, knowing I have to hunt him down. Don't know what I'll do if it comes down to a decision between catching him, and watching him hang in a square."

"The debts of the past are now weighed against the faith of those who depend upon you in the present. I don't envy you the choice, my friend."

"You call me friend?" Seven Skull Shield whispered. "Someone who will do for you what you will do for them? Or is it more? Or perhaps less? What does that word really mean, little man?"

"A great many things, thief. If you ever figure it out, let me know. I've wondered about it myself."

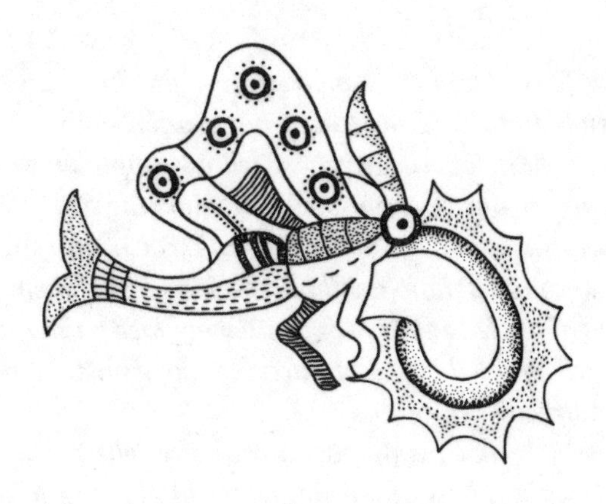

Fugitive

I wonder if there is any greater terror than to be a young woman alone. Especially in Cahokia with its masses of people. I am faceless. Without title or authority. I am not High Minko White Water Moccasin's daughter, born of the Chief Clan of the Sky Hand Muskogee. I am not the Morning Star's wife. To claim either of the above is a death sentence.

My only worth, I am quick to discover, is what my body can provide in the way of labor or sex. That revelation is gut wrenching. Inconceivable.

Unmarried young women without families are either slaves or bound servants. There is no other role for them. They have no rights and exist only for the labor they provide hauling water, fetching firewood, hoeing or harvesting crops, cooking, and doing household chores. Or to pleasure and warm a man in his bed.

This becomes startlingly obvious to me just walking along the edges of the canoe landing. The comments and calls are rude. Jarring and vile to a woman of my chaste upbringing.

If I am anything, however, it's a quick learner. I have mixed charcoal with grease to paint a Bear Clan design on my cheeks, having heard that they are least numerous of the Cahokian Earth Clans. I have abandoned my braid for the Bear Clan's twisted bun and have turned my skirt inside out to hide its telltale pattern.

My pack, along with the wealth I stole, is now crammed with old rags to make it look like a heavy burden. If anyone tries to approach me, I wave them off, muttering "I'm busy," or "No," some of the few Cahokian phrases I know. Then I stride off, back bent under the pack like I have a purpose.

I have been up and down the canoe landing for three days now. But for a loaf of bread I stole from a farmstead, I have eaten nothing. There are warriors everywhere. I have overheard them telling people they are looking for a Muskogee woman, the one who poisoned the Morning Star.

Though my heart is pounding each time, and fear nearly strangles the breath in my lungs, I make myself march within a pebble's toss of them. I keep my head bent at just the right angle so that they can see my face paint, give them a slight nod, and steadfastly proceed as if I'm hurrying along on clan business.

So far it has worked.

My stomach growls as I tramp past a cook fire where fish and a turtle are roasting over the coals. The smell brings water to my mouth and lingers like a fitful dream in my nostrils.

I dare not glance sideways lest someone see the wistful look in my eyes. A look that will betray me as an imposter and spark questions about who I really am.

I hear voices rise in Muskogean as I march along just up from the beach. These are Kaskinampo Traders from just north of the great bend of the Tenasee River. We passed through their territory when Strong Mussel brought me here.

I hesitate, wondering if I dare approach them, try and bargain passage using one of the remarkable items I stole from the Morning Star's room. As I am eyeing them, one glances my way, shooting me a lascivious grin. His hands fly in Trader sign language to ask if I would lay with him for a sack of freshwater mussels.

I shoot him a look of disgust, muttering "No" in Cahokian, and plod on in my search for Straight Corn, Hanging Moss, or Wet Clay Woman. The only hope that buoys me is that they have to come here eventually. That they haven't already been caught. Or worse, have fled.

That, or I will see Strong Mussel or Cloud Tassel or my father's warriors and beg them to take me away from this place. Yes, it is a measure of my desperation that I am willing to return to Split Sky City and swear on the bones of my ancestors that I will never disobey again.

To my dismay, I have no idea as to the fates of either my Albaamaha or the Sky Hand. It might be the talk of the Cahokians surrounding me that they are all hanging in squares, dying, and I wouldn't have a clue.

I plod around a huge raft of logs that have been floated downriver and laboriously dragged up on the beach. A crew of men swarm over it, some with the huge hafted splitting mauls used to create planks and rails. These are giant, hafted, ground-stone axes that take two men to raise and swing. With a precise hit they will split the grain, allowing hardwood wedges to be driven in to widen the gap. Then the ponderous ax is lifted again, driven down forcefully, and the process repeated until a plank pops free.

My attention is so fixed on the process I actually jump as someone matches my step.

"You've given me quite a chase, girl," Two Sticks says as he nonchalantly gazes at the woodcutters. "The entire city is looking for you, and here you are, parading right through the middle of the canoe landing, passing yourself off as a Bear Clan woman."

"Where is Hanging Moss? And what about Straight Corn?"

"Gone."

"Where?"

"Home, I assume. The moment I heard that you'd poisoned the Morning Star, I hurried to their so-called embassy and found the place empty."

"They wouldn't *have left me!"*

"It appears that they did. The same with your companionable and stiff-necked Sky Hand war leader and his stalwart party of invincible warriors. After a talk with Five Fists, they too took flight like a covey of finches before a sharp-shinned hawk."

"Then why are their canoes still here?" I jerk a thumb back upstream to where I've passed and repassed the beached vessels for the last three days.

"Because, thoughtful and crafty as your witless war leader is, he took a Quigualtam Trader's cypress canoe instead. From what I overheard, they were worried that the Cahokians might have changed their minds and put a guard on their boats."

Two Sticks gives me a smug smile. "Your war leader was never really very comfortable in Cahokia. And when word came that you'd been off to the Albaamaha to 'broker a peace,' he was already on edge. Then Five Fists and his warriors paid them a visit. After that, well, I don't know how fast they made the run from the Great Plaza to the canoe landing, but I'm sure that not even a motivated cougar could have beaten them here."

"You're telling me that Straight Corn, my husband, also abandoned me?"

"Lady, do you think he or any of the rest of them are fools?"

"He's my husband*! I love him! He loves me!"*

"I'm sure his heart is torn in two over it. He's no doubt staring back north with each stroke of the paddle as he heads home. I suspect that guilt will entangle itself with insufferable grief for the rest of his life as he honors the sacrifice you made for our people—and how you did it out of selfless love. You'll be a hero for as long as he lives, which I suspect won't be long."

I have stopped short, staring at him in disbelief. My heart is hammering like a pot drum in my chest. A sick feeling has pulled tight in the pit of my stomach.

"But he . . . loves me." My voice sounds timid and frail. My knees have gone weak.

Two Sticks shrugs. "He loves his family most. And beyond Hanging Moss and Wet Clay Woman, his love is for his people. I am sure that you filled his heart with delight and that special bond a man feels for his first woman."

"You talk as if I'm gone from his life!"

Two Sticks looks at me as if I'm an idiot. "You are, woman. Muck and rot, do you think he could ever *take the woman who poisoned the Morning Star back into his household? Yes, you would bring renown, but so, too, will come Cahokian wrath. It has to. Do you think they can allow the woman who poisoned the living god to go unpunished? As it is, your father, the good high minko, is going to be quivering in his boots when it is discovered that* his *daughter murdered the living god!"*

The sick feeling intensifies; a welling emptiness is sucking at my souls, causing my vision to fade. I feel tears leaking down my cheeks.

They abandoned me?

I try to speak, but words do not come.

"What will happen to me?" I finally manage between sobs.

"That is up to you." His voice has a sharper tone.

"Me?"

He glances around at the busy canoe landing. "To be caught sheltering you? It would be a death sentence."

"We could leave. Just you and me."

"And go where?" He spreads his muscular arms. "This is my world. Here I am a rich man. And no one is hunting me. I have a fine house, plenty to eat, Trade, and a life of leisure. I know Cahokia's back ways, how to stay out of sight if I have to. Why should I leave when I'm happy here?"

"But what about me?"

He studies me through half-slitted eyes. "I imagine it will be the square. Like I said, they will have to make an example of you. A most painful and drawn-out example. Probably stretch it so it takes days for you to die. Saw it once. Young girl like you. They made a slit in her belly. Pulled out a knuckle's length of intestine every day. Just left it hanging out to dry and draw flies. She lasted most of a moon. The agony was so terrible I saw blooded warriors crying in—"

"You have to get me away! I'll give you anything!"

He studies me as if from a distance, as if considering very carefully. His voice lowers as he says, "Like I told you, it would be a death sentence."

"I have Trade!" I cry, knotting my fists. "Here. In the pack. Things I took from the Morning Star's room."

He inclines his head to where a couple of Four Winds Clan warriors are walking along, shields hung over their backs, bows unstrung and armor loose. They are a stone's throw away, inspecting a canoe-load full of freshwater clams and mussels that are being unloaded into baskets.

"They're looking for a Sky Hand noble, you know. All it takes is a word, the slightest gesture, and they'll have you."

I close my eyes, swaying in desperation. "I know."

"Were I to accept the risk? What would be in it for me?"

"Like I said, I have Trade—"

"I have *Trade of my own." He shrugs, an amused smile on his lips. "What else do you offer?"*

"Anything. I'd do—"

"Anything?"

I nod.

"Cook? Clean? Serve me?" He pauses, lowering his voice. "Share my bed? The Morning Star was said to be a magnificent lover. Were you to show me? Do to me the things he did for you?"

I stare at him in dismay, aware my mouth is hanging open.

"No?" He sighs and turns, stepping away. "Then I'm afraid you wouldn't be worth the risk."

I swallow hard, fully aware of the Four Winds Warriors as they leave the clam Trader and continue their patrol of the canoe landing.

What is my life worth? What would I do to save myself from the square?

"Wait!" I hurry to catch up with Two Sticks. "I'll cook and clean and mend. Wouldn't that be enough?"

He gives me a sidelong glance. "Everything . . . or nothing, Whispering Dawn. It's me"—he tilts his head in the direction of the warriors—"or them."

The sick sensation inside me expands, hollowing out the last of me. I am empty. Betrayed.

Aloud I say, "I don't have any choice, do I?"

"There's always the square."

I close my eyes, draw my last breath as a free woman. "All right."

But what happens when he finally tires of me? When he thinks I have taught him what the Morning Star taught me?

How long before he turns me over for the reward?

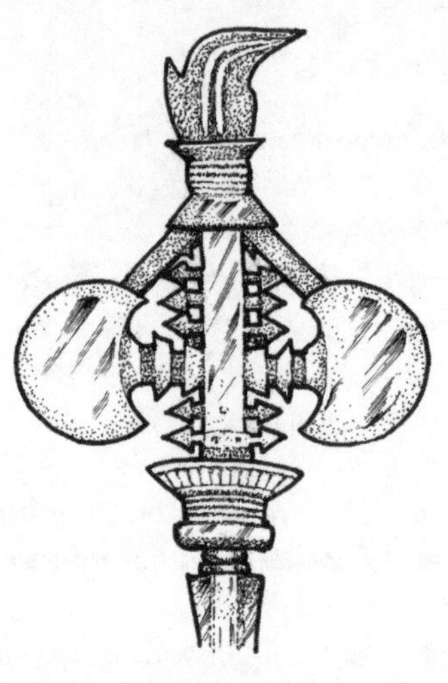

Forty-three

The night had a chill; the bite in the breeze blowing in off the river reminded a person that winter lurked somewhere up over the northern horizon. And if, on sunny and warm days, any doubt cropped up, there were always the endless *V*s of ducks, geese, herons, cranes, and other waterfowl following the Father Water south.

At times the migrating flocks were so dense they appeared as a brown smudge, like a wave rolling south through the sky, their cries like chiming music in the air.

Seven Skull Shield considered this as he wound his way through the densely packed warehouses and ambled up to Crazy Frog's large fire. Around it sat the nightly ranks of chunkey players, the fancy professionals upon whom Crazy Frog showered his favors—especially if they'd made him a small fortune in winnings that day.

Their women sat behind them, shoulder to shoulder, as they giggled and shared gossip. Mostly slaves, they were nevertheless decked out in the finest of garments and feathers, their faces painted in patterns and colors similar to that of their men.

At the sight of them, Seven Skull Shield sighed. All were young, voluptuous, healthy, and possessed of the arts that made them worth not only the price the players paid, but the cost to keep them. None, Seven Skull Shield reflected, had been chosen for their clever heads, quick wit, and engaging conversation, or deep philosophical reflections.

All eyes were on his arrival as he grinned and held his hands out to the flames. "Bit chilly tonight."

"Thief? What are you doing here?"

He turned at the sharp query and found Mother Otter standing in the doorway to Crazy Frog's large dwelling. Several of the younger wives had stopped short at the tone in her voice and now looked Seven Skull Shield's way with slight dismay.

"First and foremost, Mother Otter, I was wondering if I might finally entice you to run off with me. Maybe head off downriver. Find a chieftainship in need of new leadership and found a clan that would rival Cahokia itself. Of course, it's the *making* of that clan, and the wonders that would entail, that fills my imagination with anticipation."

She closed her eyes and shook her head. The chunkey players watched with subtly amused expressions as they picked at their plates or paused to drink from ceramic or shell cups.

"I'd take that detestable beast trotting at your heels into my bed before I'd let you so much as step through my doorway. And before I'd let *that* happen, I'd rather be chopped into pieces and thrown into the river to be devoured by Underwater Panther. And before that, I'd sell myself to foreign Traders to be Traded off to distant savages as a pack animal. Any and all of those disgusting possibilities are imminently preferable to even sharing the same side of the river with you." She gestured with a horn spoon. "Or is the subtlety of that too much for your wooden wit to surround?"

Chuckles of laughter rose from the players.

"You always remain my favorite, Mother. You'll come around."

"He's around back," she said stiffly. "And if I'd known you were coming, I would have bribed a clam diver to haul you out into the river and tie you to a rock on the bottom. No matter what it did to the fish."

"And I love you, too, dear woman," he replied with a touch to the forehead.

"Oh, and try not to touch anything," she called as he started around the house. "I know you'd steal the grain out of the wood in the ramada poles if you could, and I don't want to have to sand off the dirty fingerprints where you tried."

This was greeted by a series of guffaws from the feasting players.

Seven Skull Shield made his way around the side of the house and along the narrow passage to the cul-de-sac blocked by Crazy Frog's storage house. The place was a stronghold, with hard-plastered, double-thick log walls where Crazy Frog kept his wealth. Normally at least two guards—always blooded warriors—were lounging about the structure.

One of them now stepped out of the darkness and asked, "Who comes?"

"Seven Skull Shield to see Crazy Frog."

"A moment." The shadowy figure seemed to merge with the door. The wait was longer than usual, and Seven Skull Shield looked down at Farts, saying, "Must have caught him in the middle of counting his clam shells."

Despite the darkness Seven Skull Shield could see the wag of Farts' tail in reply.

The dark form emerged from the door, saying, "He will see you, thief."

To the dog, Seven Skull Shield said, "You stay and keep this warrior company. If any Quiz Quiz attack, grab 'em by the throat."

Farts uttered a soft whine.

Chuckling, the warrior led the way, opening the wooden plank door and allowing Seven Skull Shield into the fabric-draped entry. Pushing the thick fabric aside, he stepped into the warm yellow glow of an oil-lamp-lit room piled with boxes; baskets; huge ceramic storage jars; folded and stacked fabrics; sacks of corn, beans, and squash; and just about every sort of wealth.

A lot of it was ill-gotten gains Crazy Frog skimmed from the riffraff that preyed on the canoe landing. A goodly portion came from services the gambler's men provided for Traders, including guiding, packing, and transportation of goods. More came from Crazy Frog's share in Trading ventures; he often outfitted Traders with goods and demanded a share of the profits. The rest, however, came from the man's obsession with chunkey.

The gambler was seated on an ornate litter perched atop stacked storage boxes. The thing was draped with buffalo winter hides tanned hair-on. Turkeys in full display had been carved into the box's sides along with corn plants, all inlaid with freshwater pearls.

"Won it from an Earth Clans chief from one of the colonies down on the Tenasee," Crazy Frog said as Seven Skull Shield eyed the thing. "Took two canoes strapped side by side—and frustrated his warriors half to death—to get it here so the good chief could impress us with his largess and status. He also brought a local chunkey champion to humble us with his remarkable skill. Some nephew, I believe. Not only was the nephew anything but humbling, but the good chief's faith in his champion's invincibility led him to bet most unwisely."

"What a pity," Seven Skull Shield replied, giving a nod of recognition to the inside guard before stepping over to finger the intricately carved wood.

"Yes." Crazy Frog was watching him through half-lidded eyes. "A great many pities are suddenly floating to the surface in Cahokia. The Morning Star lies moribund, his souls in the Underworld. The city is being turned on its head as warriors search for his assassin—reportedly a mere slip of a Muskogee girl. We learn that the Keeper, though freshly rescued, has been dismissed from her longtime position by the new Four Winds matron. And in the midst of all this chaos comes word that these troublesome Quiz Quiz are in search of their Nation's War Medicine Bundle. A Bundle which no one seems to have seen or admitted to having, and which apparently vanished at the same time you captured War Leader Sky Star."

Seven Skull Shield spread his hands wide. "It does seem like everything's fallen apart all at once, doesn't it? Sort of like snapping timbers in a new construction. One beam breaks, which causes another to collapse, which causes another, and within moments the whole framework has come crashing down."

Crazy Frog watched him through suspicious eyes. "If whoever took that War Medicine Bundle could go back, I wonder if they'd have taken it, knowing how much trouble they'd be unleashing?"

"Don't know," Seven Skull Shield told him and shrugged. "But so much for Medicine Bundles, fascinating and valuable though they might be. I'm here looking for Winder. My suspicion, given your knowledge of the Trade and Traders, is that you've had dealings with him in the past."

"He might have come to my attention a time or two. Hear that he's rather prominent among the lower river Nations. A man of considerable reputation. Imagine my surprise to discover that he was actually from Cahokia. An orphan. One who scratched out a living as an urchin, miscreant, and one-time boon companion to another well-known Cahokian thief."

"Wonder where he is?" Seven Skull Shield asked offhandedly. "I'd like to look my old friend up. Reminisce over old times."

"That I cannot tell you."

"Can't or won't?"

"Can't." Crazy Frog touched the tips of his fingers together, making a tent of his hands. "Though given recent events, and the activities of important persons, I'm not sure I'd tell even if I knew."

"Why's that?"

"Thief, all of Cahokia is in chaos. The living god is on the verge of death, a new matron is stirring things up, Night Shadow Star is off to the Underworld, and Blue Heron is no longer Keeper. I hear that she is barely clinging to life as it is. Depending on how this all works out, your position among the Four Winds elite may no longer have value."

"And there is no substitute for value."

Crazy Frog shrugged. "Consider it fair warning. The world is what it is, thief. I have survived this long by wits and being quick on my feet when it comes to the shifting sands of politics."

He paused. "Fortunately for you, your trouble with Winder hasn't run afoul of that eventuality. One of my people, however, did mention seeing someone meeting his description climbing the steps to War Duck's palace at around midday. Was it really him? I don't know. If, however, he's hiding the Quiz Quiz in River Mounds City, it's because War Duck finds it to his interest."

Seven Skull Shield frowned and fingered his chin. "With the Morning Star on the verge of death, and the Four Winds Clan torn over the election of Rising Flame, he might be smarting that Round Pot wasn't chosen."

"Not to mention that his old nemesis, the Keeper, is out of the game." Crazy Frog arched an eyebrow. "You should keep in mind that he didn't approve of the things I did for you and Blue Heron. Saw it as a potential betrayal. I smoothed it over, saying it was just business, and gave him a cut. After recent developments that excuse won't even cut water."

"And it didn't matter that we kept Cahokia from disaster in the process? Maybe he'd like serving as a Mayan vassal? Or living through the wreckage of Walking Smoke's civil war?"

"Don't give him credit for that much imagination, thief. War Duck is more like a blunt club rather than a fine obsidian blade when it comes to the nuances of things. Look to Matron Round Pot for the cunning and planning."

"But what use would they have for Winder and his Quiz Quiz?" Seven Skull Shield scratched the top of his head as though the act would stimulate an answer.

"Oh, all right. I'll give you a clue: Consider how the Quiz Quiz and Winder think. So far it's been a disaster for them. Everything they've tried—stealing the Surveyors' Bundle, Sky Star's capture and torture, the loss of the War Medicine, kidnapping the Keeper and ending up with two dead Quiz Quiz—has all gone from bad to worse."

"Don't they know when to cut and run? If everyone hadn't been distracted by the selection of the new matron, they'd never have made it this far. Let alone grabbed the Keeper. And if she dies, it will bring the whole of the Four Winds Clan down on top of them. It might anyway as word spreads."

"I might agree with you, but what if the Morning Star dies?"

"Piss in a leaky pot, I hadn't thought of that."

"My guess is that War Duck has. And he knows how Quiz Quiz

operate. Winder is easy: He's looking to salvage his reputation. From the Caddo lands to the eastern Tenasee, he's known as a man who can get things done. His knowledge of the Nations is second to none. He acts as a middle man, a broker of peace agreements, and an agent sent to ransom captives. Some pay him to learn things about enemies, and he is known in some circles as a man who can obtain someone else's treasured possessions."

"And the Quiz Quiz?"

Crazy Frog smiled grimly. "You asked why they didn't cut and run? They don't think that way. What began for them as a quest to steal one of Cahokia's Power Bundles for their own use has degenerated into a matter of sacred honor. Sky Star and the rest can't run. Not without their War Medicine Bundle. And certainly not without retaliating for the loss of two of their warriors, and worse, for the indignities heaped upon Sky Star during his capture and torture."

"You think War Duck knows this?"

Crazy Frog shrugged his ignorance. "It depends on how deeply Winder has brought him into the game."

Seven Skull Shield sighed, perched his butt on a hip-high seed jar, and ran everything Crazy Frog had told him through his head. "When we followed Winder back to the farmstead where he'd hidden Blue Heron, his Quiz Quiz had changed their appearance. Looked like dirt farmers. The hair poms were gone; so, too, was their regalia. They had mussed their tattoos and were carrying sacks. Probably had their weapons in them."

"And there are thousands of barbarians in River Mounds City who meet that description." Crazy Frog raised an eyebrow. "Looks like you've got a problem, thief. These people live for vendetta. They'll be coming to even the score with you and Blue Heron. And it won't be pretty."

Forty-four

Night Shadow Star's skin prickled from the sweat lodge's damp heat as she threw the flap back and stepped out into the night. Staring up at the stars, she stood naked, arms out, and let the cold breeze fight its battle with her too-hot skin. What began as relief faded, then turned to shivers as the chill won out.

Illuminated by firelight, the sweat lodge stood in a hollow surrounding a small spring that flowed from the sandstone. Around her, the Cave Society knelt, heads lifted to the heavens as they Sang and drummed, calling upon the Powers of night and darkness to bless her. Their chants, in a harmony, rose and fell, her souls swaying in time to their melody.

Disembodied voices from the Spirit world whispered and hissed from the night, the words mostly unintelligible, their meaning lost and jumbled.

At the corners of her vision, images flickered and flashed—like hints of light or snatches of movement. The fragile veil between her and the Spirit World lay in shreds about her. So close she might reach out and touch it, though the singers and priests appeared oblivious.

Meanwhile, at the fire, Fire Cat used a stick to pile coals around the heating river cobbles. After they had finished their first sweat, he had used a forked deer antler to carry the cooling stones from inside the sweat lodge. When he'd dumped them onto the bed of coals, they'd been dark ovals against the glow. As she'd watched, the stones had turned dull red, orange, and now were almost white with heat.

As her teeth began to chatter, Fire Cat said, "We are ready, Lady."

"Go ahead." She began to Sing, asking for the blessing of the Spirits as she cleansed body and souls.

Around her, the ranks of priests renewed their chant, arms raised to the night.

Fire Cat used his blackened antlers to fish the stones from the fire, then carried them one by one into the low-domed sweat lodge.

After he had placed the last inside, she lowered her arms, rubbed herself, and ducked back inside the cramped confines. Seating herself on the hides in the rear, she shivered at the warmth radiating from the glowing stones.

Fire Cat reached out and tugged the door flap in place, sealing the lodge. Then he settled himself across from her.

In the glow of the stones, she could just make out his muscular body, his back bowed by the low walls. He was whispering a prayer under his breath, purifying himself for the ordeal.

When he finished, she said, "Thank you for doing this."

"You should be praying, Lady."

"According to ritual, we must sweat four times. We've another two to go. I have plenty of time to purify myself." She chuckled. "As if Piasa hadn't cleansed my souls of any impurities before he vomited them back up into my body."

On the other side of the stones, Fire Cat's eyes were like black holes in his barely visible face. He waited patiently, knowing she would get to her point.

"Power fills too much of my life, especially being caught between Piasa and the Tortoise Bundle. I have no room for impurity of the souls. My body, however, is a different thing. In the days after Thirteen Sacred Jaguar's death, I was unclean, my body tainted by his semen. I could feel it inside after his attempts to impregnate me, but that was finally flushed from my loins during my woman's moon."

"Should you be discussing such intimate woman's things with me?" Fire Cat asked softly. "Isn't breaking such a taboo dangerous? Especially in a place like this?"

She reached out, casting water onto the glowing rocks. Steam exploded in a suffocating haze, its touch tingling on her bare skin.

As it subsided, she said, "At midnight, you and I are descending into the earth, following the Morning Star's trail back down into the Underworld. Are you afraid?"

"Yes." He almost shivered. "I am still a Red Wing. We are a Sky Clan. Down there in the darkness . . . The monsters . . ."

"But you accompany me anyway?"

"I do."

"You have made this choice, knowing you could lose your souls in the blackness. That they could be devoured by Horned Serpent, who is the guardian of this place. Knowing that, should that happen, there will be no afterlife with your ancestors. That the essence of yourself will scream as it is slowly digested. That everything that was Fire Cat will finally be shit out in darkness, left to stink and rot into black eternity."

He was silent. His hands cupped the steam, rubbed it over his skin, as was proper in the sweat lodge. "I will stand behind you, Lady. As is my oath."

The grim finality with which he said it brought a wary smile to her lips as she poured more water onto the rocks.

After the sizzle and gushing steam subsided, she gasped for breath, then said, "Despite being terrified, you will accompany me. Sacrifice yourself to the Powers of Darkness for me should it become necessary."

"Is there a reason you are stating the obvious?"

"I am answering your question . . . making a point about what is taboo, and what I can and cannot discuss with you, Fire Cat."

She cupped steam and rubbed it over her sweat-beading skin. "You and I are not like other men and women. We are opposites crossed: male and female. Heretic and believer. Master and bound servant. Priestess and warrior. We have both cursed, hated, and saved each other. In the service of Power, each of us will sacrifice his life to protect the other."

"Lady?" He sounded incredulous.

"I state no more than what we both know in our hearts, Fire Cat. When you think about it, this was probably Piasa's ultimate purpose when he ordered me to cut you down from the square. Two sworn enemies . . . whose souls were fated to weave together like a remarkable fabric."

He was silent, poured more water. Steam exploded from the hot stones.

She gasped for breath, eyes closed against the unbearable heat as her sweat beaded and trickled in patterns.

"Why do you bring this up now?" he asked when he could catch his breath.

"If we are to survive our journey into the Underworld, impurity must be washed away. The sweat lodge is a place for cleansing. A place where purity of body and soul can be achieved before a great undertaking. We both understand that we are condemned to be what Power has demanded of us. At the same time, we are exalted and blessed by that same fate as, perhaps, two individuals have never been before. I wanted to put that into words so that there was no doubt. As much as we have shared, I wanted no secrets between us before we descend into the darkness."

He splashed more water onto the stones, the steam stung and burned into her skin.

"Then you should know, Lady, that there are worse ways to die than being devoured by Underworld monsters."

"How is that, Fire Cat?"

"I might have died in a world and place where I had never known you," he told her softly. "So whatever comes after we enter the cave, no matter what terrors are unleashed in the darkness, I am with you."

"And how does that make you feel, Red Wing?"

"For the first time in my life, Lady, I feel pure and free."

"Very well. Throw back that cover. The stones need to be reheated, and I have to cool off or I'll lose consciousness."

A relief ran through her souls as he tossed the cover back and cool air rushed in. Come what may down there in the darkness, it would be with the knowledge he finally understood.

And like him, she knew there were worse deaths.

Misery

I suppose Two Sticks' house is nice, but only in comparison to a stick-and-wattle hovel. It's not very big, only two-by-four paces, and it's not a trench-wall, with a sunken floor, but a post-constructed structure where saplings were individually placed in postholes and bent over to be tied together at the top to form the roof. That, in turn, is finished with a split-cane covering to shed water.

Ceramic jars line one wall. The puddled-clay hearth is centrally located at the foot of the straw-pallet bed, which at least rests on an elevated frame.

The thing creaks and sways, as I found out the first time Two Sticks frantically tossed me onto it and took me. An act he repeats over and over, leaving me sore and feeling as if my pelvis is thick and waterlogged. I no longer wonder or care if the bed is going to collapse. Some part of my soul has gone dull and senseless.

I understand that I have Traded my body and services for protection. That's the deal. I'll try to live with it, but I don't have to like it. Most times I'm just listless, going through the motions of feeding the fire, cooking, and fetching water. But at odd moments, and without warning, I will burst into tears.

Two Sticks watches me, sometimes absently fingering the scar on the left side of his face as he does. At these times a flat hollowness fills his eyes, as if he's seeing something in his memory. Afterward he is remote, gaze fixed on a distance only he can see.

His house is located on the southern end of River Mounds City, a place where the levee fades into the marshy floodplain. It doesn't take a Surveyors' Society chief to see that these lowlands are subject to frequent flooding, though we are past the worst season for that.

"If it floods I just pack up and leave," Two Sticks tells me when I bring this up. "When it dries out, I come back. Plenty of new clay lying around to replaster the walls. Bedding is cheap, and someone is always Trading it at the canoe landing."

"But what do you do?" I ask.

"I'm a guide." He shrugs. "You know that. I offer my services for newcomers to Cahokia. That, and I spy." His smile goes flat. "Though if the Keeper's no longer the Keeper, I may have to find someone else who values my abilities."

"And if you can't?"

"Depends." He looks at me through knowing eyes. "Might have to put you up for the Trade. You know how men are after weeks on the river. They'll come across with a sack full of shells, maybe a couple of good pearls, or a small sack of yaupon tea for a chance to slip their shafts into a snug sheath. Might have to train you up a bit, though. You've got muscles down there. The better you use them, the more you move, and if you could act like you enjoy it, the better they'd pay."

I stare at him, openmouthed. It's not so much what he's saying as the way he's saying it: as if I were just some common woman from a low-status clan desperate to become a paid woman.

"I am a high minko's daughter," I tell him. "Of the Chief Clan of the Sky Hand people! Not some homeless, clanless slave woman to be Traded for a man's pleasure. I'm—"

"You are the woman who assassinated the Morning Star," he reminds me as he points a finger at my face. "You are the assassin that the entire Four Winds Clan is desperate to hang in a square and torture to death. Everyone you ever knew has abandoned you. Your noble father, mother, and clan? They sent you off to exile. Your loving young husband and his caring family? They used you as a weapon against the Chikosi. Played you like a hand puppet to slip poison into the Morning Star's drink. Then they vanished into the night. Not even your Chikosi embassy remains. They, too, skulked away. There's no one but me." He goes back to fingering his scar, and an absent smile finds his lips.

I have a crawly and nauseous feeling down in my gut. What he says is true. "Why did you want me?"

His eyes have that flat, passionless, blank look. "I like driving myself into a Chikosi high minko's daughter. Knowing I possess the Morning Star's wife, and when I'm in you, my shaft feels what his did. Closer to home, you were married into the arrogant and mighty Reed Clan. To the matron's son, of all people. And after all those twists and turns of Power, you spread for me. Here. In my house. At my command. How's that for a disgraced, clanless, and exiled Albaamaha? Back home even the lowest of Chikosi spit on me. Gave me this scar." He points to his cheek. "Now I'm pumping myself dry in the high minko's daughter."

The sick feeling curls tighter in my stomach. "You are a . . . a . . ."

"Disgusting man?" He shrugs, expression amused. "Ask the Cahokians; they're calling you a vile murderess, a treacherous camp-bitch who assassinated her husband. That you seduced him, played him, knowing all along you were going to poison him. You, my dear, are the most despised woman in all of Cahokia, and as news spreads, in most of the world. And that puts you a lot lower than me."

I am speechless, my hands knotted, sobs choked in my throat.

He continues, "Compared to that, what do I care what you call me. I just murdered a cousin to be declared an outcast. Hardly in the same category as poisoning a living god. But any time you tire of my company"—he points to the door—"you can leave and take your chances."

"What if I do?" My voice quavers.

"The nearest farmstead full of dirt farmers will tear you apart with their bare hands for what you did to the Morning Star. Just don't mention me. They'd cut me apart alive for keeping you here."

"Then why are you doing this? Just to have a minko's daughter? What about when that gets old? All you care about for the time being is my body. You don't even like me."

He studies me thoughtfully. "You'll be worth a fortune to me. But not here."

"I don't understand."

"Don't you?" He laughs. "You are the woman who killed the living god. That makes you special, Whispering Dawn. Exotic like no other woman in our world. Men will Trade for that. Trade to possess you for a night. Trade a small fortune."

"I won't do it!"

His face is expressionless again, those flat black eyes pinned on mine. "Of course you will. If you won't, I can always tell the Cahokians where to find you. Nor can you hide. Not from here on out."

"What makes you say that?" My souls are reeling, shocked, and numb.

He points to the tattoo on my hand. "Are you figuring to cut your hand off? Rip that soft skin from the bones? All I have to tell the Cahokians is 'Look for the young woman with the Sacred Moth tattoo. It's the sign of her assassins' order.'"

Forty-five

Based on the movement of the stars, Fire Cat could tell they were at the night's midpoint. With great solemnity, the Cave Society priests began to Sing. The single bonfire cast its dancing yellow light on the cave entrance. On either side, trees rose along the steep slopes, their leaves bathed in contrasting shadow and flickering light by the fire's leaping flames.

Oak, cedars, shellbark hickory, and black walnut grew on the slopes, while sassafras and shagbark lined the edges of the cavern. Before it, tumbled sandstone blocks were sunk in the grass-covered soil.

To reach the cave, they had followed the ancient path, climbed up the conical hill's southern side, Sung prayers at the summit, and left offerings. Then, pace by pace, they had descended the northern slope to perhaps an arrow's shot down from the top. There they rounded the cave mouth to this small hollow in the hillside.

Fire Cat stood back from the fire, slightly behind Night Shadow Star's right shoulder, his copper-bitted war club in hand. He wore only a breechcloth, and a buffalo-wool blanket hung around his shoulders.

Night Shadow Star was clad in a skirt and split-feather cape, her hair loose and falling down her back. She carried only a small pack with her sacred paraphernalia. Her head tilted back to the night sky, she hummed in time with the priests' Song.

Before them loomed the dark opening. Like a Spirit maw, it seemed to swallow the light.

Fire Cat's soul cringed as he looked into that blackness. The night, the Singing, the moonless and star-filled sky, all sent flickers of fear into the very marrow of his bones.

"At midnight," Night Shadow Star had told him as they dressed after the sweat lodge. "That's when the Underworld is in complete opposition to the Sky World. That is the moment we have to enter the outer cavern. At any other time and the Spirit opening to the Underworld is closed, the path to reach it blocked by dead ends, traps, and pitfalls."

"Will the priests lead us?"

"We will go alone, Fire Cat. You and I. They understand that I am Piasa's chosen. That I have special Powers. Accompanied by Sister Datura, you and I will only be able to go so far in our bodies. If we make it all the way to the cave's depths without being killed by the Spirits, our souls will have to leave our bodies behind. Sister Datura will allow us to soul-journey the rest of the way. It means filtering through the cracks and following the Spirit paths that lead down into the watery depths. That is where we will find the Morning Star's Spirit."

And that scared him more than anything. The physical he could fight, as he had the wild northern tribes, the Tula, and the Itza. But when his souls were separated from his body, how did he protect himself? From childhood he had grown up hearing stories about Spirit beasts in the Underworld. How they could sneak up, baring mouths full of teeth, and rip a person's being into shreds. The notion of giant teeth tearing his living muscle apart, of blood spurting from his veins and arteries, and his bones snapping as Spirit teeth crushed them? That had lurked beneath his worst nightmares.

According to the stories it was the most terrifying death a person could face. Worse than the pain, agony, and suffering in the square. He'd seen what it had done to Night Shadow Star. The memory still brought her bolt upright in bed, screaming, her eyes wide with terror, fear-sweat beading on her face and chest.

A woman of Power, she had survived.

Barely.

What chance did he have?

It matters not. I will go. I will act like a Red Wing war chief. I will do my duty to the woman I love.

Even as he thought the words, the priests' Song ended. The Cave Society elder rose and stepped forward to wave a leafless branch over them, as if spiritually blessing them.

Night Shadow Star reached into her pack, removing her small ceramic jar. Singing a blessing, she raised it to the night sky, offered it to the four sacred directions, and finally to the opening that led into the earth.

With two fingers, she dipped out the greasy paste made from crushed datura seeds. Turning to Fire Cat, she carefully rubbed a dab of the concoction into each of his temples. Then, with care, did the same to her own before replacing the little pot inside her pack.

As this was happening a second young man approached bearing four split-cane torches. He stopped at the fire only long enough to lower the frayed end of one into the flames. When it caught and crackled to life, he stepped forward, handing one lit torch to Night Shadow Star; the remaining three he gave to Fire Cat.

Sister Datura? How do I tell when she takes possession of my souls? He certainly didn't feel any different.

"Go in Power," the old man whispered.

With a slight nod of the head, Night Shadow Star took a deep breath and walked toward the rectangular opening in the lichen-covered sandstone.

The only sound was the crackling of the fire and the soft sigh of breeze through the trees.

Heart hammering in his chest, Fire Cat tightened his grip on his war club, nerved himself, and followed behind his lady, his head held high, his blood pulsing liquid fear.

As they passed into the first gallery, one darkness was replaced by another. The dancing light of the lit cane torches barely illuminated the oblong room.

Here had been placed numerous offerings brought by pilgrims from all over the Cahokian world. Baskets, ceramic jars, wooden boxes, feathered prayer sticks, painted leather and embroidered fabrics, and other objects lined the edges of the chamber. Along the walls, too, were burials, the dead tightly bound, knees to chests, arms flexed and tight to torsos, the heads wrapped in fabrics.

Under Cave Society supervision, this was as far as supplicants could come. Only special adepts were allowed beyond, into the ominous blackness ahead.

The opening in the cavern's rear looked like a beastly mouth, agape and waiting. Fire Cat's heart began to pound, and he fought to swallow past the knot in his throat.

You can do this.

He kept shifting his grip on the war club, skin prickling, his hair rising. As Night Shadow Star led the way over the uneven footing of tumbled and broken stone, the air moved, as if the Underworld were whispering across Fire Cat's skin.

He ground his teeth, every muscle alive with tension as Night Shadow Star, Singing softly under her breath, ducked down before the opening and extended the torch. The flames danced in the cool, damp air that spewed out like a deadly exhale. It carried a smell of earth, stone, and the musty pungency of the long dead. Tilting her head the way she did when the Spirits whispered in her ears, Night Shadow Star crouched, extended the torch, and ducked into the blackness.

Fire Cat hunched down, placed one hand on the cold stone, and froze. Fingers of panic caused his lungs to flutter.

I don't have to do this! If I run, they'll never catch me. I could disappear. Go so far away they would never find me.

An image of golden sunshine, a warm blue sky, a verdantly green meadow—lush with grass and bounded by tall and sparkling trees—seemed to burst into his imagination. Birds, deer, life everywhere. It could all be his. . . .

A tear, triggered by indecision, trickled down his cheek. He remained paralyzed. Caught between this world he so loved and whatever horror lay just past that narrow divide.

"Fire Cat?" Night Shadow Star's voice seemed to call from across an eternity.

In that instant her large dark eyes peered out of his memory, questioning, as if wondering if he still backed her. A rapture rolled warmly through his chest. The world seemed to shift, his fear like a thing alive inside him.

Fire Cat bit off a curse, hating himself for his cowardice, and slid the three torches across the stone before he followed.

He straightened, knees weak, inside the next chamber. His hand was trembling as he collected the cane torches and turned. The way he clutched the war club's handle in his right hand should have splintered the wood. His insides felt as though a thousand insects were crawling around inside his flesh, and his vision had turned watery, unable to find that fine focus.

Then he came face-to-face with the monster.

Eyes burned into his.

Round.

Black.

Huge.

Wavering in the light of Night Shadow Star's cane torch, the eyes stared out of a black face and pinned Fire Cat's souls with their eerie stare. A sharp-toothed mouth bared pointed teeth, the expression threatening. Ugly square ears stuck out from either side of the round head. Above them, black antlers rose. The creature's body—corpulent and sinuous like a slug's—trailed along the wall.

A choked sound caught in Fire Cat's throat as the monster wavered on the rock and seemed to rush toward him. He froze like a frightened rabbit. That eerie stare burned down into the bottom of his being.

He and the terrible beast were face-to-face, locked together. In a moment it would strike, those teeth would—

The torches clattered to the ground from his nerveless left hand.

"No," he choked.

"Fire Cat?" Night Shadow Star whispered as she stepped between him and the terrible beast. "Do not move."

Liquid fear ran like water through his belly, paralyzing muscles and sickening his souls. Nausea wove itself through his stomach.

"This is the Spirit of Horned Serpent," she told him. "Guardian of the cavern." She reached out, wrapping her fingers around his where they clenched the war club. "From here on, you must show courage. The Spirit can feel your fear. If you do not show courage, it will devour your souls, Fire Cat."

Her tightening grip imparted just enough courage that he could swallow, nod at the wavering apparition.

Reaching down, she collected the torches. His eyes still locked with the monster's, he somehow took them from her. Heart hammering, Fire Cat managed to will his legs to move as Night Shadow Star led him away. The monster faded into the stygian blackness as she led him deeper into the cavern.

Fire Cat could sense the terrible apparition hovering just behind him, though when he cast worried glances back over his shoulder, he could see only wavering darkness.

A sheer wall blocked his way, and as Night Shadow Star lifted her torch high, a hundred figures drawn in black—warriors locked in battle—leaped from the rock. Thunder Birds hovered with wingtips down. The Spirits of elk, deer, wolves, and dogs pulsed vibrantly. Large-eyed serpents stared at him, sending a chill through his souls. Faces seemed to leer, and a snarling mouth with peg-like teeth made his skin tingle.

"They are all black," he whispered, noting that the only red on the wall was drawn in lines, circles, and bars.

"They are dead," Night Shadow Star told him softly, her voice distant. "We have passed into the realm of the dead." Her eyes had grown large in her face—glistening, depthless, and as dark as the cavern itself.

He felt her Power as it flowed from her eyes, from her mouth and hands. She was one with the darkness, one with the whispering voices that he could now hear. The drawings spoke, Sang, and laughed, as did the cool air around his head.

He cocked his head, trying to hear them, only to lose individual voices in the soft but sibilant merging of distant sound.

"I feel so . . ." He blinked, trying to understand the floating sensation.

"Sister Datura has embraced you," she told him. "Do not fight her."

Night Shadow Star stepped up, leading him over the broken footing along the wall, past an image of Mother Spider. The torch light focused on a black chief, his headdress spilling down his back, the forked-eye design marking him as Sky World. He held a bow with nocked arrow in his extended right hand, a mace lifted high in his left. A three-banded breechcloth draped his waist as he Danced and exhaled a white, outlined, human head from his mouth.

"Who?" Fire Cat asked, his balance shifting like loose sand beneath his feet. A series of pots had been laid at the foot of the wall; offerings for the black warrior, and proof that he was a figure of great importance.

"Black Tail," Night Shadow Star told him. "Captured in the moment the Morning Star took possession of his body." She inclined her head toward the outlined white head. "His souls are being expelled, sent to the Underworld. Creating balance between sky and earth."

She tilted her head slightly, saying, "Yes, ancestor. I know he doesn't believe."

Fire Cat flinched as he heard faint laughter in the darkness. The black chief's single visible eye watched him with a cold menace and disdain.

Then Fire Cat shivered, for above Black Tail's trapped life soul, a different monster was baring fangs as it swallowed a deer whole. Three arrows had been shot into its corpulent body, and elk antlers jutted from its eyeless head. From instinct, Fire Cat raised his ax, stumbling back.

"Easy, Red Wing," Night Shadow Star warned, reaching out to grasp his arm. At her touch, an electric crackle shot through him like a wave. Something elemental, alive, pulsing of womanhood and blood and security.

"Why are we here?" he wondered, her reassuring touch allowing him voice.

"Here, look." She took him another step along the wall, extending the torch.

"Morning Star," Fire Cat said as the white-bodied figure jumped from the stone. He recognized the white-shell maskette earpiece, the arrowed-forelock headpiece and the Soul Bundle at the back of the image's head. A bow was clutched in the effigy's left hand; the dead and severed head of Morning Star's father hung from his right.

Her voice hollow, Night Shadow Star told him, "It happened right here. In this place. In the Beginning Times, this is where the Morning Star brought his father's head after defeating the Giants in a game of chunkey. On this spot, he brought his father's head back to life."

She turned, her eyes dark and glowing. "Power fills this place.

Through each of the drawings, the souls of the dead are given presence. Hear them? All around us. Feel their touch, Fire Cat? Light, like the faintest stir of air."

He jerked as something skipped lightly along his forearm. Almost cried out as a tickle ran along his thigh.

The voices in his head grew louder.

"We should leave," he whispered. "No good will come of this."

In the flickering torchlight, Night Shadow Star smiled. An action without humor, it appeared as the rictus of a woman condemned.

"Come," she told him. "There is only one way now. If you go back, the dead will claim you. And Horned Serpent's Spirit will devour anything that makes it as far as the exit."

Fire Cat bent, gut racked by a convulsion. He fought the need to vomit, then gasped as the Dead came wheeling out of the darkness, reaching out with black, formless hands to finger his sweating skin.

"Why are they angry?" he demanded, voice breaking.

"Because the Morning Star's Spirit chose the Sky World at the end of the Beginning Times. And now he is in the Underworld. If we don't bring him back, Fire Cat, they will take it out on us."

"How?" he cried, struggling to focus as Sister Datura whirled him around and the dead began to grasp his arms and legs.

"There are worse things than being devoured by the Spirit beasts. Come, we must hurry."

On the point of tears, he stumbled along behind Night Shadow Star. He had to climb over blocks of roof fall, the footing treacherous . . . and the dead followed as they tugged at his hair and laughed just behind his ears.

Forty-six

Seven Skull Shield wondered if he should have left Farts behind rather than bringing him along on this mad venture. He was sure that with the promise of some small reward, he could have talked Crazy Frog into letting his small tribe of children take care of the beast. Unlike Mother Otter, the children fawned over Farts.

Around him, River Mounds City was falling off to slumber, the night dark, with only patches of stars overhead. The smell of smoke, sour latrines, and the wet pungency of the river hung on the still air.

From one of the society houses surrounding the square came the sound of a flute. A man laughed in the distance, and a shift of the air brought the taint of a charnel house to Seven Skull Shield's nose.

He made a face as he stared up at the mound-top palace with its clay-covered palisade wall. The wedge-roofed building rose up against the partly cloudy skies like a looming miasma. The thing seemed to reek of doom and death and defeat.

"Pus and blood," Seven Skull Shield muttered under his breath. "It's just War Duck's same old stodgy palace. Seen it a thousand times."

On none of those occasions, however, had he been trying to sneak into the fortified heart of River House. The palace had always been a fixture of the city. A mere landmark. A place he'd never had any particular interest in, other than as the high chief's residence. If it had meant anything to him, it was as a place to avoid, since he could think of no sane or healthy reason for him to be within those grim walls.

But tonight it might hold the key to Winder's whereabouts. Make no mistake: Time was everything. Seven Skull Shield and his old friend were now locked in a deadly race. Winder and the Quiz Quiz couldn't let the Keeper's rescue go unanswered. And the only way Seven Skull Shield could stop that was to find them and figure a way of destroying them.

"By Piasa's balls, I'm an idiot." And so saying, he bunched his muscles, found a purchase in the weathered clay, and began scrambling up the long slope. Behind him, Farts climbed in pursuit, paws and claws finding much better footing on the crumbling surface.

Forty-seven

The fire had mostly burned down to coals when Matron Round Pot bid the last of her clansmen good night and walked them to the palace door.

Turning, she was satisfied to see Clicking Boy, her twelve-year-old house boy, toss a couple of thick lengths of cottonwood onto the fire. Together they would burn long enough to ensure the fire didn't go out during the night. She always checked to make sure. Once, as a girl, the eternal fire had been allowed to burn out. Not so much as a hot coal could be found the next morning. In a panic, a runner had been sent to the Morning Star's palace for a replacement ember to reignite the sacred flame.

Even before it could arrive, her mother, Waving Stem, had complained of pains in her chest, retired to her bed, and was found dead not a hand of time later.

That was the way of it. Allowing the eternal fire to go out brought disaster and ruin in its wake. In the aftermath of that event her family had barely managed to maintain control of River Mounds—and from that day forward, her father, Cutting Stone, had suffered setback after setback, until his death when War Duck took over as high chief.

Since then, River House had prospered and grown in prestige within the Four Winds Clan. Bit by bit they had undermined Horned Serpent House and held their own against Evening Star House despite Columella's adroit politics and her despicable dwarf spy.

Right up until that accursed Walking Smoke precipitated disaster. Only after Walking Smoke's destruction had she and War Duck figured out that the miscreant had rented their warehouses to hide his perversions. That—but for luck—he might have unleashed his madness in River Mounds City rather than across the river. But for Round Pot's quick action the scandal might have brought down River House. As it was, they'd been left with a bit of a taint that hadn't fully dissipated by the time the Four Winds leaders assembled to pick a new matron.

"I came so close to winning," she whispered.

The burning frustration of her failure was like acid in her stomach. First she'd been outmaneuvered by cunning old Blue Heron and Columella. And then—after Five Fists made the Morning Star's wishes known—had come the realization that even if she had managed to accumulate the votes, the living god would have whisked the matron's chair right out from under her.

But the part that stung the worst was War Duck's ultimate betrayal. That he had sided with Slender Fox just because the woman had bedded him? The memory of her humiliation, her outrage, sent a frothing bile burning in her belly.

War Duck, one day, would pay for that. So, too, would that suppurative sheath, Slender Fox.

But that could wait. She would bide her time. And if tomorrow's desperate gamble worked, revenge would come sooner and harder than even War Duck imagined it might.

She sighed and stared up at the soot-darkened roof overhead. Around her, her household was preparing for bed and seeing to her guests. Several of them were influential cousins, others prominent Earth Clan chiefs upon whom she and War Duck would have to rely in the event of the Morning Star's death.

Her slaves were unfolding blankets on the sleeping platforms surrounding the walls. Others were seeing to the chamber pots or stowing personal items in the storage beneath the beds. Ensuring the guests were happy.

So much depended upon being perceived as a superb hostess. And appearance was everything. She watched as the big corrugated boiling pot was placed next to the fire and filled with jar after jar of water. By morning it would be steaming, perfect for brewing huge draughts of black drink for her guests.

Her palace was a showpiece: the walls covered with exotic shields, weapons, weavings, and relief art. Not as gaudy as the Morning Star's palace, but impressive because of the diversity and rarity of the collection. Some of the fabrics had been imported from the distant Palace Builders in the far southwest. Other woven sealskin pieces came from islands in the cold ocean in the far-off northeast. And a favorite carving of hers was an elongated mask said to have come from a people called

Taino who traded with the Calusa and Tequesta peoples down on the tip of the peninsula.

Her family had been building their collection for three generations now, and Traders knew that the more distant a piece's origins, the more River House would Trade for it.

War Duck still sat on his dais behind the fire, chin propped on his palm as he stared—deep in thought—at the new flames licking up the sides of the cottonwood lengths.

She walked over, crossed her arms, and stared at him. He raised his disfigured face and fixed his remaining eye on hers. "Think he'll still be alive come morning?"

She shrugged. "If he isn't, we've laid our plans. Everyone knows their duties. The Earth Clan chiefs have ordered the assembly. We'll have enough warriors in the squadrons to keep order. I think we can keep the rioting to a minimum, and we don't have the numbers of dirt farmers to deal with as the other Houses do. The craftspeople and the Traders will be little trouble, and who will notice the extra chaos at the canoe landing?"

"I wish we had had some warning, but no one else had any either. And that fool Rising Flame has the rest of the clan paralyzed. Was the Morning Star mad to pick her?"

"Perhaps. Whatever his reasons, this is our opportunity. Rising Flame is weak, and dismissing Blue Heron has made the Morning Star House vulnerable in a way they haven't been since Black Tail first surrendered his body to host the living god. This is our time."

"We have the wealth, we control the Trade, and most of the manufacturing is centered here. Our only weakness is defending the city if several of the Houses ally to attack us."

"Blood in my piss," she muttered. "We sound the same as Petaga did back before the wars turned against him." But then, defense had always been River Mounds City's greatest vulnerability. Not long after the Morning Star's resurrection, the palisade walls had been torn down to make room for rapid expansion as River Mounds grew from a town into the elongated city it had become. Hemmed by marshy lowlands, Cahokia Creek, and the river, every plot of elevated ground was filled with buildings and cramped farmsteads. No room remained to maneuver defensive squadrons. Combat would quickly descend into disorganized chaos as warriors battled among the buildings.

Thinking about it, part of her actually hoped the Morning Star would survive—despite that meaning she couldn't move on the other Houses.

"I'm going to bed," War Duck said through a yawn. He stood, adding, "Lot of people here tonight. Couldn't tell who was coming and going. Look at it. Every bench is full and some are sleeping double."

She watched him go, took one last look around to assure herself that the palace was in order, and walked back to her personal quarters. She didn't bother with a lamp, knowing by feel where her possessions were stacked. Nor did she have to worry about Grass Seed's things, as her husband was out organizing the Earth Clans and overseeing their call-up of warriors.

With a sigh, she undid the bun at the back of her head and let the long braid fall until it tickled the backs of her calves.

She unclipped her cape and let the skirt fall before she climbed under her blanket. For a long time she replayed the night's conversations, picking at the strategy sessions she'd moderated. If only there were some certainty; but then, that lack of information had always been one of their weaknesses compared to Blue Heron's and Flat Stone Pipe's spy networks.

In the process, she drifted off to sleep and troubled dreams.

Sometime in the night, she was startled awake when a hand clapped hard onto her mouth. A jolt of terror caused her to jerk and curl. Something sharp pressed against her throat; her guts went runny at the feel.

"Not a sound, High Chief," a whispered voice ordered.

She swallowed hard. Then asked against the fingers, "What do you want?" It came out garbled.

"You promise not to shout?"

She nodded, wishing the uncontrolled shivers weren't betraying her absolute terror.

The hand eased, although the sharp edge on her throat remained. "What do you want?" she whispered dryly.

"Snot and shit," the voice hissed back in annoyance. "Where's the high chief? Who are you? His wife?"

"He's in his room. What do you think? That we'd commit incest?"

"Matron Round Pot?"

"If you are going to murder me, be about it!"

"Of all the shit-heeled bad luck. How was I supposed to know which room . . . ?" She heard the man sigh. "Listen. All I need is for you to tell me where the Quiz Quiz are hiding. I figure you know which warehouse Winder is renting."

She swallowed against the knife at her throat. "What Quiz Quiz?" She need only play for time, keep him talking. As she did, she balled the blanket in her fists, slowly drawing it up off of her feet and wadding it in her grip. If she could break free, it wouldn't be much protection. Maybe just enough to foul his knife and keep it from killing her as she screamed for help.

"The ones who stole the Surveyors' Bundle, the ones Winder helped, and the ones who took Clan Keeper Blue Heron. Now, tell me where Winder hid them, and I'll be on my way. Simple, huh?"

Something about the man just wasn't right, his tone full of irritation. "You snuck in here to find a party of Quiz Quiz?"

"Go to the source; that's what I always say."

"Are you a lunatic?"

"It has been brought up in conversation a time or two, yes. And by some of the most remarkable of people. You wouldn't believe." The sharp edge pressed a little harder against her throat. "Now, just tell me where the Quiz Quiz are hiding. It's got to be a warehouse or temple—someplace busy where they won't draw too much attention."

"You think I know this?"

"Actually, I figured that War Duck did, but since I picked the wrong door, I'm going to have to get the information from you. So, Matron, if you want to wake up alive tomorrow morning, you'd better tell me."

Her mind racing, she struggled to understand, but beneath it all a building anger began to brew. "I haven't a clue as to where your Quiz Quiz are."

"Sorry, doesn't work. They're here somewhere."

"If anyone knows, it's War Duck. He attends to most of the Trade and commerce. If he rented to some Quiz Quiz—"

"Most likely to Winder."

"Who's he?"

"A rather well-known Trader."

"Like I said, Trade is War Duck's responsibility." The anger burned free. "So kill me and get it over with!"

"Oh, by Piasa's balls! You mean to tell me that you don't know what goes on in your own House? Even when it means Cahokia is going to be shaken right down to its roots?"

At her silence, he asked, "Could this get any worse?"

"Lady?" Water Ant's worried voice called from beyond her door. "Are you all right?"

"It's worse," the assailant whispered to himself.

She felt as well as saw his head swivel. When he did she had balled up enough wadded blanket to take her chance. Thrusting upwards with the blanket in an attempt to shove the knife away, she jerked sideways from under the blade, flipping her entire body at the same time.

"Help!" she screamed from the bottom of her lungs. "Assassin!"

And in an instant, her assailant tossed the "blade" onto her chest, and in a flash he was gone. Pounding through her door, he knocked Water Ant out of the way.

"Assassin!" Round Pot cried as she fumbled for the blade he'd left on her chest, fingers recognizing nothing more dangerous than a large potsherd. "Grab him! Don't let him get away!"

She heaved herself off her bed, staggered past the squalling Water

Ant, and out into the great room in pursuit. The fire had burned down to a glowing bed of coals that cast a faint reddish light across the room. Just enough to see, but not enough to make out details.

Screams erupted to her right, and she whirled. Instead of fleeing across the open center of the room, the big man had leaped onto the sleeping benches and was tromping his way across the tops of the recumbent sleepers. In time to their screams, he was ripping her precious ornaments from the wall, flinging them out to bounce on the floor matting.

At the same time—mixed with the shrieks, screams, and wailing of the people he was stomping his way across—he was bellowing "Farts! Farts! Farts!" like a madman.

The entire room burst into pandemonium.

She watched in amazement as the big man swayed and staggered his way onto Heavy Toad's bed—the footing not exactly good atop wiggling bodies and blankets. Her clumsy and overweight servant sat bolt upright in his bed; with a loud crack the pole frame gave way under the combined weight. She heard Heavy Toad's high-pitched wail of fear over the popping and snapping of the stored seed jars beneath as they shattered and spilled a winter's worth of reserves onto the matting.

The whole mess of bedding, bodies, and mayhem rolled onto the floor, where the assailant scrambled nimbly to his feet. Heavy Toad huddled into a ball, head back, squealing his terror.

Two of her guards had charged in through the front door, throwing it wide. She could barely hear their calls of "What's wrong?" over the screams and shouting.

Something dark and fast hurtled through the door behind them. Whatever the four-footed apparition was, it knocked both startled guards off their feet. The warriors hit on the flats of their backs, feet flying high.

"Wooo haw!" the assailant called, grabbing War Duck's heavy litter by one handle and upending it into the path of three of the Earth Clan chiefs who had leapt off their beds and were charging his direction. It caught them in a body block, dropping them in a mess of flailing arms and legs.

Around the room her slaves were screaming in terror, stumbling out of their beds, rushing for the door. Frightened and disoriented guests milled about frantically, shouting questions, demanding protection. A tangle of people were grabbing for clothing and personal items. She could hear the crash of something wooden as it splintered.

The beast that had burst through the door was bounding through the confusion, howling and barking, bowling people off their feet to sprawl this way and that.

She had a single glimpse of the assailant, his silhouette outlined in a reddish glow as he lurched toward the fire. Saw his leg go back, and watched him kick over the big pot of hot water, spilling its contents into the coals. The fire reacted with a roaring hiss—the eternal and angry sound of flame meeting water. A curling puff of crimson steam billowed up in the instant before the room went suddenly and opaquely black.

"Someone catch him!" Round Pot shouted with all her might.

"Who?" a voice answered through the chaos.

"The assassin, you dolt! Grab him!"

More screams. The sound of tearing cloth. A woman was bawling in pain or terror from somewhere by the door.

A dog began barking in what sounded like delighted excitement.

"I've got him. I got the—" A meaty smacking sound cut it short.

"Here! He's here!"

"That's me, you idiot! Turn me loose!"

"Over here!"

"Help!"

"Guard! Guard!"

"Ouch!"

"You hit me!"

Something else broke with a crash followed by the sound of shattering pots.

Round Pot stopped short, unable to see anything, hands raised, ordering, "Stop it! Silence. Bolt the door!"

"Someone get a torch!"

"That's my leg!"

"Touch me again like that, and I'll smack you one!"

More screams.

"Someone help me find my fire bow!"

"Where are the pus-rotted torches?"

A flailing black shadow slammed into Round Pot; the impact knocked her off her feet. Her body hit the floor with a painful thump that blasted lights through her vision.

Someone stepped on her hand, and she realized the futility of trying to make sense of the madness. On all fours she crabbed off to one side, pulled herself up onto the sleeping bench. There she dropped her head into her hands as more curses, yips, and thumps disrupted the darkness.

She was still shaking her head when the realization hit her that her palace was a wreck, the eternal fire was out, the door was again gaping wide to the lighter night, and the assassin had to be long gone.

Who would threaten her with a potsherd? Cause all this, just to find some Quiz Quiz?

"War Duck? You rotted well better be able to explain this!"

Forty-eight

With her pack on her back, Night Shadow Star strode purposefully down the narrow cavern. Her feet barely sank into the soft mud, and her long black hair trailed out behind her like strands of moss in the current.

Around her, roots emerged from cracks in the dark limestone walls to wind down along the stone in tangles. An occasional fish would dart past, and she often had to step around concentrations of freshwater mussels where they clumped together in the mud.

She barely flinched when Piasa—accompanied by a blue glow—flashed into existence at her side. The great Underwater Panther's wings were folded atop his back; the snake's tail with its rattles kept swishing back and forth. The Spirit beast studied her through deadly yellow eyes, the black pupils like pools of emptiness. He wrinkled his cougar face in what might have passed for a smile had it not exposed his long and curving fangs.

"How do you know the way?" the Spirit creature asked.

"I can feel him," she told him. "As you said. The Morning Star's presence is a disruption. An infection by Sky World Power that can be felt corrupting what was once healthy. Look at the tree roots, they grow more knotted and twisted the closer we get. It is as if they are writhing in pain. A few fish still flee, but most have gone."

"What is in your pack?" Piasa extended a pink nose, sniffing as if to get a scent.

"Fire Cat," she told him. "His souls weren't ready for the Underworld. He would have gotten lost, perhaps been carried off by the dead who found him amusing. Despite his fear, he nevertheless followed my instructions. Followed me to the end of the cave where we left our bodies."

"Why bring him at all?"

"I couldn't have left him in the darkness with Sister Datura and the dead. They would have driven the souls from his body, left him insane."

"So you are carrying him in a sack?"

"Even the bravest man has a limit to his courage. To journey down from where we left our bodies one has to slip through the narrowest of cracks. The thought of getting stuck, of being forever trapped in darkness, immobile and under a crushing weight of stone, is scary enough for me. By putting his dream soul into the sack . . . Well, sometimes what we don't know doesn't hurt us."

"Perhaps I should find you another warrior, one with more—"

"There is no braver man, Master. Leave him alone."

Piasa's yellow eyes burned hot; then the beast chuckled. "If he amuses you, keep him."

She shot him an angry glare. "He has earned my respect. And served you well, if you will recall. I will stand by him if no one else will."

"Then let us hope he has the courage necessary."

"Let us hope the Morning Star has the sense to accompany me back to his human body."

They rounded a bend in the winding way, coming upon an open cavern perhaps a stone's throw across. Roots like fuzz hung down from the arched roof. The sandy substrate had a rumpled and rolled look. There, half buried in mud, his shell covered with green streamers of moss, Snapping Turtle faced a golden-glowing hole in the limestone wall on the other side of the cavern. Something about his posture looked wary, as if the great turtle were ready to either flee or fight.

To his right, patterns of color seemed to ripple along the scaled hide of a huge winged serpent where it coiled atop a low mound of moss. The giant snake's great triangular head—its crystalline eyes the size of large plates—was raised; the neck tensed as its forked tongue flicked out like a thick and wicked lash. Atop its head gleamed a rack of scarlet antlers similar in shape to a deer's. The wings—banded in all the colors of the rainbow—were extended high and spread, as though preparatory to launching the mighty serpent into flight.

At her and Piasa's arrival, the serpent's terrifying head swung her way, and the sparkling crystalline eyes fixed on hers. "Can you remove him?"

"I don't know, Lord." Pus and muck, Horned Serpent frightened her. "What if I can't?"

Horned Serpent's crystalline and cold stare projected a chill into her souls. "Then we will take matters into our own hands."

"What does that mean?" she asked.

"Battle," Piasa told her. "A fight."

"Nasty business if we do," Snapping Turtle noted, the weird pupils in those round and alien eyes still fixed on the glowing hole across the cavern. "Rock is fractured, tunnels collapse, the ground shakes and convulses. The dead are terrified. Fear will be unleashed everywhere."

"It isn't just confined to the Underworld," Horned Serpent told her. "Your world will be convulsed until trees fall, houses collapse, cracks appear. Even rivers are shaken out of their courses."

"Powers were separated for a reason in the Beginning Times," Snapping Turtle groused. "They are meant to be *kept* separate. What was that silly moth thinking?"

"I wasn't aware that a moth thinks," Horned Serpent replied bitterly. A glow built behind his eyes as he studied Night Shadow Star. "Can you remove him? Take his Spirit back to where it belongs?"

She cast an uneasy glance at the glowing hole. "I don't know. I mean . . . how? I've never done anything like—"

"Bah!" Snapping Turtle spat. "She is useless. I should have eaten her the first time her whimpering souls polluted our peace and quiet. She's been nothing but trouble. If we want this corruption removed, we should just rush in there and tear the Sky Creature and that silly moth to pieces. Get it over with."

"Like usual, your thinking is mired in the mud," Horned Serpent replied as he fixed his crystalline gaze on the hole across the way. "Not all problems are best solved by those massive and shearing jaws of yours, old friend. This isn't a matter of some Tie Snake in a fight with a Thunderer—which is destructive enough. The Morning Star is a Powerful being. That he chose the Sky World over us after destroying the Giants is regrettable, but he did. If we attack, we could collapse the entire Underworld in the ensuing battle."

"That would get Old-Woman-Who-Never-Dies' attention," Piasa muttered distastefully. "It's bad enough when she drifts from her Dream toward wakefulness, but should she be suddenly snapped out of it?" He made a face.

"Let the woman try," Horned Serpent said. To Night Shadow Star he added, "Go and see what you can do. See if there is a way to get him back to your world without destroying our own."

"Because if you don't," Snapping Turtle insisted, "we *will* deal with this in our way."

The golden light in the hole flickered, brightening and then fading away. She could feel the intensity of some terrible conflict being waged just beyond that portal. Her heart began to race; an insidious weakness sapped her muscles and bones.

This is insane! What do they think I can do? This isn't some Itza lord, or my twisted brother. They are asking me to step between the Powers of Underworld and Sky! This is a task for Spirit beasts, not a mere woman!

"Well, go on," Piasa prodded. "He's been living in your brother's body, after all. There must be something human clinging to his Spirit that you can appeal to."

Still she remained frozen, afraid of the pulsing light.

Any further delay was denied her when Piasa shoved her forward with a taloned foot, almost tumbling her in the mud in front of Snapping Turtle's pointed nose.

On trembling legs she slowly walked forward, almost wincing at the fluctuating pulses issuing from the hole. As she neared the terrible opening, the panic built. Tears streaked her cheeks, and a quavering sounded deep in her throat.

Somehow she kept one foot ahead of the other, one fist knotted in the sack where it hung over her shoulder.

Why are you so afraid?

"Because if you go in there," the Tortoise Bundle whispered from behind her ear, *"and you fail, you will never leave that place."*

"All I have to do is talk the Morning Star into returning to Chunkey Boy's body," she insisted in an attempt to convince herself.

Sister Datura's laughter echoed through the watery depths, the peals of it mocking and derisive.

Night Shadow Star shot a worried glance back over her shoulder. The three lords of the Underworld were giving her the sort of look they'd give the condemned.

She was at the glowing opening now. Each frantic beat of her heart ran electric through her body.

"Go on," Piasa called.

Like a lash, his words drove her headlong into the glowing hole. Half blinded by the flickering light, she raised her arm to partially shield her face. In staggering steps—as if into the teeth of a blizzard of light and pain—she advanced. How long? A matter of steps? An eternity?

Time twisted around her.

Her eyes ached as they adjusted, and she realized she'd stumbled into another cavern. In a blaze of pulsing and golden brilliance, she could see two figures as they whirled and fought.

The Morning Star—a being of light—wore a deer-antler headdress, a raccoon's back-hide hanging down over his forehead. Eagle wings draped from his arms, and a splayed-feather tail extended behind him. His neck was wrapped in shell necklaces, a sash and pointed apron at his waist. The Morning Star's face was strained, exhausted, and what she had first thought was red paint around his gasping mouth, she now recognized as blood.

Clasped at arm's length fluttered a giant humming moth—a huge creature whose brightly colored wings blurred as they battered at the Morning Star's arms. Each of the buzzing beats was weakening the Morning Star's grip on the giant moth's proboscis and thorax.

And then she saw the source of the blood. Though held at arm's length, it wasn't far enough. The giant moth's proboscis streaked out like a whip to lap at the blood welling on the Morning Star's lips. In desperation, he would release his grip with his left hand and bat the vicious proboscis to the side. As he did the moth would press closer, causing the Morning Star to slap his hand back to its thorax in a desperate effort to push the beast away.

Then the terrible proboscis again struck at his mouth and began to feed.

Night Shadow Star hunched under the force of the battle. The humming wings pounded vibrations of ancient Power through her cowering body, making her teeth ache and her bones feel like they were cracking. The radiance burned her skin—so painful it raised blisters as she watched.

Waves of misery poured through her, leaching away her souls and will. In terror, she sank down, strength draining away. All that remained were the humming beats of those terrible wings, that lashing proboscis as it lacerated and sucked away the Morning Star's blood . . . and the horrible realization that she could do nothing.

Screaming in agony, Night Shadow Star tried to rise, only to be beaten down again. She felt the sack slip from her limp fingers as she collapsed on the shivering sand. Her dying gaze fixed on the flashing and battling figures. Morning Star was fading, tiring. It was only a matter of time.

"And then what?" the Tortoise Bundle whispered just beyond her fading hearing.

"Death," she whispered.

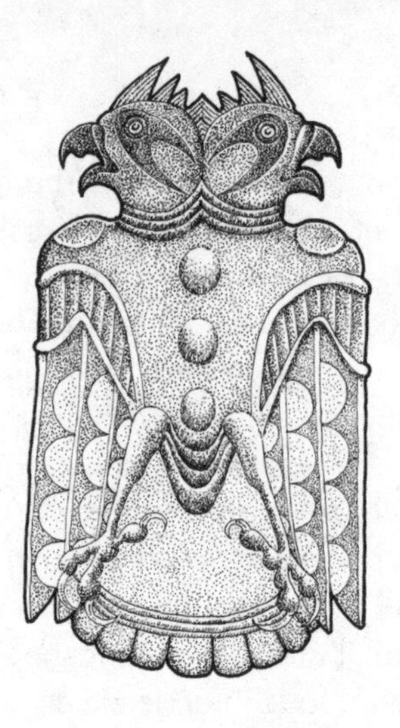

Forty-nine

As she knelt before the altar in Old-Woman-Who-Never-Dies' temple, *Tonka'tzi* Wind wondered if she was fated to be the last Great Sky of Cahokia. The thought was sobering.

Just at sunset, she had had her litter carried down the Great Staircase from the Morning Star's palace, her escort of warriors calling for the mostly silent crowd to make way as they rounded the Morning Star's great mound and took the avenue north, across North Plaza and Cahokia Creek. They had finally deposited her at the doorway to Old-Woman-Who-Never-Dies' temple, on a low terrace on the creek's north bank.

The temple was one of a line of mounds and structures on the creek's low terrace, and stood on a direct line of sight along the avenue that paralleled the western base of the Morning Star's mound, precisely located one and a half measures to the north. Dedicated to Old-Woman-Who-Never-Dies, the complex consisted of a two-terraced mound, with the temple on the lower, eastern platform and its associated charnel house atop the higher western platform.

It was to this complex that Morning Star House always retreated to show their respect to the greatest of the Earth Spirits. And it was to here that Wind had come, followed by the surging crowd, most of them Singing and Praying for the Morning Star's recovery.

As she knelt before the altar with its masterfully carved sculpture of the goddess, Wind could close her eyes and feel the thousands who now surrounded the temple. Sense the Power of their combined bodies, all standing, kneeling, and watching. They might have been a single vast being with a thousand lungs breathing the hopes of a world. All waiting on her, expecting her to intercede on behalf of their longings and aspirations. She was supposed to make this right and bring their living god back to his body.

Why does it have to be me?

She glanced sidelong at the priests and priestesses, all ancient, their visages shriveled, faces painted, as they knelt to either side in the dark room. Each held a cornstalk in the left hand, a hoe in the right—the traditional symbols of Old-Woman-Who-Never-Dies.

They, too, were looking at her with expectation in their eyes. Pus rot them all, *they* were the chosen. Why weren't they interceding on the Morning Star's behalf and beseeching their patron to send the living god's essence back to Chunkey Boy's body?

Wind turned her attention back to the hunched statue of the goddess where it rested atop the altar. She had already laid an offering of corn, squash, and goosefoot seeds in the basket that rested before the old woman's statue. Now she looked into the shell-inlaid eyes, stared hard into those black pupils that fixed so intently on her.

"First Woman, on behalf of all the peoples of Cahokia, I plead with you. Please send the Morning Star's Spirit back to us. Free it from the bonds of the Underworld and this ancient and meddling moth. Though we do not understand the creature's reasons for taking the living god from us, you, who have lived with the ancient Powers, must. Intercede on our behalf. Heed the offerings of the people. All across the city, in every temple, they have laid the proceeds of the harvest before you."

Did she see a sharpening in those piercing eyes?

She blinked. No. The statue looked just the same. Occasionally it would seem to move, but that, she had discovered, was an illusion caused by the wavering firelight.

Her knees on fire from kneeling, and lower legs numb, her misery was intense.

How many hands of time had passed since she had knelt here? Every muscle ached from being bent into a submissive posture. Try as she might, she couldn't see that her pleas had made any difference.

The soft whisper of voices from behind caused her to glance over her shoulder. Rising Flame now entered, several of her servants bowed as they were dismissed and then retreated to the outside.

Wind tried to rise, winced, and realized her legs had lost all feeling.

Two of the temple assistants rushed forward, bowed low and touched their foreheads, and took her arms. Gently they eased her up, one saying, "Don't try to walk, *Tonka'tzi.* Just let us carry you."

Oh yes, with legs that felt as senseless as oak, what else could she do?

Obviously practiced for such an event, the young men swiftly bore her to a seat in the rear, efficiently composing her as the first prickles of returning circulation began to torture her legs.

"Any news?" she asked Rising Flame when the matron walked up.

"He still lives," she replied, casting a nervous glance at the ominous statue atop its altar. Old-Woman-Who-Never-Dies was glaring hostilely at them through her shell eyes. "Though Rides-the-Lightning says not by much."

"What time is it?"

"It's the middle of the night, *Tonka'tzi.* Probably close on morning. I couldn't sleep. Half the city has flocked into the Great Plaza. The other half, hearing that you are here, has camped around this temple. Like you, they are praying for Old-Woman-Who-Never-Dies' help."

Rising Flame shook her head. "I've never seen anything like it. Felt anything like it. It's huge. All those people, all waiting, their hearts literally aching. You can feel their hope and their fear, a tremendous Power in the night. It's all coupled with a sort of confusion. They don't know what to do to fix it, so they can only wait and pray."

Wind gasped as the tingle in her legs built into a thousand-needle prickling ache, and making a face, she wiggled her feet and shifted her legs back and forth.

To Rising Flame she said, "Just before you arrived, I was contemplating the fact that if the Morning Star dies, nothing is going to save this city. All those people out there? They're waiting on the outcome. And when they hear that the Morning Star is finally dead by assassination? They are going to turn on each other, on the Earth Clans, and on us. It will be an ocean of grief and betrayal that drives them. No amount of warriors or squadrons will stop them. They will tear the city apart, and then they will turn on each other."

"Pus and blood." Rising Flame dropped to a seat beside her, her empty gaze locked on the statue that continued to glare at them. "What do we do?"

"What *can* we?" Wind shrugged. "We are outnumbered. We dare not try to make an escape; they'll see. Imagine what they'd do if they thought we were running out on them."

Wind chuckled softly, adding, "This might be the safest place in the whole of Cahokia, Matron. To be found humbly praying to Old-Woman-Who-Never-Dies might cause them to hesitate, and perhaps drop to their knees in prayer beside us." She paused and made a face. "Or not. They might just tear the temple down and stomp us into the floor."

"Or just trickle away and go home?"

"Now that's a nice thought."

After a silence, Rising Flame said, "Word came late last night that among the dirt farmers, they've started sacrificing young women. Purifying them, sweating them, feasting them, and offering them up to First Woman before they put a rope around their necks and strangle them. Then the bodies are buried with the appropriate offerings."

Wind sighed. "Wonder if it's going to make any difference."

At the other end of the room, the statue remained unmoving, still crouched, hoe in hand. But then death had always been Old-Woman-Who-Never-Dies' particular calling. Before a person could be reborn, they had to die.

So . . . how long do we have? Moments? A finger of time? A hand, or a day?

Cahokia's miracle, growth, and expansion had been like nothing ever seen. Now, if the Morning Star died of assassination, the city's sudden and convulsive death would be epically cataclysmic.

Fifty

The dreams were fragmented, broken snippets: images of people and places long gone. Feasts, good times shared, moments of joy with old friends lasting long into the night. Her brother Red Warrior Tenkiller held his stomach as he laughed so hard at one of her jokes that his face turned red and he almost threw up. Memories of lovers and spectacular sex that had left her body trembling in the afterglow. Being present at the birth when White Pot squirted Chunkey Boy out of her sheath. Black Tail's death, and the emptiness that had sucked away her souls.

Blue Heron tried to cling to them—to the safety her memories represented. Down deep, she knew how those times would turn out. With that knowledge came reassurance. Fear arose from not knowing, from the uncertainty that pain, suffering, and ultimate defeat hovered just over the future's horizon.

Fight as she did to hold tight, however, the images faded, slipped away, and became gray mist as her head began to ache. The disappointing realization that she was desperate for a drink overwhelmed her.

Blue Heron blinked her way into a world of hazy gray light and tried to shift, which brought more discomfort as every part of her body hurt.

Smacking her lips, she forced a swallow down her dry throat.

"Lady?" a voice asked.

"Water," she croaked in return, and a cup was placed to her lips. From it, she drank greedily, heedless of the fact that some of it spilled down her chin to drip on her chest.

The room came clear, looking like an unfinished palace. The roof didn't even have a coating of soot. Where? Hers?

"Come back to us, have you?" another voice asked, and Columella stepped into view.

"What happened to me?"

"Your souls slipped away for a while, Blue Heron. That happens sometimes after a body has been battered and wounded the way yours was."

The cup had been refilled. She drank again, this time with more decorum. When she'd finished, she asked, "Help me sit up, please."

The servant woman and Columella both helped her upright on the sleeping bench—an action accompanied by gasps of agony as her broken ribs grated. And once there, her impulse to pant for breath hurt so much she saw stars. Had she ever hurt this badly?

It did feel better to have the world come back into perspective. "It's been a blur. I was in a crummy little moon temple. I remember the Quiz Quiz kicking the stuffings out of me. And then . . ." She squinted, realizing her left eye was puffy and almost swollen closed. "Did I imagine it, or was the thief there?"

"Seven Skull Shield and Flat Stone Pipe followed the Trader who captured you back to where you were being held. The thief killed two of the Quiz Quiz to get you free. You've been here since, under my protection and well guarded by my best."

"Vomit in a pot, what else has been happening? That Trader, Winder, I remember him saying something about the Morning Star, some sort of problem."

"He was poisoned. By some girl he'd married. Apparently it's all tied up with the Sky Hand and Albaamaha treachery."

"That little slip of a thing?" Blue Heron shook her head, then wished she hadn't as the pain stabbed in response. "Dancing Sky said she'd be trouble. Where is the dear young thing? Hung in a square?"

"Vanished. Five Fists has warriors all over the city looking for her." Columella arched a disbelieving eyebrow. "The war leader says that before all this started, the Morning Star ordered him not to harm the young lady."

"Bah! That's crazy. Besides, Five Fists can't find his piss pole with two hands in broad daylight. Who did Rising Flame appoint as Keeper?"

"Word is that she favors her uncle, but both she and the *tonka'tzi* have had their hands full. The Great Plaza is full of people. Maybe ten thousand of them. Standing vigil for the Morning Star. All praying for his souls to return to his body."

"And what do you hear the chances of that are?"

Columella shrugged. "Night Shadow Star has traveled to the Sacred Cave, personally descending into the Underworld to try to get Morning Star's Spirit to return to Chunkey Boy's body."

"Not everyone who enters those foul caverns comes out again. And no doubt she's dancing with Sister Datura again. Could this get any worse?"

"Indeed it could." Columella turned, ordering, "Bring the Keeper something to eat. Some of that corn stew with acorns."

As the bowl was brought, Blue Heron asked, "Worse how?"

"Seven Skull Shield has sworn vendetta against the Quiz Quiz, who have sworn it against you. He invaded War Duck's palace last night. Somehow he got into Round Pot's room and demanded to know where the Quiz Quiz were hiding. Either the good matron didn't know, or she played it coy. Someone called out an alarm, and your thief turned the place upside down making his escape. Made quite a ruckus." She paused, eyebrow lifted. "Extinguished the eternal fire."

"That's bad luck. Round Pot must be apoplectic."

"Doubly so. Flat Pipe's agents report Round Pot and War Duck were planning a move against the other Houses the moment the Morning Star was declared officially murdered. Most of the River House supporters fled like bobwhite from a falcon. They feared that any action stemming from such a catastrophic beginning was doomed by Power to the worst kind of failure."

"And where's Seven Skull Shield now?"

"Trying to find the Quiz Quiz and his old friend Winder." She arched that eyebrow again. "He's still working with Flat Stone Pipe. They seem to have developed a rather unusual respect and appreciation for each other. A fact that gives me no little unease."

"Those two? Combining their talents to who knows what ends? Now that's almost as frightening as the prospects of the Morning Star's assassination." Blue Heron took the stew and a bone spoon a servant handed her—and realized she was famished as she began to eat. "If the Morning Star dies, I've got to be back at Morning Star House. Wind is going to need me. The whole city is going to erupt."

"You shouldn't travel, Keeper. Not yet. Your souls have just slipped back into your flesh. Give it a day or two to ensure that they stay where they belong."

Blue Heron grimaced as she handed the empty bowl back. As much as it hurt to just sit up, how was she going to pee? Defecate? Or even walk.

"I've got to get back, Columella. That idiot Rising Flame won't have the first clue about what's going to come down when the Morning Star dies. River House is just the tip of the ice floe. Green Chunkey and Wolverine won't be far behind in their mischief."

"Aren't you forgetting something?"

"Such as?"

"In all this confusion there's a bunch of frustrated and angry Quiz Quiz who feel humiliated by your actions. The last message I got from Flat Stone Pipe was that old enemies are using them as a tool to murder you."

"If you won't help me," she growled, "I'll do it on my own."

"No way you'll do it on your own, Blue Heron. My healer says one of those broken ribs could puncture a lung and kill you if you move wrong, or fall."

"Will you at least do me a favor?"

"I might."

"The thief is still around, isn't he? Send for him. Seven Skull Shield will make sure that I make it home."

"He's just across the river."

"My litter still outside?"

"It is."

"Then I'm going."

So saying, she wobbled to her feet, stifling a yip of pain deep in her throat. More than ever in her life, Wind needed Blue Heron's help. By Piasa's swinging balls, when had she ever hurt this much?

One step. Two. Spit and phlegm, she was better than this.

"Come on," she whispered to herself, the world beginning to spin. "You can do it."

Wasteland of the Soul

I wonder what I have become. I have lost so much of myself I am surprised when I lift my hands and see palms and fingers. Or that my legs appear whole. That patches aren't missing from hips, belly, or shoulders. I keep expecting invisible places, missing bits from my ever thinner shell of being. For there is nothing left inside to disappear, which leaves only the outside of me to slowly vanish into nothingness.

Perhaps it is because I haven't found a missing patch yet that I feel obliged to act. Had I awakened this morning and discovered that some body part had vanished into nothing, it would have been too late. It has dawned on me that if I am ever to act, it has to be before that occurs. Before my hand fades away, or my foot vanishes in the night.

Before I lose the last of me.

So I have done what I have done.

Two Sticks didn't understand what the little ceramic jar was when he went through my pack. He placed it in his carved storage box with the rest of the valuables I stole from the Morning Star's room. He figures to Trade them when we leave for downriver sometime in the next moon. After, he says, the vigil for my capture fades away. For reasons I don't understand, he thinks he can Trade my "bed services" to the Quiz Quiz for a start, and that the Trade will be most profitable. Something about "payback" that I haven't had the energy to ask about.

Mostly when he talks, I pay little attention. His ramblings change with the angle of the sun. One finger of time he's excited about this possibility, then next he's waxing on about something entirely unrelated that will make his fortune and fame.

He does not notice that I am fading away. That surprises me. Each time he orders me onto the bed he should realize that there is less and less of me. That one of these times, soon, I will collapse under his weight. That I will crush like a hollow pot. Can't he feel it when he jams his shaft inside? There's nothing left inside, only dead space to stimulate him.

I certainly can't feel anything down there. Because of that, I am always surprised when he stiffens and groans, and finally goes limp.

My souls are so transparent thoughts just pass through them, airy, floating.

I think this as I sit on the side of the bed and study Two Sticks through emotionless eyes. He is breathing irregularly. His eyes flicker under damp lids, as if his souls are tortured. On occasion his fingers twitch, and one of his feet will jerk.

I roll the little ceramic jar between my fingers and consider it a miracle that I continue to have sensation in my fingers.

When I took the jar down before breakfast, I knew that it was empty, that at most a drop might be left inside. Turned out there were three. In addition I used a splinter of turkey leg bone to scrape out the inside, gouging out the porous clay and sifting it into his morning cup of tea.

To my relief, he drank down the whole thing. Never even hesitated. Just as I had with the Morning Star, I used my body to distract him, throwing everything I had left into the act. He was so surprised, so pleased, he never even noticed that he was coupling with emptiness. Thought that the delirium was from his physical release.

And like the Morning Star, he just drifted off.

So I sit, watching him, rolling the jar in my fingers, and know what I have to do.

I take a deep breath. As I can hold a breath, my ribs and chest haven't faded away. But they might. At any minute they could vanish.

"Just do this," I tell myself.

But what comes next? Will some of the missing pieces of myself re-form, sort of like an image out of mist? Or are the vanished pieces of me gone forever? Maybe the process is irreversible, and I will continue to fade until there is nothing left, not even a flicker of shadow.

With that thought I reach for the water bag: a tanned buckskin piece with tightly sewn and stitched seams. It just fits over his head, and I tie the sealing string around his neck.

Then I wait, watching as his lungs suck deeper and deeper breaths, each one contracting the soft leather sides of the sack before puffing it out again.

I wonder if, when it is all over, he will fade away into nothingness, too.

Fifty-one

Midge—who had just turned two—erupted in her shrieking cry, her face contorting, eyes closed, mouth agape to expose barely budded teeth in pink gums. She began to bawl with a lusty squall. Her older sister, Fly, had pushed Midge down, and Midge had landed hard on her butt.

Sitting at his breakfast fire, Crazy Frog watched his youngest wife—a girl in her late teens named Flower Reed—sigh as she turned from stirring the hominy pot. With comforting words she bent to the little girl and reassured her. Meanwhile, his third wife, Blanket, went after the obnoxious Fly with a wooden ladle. That provided just enough distraction that one of Crazy Frog's sons, Scoot, grabbed away his little brother's breakfast bowl. He slurped down its contents before shoving the empty bowl back into his outraged brother's hands.

A tussle broke out that caused Mother Otter to stop braiding oldest daughter Sly's hair and dive into the middle of the fray to reestablish order.

Sitting in his spot behind the morning fire, Crazy Frog grinned to himself and reflected that life was good. His greatest joy in life might be winning a fortune gambling on chunkey, but mornings around the breakfast fire with his five wives and their tribe of children filled him with a deep-seated sense of contentment.

"So help me," Mother Otter told him as she stomped back to Sly's hair, "the next one that misbehaves is being Traded to a wily Caddo and sent downriver!"

Crazy Frog adopted a somber face as he looked around the room and shook his head. "We'd have to Trade your Caddo something valuable, like the Morning Star's most-prized chunkey stone, just to get him to take one of these little animals. No, I'd say the only Trader dumb enough to give us anything for one of these little weasels might be one of those Karankawas we hear about down on the gulf. And they'd only want one to throw on the fire and eat."

"Oooh!" Tight Hair, the pretty, second-oldest daughter, cried. "You're not Trading me to any cannibals."

"Might," Crazy Frog told her, smiling as he went back to his breakfast.

He had just used his horn spoon to fish out a chunk of goose meat and hominy from his bowl when wife four, Wild Rice, leaned in the door from where she'd been milling corn at the pestle outside. "Husband? Someone to see you."

Her tone of voice left no doubt. The "someone" was important enough for him to interrupt his favorite time of morning.

Setting his bowl to the side, he stood, arranged his apron so that the long point of it hung down between his knees, and grabbed a warm buffalo wool cape against the chill.

Stepping out into the purple morning, he stiffened at the sight of the litter that had been lowered before the smoking remains of last night's fire.

The man stepping off the litter was huddled in a fine blanket, wore a Spirit Bundle headpiece, and carried a polished ground-stone mace.

"We need to talk," War Duck told him as he walked past, a brooding thunderstorm behind his good eye. The grim expression contorted the scar on his left cheek.

Crazy Frog took a deep breath and followed the high chief around to the hemmed-in entrance to his storehouse. The guard started, wide-eyed, and snapped to attention, but at least he'd been awake.

War Duck led the way into the storage house, setting aside the door and thrusting the fabrics out of the way. To the guard inside, he ordered, "You. Take your associate and go for a walk. Your master and I have to talk."

War Duck seated himself on one of the big wooden storage boxes, rearranged his blanket, and rubbed his scarred face. "Pus and rot, what a night."

"What's happened?" Crazy Frog reached up to lower the fabrics in order to prevent anyone from seeing in, but War Duck gestured for him to desist.

"No. I want to be able to see out." A pause. "An assassin attacked

Round Pot last night. Sneaked into the palace somehow, maybe during our planning. We had every Earth Clan chief, the squadron firsts, and some of the society house leaders come to discuss plans for when the Morning Star dies. People were coming and going all night, and many were invited to stay. The palace was full. Then, in the middle of the night, the assassin sneaks into Round Pot's room and threatens her."

"Is she . . . ?"

"No. Praise be to *Hunga Ahuito* and his grace. The assassin made enough noise questioning her that one of the servants overheard and called to ask if everything was all right. That saved her. Apparently the man's nerve broke, and he ran."

"And you want me to see if I can find him? Of course. I'll have every single one of my people—"

"That's not my biggest concern. This assailant broke in to ask Round Pot where the Quiz Quiz were hiding."

Crazy Frog—veteran of survival in River Mounds City's rough-and-tumble underside—kept his expression in check. His gut, however, did a flip. "How much did he know?"

"He asked specifically about Winder. Knew that Winder had been to see me."

Seven Skull Shield! Crazy Frog felt the ground turn to sand beneath his feet. He'd have to be very careful. Playing all sides against the middle was a tricky business.

"Piss in a leaky pot, how? Unless . . . yes. He's one of the Keeper's agents. She must have told Columella before her souls drifted out of her body. Last I heard she was unconscious, hanging to life as tenuously as the Morning Star."

"This whole thing has gone from bad to worse." War Duck banged his fist on the box top.

"Why did you order me to help Winder in the first place? I told you the Quiz Quiz could be a problem."

"The Quiz Quiz were supposed to steal the Surveyors' Bundle so that I could embarrass Morning Star House. Use it as a means of getting Round Pot elected clan matron. My chance to declare, 'Morning Star House couldn't even protect one of the most sacred Bundles in Cahokia! Why should we continue to allow them to maintain such a position?' What a club to crack them over the heads with.

"But what happens? Somehow the Keeper gets the Bundle back, that fool Sky Star gets captured and hung in a square, their War Medicine gets stolen, and that greasy sheath, Rising Flame, is made Matron."

"It's not all bad. In becoming matron, Rising Flame has dismissed Blue Heron as Keeper." Crazy Frog crossed his arms.

"And what?" War Duck demanded. "That fool Winder kidnaps her in Evening Star Town, which infuriates Columella and brings her into the mix. The Quiz Quiz beat the souls out of Blue Heron's body, and then *lose* her to one of Columella's agents!"

"What do you want me to do, High Chief?"

"Don't you see?" War Duck reached out with a supplicant hand. "This poisoning of the Morning Star, it's the greatest single opportunity to come our way in three generations. The instant he dies, River House can move first, take control of the entire city. Or what's left of it. We have the river, the Trade. Most of the workshops and finest craftspeople are here. After the fighting boiled down and most of these pesky dirt farmers had gone back to wherever they came from, River House would have risen as the preeminent authority."

"Why do you say 'would have'?"

War Duck blinked his weary and exhausted eye. "Because someone wanted to find the Quiz Quiz so badly they sent that assassin last night. It wasn't enough that he threatened Round Pot, but in making his escape, he caused a disaster. Not only did he rip up the palace, but people got hurt in the melee. Important people. And then, in the middle of it all, he kicked over a pot of water and extinguished the eternal fire. Put it out cold."

"Oh, rot," Crazy Frog whispered.

"Every person there was shocked when it finally hit them: It was a sign. Not only did the assassin escape, he made fools of us all. But when he extinguished the eternal fire, he called down bad luck on every individual in that room, not to mention the whole of River House!"

"Which means that no one is interested in following your lead against the other Houses if the Morning Star dies."

"Our support evaporated before the last person fled that room." War Duck pointed a finger. "That's what those thrice-accursed Quiz Quiz have cost me."

Crazy Frog fought the urge to step back and put a little distance between himself and War Duck. It never paid to be too close to the victim of so much bad luck—high chief though War Duck might be. A man never knew when it might rub off and contaminate him.

He forced himself to stay—but his skin prickled at the high chief's proximity.

"What do you want me to do, High Chief? They won't leave until they recover their War Medicine. Unless you want to have them murdered."

"Columella sent me a runner this morning. I am told that Blue Heron isn't doing well. Columella is sending Blue Heron back to Morning Star House and that blind fool Rides-the-Lightning in hopes that he can call her souls back to her body. The runner—not knowing of our disaster—asked for an escort to keep the lady safe on her journey."

War Duck smiled, the action distorting the scar on his face. "He said there would be two litters—one bearing the lady and the other a 'prized possession' whose safety *must* be maintained."

"You think that's the War Medicine Bundle?"

"You told me that you never saw it when that loathsome thief captured Sky Star. You were the one who transported Sky Star to that foul Blue Heron." The single eye slitted. "That still really angers me."

"Think, Lord. If I had refused, the Keeper would have suspected you might have been behind the theft. If I've learned anything, it's never to underestimate her."

War Duck gave him a flat, unimpressed stare.

Crazy Frog spread his arms wide. "You only said you wanted me to help Winder find a place for the Quiz Quiz to hide. Nothing about protecting them, or that they were allies. And I thought you wanted me to work with the Keeper . . . as long as I kept you informed."

"Getting back to the point, yes. I think Blue Heron and the War Medicine will be on those litters." War Duck rubbed his temples as if to stimulate thoughts behind his weary expression. "River House is in turmoil. We were attacked last night. The Morning Star is on his deathbed, and chaos might break out the moment he dies. Upon Blue Heron's arrival at the canoe landing when they bring her across the river, we will not have any warriors to spare for a guard. Do you understand?"

Crazy Frog hesitated. "Tell me straight out: You are ordering me to tell Winder that Blue Heron and the Medicine Box will be essentially unguarded and traveling down the Avenue of the Sun today."

"That's what I'm telling you. I need to salvage something out of this disaster. Getting rid of both Blue Heron and these accursed Quiz Quiz at the same time might be small justice, but given the wreckage wrought in the last couple hands of time, I'll take it."

"I'll have one of my people send word."

War Duck pushed himself off the box. Hesitated, rubbed his fingers over it. "Lot of soot on this." He glanced up. "I'd say your roof is going. About time to replace it."

"Just had it done." Nevertheless, Crazy Frog noticed that a couple bits of soot had drifted down to dust the high chief's shoulders and hair even as they'd talked.

But for the moment, the storehouse roof was the least of his problems.

Fifty-two

Am I Dreaming?

The words seemed to float above the pain and confusion that left Night Shadow Star paralyzed and cowering on the tortured sand. When she blinked her eyes, her vision shimmered, and she barely recognized the flickering images that careened and fought. Some part of her shattered souls remembered that it was the Morning Star and Sacred Moth who battled with such desperation.

The briefest memory of the monstrous moth sucking the Morning Star's life away remained with her: *It's drinking his blood. Sucking out his essence. And as it feeds, it gets stronger while Morning Star weakens.*

It came to her that her souls were locked in the Underworld, that the Power in the mighty battle had battered her down—beaten the will to act or move from her being. That like an earthworm after a storm, she was being desiccated by the radiant light of the battling Spirits. Nor would it be long before she faded, dried, and hardened.

This was death.

The end of a world.

Her world.

Here, in the depths, the Morning Star—born of Corn Woman and First Man, conqueror of monsters, he who defeated the Giants and resurrected his dead father, who shaped and formed the Beginning Times—would fall victim to a moth.

But for the searing pain and dying souls, it would laughable.

"Is this all you have left?" the Tortoise Bundle asked from far away.

"I . . . can't . . ." She couldn't find the words to finish.

She felt herself growing lighter, fading—the blinding light from the fighting duo burning away the image of who she was. The sensation of nothingness filled her with wonder and awe. For the moment, she even forgot the desperate battle that raged just paces away. Dissipation of self—of all that she was—absorbed her entire attention.

This is death. How I cease to be.

Even fear had evaporated until all that remained was to be witness to nothingness. Then even nothingness faded.

It wasn't so terrible.

It wasn't anything.

She was almost there when movement at the edge of her vanishing reality distracted her.

The sack lay forgotten on the vibrating sand; now the fabric moved as something inside stirred and crawled toward the slack opening.

She had lost so much of herself that she barely recognized the form that emerged from the coarsely woven fabric. Like being born, the head came first, followed by shoulders and torso. As the man's hips emerged, he climbed to his hands and knees, a copper-bitted war ax gripped in his right hand.

Fire Cat! She recognized him, as if from across a distance.

In the blinding patterns of light, he winced, face contorted with fear and pain. She saw the terror in his face as the wood of his war club blackened, scorched, and burst into flame.

Fire Cat hunched down, head protected by his arms as the war club burned to ash, leaving only the long, pointed copper spike.

Through slitted eyes the man stared at the battle where Morning Star could no longer bat away the deadly proboscis, but kept both arms locked, trying to hold the giant moth at bay, while the proboscis flicked and danced along his bloody lips.

The Red Wing cried out at the sight, wincing, shooting glances around the fire-reddened cavern walls. One frightened glance he cast her way, locking his vision with hers and whispering, "I love you."

The words stunned her, shook the remaining shadow of her souls.

Then he clawed at the sand, picking up the copper spike.

Bellowing his rage, he staggered to his feet, wavering with each pulse of the deadly light. Muscles knotting and bulging, he forced himself toward the combatants where they spun and struggled.

A terrible shriek tore from his lungs as he fought his way those last few steps—his body physically pummeled by the light.

"He's not going to make a difference," the Tortoise Bundle whispered. *"He's fading too fast, too weak to strike."*

Had there been enough left of her, Night Shadow Star would have whimpered as Fire Cat teetered at the last of his resolve. The hammering of the moth's frantic wings ripped the frayed vestiges of his strength away. In a heartbeat, it would be over.

But the man didn't strike, couldn't. Instead he thrust the copper blade out before him like an offering. The Morning Star's hand flashed in a desperate grab as Fire Cat was blasted backward to slide across the sand.

Night Shadow Star gaped. The Morning Star pulled his left hand back. Copper flashed in the light. He had it. And struck. Struck again. The terrible moth convulsed, trying to break away.

Pulled and jerked this way and that, the Morning Star was flung about the cavern. But he continued to pull his left arm back, thrusting again and again. The blade flashed—copper leaving a streak as if it were smearing the light.

With one last desperate effort, the moth rose and smashed them both against the high ceiling. The impact knocked the Morning Star's grip loose, and he fell hard to the sand.

In an instant, the light vanished to be replaced by the Morning Star's weak glow.

Night Shadow Star blinked, a ringing in her ears. But beyond that was only silence and peace.

"Too late," the Tortoise Bundle's voice grew ever fainter. *"You don't have the strength to save yourself, Night Shadow Star."*

"Wait! Come back."

Only silence remained. A sense of desolation and loneliness in the wake of the Tortoise Bundle's departure from her life.

From the shadows of the now-darkened cavern, Sister Datura laughed, and then even she faded into growing darkness.

The Morning Star's form remained visible, glowing softly like a hearth stone in a dying fire. He stood over Fire Cat's dead body, looking down sadly.

"Help me," Night Shadow Star whispered.

"I can't." He smiled sadly. "There is not enough of me left to carry you from this place. It is too dangerous. I sense my enemies. Close." He inclined his head. "Just there, in the next cavern."

"How will you . . . ?" She couldn't finish the thought.

"I've been here before, you know. A long time ago. They won't expect me to know the back ways. The cracks and crevices. And I can feel my image—the one drawn on the cave wall above. It will lead me. If I can avoid the traps, if I don't get lost . . . Tell me, is there any reason I should return to your foul brother's body when my spirit could fly free?"

"Cahokia needs your—"

"Cahokia is doomed, Night Shadow Star. Why not let it die now? God, Spirit, soul, or being, the only certainty in existence is eventual oblivion."

"Please," she whispered. "For me."

His image continued to fade before her, the cavern going ever darker.

"What about Fire Cat?" She tried to indicate Fire Cat's body where it lay supine on the sand.

Morning Star studied the copper spike he still held, its sides wet with the moth's fluids. "He didn't act a moment too soon. I'll barely make it as it is."

A pause.

Then he said, "Thank you for bringing him here.'

She watched the Morning Star bend, extend his hand and blow across his open palm. A golden haze settled onto Fire Cat's head. Even as it did, the Red Wing's body shivered, arms and legs quivering.

"He won't remember a thing," Morning Star told her as he straightened.

The glow that was the Morning Star began to fade as filaments of darkness began to enclose him. She watched in horror as they wound slowly around his legs, hips, and torso, as if he were being wound in black. As the last tendrils surrounded him, the last of his golden glow vanished. Silence became complete.

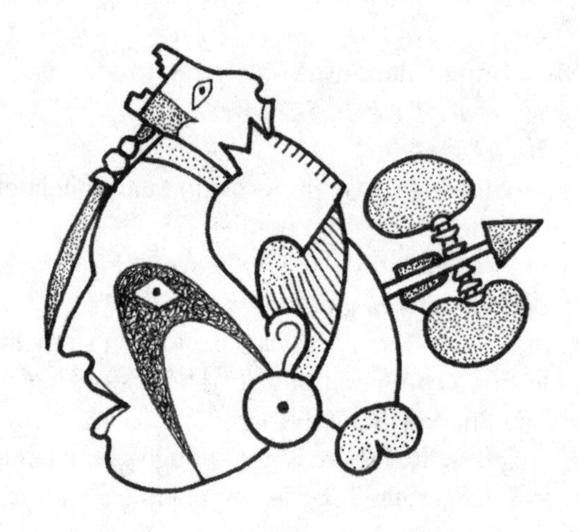

Fifty-three

Reeling and sick, Fire Cat sat up in a thick and clinging blackness. His stomach pumped, and he jerked forward as one dry heave after another pulled his guts into a tight and painful constriction.

Finally, gasping for air, his stomach hurting the way it would if he'd been kicked, he tried to place his surroundings. Where was he? He couldn't even see the motion of his fingers when he held them before his eyes.

Pus and blood, his head felt like it had been stuffed with wadded and dusty cobwebs—and a terrible taste filled his dry mouth. Feeling around with his fingers, he recognized gravelly soil, a couple of pieces of broken pottery. Next he encountered a stick, carved, and with a feather on one end: prayer stick. Had to be.

Then he found the stone wall: flat, vertical. It felt like sandstone.

Turning, his questing fingers encountered fabric. Then a body, cool to the touch. Feeling up along the hip he encountered skin and then a breast. Female.

From the confusion of images wheeling around inside him, he took the first that flashed in his head. "Night Shadow Star?"

She didn't answer, and he pulled her onto his lap and hugged her close. Some of the terror faded at the feel of her, and he buried his head in the angle of her neck, breathing deeply. Was she even alive?

"Where in Piasa's name are we?"

A cave. That was it.

Memory came spinning back: the canoe journey, the Cave Society, and a cleansing in the sweat lodge. Then he remembered the horrifying descent, how the Dead and the guardian Spirits had terrified him as they pulled and plucked at him.

He hugged Night Shadow Star's limp body against his, as though he could press her into his very soul. *I am in the Underworld!*

The Dead, the Spirits, were all around him. Hovering in the blackness, slipping through the air just beyond his reach.

A cold terror broke free, chilling his souls, choking a sob from his shivering lungs.

Time meant nothing.

In the end, the terror exhausted itself and gave way to inevitability.

Night Shadow Star's body warmed where it was clasped against him.

Screwing up his courage, to the surrounding Dead and Spirits he respectfully whispered, "Go away! We're not here to hurt you."

His answer was silence and blackness so thick he could almost feel it between his fingers.

The only sensation was Night Shadow Star's breathing as her breath purled in and out of her slack mouth. Fire Cat shook her, calling, "Lady? Wake up."

He blinked, trying to think, to remember.

Flashes of nightmares erupted like fire from down in his souls. Impossible things. Images that included darkness, flashing lights, pain, and terror. Fluttering wings, blinding light and heat. The Morning Star's face, his mouth dripping blood. Reaching out with a copper spike . . .

"Sister Datura," he realized, then reached up to dab at the grease where Night Shadow Star had rubbed the concoction into his temples.

So what was real, and what was Spirit Dream?

"Got to get you out of here," he told Night Shadow Star.

Fear sent ripples down his back as he felt around. Rock to left and right, and more rock just over his head. They were in a confined chamber, more like a tomb than a cavern.

The panic left him unable to move. Prickling fear-sweat broke out on his skin.

Buried alive. Surrounded by the pressing weight of the earth!

When the terror finally drained away, he made himself breathe normally. *Think!* Rot it all, he and Night Shadow Star had climbed down here. Unless one of the guarding monsters attacked them, they should be able to follow the same route back out.

Something that sounded like claws scratched the unyielding rock just overhead. He froze, desperately feeling around for his war club. It wasn't hung on his hip. Didn't seem to be anywhere on the ground around him. Where could he have lost it?

Some impossible memory of it, of the wooden handle bursting into flames, tried to form in the eye of his souls.

In his searching he did find the handle of one of the cane torches. Shifting Night Shadow Star, he felt around for her bag. Inside it his fingers located the datura jar, a water bladder, sacks full of what felt like cornmeal or milled nuts, and another stuffed with shells. For Trade, no doubt. Nothing, however, could be used to start a fire.

Of what use was a torch without a flame?

He sank down, defeated and empty.

"All right, Lady, you have done it to me again." He made a face in the darkness, wondering if the Spirits could see it. They probably could. He'd heard that only the living were blind in the Underworld.

That brought a smile to his lips. As long as he couldn't see his hand in front of his face, and he was terrified to the point of throwing up, he was still alive.

"Well, Lady," he told her. "It's a long way to the surface. Somehow I have to carry you, feel my way, and hope that I don't offend the Spirit beasts who can reach out of the darkness and kill us both without warning."

He remembered the narrow fissures she had led him down so far below the last of the painted caverns. And if they made it that far, the chaos of blocks, gaps, and angled roof-fall might prove just as treacherous.

He smoothed a loose lock of hair away from her brow. "I wouldn't do this for just anyone, you know. Since you are locked away somewhere with Sister Datura and cannot hear, I can tell you that if we die down here, it was worth it just for the chance to love you."

He secured her sack to his breechcloth. The useless torch, he'd leave. There wasn't room to stand; nor was he sure which way to go. He wasn't even sure which way was up.

"Spirits," he prayed. "I have no idea if I am worthy or not, but I serve Lady Night Shadow Star, who serves Piasa. I ask nothing of you but guidance on how to carry my lady out of here."

As his words faded into the awesome silence of the Dead, he sighed. Nothing came in return.

Feeling along the wall, there were only two ways to go. "Very well, Lady. We're going that way."

Fire Cat shifted around in the narrow space, his shoulders wedged against the cold stone, and cradled Night Shadow Star as best he could before waddling ahead in the darkness.

He had never been so scared in his life.

Fifty-four

The location was perfectly chosen: a farmstead just off the Avenue of the Sun. No telling where the family was that lived here. Probably gone to wait for the Morning Star's death, and to mourn his passage when it finally came. So many people had done just that. Half of River Mounds City had packed a burden basket full of food and trudged off to the Great Plaza to wait, and stare up at the high palace, and whisper prayers that the living god would continue to be the miracle they had celebrated all these years.

Well, let the foul god go for all Winder cared. As a child, growing up here, the Morning Star had done nothing for him. It didn't matter if the Spirit Being were living in old Black Tail's body, or Chunkey Boy's young one, the living god had never so much as put a morsel of food in Winder's mouth, let alone eased his misery.

"I hate this place," he muttered as he stared out the farmstead doorway. How the family who lived here kept body and soul together was beyond him. The dwelling was a bent-pole wall construction, which, while roomy, looked like the first wind would blow it over. A small field out back was full of corn, beans, and squash, and ready for harvest. Out front—next to the ramada and pestle and mortar—a garden full of sunflowers, goosefoot, tobacco, and raspberries took up what little yard there was before surrendering to the avenue's beaten white sand. The place was so close to River Mounds City that the two huge guardian posts that marked the boundaries were visible not more than three bowshots to the east.

All of which made it perfect for Winder. He had led his Quiz Quiz here by the back way—a secondary route that cut off from the avenue, wound its way to the north end of River Mounds City, and ended at the northern and swampy limits of the canoe landing where it followed Cahokia Creek back from the river.

When they had finished their task, they would return that way—hopefully without incident—and be on the river before nightfall.

Sky Star hobbled to his feet where he had been sitting with the rest of the warriors. Hitching his way to the door, he inclined his head, indicating that he wanted to speak privately.

Winder led the way out to the ramada, where Sky Star leaned against one of the poles to support his wounded body. "Are you sure you should have trusted that runner?"

Winder reached over and snapped off one of the sunflower seed pods. Using a thumbnail he began plucking out the black seeds and popping them into his mouth as he watched the few people passing. "Definitely not as much traffic. It's like the Morning Star has put the world on hold while he dies."

"I wasn't concerned with traffic. What if we're out here for nothing? Misdirected. And all the while that Cahokian bitch is back at Evening Star Town, sitting up in that palace feasting and drinking grape juice?"

Winder crunched more seeds before saying, "War Leader, the runner was from War Duck himself. And he got the information from Columella. They're Four Winds Clan. Keeper Blue Heron is one of their own. Something happened up at the River House palace last night. Something bad enough to get the eternal fire extinguished—and War Duck blames Blue Heron for it. Columella couldn't have known that."

"So you think the old woman is coming this way with the box?"

"War Duck has no reason to lie. He's in this up past his one good eyebrow. I can hear behind the words. None of this has worked out the way he anticipated. What he wants now is payback for the damage Blue Heron has done him and his House over the years, and to have us gone."

Winder paused before adding, "And given that Cahokia is going to explode like a ball of wet clay in a hot fire the moment the Morning Star dies, gone is where we want to be."

Sky Star closed his eyes. "This has been a disaster. I am ruined for the rest of my life. The War Medicine Bundle is profaned even if we get it back. It will have to be reconsecrated. I have lost two warriors, and the slave who warmed my bed has run off. My Power is broken. I am disgraced."

"Maybe not. You will take the Four Winds Clan Keeper back as a prisoner. Or, if she dies, you'll take her head and bones. She might not be the Surveyors' Bundle, but no one has taken a member of Black Tail's immediate family prisoner for almost a hundred years. I think there are war honors enough in that to allow you to live in prestige for the rest of your life."

And it will have served to make me a fortune. I will be known as a man who can salvage a triumph out of disaster.

That brought a smile to Winder's lips.

"My warriors are ready," Sky Star announced. "Now, if she will just come as they said. You are sure she will not have an escort of warriors?"

"War Duck insisted there will be no warriors. Columella and her people don't know that he is desperate to get Blue Heron out of the way." Winder pointed with a hard finger. "You keep your men in line, War Leader. This has to be done my way. Quietly. Without screaming and yelling. As they come past, our people file out, surround the litters, and threaten the porters. I'll order them to leave, and as soon as they do, Red Stroke and Moccasin grab and gag the old lady while Smoking Water takes the War Medicine box from the second litter. And then we move."

"And then we move," the war leader agreed. "Quietly. As fast as we can for the canoes. I want to be gone from this place."

"You and me both. But War Leader, if you start to slow us down, I will order you carried. Do not argue. I'll tell everyone it is a show of respect for your courage and audacity as the war leader who captured Blue Heron and recovered the War Medicine."

"You lie with a very clever tongue, Winder."

Sky Star hobbled out to look down the avenue. "We have been here almost a full hand of time. Why have they not come?"

"Patience, War Leader. The later they are, the better I feel. It means that they *don't* have an escort. That when War Duck didn't provide one, they tried to find someone else." At least that's what he hoped had happened. Though the old woman might have turned around and had someone paddle across the river to Evening Star Town to see if she could beg an escort from Columella.

"I do hope she lives long enough to make it back to Quiz Quiz," Sky Star said wistfully. "My souls ache with the desire to hang her rot-infested body in the square. It will be a challenge, but I want to see if I can keep her alive and suffering for a half moon. She won't see any of it, of course, because I'm going to cut her eyes out before I drive a burning stick into her sheath. I have a lot to pay her back for."

Winder gave the war leader a smile. He would be long gone from Quiz Quiz. Unless Cahokia tore itself apart with civil war after the Morning Star's death, the Four Winds Clan *would* retaliate. Not even

War Duck—complicit in her abduction—could allow the Quiz Quiz to go unpunished. In fact, he would probably yell the loudest about foreign perfidy as he assembled an army to hammer the brains and guts out of the poor Quiz Quiz. If Cahokia acted quickly enough, they could probably justify the conquest to the other lower river Nations in a way that would avoid the inevitable retaliation.

I wonder if I should offer myself to War Duck as a guide?

He was pondering this when he noticed the approaching party. Yes, two litters coming just behind what looked like a double rank of slaves bearing large burden baskets hung from tumplines.

"Alert the warriors," Winder told Sky Star. "They are coming. Right behind those slaves. And yes, look there. I see Seven Skull Shield and that dog of his."

"I shall kill them both!" Sky Star gritted, his eyes afire.

Winder grabbed a handful of the war leader's hunting shirt. "You will *not*! I said this was to be done quietly. If you can't make that happen, hobble your scarred carcass back inside and send me Moccasin to command this operation!"

For moments they glared into each other's eyes, Sky Star finally relenting. "But the thief and the dog die?"

"Fine. But not here. Not on the road."

"And if he fights?"

Winder considered, then shrugged it away. "He won't fight. Not if a blade is held against the old woman's throat. Leave that to me. I know my old friend. His biggest weakness is that pus-rotted sense of loyalty."

Winder slapped the war leader on the back. "Now, send your warriors out here. I want them bent over, harvesting raspberries and sunflower seeds, their weapons out of sight down in the plants."

As the Quiz Quiz warriors filed out and bent to the deception, Winder motioned Red Stroke and Moccasin over. "You understand your task?"

"Yes, Trader," Red Stroke replied. "As soon as the litter is on the ground, we lay hold of the old woman and carry her off."

"We've got to be fast."

"What about those slaves out front?"

"They are slaves, what do they care?"

"And the ones coming behind?"

Winder took a look, seeing a second party perhaps a stone's throw behind Blue Heron's litter. Twenty half-naked men, cloth pads on their shoulders where they were bearing a heavy log to some distant construction project.

"Even if they cared, we're armed; they are not."

"Yes, Trader."

"Now bend down. Let's look like we're working."

Despite himself, Winder couldn't help but shoot a glance at Seven Skull Shield. His old friend was plodding along, obviously engaged in conversation with the old woman riding atop the first litter. He was close enough now that that Skull's old familiar laugh carried.

By Piasa, old friend, I am so sorry it's come to this.

Or maybe it hadn't. Perhaps, just maybe, like in the old days, Seven Skull Shield would see that all was lost, and he'd turn on his heel and run.

Please do that.

A curling anxiety turned sour in his gut as the line of dirty slaves shuffled past, backs bent under what had to be heavy loads. Splotches of dried mud had caked to their skin, and sweat stains had traced lines through the grime.

Not more than ten paces behind them came Blue Heron's familiar litter, her porters striding along, faces blank of emotion. Just men doing a job and periodically talking among themselves.

Atop the litter, the old woman sat, her form completely swaddled in a blanket, a beautiful lace shawl pulled over her head, no doubt to hide the bruises as well as obscure her identity.

Seven Skull Shield was pacing along on the near side, telling some story about fish while that ungainly dog of his panted just behind, its bearlike jaws agape, tail swishing.

And yes, the following litter—carried by only four porters—bore some sort of boxy thing on the seat. Its nature was uncertain since it was wrapped in a fine yellow-and-black striped blanket. But the size was most definitely right.

Bless you, Horned Serpent!

Just as Winder met Seven Skull Shield's eyes, he shouted in Quiz Quiz, "Move! Take them."

The warriors around him ripped their war clubs from the obscuring vegetation and went charging out to surround the litter. Even as they did, the porters, frightened half out of their wits, dropped the litter and bolted, running like deer.

"Go! Go! Go!" Winder shouted, his heart leaping with joy.

Seven Skull Shield, meanwhile, stood as if rooted, a queer smile on his lips.

"Run, Skull!" Winder shouted in Cahokian, knowing Sky Star couldn't understand. "Save yourself! They'll kill you otherwise."

"Can't do that, old friend." Skull stood stoically as the Quiz Quiz surrounded him, war clubs ready.

"Come on," Winder pleaded. "They just want the old woman and the box!"

"No." Seven Skull Shield beckoned. "Come over here. You kill me first."

Images flashed between Winder's souls: he and Skull as boys. Laughing, shivering together under a blanket. Was this how that friendship would end? "I . . . *can't*!"

"What in Piasa's name!" Moccasin cried, having leaped to the far side of the first litter and ripped the lace shawl away. At the second litter Red Stroke was tugging the blanket to the side to expose the War Medicine.

For a long and shocked moment, everyone stared.

A dwarf stood braced against the seat back as he pawed for balance. Even as he recovered, he shouted, "This is intolerable! As a servant of Lady Columella, high matron of the Evening Star House, I command you to lay down your arms."

Meanwhile Seven Skull Shield was grinning, gesturing to the big dog to stay. The beast was bouncing on his paws, unsure about what was happening, but reading the excitement and tension.

"War Leader," Smoking Water cried from the second litter. He and Red Stroke had finally torn the blanket off the box, exposing a square crate made of rough pine slats. From inside he lifted a couple of cracked brownware pots. Staring in disbelief, he cried, "This is *not* the War Medicine!"

"You piece of shit!" Winder bellowed, starting forward. "What have you done?"

Skull just kept grinning, and all the while the dwarf was shouting insults, dancing up and down on the litter seat, demanding their surrender and shaking his fist. The Quiz Quiz stared in stunned amazement.

"Not a step closer," Seven Skull Shield warned, "or I'll turn the dog loose on you, Winder. And if that happens, a lot of people are going to get killed."

"Killed?" Winder bellowed. "Have you lost all the smarts you've ever had? You're surrounded by warriors! One word from me, *old friend,* and you and your silly little dwarf are dead!"

"What has happened here?" Sky Star cried, hobbling up from the side, where he'd been observing. He, too, couldn't keep his eyes off the pirouetting dwarf on the litter.

"We've been tricked!" Winder said through gritted teeth.

"Kill them," Sky Star ordered. "Enough of this! Show them how Quiz Quiz deal with fools!"

"Winder?" Seven Skull Shield chided, that old easy smile on his lips. "Before you do anything foolish . . ." And he pointed.

A cold realization slipped down Winder's spine as he followed Seven Skull Shield's finger. While they'd all been gawking in confused disbelief at the gesticulating and shouting dwarf, the slaves ahead had slipped their tumplines and dropped their burden baskets. From inside they had plucked shields, strung bows, and quivers full of arrows. They might look like slaves, but they now advanced in a half circle like blooded warriors—eyes deadly as they stared down nocked arrows.

Winder filled his lungs to order a retreat, but when he shot a quick glance behind to chart an escape, he froze. The crew who had been toting the heavy log had dropped it onto the avenue. Winder could now see that the top and inside had been hollowed out, perhaps as the start of a canoe. From the hollow, the men had plucked bows and quivers. As this impossibility struck home, they were fanning out in the way only a practiced squadron could, cutting off any retreat.

Surrounded!

His warriors, armed only with war clubs, stood no chance. They'd be shot down at the first volley.

"Winder, tell them to lay down their arms," Skull said. "These are elite warriors from the Evening Star squadron. At an order from Flat Stone Pipe here, they will kill every last one of you."

"No!" Sky Star cried. "I will not go back to the square."

"Your Power is broken, War Leader," Winder told him. "At least if we surrender, perhaps your people will ransom you. To die—shot down like trapped deer—because you have been tricked by a thief and a dwarf is not an honorable death."

"Drop your weapons," Sky Star cried, tears streaking from his eyes.

Winder's hopes and dreams died as the Quiz Quiz war clubs thumped hollowly on the sandy roadway.

Fifty-five

Someone was stroking the side of Night Shadow Star's head, and she realized it was a tender finger tucking a curl of her hair behind her right ear. The touch was light, almost reverent, and she stirred.

"Welcome back," Fire Cat greeted softly.

She blinked, blinked again—and realized that her eyes were indeed open to the incredible blackness. She lay canted on her side in his lap, her head on his shoulder, her body tucked against his.

"We're in the cave," she said, remembering. "How long has it been?"

At that, he laughed. "An eternity? Days? A couple of hands of time? I have no idea."

She should have forced herself to sit up, but she remained where she was, reaching out only to hug an arm around his neck until it encountered the unyielding stone against which he leaned. To lie thus—feeling his warmth, his arms around her—conjured a deep satisfaction inside her tired souls.

"I saw my children," he told her. "Talked with them. Played. They told me . . ." His voice caught. "They told me it was all right." A pause. "They looked so real. I thought for a moment . . . I mean, they really are dead, aren't they? Not some trick? Spotted Wrist . . . I thought he . . ."

"Yes, they are dead. No trick. You are in the Underworld, Fire Cat. The place to which their bodies and souls were consigned. The longer you are here, the more of the Dead you will see, until your souls can't stand it anymore, and you leave your suffocating body behind . . . preferring to join the Dead rather than to remain trapped in such a pitiful and fragile shell as flesh."

"I thought it might have been Sister Datura tricking my souls. As it is, I have the craziest images running through my memory. Flashes of light. Screaming in pain."

She felt it as he shook his head before continuing. "It's hazy and unreal in my memory: a hammering that vibrated the sand under my feet, blinding white heat, and some terrible conflict."

"Do you remember handing that copper spike to the Morning Star?"

"Handing . . ." He stopped short, and she felt his unease like a tension winding through his body. "No. But there was something. Big. Beating at me . . ."

"The moth?"

Again he shook his head. She could almost feel him frowning, sense his struggle to search his memory.

"So many odd . . . Oh, I don't know. I'm confused." He lifted an arm from her back to gesture at the surrounding darkness. "I don't even know where we are, Lady. I carried you. Sort of. At least got us out of that narrow tunnel. For a while I couldn't even figure out which way was up until I thought to lift one of the pebbles from the floor and drop it. It clicks when it hits bottom so I know that way is really down."

"You sound oddly resigned."

"I think we're going to die in here. You thirsty?"

"Very."

He shifted, arm extending to the side before it returned with her water bottle. Greedily she sucked down the cool liquid, refusing to completely slake her thirst. She handed the rest to him, only to feel him replacing it in what she assumed was her pack.

"You aren't going to drink?"

"I'm not thirsty."

"Suffering on my account isn't part of your oath to me."

"No, Lady, I suppose it is not. Down here, with nothing left, I think we're way beyond oaths and other silliness. I wonder if Chunkey Boy survived the poison?"

"You don't remember the cavern? The fading glow? The Morning Star's final words to me?"

He shook his head. "I don't think so."

"We all would have died but for you. You carried the copper spike."

"What spike?"

"The one that was left after your war club burned up. You went to fight the moth, to free the Morning Star, but it was too much to bear. At the last instant, before the moth could kill you, I saw you hand the spike to the Morning Star. With it he was able to stab the moth."

"Are you making this up?"

She shifted, staring at him in the darkness, wishing she could see his eyes. "No. I'm not making it up."

"Then how did I get there?"

"I carried you in my pack."

For a long moment he was silent. Then, as if talking to himself, he said, "Maybe it's the datura. Causes visions."

She slapped him halfheartedly on the shoulder. "It doesn't matter. I know what you did."

He tightened his grip on her, and she snuggled closer, placed her hand to his chest. Felt the steady beat of his heart. It wouldn't be so bad. She could just stay this way, curled against his strong chest. Were she to go back, it would just be to pain, and fear, the voices and visions, the constant worry and periods of depression. She was tired of the endless—

A flash of blue light flickered at the edge of her vision.

"Touching. Don't you two look cozy? Now, now, mustn't get too comfortable."

"Piasa," she said tensing. At the same time part of her wondered where the Tortoise Bundle was and why it wasn't playing with her souls.

"Where?" Fire Cat asked, shifting.

The Spirit beast's flickering glow drifted off to her right and then up.

"Blood and spit," she said wearily, disentangling herself from Fire Cat's arms. "Come on, Red Wing." She climbed to her feet.

"Lady?" She heard the reserve in his tone. "There are pitfalls, cracks. I barely avoided death just getting us out of that narrow tunnel."

"I suspect my master won't allow us any such easy escape as a simple maiming in the dark. Not when he can keep me alive and in his service."

"What a cheery thought."

"Come on. He's waiting on us."

When they reached the surface—if they did—she would again be Night Shadow Star, and heir to all the trouble that entailed. Back in that world, she and Fire Cat would once again be master and servant, separated by the rules of her class and status. She would be required by oath to hold him at arm's length—the price she'd paid to save her city.

Piasa's haunting laughter reverberated in the black confines of the cavern as he disappeared to leave Night Shadow Star and Fire Cat once again in darkness.

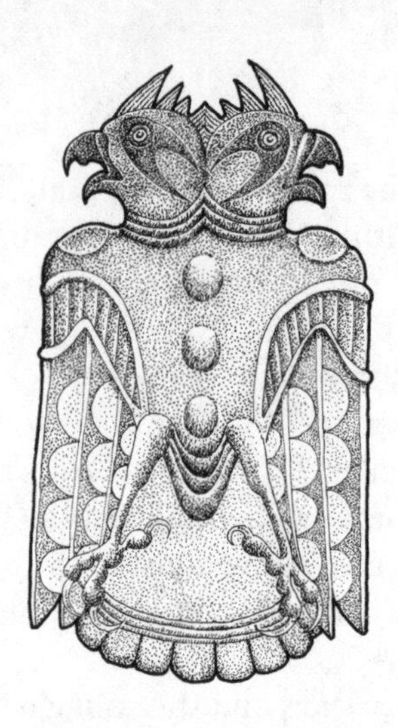

Fifty-six

Better, perhaps, than anyone in Cahokia, *Tonka'tzi* Wind understood the value inherent in making the right appearance. How to do that, however, was paramount. Nor did she have a clue about how to make a spectacular entrance as her porters carried her up the crowded Grand Staircase toward the Morning Star's palace. Everything was in chaos. How did she assert her authority?

She'd never seen the city like this. People, most of them Earth Clan nobles and some from the lower ranks of the Four Winds Clan, had to be displaced from the crowded steps just to allow passage. The men and women, mostly young, had stepped off and were clinging precariously to the steep mound sides.

Many of them called, "*Tonka'tzi,* what news?"

It was madness.

She had been half asleep—cramped and aching from her continuing devotions at Old-Woman-Who-Never-Dies' temple on the other side of the North Plaza. The only warning she had received of anything going even more wrong was when her servant charged in, declaring, "*Tonka'tzi,* Wolverine and Slender Fox are passing. They are being carried at the head of a full squadron!"

She had stumbled to her feet, almost falling when her cramped legs wouldn't hold her, and been half carried to the temple doors. The sight of passing warriors, fit for battle, had brought a palpitation to her heart.

The route south from Serpent Woman Town veered around the

string of old oxbow lakes and involved several creek crossings—or most of the journey could be made by canoe following the waterways.

The squadron she had watched marching south along the avenue had apparently taken the land route. They had shields hung over their shoulders, bows and quivers poking out above their loosely tied armor. While stepping out in good time, they had that loose-limbed, swinging stride of men warmed to the routine of march.

At the head of the squadrons—and atop two litters—rode Serpent Woman Town matron Slender Fox and High Chief Wolverine of North Star House. Wind had immediately called for her litter and had her people race in pursuit.

Blocked by the North Star squadrons, she hadn't been able to overtake the leaders. Had barely been able to force her way through the crowds surging around the base of the Morning Star's mound.

Now Slender Fox and Wolverine preceded her up the staircase, their warriors and functionaries haven taken position at the foot of the stairs. Swelling around the base of the great mound, the huge crowd still waited, ominous, like some lurking and formless monster.

A rustle—the stir of conversation from a thousand lips—had run through them as she and the North Star House rulers had started up the steps. Oh, yes, the people knew something was happening, and she could feel the whetting of their interest, the building unease.

She had seen crowds, and she'd seen mobs. This giant throng of massed humanity was something else entirely. Down deep inside of her souls she feared it. Its immense Power—like a barely contained thunder—chilled her like nothing she'd ever known, as though it could explode in a massive wave that would wash over and engulf her entire world. And when the last of it had ebbed away, only broken devastation and corpses would remain on a desolate and exhausted soil.

All it would take would be a spark. A single wrong move. Then, heedless, mindless, the mass of humanity would react.

Do you understand? She wanted to scream at Wolverine, shake her fist in Slender Fox's face. *We can't make a mistake here.*

Unless—*Hunga Ahuito* forbid—they should reach the palace gate and learn that the Morning Star had just died. What would the masses do then? Swarm the palace in a violent demonstration of their devotion? Go berserk in their grief? Rend the very fabric of their world the way a young and freshly made widow did her skirt?

Today I could see the end of the world.

Her heart was hammering as they were allowed through the high gate. The last thing she saw was a Horned Serpent House woman as she lost her footing on the loose mound side and went tumbling down the long slope to the accompaniment of cries and gasps from the spectators who'd regained the steps.

Wind didn't wait to see if she survived.

Inside the high palisade the courtyard was packed. It was all Wolverine's party could do to hammer people to the side and make a passage to the palace doors.

Wind's porters set her litter down, shoving people in the process, who shoved more people, all of them calling questions, shouting for news.

Five Fists had managed to keep some semblance of order, his warriors—armed and panicked—standing just inside the doors.

"What news?" Wolverine was demanding. "Is he still alive?"

Five Fists ignored both him and Slender Fox, and used an arm to shove them aside. "*Tonka'tzi*, I don't know what to tell you. Rides-the-Lightning and Matron Rising Flame are with him, but his breathing has slowed. His heartbeat . . ." He made a face. "It beats, then skips, and a breath later, beats again."

"What does that mean?" Slender Fox demanded, refusing to be put off.

"I *don't* know, Matron," Five Fists thundered.

"You will know," Wolverine bellowed back, "or I will order my squadron to clear this palace and this mound if I have to throw every man, woman, and child down the slopes to do it."

Around her, filling the room, were most of the other Four Winds Clan leaders. Green Chunkey now came waddling toward her, his corpulent belly preceding him like a battering ram, calling, "You'll do no such thing, Cousin."

Wind shouted, "Stop it! All of you." But she might have been whispering into a gale. And that left her with her original problem: Appearance was everything in leadership, so how did she reassert the *tonka'tzi*'s authority?

As the press of shouting nobles broke into bickering and shoving, she retreated back into the room—glanced around at the grand palace and its furnishings. Walking over to the fire, she noticed it was down to coals. It took a snap of her fingers, and one of the cowed boys who had been literally hiding back in the corner came warily forward.

"The fire needs wood, boy."

"But . . ."

"No buts. If this fire goes out, you will be skinned alive and left for the ravens to pluck your lidless eyeballs from your head. So build it up to a roaring blaze."

And so saying, she walked back into sacred space, picked up the conch-shell horn, and stopped before the Morning Star's high dais. Standing before it, she lifted the horn to her lips and blew.

At the horn's ringing clarity, the room went silent, all eyes turned her way.

Holding the horn as if it were a talisman of office, she climbed onto the forbidden dais and seated herself in the Morning Star's panther-hide chair.

Yes, this is the way. Either that, or I've just consigned myself to the square.

One wrong word, and they'd kill her for blasphemy.

Fifty-seven

With trembling fingers, Night Shadow Star reached out into the thick blackness. She felt her way forward in a universe devoid of light, a totality of near-liquid black that seemed to run between her fingers. With a tentative foot, she tapped the soft footing ahead, wary of a drop-off, or crack. Each contraction of her heart beat like a pestle in her chest. Panic lay just at the edge of her being, and as long as she wasn't listening for it, the whispering of the Dead distracted her.

The moment that she stopped, cocked her head, and struggled to hear what they were saying, however, they vanished into the silent dark like a snap of the fingers.

And silent it was. Like a weight. Pressing around her. As if all sound had been absorbed by the darkness, stone, and cool air.

"Lady?" Fire Cat asked from behind her. "Are you sure your master has abandoned you?"

She swallowed hard, wishing for water. The knowledge that a remnant sloshed back and forth in the bottle that Fire Cat carried almost drove her mad. He was saving it for her. Suffering his thirst that she might finally swig down that last precious couple of swallows. Which was all the more reason she would die before she'd drink it.

"Nothing," she told him, gesturing her futility—as if he could see anything, let alone her expressive gesture. Filling her lungs, she called, "Master?"

The cool silence mocked her as she stared around, desperate for even a vestige of Piasa's eerie blue glow.

Nothing.

Only the eternal blackness returned her gaze.

"Lord, why have you left us?" she demanded of the invisible air.

She could hear Fire Cat's breathing, his growing fear audible as he drew each worried breath. She'd heard men pant in terror. Knew that cadence: the slight gasping intake and frantic exhalation.

"It is all right," Fire Cat told her. Then he swallowed hard, perhaps from fear, or maybe because of his thirst.

"He would not have left us without a reason," she forced herself to say reasonably.

"You are too important to him." Fire Cat sounded like he was trying to reassure himself.

Why? she asked herself. *He led us this far, to this place, only to dwindle into nothingness.*

Through an act of will she calmed herself, paced her breathing with deep and rhythmic breaths, and managed to slow her pounding heart.

Something. There must be something.

Fragments of conversation—bits of sentences—tried to pop out of the air around her. Like the visions, the Spirit voices hovering in the air were worse when she was frightened or worried.

"Leave me in peace," she pleaded. "Let me listen."

Cackling laughter answered from just over her head.

She sensed rather than saw or felt Fire Cat as he tensed.

"Not you," she whispered. "The voices. Don't you hear?"

"No, Lady. But I never do."

She wanted to bend double with that bitter laughter of frustration and despair. If she did, it would mean surrender, a broken admission of defeat that would leave her hollow and supine on chilly cavern floor.

You will be lost.

Closing her eyes—as if that made any difference—she stilled herself. Drove the voices into silence by straining to hear them, and slowly exhaled a deep breath.

Then she carefully opened her eyes and began searching the darkness. Timing herself by the beating of her heart, she scanned the ink-thick blackness.

There!

Just a faint golden flicker. It seemed to sway, to strengthen and then diminish. But what was it? Certainly nothing that hinted of Piasa and his eerie blue.

She reached back—fumbled for Fire Cat's hand—and felt her way forward and slightly to the right. Whatever happened, she couldn't lose sight of that lazy waving filament of illumination.

"Lady, do you—"

"Shhh."

Fumbling about with her toe, she made one slow step after another, the faint golden glow ever brighter as she felt her way over a chunk of angular roof fall. Rounding another such block, she finally stared up, standing just beneath the slowly waving light.

She could make out golden filaments, just out of reach. Fragments. Threads similar to torn cloth, that when they twisted, glowed on one side, and were black on the other. She stared, trying to place the familiar . . .

"Part of a cocoon," she whispered.

"Lady?"

"In the cavern. After you handed the spike to the Morning Star. He was fading, being cocooned in darkness."

"I don't remember any of that."

"You were dead," she told him thoughtfully.

"So you say, but I . . ."

She stilled his outburst with a squeeze of her hand, adding, "It's all right. We're on the right path."

"How can you say that? I can't see the nose on my face, let alone any cocoon."

She smiled at the frustration in his voice, tugging him forward as she picked out another filament of black-backed golden cocoon just ahead. Even as she passed beneath it, the first remnants of cocoon faded into nonexistence. "The Morning Star went this way."

"Are you sure?"

She led him with greater confidence now, feeling her way with her feet.

One after another, the bits of cocoon drew her onward, hope springing in her chest until, as she stepped into one of the narrow chambers, a golden glow illuminated both the pictographs and the cloth-wrapped bodies of the Dead where they were propped beneath the drawings.

And there walked the Morning Star, illuminated by an interior glow. On taloned eagle feet, he strode carefully along on the rock-strewn floor. Feathered wings extended from his arms. His antlered headdress with its raccoon hide and arrow-studded crest cast shadows on the irregular ceiling.

Stunned, Night Shadow Star watched as the Morning Star's fingers flicked lightly over the bent heads of the Dead where they had been propped against the walls. Wrapped as they were in fabrics, they might have been supplicants seeking his blessing.

As his fingers traced across the bowed heads, bits of soul flickered and darted from the bodies. Like wingless birds they rose to the charcoaled figures drawn on the stone over each. Upon reaching that portal, the souls sank into the stone, the drawings momentarily alive as they expanded, raised their arms, or Danced on agile legs. A breath of time later they faded back to charcoal, immovable and again lifeless as the freed souls followed their path to the Underworld.

Night Shadow Star watched in wonder as the Morning Star made his way to the far end of the cavern; the drawings on the walls animated, Dancing, the occasional red lines, circles, and dots burning as crimson as a winter sunrise.

The Morning Star seemed to hesitate at the end of the room, then glanced over his shoulder, meeting Night Shadow Star's gaze. With a curious smile on his lips, he gave the slightest nod of recognition.

He vanished in a flash that left afterimages burning on the backs of her eyes. She had seen it, hadn't she? A sort of lightning flash that blinded. A burning streak of brilliance that shot instantly into the image of the Morning Star drawn upon the stone wall.

The cavern once again pitched into stygian black.

"That was miraculous," she whispered.

"What was?" Fire Cat asked, voice strained with anxiety.

"The Morning Star. Freed of the cocoon. The way he touched the heads of the corpses and liberated the body souls to enter the drawings." She pointed with her free hand. "Did you see how he vanished back into the stone? Reanimated his image on the wall?"

Fire Cat's long pause irritated her.

"Is that the choice he made? Rather than return to the world, to vanish back into the stone itself?" She fought sudden tears. "Then what was our purpose in coming here?"

The pause was awkward this time—and just long enough she was about to snap at him when he said, "Lady, with all respect, I haven't seen anything since that last torch burned out. I've been following faithfully behind you. I trust that with your Power, you actually saw these threads of light and cocoon you talk about. But in this constant blackness, I couldn't have seen the Morning Star if he were pressing against me."

"But he was just . . ." She frowned and shook her head.

"Yes, Lady. I'm sure he was. Please. Drink the rest of the water. You will feel so much better."

"You saw nothing?"

"No, Lady."

"What does it matter," she replied wearily. "Even if we haven't saved the Morning Star, let us hope that we can still save ourselves."

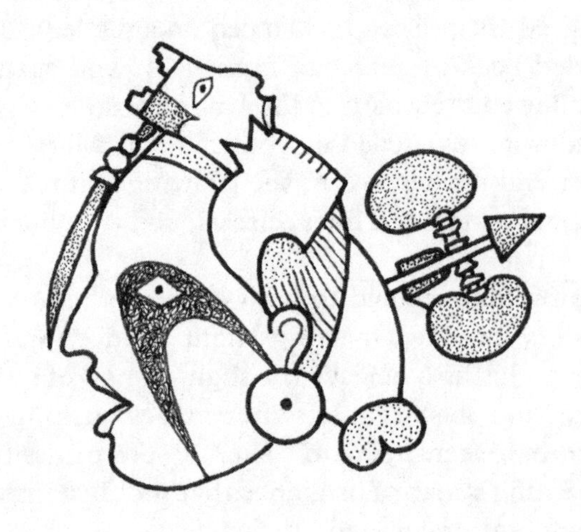

Fifty-eight

The chance had always existed that it could end like this. Winder stared around the Evening Star Town Plaza and the crowd that had assembled to stare at him and the Quiz Quiz prisoners. Word had passed that these were the barbarian warriors who had dared to kidnap Keeper Blue Heron. From the looks Winder and the Quiz Quiz were getting from the crowd, he had no doubt that if the guarding warriors turned their backs, things would get ugly in a hurry.

The Evening Star warriors had made no bones about the fact that Winder and his companions were bound for hideous death in the squares, so maybe the tender mercies of the mob might be a far better and faster—if just as brutal—fate.

That was the risk Winder had taken in his given profession—what justified the exorbitant Trade he asked in return for his services. Risky ventures demanded remarkable Trade in return. Winder had made both reputation and fortune by accepting that if anything went wrong, he would pay with his life in a most agonizing way.

Oddly, the risks had been growing fewer and less dangerous as his fame spread on the southern rivers—especially as a broker of communication between enemies and a negotiator for ransom and diplomacy between hostile parties. High chiefs knew that he was a spy, but also an honest agent for those whom he represented. As a known quantity, the risk of misunderstanding had been significantly ameliorated.

How ironic, then, that he should find himself in such dire straits, and not at the hands of some petty barbarian chief up a minor tributary of the Tenasee, but in Cahokia, the great city of his youth. Nor had the manner of his capture been through treachery at a feast, as he'd always imagined it would be. Instead, he'd been cunningly trapped—caught in the act of attacking one of the highest-ranking Four Winds Clan elders alive.

Was I so arrogant and proud that I missed the signs? Did I bait Power to believe that I was so assured of my invincibility and success that it had *to bring me down in such a manner?*

Winder chuckled to himself, amused at his hubris, as he tested the bonds that bound his wrists and feet. One of the most humiliating events of his life had been the walk back down the Avenue of the Sun, tied in line with the rest of the Quiz Quiz captives, looking for all the world like an incompetent fool. The worst part had been the jeers and catcalls from the spectators and passersby.

Winder had never feared death. Public humiliation, however, was beyond his tolerance.

"And I was brought down by good old Skull of all people?" Again, that had to be the hand of Power smacking him down. Nothing else could explain his old friend's involvement in Winder's complete destruction. The joke was that he had left Cahokia to avoid just such an end.

Now here he was.

I should never have come back here.

Most of the huddled Quiz Quiz stared at their bonds and just mumbled to themselves, blaming their disaster on the stolen War Medicine box. When the Surveyors' Bundle *and* the War Medicine had been lost, they muttered, they should have left, allowing Sky Star to pay the price for their failure.

But I couldn't let it end at that. No, I had to push it. My fault. All my fault.

And Skull's, of course.

Even as he thought it, he saw Skull come ambling down the long staircase that led up to Evening Star House's high palace on the plaza's northern side. His old friend's blocky face looked thoughtful, maybe even sad. Even the ugly brindle dog that padded at Skull's heels looked dejected.

Winder watched his old friend walk up, nod to the squadron first in charge of the guarding warriors, and then settle himself on the packed clay just beyond Winder's reach. Skull pulled up his knees, clasping his arms around them as he studied Winder.

"I was just thinking about you," Winder began. "About the old days. About how Power must be laughing, using you to bring me down. Odd, isn't it? Remember the time I distracted that Panther Clan bunch?

They'd caught you stealing a pot of corn from their storage pit. As I recall, they were going to beat you to death and leave your corpse hung from the guardian post out front as a deterrent for anyone who might have similar ideas regarding their oh-so-precious corn."

Skull smiled. "Wasn't the only time. Remember when that bunch of bigger boys at the canoe landing took our blankets? Then we took them back when they weren't looking?"

Winder nodded. "Wasn't particularly bright of us, going back to the same old abandoned building for the night. They almost beat us back there."

"And you told them you'd taken the blankets back by yourself. That I wasn't even part of it. I never forgot that."

"Didn't do much good." Winder shrugged. "They still smacked us both around. Took weeks for the bruises to heal.

"Without blankets we had to sleep in the corner of that old house huddled together like field mice. Just you and me. In the middle of the winter. Couldn't get a good night's sleep."

Skull's features turned amiable. "Every time I'd drift off, you'd shiver so hard I'd be wide awake with my eyeballs vibrating."

"Me? You were the one shivering. Wasn't much more to you than skin and thin bones. I at least had a little fat around my belly to keep me warm."

"Blessed little, if I recall." Skull reached out to pet the dog when it dropped beside him and exhaled with a huff. "Seems to me I remember a permanent hollow running from your ribs down to your navel in those days."

"Always hungry, weren't we?" Winder shook his head. "Remember the year we got away with that roasted goose on the winter solstice? Stole it right off the fire."

"Had to toss it back and forth between us as we ran. It was too hot to hold for more than a heartbeat without blistering our fingers."

"The thing spent more time in the air than when it was alive and flying."

"But neither one of us dropped it," Skull reminded with a pointed finger. "It was too rotted precious for that. And it was mostly cooled to the touch by the time we got to that sheltered niche between the warehouses."

"I think that was the finest meal of my life," Winder said wistfully. "That whole goose! I can still taste the grease dribbling down around my tongue. Smell that steaming fragrance. Remember how it chewed as I pulled the meat from the bone."

"No high chief ate better than we did that day. You were grinning so hard I thought your mouth would get stuck like that, and you'd go through life looking like an idiot."

"Never! Look like an idiot? I left that sort of thing to you."

Skull chuckled. "I suppose you did." A pause. "A long time ago."

"A very long time ago." Winder's gut went bittersweet. "I suppose, if I had to meet this end, it is fitting that it's you who brought me to it rather than some stranger. Facing one's death is something best done at the hands of friends. They, at least, know you for who you are. With strangers it can be so callous, a matter of simple business. Not only have they no clue as to who you are, they could not care less."

"Never thought of it that way.'

"Skull? I would ask you for something, though. I don't want you to come after they hang me in the square."

Skull's gaze hardened, almost turning brittle.

At his silence, Winder added, "I don't want you to see me like that. Remember me instead as that boy you shared the solstice goose with. Remember the smiles we had that day, and the grease that ran down our chins. Or how we took care of each other." His jaws clenched, and he added, "Better than brothers, eh?"

Skull looked away, lips pursed as he petted his dog. "If it had been anyone but Blue Heron . . ." He made a face. "Why didn't you leave that day when I asked you to?"

"Too much at stake." Winder gestured with his bound hands. "It was always the longest odds that paid the best. I had a reputation to maintain. You get a taste for that life, for being a big man, an important personage, especially after where you and I came from. Those who do not dare, never eat solstice goose. Nor, if they are great men, do they become even greater men."

"Beating Blue Heron like you did . . ." Skull gestured futility and looked away.

"I didn't know she was your friend. Nor was that my doing. I stopped the Quiz Quiz who was kicking her to death. Tell her that I'm sorry."

"Won't make any difference." Skull worked his strong fingers, watching the tendons flex. "But for that I might have been able to work something out. Maybe just a banishment, arguing that you were only hired. That you didn't have a choice."

Winder laughed. "But I did, Skull. And you know it. I gambled that I could save it all, get the War Medicine back and get away with the Quiz Quiz. Instead, well, Power had other interests."

"Hey!" Flat Stone Pipe shouted from the palace staircase. "Thief! They want you inside."

"Be right there," Skull called, rising to his feet. To Winder, he said,

"I give you my word, old friend. I won't come to see you hanging in the square. After what you've done, they'll make sure it will be long and painful. I don't think I could stand that." He hesitated, whispering, "Better than brothers."

"Good. And Skull, if you'd remember anything about me, do it anytime you eat roast goose, all right?"

Skull's face was working in that old familiar way that it did when he was fighting with himself. Instead of words, he just gave a quick nod of the head, and then strode off for the stairs, where the dwarf waited.

It was the dog that paused, looked back over its shoulders, and fixed the odd blue and brown eyes on Winder. The beast seemed to be considering, judging Winder's soul.

"Take care of him, dog."

The beast cocked its ears, then with a parting glance, raced after the burly thief as he started up the stairs.

"Farewell, old friend," Winder whispered softly.

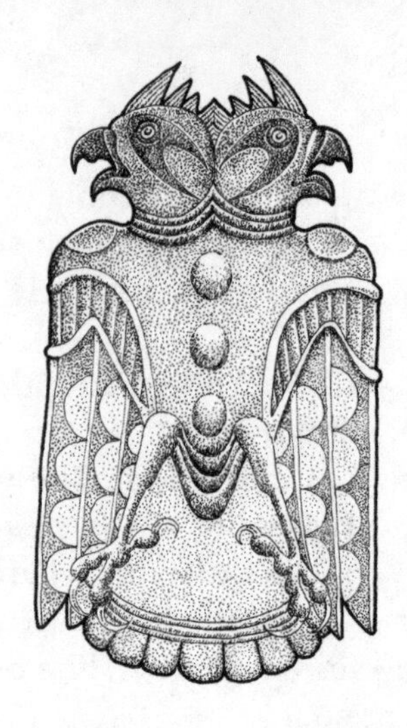

Fifty-nine

People stood frozen, gaping and wide-eyed, as they stared at *Tonka'tzi* Wind where she perched imperiously on the Morning Star's high dais with its panther-hide covering. The shocked quiet was that of the tomb.

She had to seize the moment now. Before they could react. Or think.

"I am *Tonka'tzi* Wind, and I *will* have order." She pointed to the appalled old lop-jawed warrior. "War Leader Five Fists. You will enforce order. The first person who acts out of turn will be removed from this room. If they protest, you will use your war club to break his or her jaw. Am I understood?"

Five Fists expression was incredulous as he pushed his way clear of the stunned crowd, shouting, "Yes, *Tonka'tzi*!"

"Are my orders clear?" she demanded, shooting her gaze from face to face.

Around the room, heads bobbed uncertainly.

"But sitting on the Morning Star's chair?" Lord East Water cried. "That's sacrilege!"

"War Leader Five Fists"—she pointed—"remove that man."

"Yes, *Tonka'tzi*."

And quick as a snap—at Five Fists' nod—two of his warriors took East Water by the arms and hustled him to the doors before pitching him out. Idly Wind wondered what Rising Flame would say when she learned her father had been so summarily expelled.

"Now," she said, leaning forward. "We teeter on the knife's sharp edge of disaster."

Green Chunkey stepped forward, doing her the courtesy of touching his chin. "With respect, *Tonka'tzi,* the Morning Star is dying. Whatever happened with Lady Night Shadow Star and her journey to the Underworld, it was obviously a failure. Just before your arrival I was in there, saw his body. Even Rides-the-Lightning has given up hope."

Wolverine stepped up to the man's side, touching his chin and saying, "*Tonka'tzi,* it is past time to fortify the Morning Star's palace. My squadron is positioning itself to take control of the situation here as we speak."

"You will not," Green Chunkey said bitterly. "Once your people have control . . . No, I absolutely refuse. You will *not*—"

"Silence," Wind barked, pointing hard at both of them. To her relief, they obeyed. "If *anyone* moves on this palace, that crowd out there will take matters into their own hands."

"With respect"—Wolverine barely hid his annoyance—"that squadron out there is just back from Red Wing Town. My best veterans. The idea of a crowd of unarmed, undisciplined dirt farmers standing against the authority of any Four Winds squadron, let alone mine—"

"That *mass* of humanity out there doesn't give a louse's leg about your authority," Wind rebutted harshly. "Set them off and they'll crush your warriors through their very weight. They are out there—ten thousand strong—out of concern for their god. That is their *only* concern: whether the Morning Star lives or dies. They could not care less about any show of strength. In fact, all it would take is a warrior shoving the wrong person, and like a spark from a fire, their passion will burn so free and hot it will consume us all. Until only ruin is left."

Wolverine said, "I don't think you understand—"

"Do *you* understand the meaning behind irresistible, relentless, mindless, and invincible? If we do something to set them off, they will come as a *flood*!"

"*Tonka'tzi.*" Slender Fox took a position beside her brother. "Whether the Morning Star lives or dies, we have to make a change. The Morning Star House allowed the assassin to ply her poisons. They put us into this situation. I know you are biased toward them, are one of them, but as *tonka'tzi* you now must serve all of Cahokia."

Slender Fox turned, facing the rest of the room. "So consider this: My brother, Sliding Ice, is preparing himself, cleansing his body and purifying his souls. He is ready—the moment the Morning Star dies—to offer his body as a new home to the Spirit hero of the Beginning Times. There is your answer to the dilemma. A rapid resurrection of the

Morning Star. A new home for the living god. We need not even wait until a tomb is built for Chunkey Boy's body."

"And why should it be a North Star House body?" Green Chunkey demanded. "You and Wolverine assume too much!"

Shouts broke out, Wind bellowing, "Silence!"

This time, to her surprise, it took Five Fists pitching into them with the handle of his war club to bring order.

And he'd no sooner done so than a messenger bearing a staff of office was passed through by the guard at the door. Working his way through the press to the fire, he blinked, confused at the sight of Wind on the high dais. Then, as if pulling himself together, he knelt before Green Chunkey to announce, "High Chief, it is my honor to report that our two squadrons have arrived at the Great Plaza. Squadron First Split Snake reports resistance from the crowd. They refuse to give way to allow our warriors to proceed to the palace. The squadron first asks your permission to move them, High Chief."

"Move them," Green Chunkey said sourly as he glared at Wolverine.

"No!" Wind barked, fear pumping with each beat of her heart. "Do that, and we'll all die!"

"*Tonka'tzi*," Green Chunkey told her, "I will not leave my squadrons to the south while Wolverine holds this ground." He looked around. "North Star House essentially holds us all as hostage. Consider, Lords: All he needs to do is issue an order, and we are his prisoners. *He* will hold us while Sliding Ice offers his body to become host of the living god! North Star House will have taken all of Cahokia!"

"You piece of fat shit," Slender Fox told him as she thrust a finger into his face. "While you've lived on the wealth of southern colonies, we've been holding the north, battling the Red Wing and their forest barbarians! While you've prospered, we've paid the price in dead relatives and war. And what has it earned us? Strength, you overstuffed cutworm. And now North Star House claims its reward."

Green Chunkey ducked awkwardly around her finger, gesturing to his messenger, as he said, "Order my squadrons forward. No matter what the cost!"

"No!" Wind thundered again. "Five Fists, stop that man!"

The lop-jawed warrior made a gesture, and one of his warriors—pale-faced and scared—laid a hand on the messenger's arm.

"You sure you want to do this?" Green Chunkey asked, cunning eyes on Wind. "Let him go, or by Piasa's balls, there's no stepping back from this."

"High Chief," Five Fists said reasonably, "it is the *tonka'tzi*'s order for the moment. And she is the *tonka'tzi*."

Green Chunkey laughed bitterly. "Ah, yes, words from the eloquent Five Fists. But for you and your fawning subservience to the Morning Star House, Robin Wing would now be Four Winds Clan matron instead of that foolish Rising Flame! I know whose side you're on."

"I *serve* the Morning Star!" Five Fists had his offset jaw clenched.

"Yes. Sure." Green Chunkey sniffed disdainfully. To the warrior holding his messenger, he said, "The fates of Cahokia and a thousand lives lie in your grasp, warrior. Let my messenger go, or you can live with the responsibility of knowing it was all your fault."

"Hold!" Wind snapped. For the moment, the only authority she maintained came from the chair's height. "Five Fists, it is on my order that *no one* leaves this room. Not for any purpose! If anyone tries, be it matron, high chief, or lowly servant, kill them."

"*Tonka'tzi*?" He shot her a stunned look.

They all did.

I am all that's holding this together. If I slip, make a mistake . . .

She took the chance of seating herself again, desperate to appear in control as her heart hammered crazily in her chest. The hatred between Green Chunkey and Slender Fox and Wolverine was crackling like sassafras root in a fire.

Both sides could taste victory. Each believed that by taking initiative, they could seize control of the city—and the will of the people be cursed. In that single daring move Morning Star House would be deposed, and they'd name the next host for the Morning Star's body.

Not counting Evening Star House and River House. The stars alone knew what havoc they might be committing at this same moment. And if a River House squadron came marching in from the west? What then?

The masses of people out there will decide.

"You would have this old, broken-down warrior kill me?" Wolverine asked, flexing his eagle-scarred and muscular arms. "Brave words, *Tonka'tzi*."

Gelling all of her courage into a lump of resolve, she forced her expression to remain steadfast. They couldn't know—not even by a quiver of the lip—how desperate, how fragile she felt.

"High Chief Wolverine, I wasn't joking when I told you that crowd out there is the biggest threat we face. I will take any measures I need to take to keep *anyone* from acting foolishly. You think it's simple matter of besting Horned Serpent House? Green Chunkey's not the threat. He's as deluded as you are. Any sign of hostility, any conflict, and *the people* will tear this city apart!"

Wolverine's lips flattened into a cunning smile. "*You* will do this? *You* will save us all."

Looking as regal as she could after so many hours without sleep, her stomach empty, her wits at an end, she said, "If I am the only thing standing between peace and disaster, so be it. I will do my duty."

"Then I," Wolverine said, leaping across the fire, "will free myself of that impediment."

His action was so fast it caught both her and Five Fists by complete surprise. She barely had time to shift before he'd pounded his way up onto the dais and grabbed her by the throat.

She felt his grip—the same that he used to hold eagles—tightening on her throat. Lifting her bodily, he turned to face the shocked room. Wind heard a curious gurgling sound at the base of her tongue.

"Five Fists," Wolverine declared, thrusting his other arm out to stop the old war leader, "you will allow my sister to leave. Slender Fox, command our warriors to take control of this mound and to fortify the Council House wall and remove all these pus-sucking spectators. At the same time, tell Fast Throw to send a messenger to Wet Stick and tell him we need a second squadron here now. That we are threatened by squadrons from Horned Serpent House."

Slender Fox nodded, shooting an "I dare you" glance at the apoplectic Five Fists. "What about the Morning Star squadrons?"

Wolverine told her, "They can't be called up by anyone but the Morning Star or the matron, and she's here." He grinned wickedly. "And I do not foresee Matron Rising Flame departing the palace anytime soon."

"You . . . fool," Wind wheezed through the tight grip on her throat.

Wolverine's hard brown eyes drilled into hers. "You're courageous, that's for sure, *Great Sky.*" He mocked her title.

From the corner of her eye, Wind watched the warriors step aside to allow Slender Fox through the great double doors.

We've lost it all.

How long would it take? Slender Fox, slim and athletic as she was, would literally fly down the stairs—or at least weave her way as she could, given the number of bodies clogging the steps. At the foot of the stairs, she'd give the order, and the North Star squadron would start up en masse, knocking people aside as they did. Even as they started to fortify the Council House, expelling people in the process, the mighty throng would realize that something terrible had happened.

Wind closed her eyes, trying to swallow past the grip that held her like a vise.

Among the people it would start with a sort of questioning moan, and would flow out like a ring in a pond. The noise would grow to a rumble of disbelief. Then would come the shouts, swelling, spreading, verbal expression of the growing disbelief in their hearts.

Someone would yell, "The Morning Star is dead!"

After that, it would be unstoppable. The grief would be let loose, and it would drive them forward, heedless of the consequences. They would be coming for their god.

"Nothing will stand in their way," she whispered, sagging in his grip. "Go on, kill me. We're dead anyway."

But he didn't. Instead, Wolverine just released his grip, letting her sag into the chair.

"It is done," he said with subtle amusement.

Wind coughed and rubbed her throat, her defeat so complete that she felt empty, drained, and without form or substance. Nothing lasted forever—not even mighty Cahokia. As it had risen from the mud along the Father Water, so too would it now fall.

She could imagine how it would look in generations to come: the buildings gone, grass covering the abandoned and slumping mounds, occasional trees, but little else to show the grandeur that had drawn tens of thousands to this place.

I was here to see it end.

Slender Fox would be at the bottom of the stairs now.

"We've lost it all," she whispered. "How will the future judge? What will the people say years from now as they walk these abandoned places and ask, "Who were they?"

"Oh, stop whimpering, woman," Wolverine told her. "Get over it. I've won."

"Won what?" a voice asked from behind, and Wind could barely find the energy to crane her neck.

Rising Flame emerged from the Morning Star's doorway and stopped short at the sight of Wolverine towering above Wind on the high and forbidden dais.

Wolverine smugly began with, "North Star House is taking control of the palace, Matron. My warriors will be swarming up the stairs at any—"

Rising Flame stepped forward as the Morning Star—looking frail—emerged to take her arm. His face was painted in white, the black, forked-eye designs vivid. The maskette shell ear pieces contrasted with his black hair. A copper headpiece with its Spirit Bundle was atop his tightly wound bun, and a brilliant cloak made from tanager feathers hung from his shoulders.

Together he and Rising Flame walked forward, hisses of disbelief erupting from the people before they dropped to one knee, bowing their heads, touching their foreheads. Wolverine had thrown himself from the dais and flat on the floor, face buried in the matting.

Wind staggered down off the dais, bowing before the living god and stating through her raspy voice, "Lord, they need to see you at the palace gate. No time to waste."

"Of course, *Tonka'tzi*. Feel the Power they radiate." He closed his eyes, sniffing as if savoring. "It took a while to decide. It's the only reason I came back, you know. To feel that Power, that adoration."

She remained where she was as he passed, heedless of her knees—still sore from the hands of time she'd spent on them in Old-Woman-Who-Never-Dies' temple.

When the tears came, they blinded her eyes, silvering her vision as she watched his silhouette pass through the doors and into daylight and heard a rising cheer from the courtyard.

Close. So close.

Sixty

Blue Heron hobbled along the line of Quiz Quiz prisoners where they sat, cross-legged, on the hard-packed clay of Evening Star Town's plaza. The entire string was tied together along a long length of rope—each bound by a loop knotted around his neck. Any one of them who lifted his hands to pick at the braided rawhide collar received a quick whack from one of the patrolling warriors.

Bouyed by the news that the Morning Star lived, a considerable throng of locals—including various Earth Clan subchiefs and lesser Four Winds nobles—had clustered around to watch the spectacle.

Seven Skull Shield, Columella, and Flat Stone Pipe followed along just behind her. They had carried her down from the palace on a litter, but for this task, for this short distance, she could walk. The last time—when she'd threatened to leave on her own—she'd made it halfway across the floor before the world spun around in ever-faster circles. Columella had barely kept her from nose-diving into the floor. At least now she could keep her balance.

Her ribs hurt like sixty lashes; her swollen eye had turned a horrible black that faded into yellow and green; and the bruises on her arms, chest, and hips were something to see.

"That one." She pointed, staring into the Quiz Quiz warrior's disdainful eyes. They reminded her of smoldering stones. "He's the one."

Seven Skull Shield stepped up beside her, calling, "Winder? Who is this man?"

"That is Moccasin, Skull. But you probably don't want to tangle with him. With one hand he'll rip your arm out of its socket and beat you to death with it at the same time he uses a splinter to pick his teeth with the other."

"Feisty, aren't you, Trader?" Blue Heron called. "I'd save it for the square. You're going to need all of your reserves."

She saw the agony in Seven Skull Shield's expression, the pinched lips, the knotted jaws. "Sorry," she whispered for his ears only.

Then she ordered, "Take this one. Cut him out of the line."

Two Evening Star warriors bent to the task—the other Quiz Quiz calling questions, uneasy at their companion's treatment.

"So he's the one who beat you?" Columella asked as she watched the man being dragged away.

"I'm not a particularly nice person. A fact you figured out for yourself years ago." Blue Heron placed a hand to her broken ribs as she turned. "Nor am I forgiving. That bit of worm vomit would have kicked me to death if Winder hadn't come when he did. Maybe there's a time and place for such things, but old Moccasin there, he was enjoying himself too much. He outright *liked* it."

A commotion broke out among the crowd on the southern end of the plaza, people shifting and moving.

"Now what's this?" Flat Stone Pipe asked.

A party of warriors carrying a Morning Star House standard appeared between the buildings on the path that led up from the canoe landing. Behind them came a litter borne by trotting porters. They skirted the stickball grounds, saluted the giant cypress World Tree pole where it dominated the center of the plaza, and respectfully circled the chunkey courts.

"Well, well," Blue Heron mused as the approaching warriors broke ranks and saluted. Rising Flame's litter was carefully lowered, and the porters stepped back as she rose and strode forward.

"Matron Columella," Rising Flame greeted. She wore a multicolored cloak made of painted bunting feathers mixed with lines of red cardinal breasts overlaid by chevron-shaped patterns of copper-gleaming spring turkey feathers. Her hair was adorned with a swan-feather splay, and she wore a tanned buckskin dress dyed in deep blue and decorated by geometric patterns of oyster-shell beads and copper buttons.

"Clan Matron," Columella replied, touching her chin, eyes reserved.

Rising Flame turned her attention to the line of prisoners; an eyebrow lifted as she studied them thoughtfully. To Blue Heron, she asked, "Are you all right? Word has just reached us of your trials."

"I'll live," Blue Heron growled, aware, through a sidelong glance, that Seven Skull Shield was appraising the young matron's well-figured body with lecherous eyes, a slow grin bending his lips. Reaching behind her back, Blue Heron gave him the "desist" gesture before Rising Flame caught on and added him to the line of Quiz Quiz destined for the squares.

"We need to talk," Rising Flame said perfunctorily. "Might we use your palace, Columella? Or if that is inconvenient, I can order the Four Winds Clan House emptied for our privacy."

"Well, if you're about official business," Blue Heron said, "I suppose the thief and I will be off. Leave you all to the—"

"I want you there. Just the three of us. Things I need to say," Rising Flame told her, a frustrated resignation behind her glistening dark eyes. To which she reluctantly added, "Please."

"In that case, you are more than welcome to use my palace," Columella told her. "Fetch Lady Blue Heron's litter."

Somewhere in the time it took to relocate into the palace, Blue Heron realized that Flat Stone Pipe had managed to slip away. Seven Skull Shield had plopped himself down outside the palace door beside his bear-headed dog and was chewing on a ragged thumbnail.

As Blue Heron was carried inside and lowered by the fire she cast an eye on Columella's raised dais and speculated whether the dwarf had already slipped into the hidden cubbyhole.

Columella climbed onto her raised chair after ordering black drink for her guests, and it came to Blue Heron that her presence there covered any sound the dwarf might accidently make. Clever, Columella. Clever indeed.

Only after the yaupon tea had been served and drunk and the prayers had been offered did Columella clap her hands, ordering, "Leave us."

The palace staff bowed, touching their foreheads, and crowded out.

"Now, Clan Matron, how can I be of service?" Columella asked as she laced her fingers together and leaned forward.

Blue Heron watched Rising Flame squirm as she shifted to a more comfortable seat and said, "I have come to report that the Morning Star is recovering, though he remains weak. For the moment, he and the *tonka'tzi* have reassured the people. Green Chunkey and Wolverine have removed their squadrons."

She glanced uncertainly at Columella. "I would assume that you are not about to take action against Morning Star House?"

"You assume correctly," Columella told her with a wry smile.

Rising Flame leaned forward, hands extended, as if grasping. "What neither *Tonka'tzi* Wind nor I know is what River House's intentions might be."

"They are paralyzed for the moment." Columella cocked her head. "Why would you come to me to learn about War Duck and Round Pot's plans?"

Rising Flame glanced uncomfortably at Blue Heron. "Because you have, shall we say, resources that others do not."

"She means your spy network," Blue Heron interjected dryly.

"Pus and blood, yes," Rising Flame admitted in frustration. "So . . . why is River House paralyzed?"

"Because, due to an intruder, their eternal fire was put out the night before they were planning to march on Morning Star House." Blue Heron couldn't help but chortle.

"Their fire . . . ?" Rising Flame paused. "When did this happen? What else do Wind and I need to know?"

"Blood and piss, woman," Blue Heron couldn't help but growl at her. "All right, here's the thinly stewed version: War Duck encouraged the Quiz Quiz to steal the Surveyors' Bundle to discredit Morning Star House prior to the matron's election. But my people foiled the attempt, which caused the Quiz Quiz to lose their War Medicine box. After Sky Star was rescued by Winder, they kidnapped me to ransom for the box. My people got me back and went after the Quiz Quiz. Consider it a matter of honor. But before they could trap the Quiz Quiz, they had to sneak into War Duck's palace and dangle the bait. As sometimes happens, that plan went to shit and ended up with the sacred fire being put out. Meanwhile, our people sent a messenger to War Duck asking for an escort for my return to Morning Star House. Knowing War Duck would have to have the Quiz Quiz retaliate, our people followed him to Crazy Frog's, where Flat Stone Pipe overheard the plans."

"Who?"

"The dwarf. Don't you know anything?" Blue Heron scowled.

"How did the dwarf learn all of this?" Rising Flame looked confused.

"Seven Skull Shield tossed him up on Crazy Frog's roof—although the soot he knocked loose while he was squirming around up there almost gave them away." Blue Heron shrugged. "But once Flat Stone Pipe knew the plans, he set the trap for the Quiz Quiz. Now we get to finish this once and for all. It's just a matter of deciding whether to ransom any of them, or put them all in squares."

"Squares," Columella said with a grunt. "Can't have these sassy barbarians thinking they can come and steal our sacred Bundles on a whim."

"That or cut the big tendon in their heels and make them slaves," Blue Heron replied. "Maybe give them to the stone cutters or the chert miners. That's a pretty sobering message to send. Most warriors would rather die."

"Either way, we've got to send an army downriver and burn Quiz Quiz." Columella had narrowed her eyes. "Stealing the Bundle was one thing, but abducting you from my own stickball field? That's a slap in the face to anyone in the Four Winds Clan. Let alone that it was someone of your status in Black Tail's lineage. The clan's one-time Keeper, of all people."

"True," Blue Heron agreed. "But what will the lower river Nations do? Sure, we'd be within our rights to attack Quiz Quiz. And played right, we could conquer it. But could we hold it for the long term? We've always avoided moving against any of the lower river Nations. They would see it as colonial expansionism. It could set off a firestorm, shut down Trade, cut us off from the Caddo."

"Send them home as they are," Rising Flame said thoughtfully.

"What?" Columella cried. "Are you out of your mind? Didn't you hear what I said? They *took* Blue Heron!"

"They are Quiz Quiz," Rising Flame added softly, gaze distant. "I've been downriver. Lived there. The Quiz Quiz live for a peculiar code of honor. Retaliation begets more retaliation."

Blue Heron countered, "But we can't just let them go. They'd claim we were weak, afraid of retaliation."

"Yes, yes, but what happens," Rising Flame suggested, "if we send them downriver bound, gagged, and helpless with some neutral Traders. Maybe Pacaha? And what if they were delivered to Quiz Quiz that way, dumped at the town gates still bound and gagged, with the message, 'Here are your inept, foolish, and bumbling warriors. Their actions were so pathetic and amusing we couldn't find it in ourselves to punish them, but have sent them back to you rather than see you further embarrassed by their failures."

For a long moment, Blue Heron let it run through her souls, a rising sense of delight brewing within. "That, Cousin, is a stroke of sheer genius. The Quiz Quiz will be humiliated to wit's end, a laughingstock from one end of the river to the other; and our return of their warriors will be an honorable act, one that they cannot retaliate against without a further violation of their code."

Columella was grinning, as if seeing it in her head.

Rising Flame said, "All but Sky Star, the Quiz Quiz who beat Blue Heron, and the river Trader, that one called Winder. Someone has to pay the price. Those are the three. Sky Star was the leader, the one taken from the surveyors' square. The warrior called Moccasin would have beaten Blue Heron to death, which cannot be forgiven. As for the Trader? He was the brains behind it all, the mastermind who blatantly took Blue Heron right out from under Columella's nose. Those three must die hard . . . and slow."

Blue Heron worked her jaw back and forth. That would break Seven Skull Shield's heart, but she'd be double-rotted if she'd speak for clemency. The thief would just have to understand.

"What about the Sky Hand and Albaamaha?" Columella asked. "That definitely deserves an army and a response."

"Then you are playing into the Albaamaha's hands," Blue Heron told her.

"How do you know that?" Columella asked.

"That girl, Whispering Dawn, she's no assassin. Neither is High Minko White Water Moccasin. She was sent here to marry the Morning Star as punishment for humiliating her father. White Water Moccasin thought he'd teach his daughter a lesson at the same time he established a reciprocal alliance with Cahokia. Like bringing down two birds with one arrow. The thief knew she was being used by the Albaamaha, but just not how."

"Why didn't you do something about it?" Rising Flame asked, a flare of anger behind her eyes.

"Because I was *dismissed*," Blue Heron said flatly. "As you may recall. Want me to repeat the exact language with which I was relieved of my responsibilities?"

Rising Flame's anger vanished as quickly as it had risen. "No need. I recall just fine, thank you. And when it comes to the girl and her real motive, I suppose we'll never know. Five Fists scoured the city looking for her. She's long gone. I doubt we'll ever find her."

"Want to bet?" Blue Heron asked. Then she shouted, "Thief! Come in here."

As she'd known he would, Seven Skull Shield immediately popped in the door, followed by his mongrel monster of a dog. She winced as the beast lifted its leg on the doorframe before hurrying to catch up.

To the stunned Rising Flame, she added, "You don't think he'd miss so much as a heartbeat of this, do you?" To Seven Skull Shield she said, "Think you can find that Sky Hand girl? The rest of Cahokia seems stumped."

He gave Rising Flame a lascivious wink and added, "If she's still here, I'll see what I can turn up." To the dog he said, "Farts, get your face out of the stewpot. We've got work to do."

"Oh, for the sake of . . ." Columella shook her head as the dog took a couple of loud slurps from the communal stewpot before turning and galloping after the thief. "That man, I swear."

"So much for the stew," Rising Flame remarked.

"Took Magnolia two days to make that."

"What?" Blue Heron asked. "You're gonna throw it out because of a couple of dog slurps? Bah! Give it a good boil and you'll never know the difference."

"You actually *encourage* that man?" Rising Flame asked.

"Let's just call him an acquired taste."

"Yes. And a bad one. Like moldy acorns," Columella muttered to herself.

"So how is Wind doing?" Blue Heron asked.

"She saved the city." Rising Flame stared absently at the fire. "I misjudged you, Cousin. From the outside, all anyone sees is the heartless spider, the evil woman pulling the strands of her web as she ensnares the unwary. As was the case with my brother, Fire Light."

"Sorry about him." Blue Heron shrugged. "We sent him off to the east to keep him out of trouble. Better than assassinating him."

Rising Flame took a deep breath. "But getting back to Cahokia: We almost lost everything, and I wonder how different things would have been if a strong Clan Keeper had been in your palace, keeping track of Albaamaha and Sky Hand, and North Star House and Green Chunkey. Would that girl have poisoned the Morning Star? Would the Houses be on the verge of open warfare?"

"Matron, sometimes it's hard to tell when you start asking 'what if' questions after the fact," Columella said grimly.

"Even if *Tonka'tzi* Wind hadn't suggested that I come here today," Rising Flame said with a grim smile, "I would have anyway, head bowed, to ask Blue Heron if she would once again serve her clan." She swallowed hard. "Someone once told me, 'Not all of governing is about show and spectacle.' And after the last couple of days I have come to understand that very hard choices have to be made."

Blue Heron shifted, trying to ease the pain in her ribs. She glanced at Columella, watching the uncertainty in the Evening Star matron's eyes shift to a sly victory.

I've won.

But at the last instant, ready to pounce, she hesitated. Some deep-seated instinct made her ask Columella, "That suggestion about sending the Quiz Quiz back as incompetent refuse. Would you have thought of that?"

"I'm more of a slap-them-down-as-a-payback kind of woman. It wouldn't have crossed my mind."

"I wouldn't have thought of it. Wind surely wouldn't have."

"Sometimes it helps to have new blood," Columella added, apparently willing to follow Blue Heron's lead. "I didn't do everything right in the beginning either. Takes time. Also takes a really smart one to know when she's made a mistake. Only the ones with guts admit it to others and ask how to fix it."

Rising Flame's dark eyes betrayed the flash of victory her lips carefully hid.

"Oh, pus and rot!" Blue Heron tilted her head back, staring disgustedly at the honey-colored posts holding up the ceiling. "It just means that the Morning Star knew what he was doing all along!"

She would have laughed her frustration, but it would have hurt those broken ribs way too much.

"Then you will serve your clan?" Rising Flame asked, her full lips pursing.

"Of course. I'm happy to be the Clan Keeper and—"

"I didn't say that." Rising Flame's gaze hardened. "I am appointing Spotted Wrist as Clan Keeper. He has demanded that, along with some other rewards for his service against the Red Wing. What I'm asking is that you work with him, train him. Help him to—"

"You want a new Keeper, Matron, let him figure it out himself," Blue Heron growled, realizing she'd been played.

Columella's expression had pinched.

"Then you won't serve your clan?" Rising Flame gestured finality. "Very well. I was willing to allow you to remain in your palace, allow you to keep some of the privileges and—"

"Spotted Wrist!" Columella cried. "Pus and blood, why sacrifice Blue Heron's years of experience when it comes to—"

"Because *someone* will have to replace her!" Rising Flame shot back. "Maybe not now, not next year, but sometime. But for luck, the Quiz Quiz might have killed her when they abducted her. I want her to train a replacement."

Blue Heron fought for breath, one hand to her side. The loss of her palace? Just being another Four Winds woman? Did they think they would make a figurehead out of her? Or worse, discard her completely? Perhaps order her to move to one of the outlying Houses?

Pus in a cup, think!

"I'll do it," she heard herself whisper. "But I stay in my palace. Keep my spies and access to the Council House. And only if Spotted Wrist follows my orders for the first couple of years or so." She glared her anger and outrage at Rising Flame. "Do you understand? I *know* how this all works, where the pitfalls are, what can go wrong."

Rising Flame countered. "A year. And then he takes over."

"And I keep my palace, my people, my access."

Rising Flame gave a shrug of the shoulders. "As Clan Keeper, Spotted Wrist can build his own palace wherever he wishes."

Blue Heron's stomach turned, the nausea in her souls like a stone in her heart. With a sour taste in her mouth, she said, "Then we have a deal."

Sixty-one

Reaching out, flailing, testing every step of the way, Fire Cat preceded Night Shadow Star. When the way suddenly dropped off, he would toss a pebble, listening to hear how far it fell. And in that manner, he had avoided several drops that would have ended in broken bones and miserable death in the cave's near-solid blackness.

Behind him, Night Shadow Star clung to his left hand, letting him lead, her fingers periodically tightening on his, as if she were clinging to the only reality that remained in such a dark emptiness of cold, hunger, and danger. He could sense her disappointment after her vision of the Morning Star vanishing into the surrounding rock. He was starting to imagine things himself.

The dark, the silence, played tricks on him. He would think he saw light, sometimes like sparks, but when he concentrated, it was to realize that the blackness remained impenetrable.

Sometimes he'd hear voices: his uncle, his mother, or some long-gone friend. Like snippets of conversation from the past. Some he attributed to the Dead as they flocked around him. But Mother's words, knowing that she was alive, seemed to come from the past. Things she'd said, fragments of laughter.

So that had to be his imagination, didn't it?

Did that mean the voices of the Dead were his imagination as well? Or was it just the hollow aftereffects of his Dance with Sister Datura? Was she loath to loosen her talons from his souls?

Twice Fire Cat recoiled as his questing fingers encountered one of the burials, the body tightly bound, the head covered in cloth. From the feel, he could tell the cold, desiccated flesh was coated in mold.

"Forgive me, Elder. We wish only to pass," he would tell the restless and disturbed corpse, then carefully feel his way around the burial, leading Night Shadow Star wide.

"The Morning Star has already freed them," Night Shadow Star told him. "If we had light, you would see a drawing of the person above the body, one of the black ones. It acts like a portal through which his body-soul can travel back and forth between his physical body and the realms of the ancestral Dead."

"Who will draw our pictures if we die in here?"

"We're not going to die. There, just up ahead. Can't you see it?"

"See what? There is only black."

"Piasa's glow." She urged him forward with another squeeze of the hand. "Keep going."

"You sound remarkably calm. For all we know that glow you see could be leading us to some deeper dead end. And while we have a couple of hands full of ground corn left, we're on the last of the water."

"It's Piasa," she replied. "Something's changed. My souls are more at peace."

"Changed? How?"

"The Tortoise Bundle has abandoned me. The Morning Star has become something different. As does a butterfly from a cocoon."

"That's . . . um, bad, isn't it?"

"I don't know. Like I said, something's different. Something in Cahokia."

"You think the Morning Star's Spirit vanished into the rock forever? Or maybe he died and the whole city is up in arms. Maybe they think you're dead. Maybe the reason you don't feel the Tortoise Bundle is because they've burned your palace to the ground in mourning?"

He paused. "Not that that would be so bad."

"Are you insane? Think of how Wind and Blue Heron, not to mention so many others, are feeling."

He smiled into the darkness, giving her hand a reassuring press. "If they think we're dead, we can sneak out of the cave late at night. Make our way to the river, steal a canoe. We can be gone, with no one the wiser. Make our way south, find a place where no one knows us."

She sighed wistfully. "We could live like normal people. Maybe have a small farmstead. I've Dreamed that, you know."

"You have?"

"We have children, a nice house, good garden, and you hunt. So it's someplace off the beaten path. Away from a town. Quiet. And we are happy there."

"Children," he said, wistful on his own account, the memory of his own dead children so fresh after he'd visited with them. And if he and Night Shadow Star had children, then that meant that they were sleeping in the same . . .

He shook his head.

"What?" she asked, having felt it through his hand.

"Just that if we . . ."

"That happens between normal people. People who aren't bound by station, rank, and service to an Underworld lord. There are times . . ."

"I know," he told her when she couldn't finish. "We are who we are. Chosen by Power."

He blinked, swearing that he could actually make out an angular block of stone that jutted at an angle. Feeling for it, his fingers encountered cold sandstone. "We're getting closer to the entrance. There. Up ahead."

"Where it's glowing blue? Or is that just Piasa?"

Fire Cat saw no blue, just a lighter darkness, and what looked like a path between the stones.

Yes, he could indeed make out the narrow maw-like entrance. That meant that Horned Serpent's effigy was just there to his right, the snarling mouth gaping wide, the eerie round eyes burning into Fire Cat's souls.

Then you'd better get me now, beast. That or let me pass.

Apparently the antlered serpent judged him worthy, for Fire Cat felt his way to the opening, adding, "Watch your head, Lady."

And then they were in the larger, brighter cavern, a faint light casting the shadowy floor in relief. Fire Cat could pick his way now, tightening his grip on Night Shadow Star's hand.

But just before the opening, she whispered, "Wait," and pulled him back.

"Yes, Lady?"

"They'll be out there. The priests. My escort."

"No escape, then?"

He could see her shake her head, and then she stepped into his arms, molding herself to his body. The hug she gave him would have cracked ribs on a lesser man. Her lips, next to his ear, whispered, "Once we step back into our world . . . Well, I need you to know. I could not have done this without you. If there were only some way . . ."

She tensed, gave an irritated shake of her head, muttering, "I know, Master. It was the price. Pus and blood, can't you leave me alone long enough to say what I—"

The Spirit beast had obviously interrupted her again.

"It is all right, Lady." He gently disengaged himself, raising her hands to his lips in the process. He wished he could tell her all the longings in his heart.

"Lady? Is that you?" a voice called from just outside.

The flickering of a torch cast its first shadows as it was carried hurriedly forward.

By the time the priests stopped at the entrance, Night Shadow Star was composed, striding confidently forward, head high. "What news of the Morning Star?" she asked. "Did his souls return to my brother's body?"

"Yes, Lady!" The society priest dropped to a knee, touching his forehead as he bowed. "The runner just came! We were preparing to go in search of you. But . . . where is your torch?"

Fire Cat, marching respectfully a step behind, came to a stop as Night Shadow Star told them, "The torch? I suppose it's down there, somewhere. Red Wing? Where did we leave the torch?"

"Down where we left our bodies, Lady. In that narrow tunnel."

He heard the gasps and saw how it affected them. Mud and rot, did that torch have to be so bright? He lifted a hand to shield his eyes. Looking out, he could see it was the middle of the night.

"But no one has ever returned alive from the depths before." The priest gulped, eyes growing round and large.

Night Shadow Star glanced sidelong at Fire Cat. "For part of the journey, I had the Red Wing to guide me. Piasa led for the rest of the way. Now, alert my escort that I have returned. The Red Wing and I need to purify ourselves, and food and drink would be appreciated."

"Yes, Lady!" the awed priest cried. "An entire feast has been prepared. It was brought by Squadron First War Claw upon Clan Keeper Spotted Wrist's orders! So has an entire flotilla of canoes to escort you back to Cahokia."

In the leaping torchlight, Fire Cat saw Night Shadow Star stiffen, as if suddenly ill.

As they stepped out into the cold night, he shot a longing glance back over his shoulder at the dark opening into the earth. Would that they had never stepped out of there, that they had remained, locked away in the womb of the Underworld.

I shall hold those moments with her close to my heart forever. In such a place of terror? Who would have thought?

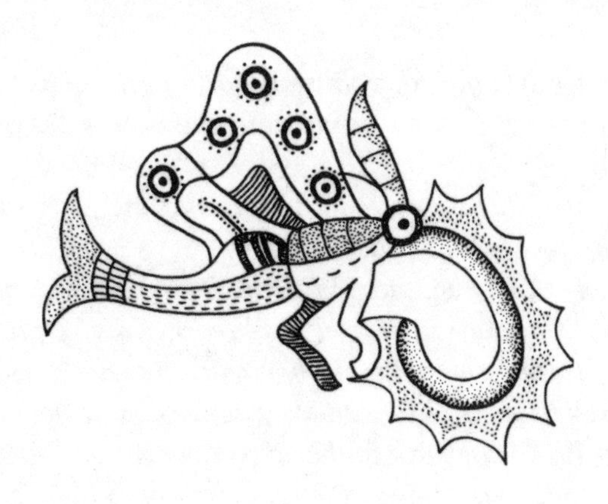

Solitude

As dusk falls, I sit in the growing dark. Two Sticks' corpse remains on the bed. He still talks to me, his body periodically gurgling, sighing as gas escapes his anus or throat. When he does, I nod in sympathy. I figure he is telling me how sorry he is, or expressing his regret over the turn of events.

Regret and sorrow. That's all that Two Sticks and I have in common. My little fire pops, mere sticks atop a bed of coals. After the light has fled and darkness drapes the land, I shall sneak out on my nightly foray for firewood and water.

Beyond that I don't need anything. Enough food remains in the storage jars to keep me fed for at least a half moon. Firewood will remain a problem, however. With as many people as are living in the area, anything burnable gets picked up. The few twigs and sticks I've scrounged are old pieces of driftwood. Do I dare try to Trade for firewood? Will someone recognize the tattoo on my hand?

I raise that selfsame hand, staring at it as if it were an apparition, something foreign, an appendage belonging to a stranger.

Hard to believe this is the same hand that poured the Morning Star's deadly drink. The hand that tied the water sack over Two Sticks' head, and then untied that same bag a couple of hands of time later to expose his dead and staring face.

One thing, however, that I've noticed since suffocating him is that I'm no longer fading away. I seem to have reached a state of equilibrium. I am stuck at this halfway point. Anything that would make me more solid—like eating to satiety—causes me to throw up. Just the thought of certain kinds of food or tastes, or smells, set me off. Other things, odd things, I now crave. It is almost routine in the morning. I wake feeling nauseous. Once I throw up, however, things are better.

On the bed, Two Sticks gurgles in agreement, and his anus expels another burst of gas. I make a face as it fills the air.

What am I going to do with him? I figure I can roll his corpse out of the bed and onto the floor, but what then? I can't carry him. I just don't have the strength. And if I drag him away in the night, how do I hide the marks he'll leave in the dirt? Even a five-year-old will be able to follow the trail from wherever I leave his corpse back to the house door.

It is a terrible dilemma. I have the perfect place to hide for the next moon, but for the knowledge that I will not be able to stand the stench as he continues to decompose.

What kind of justice is that?

I poke the coals with the last of my sticks and shake my head.

I thought I would have a sense of accomplishment after killing Two Sticks. Instead I seem to have fallen into a pit of eternal paralysis. My souls are in limbo, just hanging, stuck in place as if covered with pitch and unable to move. I am not sure that the things I remember from my past, of growing up in Split Sky City, of my mother or father, ever happened. Did I just imagine running off to the Albaamaha? Was the initiation in the Sacred Moth Society just a dream? Was I really captured and hauled off here to marry the Morning Star?

I giggle, pressing fingers to my lips to stifle the sound. That's a head-struck fantasy! A fantastical creation spun by the souls of a clanless, friendless girl who lives with a corpse. That couldn't *have been me.*

And I certainly *couldn't have* murdered *the living god!*

Assuming anyone had done such a thing, it would have been a young woman of courage and determination. Not some empty husk of a girl like me. Not a plaything. And oh yes, I was indeed a plaything.

Two Sticks taught me that if he taught me nothing else.

A worthless girl. That's what I am.

A girl? Wasn't I once a woman? Married?

Or was the Women's House and my celebration of passage just another delusion like so many of the fantasies that spin between my souls?

I absently reach down and press a hand to my abdomen. No, no blood. Not even so much as a cramp. And if my memories are correct, the right number of days have passed since my last bloody flux.

Women bleed. Girls don't.

I glance again at Two Sticks and say, "You were raping a girl, you beast. All the more reason I'm glad I killed you."

Which makes me wonder: Will I ever be a woman again?

For long moments I just sit, satisfied to breathe, to feel the warmth from the fire.

Wait. Did I hear something?

Yes, there's sniffing at the door. I know that sound: a dog.

"Go away, beast. Do it before I step out and bash you for the stewpot."

The sniffing stops, and I don't hear the beast anymore.

I am about to rise when the door opens, lifted wide.

I am stunned, having heard nothing but the dog—no sound of footsteps. Fear bursts in my breast like an over-pressured pot.

I stare up in horror at the dark shadow of a muscular man. For a moment I can only gape, frozen. And then I recognize him: the lecherous and lascivious thief from the Keeper's palace.

A whimper builds in my throat, and dies of its own futility. I feel myself going hollow again. The fading that I stemmed when I killed Two Sticks has resumed. I am . . . finished.

"You," I whisper in defeat.

"Me," he replies in his limited Muskogean.

I feel the last hope drain away, head slumping, vision blurring with defeat.

"You kill?" Seven Skull Shield asks, pointing to Two Sticks' corpse.

I nod. What's left but the truth? In Trade pidgin, augmenting it with sign language, I say, "He was going to Trade me to strange men. Many of them. 'Have a rare pot? Stick your shaft into this woman who murdered the Morning Star.' I just . . ."

What's the point? The more I talk, the more I admit, the more of myself is gone forever.

Seven Skull Shield walks over, peers down at Two Sticks' body. The gut is starting to swell; the eyes are dried out and death-gray; the mouth is slack. "How kill?"

I toss him the small ceramic jar, signing, "Last of nectar. Made his souls travel far enough I could, how you say, stop his wind."

Even as I finish, I laugh at the absurdity, the sound of it bitter and biting with disgust. It had been such a small and fragile hope. Dead now. Gone with so many of the things that had once made me me.

Then, with a sigh, I lie back on the fabrics where I've been sleeping. I know what he wants, what was in his eyes back when he first saw me. He is, after all, just another man. I pull up my skirt and spread my legs wide.

Seven Skull Shield cocks his head as he studies not my exposed genitals, but my expression. I have sucked in my lips and am chewing them against the coming pain.

Why is he dragging this out? Get it over with!

Stepping over, he reaches out a hand, saying, "Here. Let me help you up."

For a moment, the words don't make sense. "You not take?"

"Not like this?"

"But you . . ." I frown, then nod in defeat as it all comes clear. "Trade me to other men later. I understand."

"Snot and spit, no." He rubs the back of his neck. His expression screws into something unpleasant. "Sometimes men can really be vile, can't we? Come on, girl. On your feet."

I let him pull me up, almost staggering from fear and worry. His dog is lapping what's left of my supper gruel from the brownware jar beside the fire.

"Where you take?" I ask, wondering if I should make a break for the door, or if the accursed dog will drag me down.

"To somewhere safe." He rubs his chin. And there's enough light to see that he's thoughtful. "I've got to figure this out. To do that, I need the whole story. And I've got to have someone who knows Muskogee."

"What of him?" I point to Two Sticks' body.

"If I read the signs right, girl, and from what you've just told me, he's a weasel. Sometimes the best thing for a pus-sucking maggot like that is just to be left to rot, don't you think?"

I dare not allow so much as a tremble of the lips—nothing that might give him an advantage.

"You got anything here you want?" he asks. "Pack it up. I think it's dark enough I can get you to a safe place."

"Yes, yes," I say woodenly. I have figured it out. He doesn't want to be serviced on the ground just below a dead man's feet. "Find better place. I understand."

He gives Two Sticks a disgusted look. "If he's abused you to the point you can't understand there's more to coupling than rape, I'd only want him alive for just long enough that I could kill him all over again."

Then he spits on the corpse, following it with, "Take that, maggot." To me he says, "I meant it. Get your things. We're leaving."

It takes me only a couple of heartbeats to shove anything of value into my pack. As I follow him out into the night I know this isn't going to have a happy ending, but I am too exhausted to care.

Sixty-two

Things were slowly, painfully starting to make sense to Wooden Doll. Which, when it came to Seven Skull Shield, wasn't all that unusual. It just took time to figure out how the big thief's actions actually related to any kind of common sense.

Like they did that night.

Wooden Doll sat on the edge of her bed and studied the attractive young woman—barely more than a girl—who crouched by her fire. Across from her, Seven Skull Shield perched with half of his butt on her large wooden storage box, his arms crossed, expression pensive.

Skull had arrived not long after her last client had left. Wooden Doll had first felt irritation—wanting nothing more than a full night's sleep. It had brewed into anger when he led the lithesome young woman into her house, followed by that loathsome dog.

What was the matter with him? Bringing a ripe young thing like the Sky Hand girl—all right, she might be a woman, but just barely—into her house?

The flare of sudden jealousy had surprised her. Of course she knew he bedded other women. The man had a reputation for charming women into his bed—or, more often, into the woman's own. But he'd *never* dared to bring one here. Let alone one so young.

And then had come the stunning realization that this creature with lackluster eyes and broken posture was Whispering Dawn. The living god's wife. The woman all of Cahokia was hunting over the Morning Star's attempted poisoning.

Wooden Doll sighed deeply, shaking her head. "It figures, Skull, that only you could get yourself into a mess like this. My advice? Hand her over to the Keeper immediately. Before you end up hanging in a square for the few days it would take the crowd to slice you into strips and burn what's left to a charred crisp."

He arched a scarred eyebrow and flexed the muscles in his crossed arms. "Oh, come on. She's not an assassin."

"What? You just told me she murdered Two Sticks!"

"So?" he shot back. "He was abusing her. Told the poor girl if she didn't bed him, let him Trade her services to other men as 'the Morning Star's assassin,' he'd turn her over to the Four Winds."

She glanced again at the girl who hugged her knees, staring aimlessly at the matting. She did look pathetic.

"Why did you bring her here?"

"To find out the truth." He shrugged. "You speak Muskogee. Ask her to tell it from the beginning. The Sky Hand, the Albaamaha, why she came here. She looks so hopeless I'll bet she tells it straight."

Wooden Doll raised her hands in surrender. So much for a good night's restful sleep, huh? And she was competent in Muskogee. As she was in most of the major languages. It made her clients more comfortable and at ease, which meant she could Trade her services for more.

To the young woman she said, "How old are you?"

Whispering Dawn jerked at the sound of her own language. "Just seventeen, Lady."

"Seven Skull Shield wants to hear your story. Would you do that? Tell it like it happened? From the very beginning?"

Whispering Dawn nodded, a self-mocking smile on her lips, and began, "I ran away with Straight Corn. He was forbidden, an Albaamaha. But I loved him. . . ."

She spoke slowly, telling the story, her gaze locked on an interminable distance. Idly she began to finger her long black hair, twisting it around and around her fingers.

As the young woman spoke, Wooden Doll translated for Skull. He remained still, head down, lips pursed as Whispering Dawn told of her journey upriver, and of her arrival at Cahokia.

When she came to the part about putting the nectar in the Morning Star's drink, Wooden Doll asked incredulously, "Didn't you think it would kill him?"

Whispering Dawn glanced up, slightly surprised. "Hanging Moss told me it wouldn't. That he's the living god. That it would only send him on a Spirit journey."

"And you believed that?"

She nodded, eyes guileless as she met Wooden Doll's stare. "Hanging Moss wouldn't lie. He was my husband's uncle."

"They used you," Wooden Doll told her.

"But Hanging Moss *didn't* lie! Seven Skull Shield told me the Morning Star lives. That I *didn't* kill him."

"Word is that it was close, girl," Wooden Doll told her. "Very, very close. Enough so that a lot of people had the scare of their lives, and the city was barely spared civil war. Your dear Albaamaha uncle meant for you to kill him. And he meant for your father, the high minko, to get the blame."

Whispering Dawn shook her head doggedly. "Hanging Moss is a good man. He wouldn't have done this to me. Even if he had, Straight Corn wouldn't have let him. He loves me."

But the tone behind her words indicated that she was doing everything in her ability to believe it.

"They played you. Used you as a tool."

Whispering Dawn continued to doggedly shake her head, a stubborn frown marring her forehead.

After Wooden Doll had explained to Skull, he said, "That's what I thought."

"Well, gaming piece or not, her life isn't worth dog drool on a mat, which, if you'll take a look, is exactly what that mongrel of yours is doing on my prize floor mat." The beast had fixed its blue and brown eyes on her stewpot, nose quivering in expectation.

"Farts! Stop that!" Skull shifted just enough to fish in his belt pouch and toss the brindle beast a chunk of bread. "Never known a dog with such an appetite."

"You joke. All dogs are just loose hair pasted around a walking appetite. What are you going to do about the girl? She *poisoned* the Morning Star. Now she's sitting at *my* fire."

"She's barely more than a child. They *used* her."

"Neither you nor I was ever that gullible, Skull. Not even when we were younger than she is. It's not my fault that she had the stupidity to believe what other people told her."

"Come on, Wooden Doll. We were privileged in the way we grew up. We were lucky. We had to live by our wits with death and disaster around every corner. She didn't. She was deprived. Locked away in a palace, a spoiled high chief's daughter. She never got the chance to learn anything worthwhile."

"Pity her? For having life spoon-fed to her?"

"Yes."

"Pus and blood, Skull, there's times you make me crazy." She looked down at the girl, who watched them with wide and uncertain eyes. "What's your ultimate goal here? You going to ransom her? Trade her off for some advantage? Or did you think to adopt her like you did that foul-bred dog and keep her as a bed warmer?"

Skull gave her a disgusted look. "I'll admit that she's nice to look at, dream about, and maybe if she ever . . . But no. She's been beat up enough by men. And after what Two Sticks did to her? I just don't think being young and naïve should *always* be a death penalty."

"You and your warped sense of justice."

He grinned impishly. "That's why Power smiles on me." The grin faded. "I want you to keep her for a couple of days."

"And do what with her?"

"Let her watch the door. Like Newe used to do. And do something with that tattoo on the back of her hand. It almost screams 'I'm a wanted murderess, and I'm stupid.' "

"Me?" she cried. "Keep her here?"

Skull arched a sad eyebrow. "I have to go pay an old debt, and it's going to cost me dearly. Wound me down to the depths of my souls. But it's got to be done."

At his expression, she guessed, "Winder?"

He nodded. "I need to get something out of your storage. If I'm not back by tomorrow, it's because you'll finally be proven right, and I've met a bad end. When they tie me in the square, pay someone to stick a wad of water hemlock in my mouth will you? I don't want to hang around and suffer."

He turned, walking to the door. His brindle dog with its weird blue and brown eyes rose to follow, tail swishing. Then the man let himself out into the night.

"What's he doing?" Whispering Dawn asked in Muskogee.

"Going to say good-bye to a friend. That or get himself killed."

"And if he comes back? I am to service him?"

Wooden Doll lifted a skeptical eyebrow. "Why would you ask that?"

"It was in his eyes from the first moment he saw me."

Wooden Doll read the young woman's despair and self-loathing. For being so young, life had treated this one hard. "Girl, there are men who appreciate and enjoy women for who and what they are, and then there are other men, those who dominate women for what they can use or take. Skull is the first kind: He *likes* women. Enjoys their company in all of its ways and forms. He's by no means a perfect man, or unflawed, but he has never forced a woman to do anything she didn't want to."

Wooden Doll read the young woman's disbelief before adding, "My suspicion is that you've never had that much to do with that kind of man. You've just been trapped with the other kind, the users, exploiters, and takers."

"How do you know so much about men?"

Wooden Doll smiled wearily. "That's how I make my living, girl. By knowing them, and what they want, and what they'll Trade to get it. When it comes to Skull? I know him, because—with the exception of his detestable need for excitement and challenge—I'm just like him." A pause. "So, let's see what we can do to remake that tattoo."

Sixty-three

Winder had been hurt before, but nothing had ever been as painful or taxing as his first night in the square. It hadn't been bad for the first finger of time as the sun set and the Evening Star Town plaza had darkened. The trick had been to shift his weight from one foot to the other, tied as they were in the lower corners of the square.

By the second finger of time, however, a deep and throbbing ache had started in his crotch where the tendons running from his pubis to his thigh bone had begun to burn. Nor could he feel his arms, extended as they were to the upper corners of the square.

If he tried to sag and relieve the strain on his feet and legs, the pull in his shoulders became unbearable. Nor could he breathe, as it pulled the muscles in his chest to the point he couldn't suck a breath.

Then, as the night darkened, the chill began to eat into his naked flesh. The shivers had begun just after sundown and now were racking his extended limbs and torso.

And this is just the first night.

They hadn't started beating him yet. An unsympathetic warrior had explained that on the Keeper's orders, they were to wait until the next day. That they wanted him and his Quiz Quiz companions to last. The cutting, beating, and burning would commence slowly. And only at the end—he had been assured—would they use clubs to smash his leg and arm bones.

Winder endured a fit of shivers and puffed out a weak breath, seeing it fog before the starry skies.

"Be strong," Moccasin said in the square to Winder's right. The warrior had kept repeating it to himself over and over. As if, through the mantra, he would actually believe it.

I wish I had such faith in myself.

In the second square over, Sky Star hung in silence, periodically gasping, as if in disbelief that once again he found himself in such a miserable circumstance.

It was always a possibility.

Winder smiled wistfully into the night and twisted his head against the burning ache in his shoulders. Flexing his thick muscles, he was able to ease the cramps in his legs, and hang. Thankfully, his numb arms couldn't feel the ropes as they cut into the skin around his wrists.

What I would give to have someone step up and drive a stake through my chest and heart.

How long would it take before the end? Could he keep from screaming when they thrust a burning torch under his penis and testicles? Would he blubber and plead when they held his head and drove a thumb into his eye sockets, one by one, to pry out his eyes? Would he whimper when they sliced open his belly and reached in with a finger to pull out a length of living intestine?

I am a coward.

It was a sobering realization. Storms, the dangerous tricks and perils of the rivers, shiftless chiefs, and political intrigue had never scared him. He'd learned courage when he and Skull had slipped around the underside of Cahokia and survived.

It wasn't death that he abhorred, but the manner of it. Face-to-face with horror, he now recoiled, his flesh tingling. A sickness of dread lay stone-like and cold in the pit of his gut.

A night bird called.

He craned his neck to the side to see the guard slumped against the bottom of Columella's mound. Asleep. And looking so comfortable.

What time was it? The sun had gone down a lifetime ago, given the way time stretched.

He hung his head, concentrated on breathing. Allowing himself to hang, he wondered if he could let himself suffocate. If he could pass out, the pull on his chest would keep him from breathing. Death would come quickly, peacefully.

But each time he tried, a last-instant surge of panic caused him to start, shot energy into his legs, and brought him gasping and upright.

He wasn't aware of when he faded, but somehow, head hanging, he nodded off into a half-dozing state, as if his souls were floating on a lake of pain.

The hand on his head caused him to jerk awake; a gob of cloth was thrust into his mouth as he opened it to scream.

"Shhh!" a low voice warned.

Winder blinked at the dark apparition before him. An inky presence in the night. No, several men. They carefully climbed up on the square, began working on the bindings.

When Winder came loose, he fell limply, the big man in front neatly catching him. The world whirled and pitched as he was tossed over the big man's shoulders.

Earth and sky spun crazily as the air huffed in his lungs, pressed as they were with his gut over the man's shoulder. He had a vision of his arms swinging limply with each stride, dark earth rising and falling. The world kept swinging from side-to-side, upside down as his head was.

He was carried quickly and silently across the plaza. South, toward the bluff trail.

Whatever you do, just kill me quickly. The thought repeated like a prayer between his panicked souls.

Again he lost track of time. Eventually his arms began prickling and aching with renewed circulation. Images of dark buildings against a starry, partly cloudy sky imprinted on his staggering consciousness. He was being carried out of Evening Star Town. He recognized the guardian posts as black silhouettes against the night.

The smell of the river came to him, and he shifted, mumbling against the gag in his mouth.

"Quiet," the voice told him. "Don't fight me. You can't stand yet. Piss in a pot, I know. Takes about a finger of time before your limbs come back."

"Skull?" he asked into the gag.

"If you'll promise not to make a noise, I'll take that out."

"Yes," he mouthed into the cloth.

Seven Skull Shield shifted his hold enough to yank the cloth free, then resumed his careful descent of the bluff trail that led down to Evening Star Town's canoe landing.

"Why are you doing this? Don't you know what they'll do to you if they catch you?"

"Better than brothers," Skull told him wistfully. "Remember all the times you stood up for me? The times you made sure I ate before you did? The beatings you took in an attempt to protect me?"

They had reached the landing with its ramadas, stands, and beached canoes. Water lapped against muddy shores, and the smell of the river reassured. The river was safety, escape. He'd always felt secure when in sight of the water.

From his perspective, hanging over Skull's burly shoulder, Winder could see the dark shapes of canoes where they'd been drawn up beyond high water. A shadow moved in the night. Barely recognizable as a dog, it rose from one of the canoes. The whine of greeting was immediately shushed by Skull, followed by an order of, "Farts, quiet now!"

The dog complied, standing in the prow of a canoe, his tail wagging.

"They'll kill you for this, you know," Winder told him. "They'll know it was you."

"Yeah, probably." Skull eased Winder off of his shoulders, artfully lowering him into the deep hull of a small canoe. "How are you feeling?"

"Like a thousand ants are eating my arms, but I can move them again. Won't be long before I'm back to normal. Shove this thing out into the river and let's be gone."

"You're going alone."

"Skull, didn't you hear a word I said? They'll put you in that same square you took me out of."

Seven Skull Shield lowered himself to the canoe's gunwale, panting slightly from the exertion. "You're not as light as you used to be."

"You can't stay here!"

"We're not having this discussion again, are we? Fact is, this is my city. My people. And me, I'll find some way to square it with the Keeper. I'll probably end up owing her my body and soul, but that's the price I'm willing to pay."

"You really trust her? She's a Four Winds—"

"She's my *friend.*"

"You're an idiot. She doesn't have a reputation for friends, Skull. Just the opposite, in fact."

"It's not something that can be explained. Don't worry about it. But you do know that you can't come back. This is it. Cahokia is closed to you. Forever. That's my price for setting you free."

Winder winced as he worked his arms. From the feel of the muscles and joints, he knew that in the coming hands of time, they were really going to hurt. "I know."

Skull reached out, taking Winder's hand. "Then be well. Take care of yourself. You've got everything you've ever wanted: status, reputation, wives scattered over half of the south, and wealth. Go lay with your wives and found dynasties. Play with your children. Teach them to be brave and smart. This was your warning call—that single opportunity and last chance Power gives a man. Heed it. It's telling you 'Don't muck it up with foolishness.' "

"What about you, Skull? Do you have what you want? Where have all of your dreams gone? The woman you love Trades herself to any man who comes along. You have no home, no one but a dog for company.

And you sure can't place any faith in the Four Winds Clan—even if the Keeper was willing to speak for you. They're as trustworthy as a basket full of water moccasins."

Winder paused, then added, "Come with me."

"It's my city. I belong here."

"It's a miracle you've made it this long. They'll kill you in the end, you know. War Duck will figure out who kicked over that pot that put out the fire, fouled up his plans the other night. Or you'll get crossways with one of the others."

"It's a possibility."

"Listen to yourself! You're not one of them! You're an orphan. Clanless. Not even human in their eyes. Even a dirt farmer has more status than you do. I'll give you half of what's mine. Think, man. I'm offering you a home, status. It will be like it was. Just you and me." He reached out, pleading. "Piss in a pot, if you want a palace to live in, I'll build you one. Just come away with me. Save yourself."

For a long moment, Seven Skull Shield bowed his head in thought, then sighed. "Time only runs one way, old friend. We'll always have what we had back then. We kept each other alive." He waved around at the dark canoe landing. "Looks like we still do. But I've got to see how things play out here."

"They'll hang you in a square!"

"Yeah, probably. But until then, I'm going to play it for all that it's worth."

And as Seven Skull Shield said that, he pushed Winder's canoe out into the river, adding, "Paddle's down at your side, old friend. There's food and water in the fabric sack. Give my love to the south!"

"You're a fool," Winder called as the current spun the dugout around.

"That's what you told me last time you left," Seven Skull Shield called back.

"You ever need anything on the lower rivers," Winder told him as he fished for the paddle, "you look me up. I'm the best guide down there."

To his relief, his strength, feeling, and dexterity had returned to the point he could grasp the paddle, swing it out, and point the canoe downstream.

When he looked back, Seven Skull Shield was a mere dark shadow on the bank. One that faded into black and disappeared.

Sixty-four

Night Shadow Star came awake in the darkness. As if she could sense the coming of dawn, she sat up and listened. The night birds and a few late-season insects could be heard in the surrounding trees. Out just beyond the hide lodge that Squadron First War Claw's warriors had put up for her, the fire popped a couple of times. Someone was snoring not more than a pebble's toss off to the side. The breeze faintly rustled the leaves surrounding the little glen.

She took a deep breath—smelled tanned leather, buffalo-wool blankets, and dew-damp earth. Pulling her cape around her shoulders, she yanked her skirt over her hips and tied it.

Before she could crawl to the door, Fire Cat had risen from the blankets where he slept guarding the entrance. "Lady? Is all well?"

"It's . . ." She made a face. "Peaceful. I don't understand."

"Understand what?"

"I haven't slept this well for nearly three moons now. The quiet in my souls. Something's wrong." And then she placed it. "The Tortoise Bundle. Not since the golden cavern and the battle . . ."

"Yes?"

"I was dying. I remember when it left me."

"Why would it leave you? That makes no sense. Do you think it was the Morning Star? That he sent his agents, perhaps Five Fists, to steal it while you were in the Underworld?"

She shook her head, trying to remember. "One moment it was there, telling me I was weak and unworthy. And then . . . yes, I felt it go. I was . . . abandoned. A part of my souls empty."

Fire Cat sighed, slumping back on his butt. "If you ask me, that's a relief. It was tearing you apart. And if you will remember, when Lichen thrust it into your hands, she said it was only for a short time."

"For the moment it has chosen you, daughter of the Underworld."

But how long was a moment to an eons-old Spirit Bundle?

"We have to get back," she told him. "Wake the others. Dawn is coming. I can't stand not knowing. It's as if I can sense . . ."

He frowned at her perplexed expression. "By Piasa's balls, sense what?"

"In the emptiness the Tortoise Bundle left behind I sense intense pain and fear."

Fire Cat didn't hesitate. Leaping to his feet, he called, "Get everyone up. We're heading out. My lady orders that we be in the canoes by dawn. At canoe landing by midday at the latest. Let's move, people!"

She slowly stepped into the frosty morning, cocking her head toward the stars, seeing the constellation of Cosmic Spider high in the black sky, the three gleaming stars of the spider's midriff gleaming.

Tell me this isn't some new disaster!

But even as she thought it, an image formed in the eye of her souls: the niche in her personal quarters, and it was empty.

The Tortoise Bundle was gone.

Sixty-five

Seven Skull Shield stood in the cool darkness and watched Winder's canoe fade into the night as the river bore it south and into the blackness.

He tilted his head back, taking a deep breath of the chilly air, thick and wet as it was with the scents of the river, of the landing, mud, and wet charcoal from old fires.

Farts stepped over and nuzzled his hand with an inquisitive nose, batting it this way and that. For the moment Seven Skull Shield could only wonder if the dog was urging him to steal a second canoe and drive off in pursuit.

A dark shape fluttered around above his head—one of the last bats of the season in search of whatever insects he might have drawn.

Seven Skull Shield smiled slightly, raising his voice and calling out, "Well, there you have it. He would have built me a palace. It would have been like old times. What do you think, Keeper, should I have gone?"

A dark head popped up from behind the large Trade canoe that sat canted on its side just up the bank. He could see other people shifting as they emerged from hiding, fanning out, aware that they had been discovered.

Blue Heron gasped, grunted in pain, and raised herself to her feet, hobbling out around the shadowed canoe's bow. She shuffled carefully in the dark, making sure of her footing. Huddling under a blanket, she made her way to Seven Skull Shield's side, stared out at the inky black waters swirling before them. On the distant shore, at the canoe landing, low fires marked Traders' camps.

"How'd you know I was here?"

"Farts gave it away. Kept looking up your direction and wagging his tail. If it had been someone he didn't know hiding behind that canoe he'd have stood at alert. Maybe growled. I just had to count off the people he likes—it only takes about three fingers—and I came up with you as the logical choice."

"Bad calculating on his part. I *don't* like your dog."

"Then don't tell him. He likes to maintain his delusions." A pause. "You heard what Winder and I said?"

"Yes."

"Then you know why I had to let him go."

"Would he have kept his word? Given you all of those things . . . built you a palace? Made a home for you?"

"That's the thing about Winder. And maybe me, too. When we were running wild as kids we didn't have anything. No food, no home, no kin. Just rags for clothes. We only had each other and our word. That's what got him in trouble here. He told the Quiz Quiz he could do the job they asked. When I made it all go wrong, he just couldn't quit. Since he couldn't save himself, I had to do it for him."

She stared at the river in silence, as if digesting his words. "You know, there will be questions. A price to be paid. I am no longer the Keeper. I'm just here on Rising Flame's sufferance. I hope you figured that into your decision. If you didn't, you might want to plop your body in one of these boats and head south after Winder."

Seven Skull Shield reached down, flopping Farts' ears back and forth. "What do you think, dog? There's a price to be paid."

"Don't joke, thief. Winder was right about the Four Winds Clan. We are a nest of vipers. Rising Flame insisted that three hang—including your friend Winder. He was, after all, the smarts behind the trouble. He did abduct me from Columella's plaza. Caused me considerable discomfort, even if he did stop Moccasin from beating me to death. He *took* me."

"Um . . . I know. I'm sorry for that. On Winder's behalf, I can tell you it wasn't supposed to go so wrong. He hadn't planned on me and Flat Stone Pipe."

"I'm not joking, thief. Rising Flame will want your pus-dripping corpse hanging in that same square you and your thieves cut Winder down from. I'm no longer Keeper, and as to how much weight my pleas might have—"

"I'd say it would take quite a ransom to cover Winder's life, wouldn't you?"

"It would. And yes, I've told you that you could take anything you wished from my palace, but it will get out that you did so. I won't be made a fool of. It's too dangerous. And there's more than just your hide at stake."

"You're right," he agreed, ignoring the dog and crossing his arms against the chill. "It would have to be something symbolic, a ransom price that had real Power and prestige behind it. Something that made a statement."

She tilted her head, studying him in the darkness. "If you're thinking of stealing a couple dozen statues of Old-Woman-Who-Never-Dies like you did last time, let me tell you—"

"You never have any faith in me, Keeper."

"The only faith anyone seems to have in you is that you'll end up hanging in a square. And right now, that's looking more and more likely." A pause. "You ever find that Chikosi girl?"

"Turns out that Two Sticks caught up with her first. Figured that his future was a lot brighter with her dead than taking the chance she'd talk about his involvement."

He craned his neck around where the dark figures had emerged from the surrounding canoes. Looked like about twenty men. "Who you got with you?"

"Some of Columella's warriors. Them and my porters."

He squinted up at the sky. "Be morning soon. Rising Flame still up at Evening Star Town?"

"She is. And when she wakes up and finds that square empty . . ."

He smiled, hearing the warning in her words. He puffed out a breath, watching it cloud before his nose, then stepped over to the next canoe, which looked like something the Pacaha would make. He reached inside, pulled out the box he'd hidden there earlier, and slipped one of the straps over his shoulder.

Turning back, he said, "It's awfully cold out here. How about you get on your litter, and we'll let these warriors escort us back to Columella's palace where we can warm up. Then when Rising Flame comes charging in to report the outrage of Winder's disappearance, I can offer restitution."

He could see that her head was cocked, birdlike. "What kind of restitution?"

"Think she'd take the Quiz Quiz War Medicine as ransom for Winder?"

He saw Blue Heron start, then slowly shake her head. "You've had it all along, huh?"

"I guess I might have forgot to mention that?"

"And you can prove it is the real thing?"

"Just got to show it to Sky Star where he's hanging in that square up yonder. She'll be able to tell just by his expression."

"Thief, I . . ." She shook her head. "Why do I even bother?"

"I think you know why, Keeper. But let's keep that to ourselves. No need to embarrass ourselves by letting the rest of the world share our little secret."

"Told you. I'm no longer the Keeper." But she was chuckling under her breath as her porters brought her litter forward.

Sixty-six

The sensation was ever so light—the faintest touch, like the tip of a feather being trailed across the skin. Night Shadow Star needed only to close her eyes, tilt her head, and she could detect the Bundle's presence. Tell the direction in which it lay.

"You will need your armor," she'd told Fire Cat, hesitating upon their arrival in Cahokia only long enough for him to string his bow.

Spotted Wrist's escort had been extravagant, most of a squad who had borne her forthwith, accompanied by drums and flutes, down the Avenue of the Sun to the Great Plaza.

That he had done so sent her stomach to tingling as if ants were crawling around inside. She didn't like owing Spotted Wrist. Any favor he did was going to come with expectations—all of it orchestrated to reinforce his offer of marriage. Spotted Wrist wasn't used to being told no. And in all of her life, she couldn't ever remember a single time when he hadn't gotten what he'd set his mind to.

I could order Fire Cat to kill him.

That caused her to squint in distaste and wonder where that notion had come from.

After being delivered to the foot of her palace stairs—and waiting for Fire Cat to don his armor—she turned her steps for the Great Staircase, climbing resolutely up through the council gate, crossing the courtyard, and ascending the final staircase.

Behind her, Fire Cat's sandal-clad feet clapped on the squared-log steps as he asked, "Lady? Do you perhaps want to give me some idea about what we're up to?"

"The Tortoise Bundle has a new Keeper. I . . ." She made a face. "I have to know who. It's just . . . I was a part of it for so long."

The feeling of emptiness had been growing in her souls during the entire journey back to Cahokia. Along with it lay the sure knowledge that something had happened, some change in the world. And lurking in the back of her souls was the knowledge that Spotted Wrist wouldn't have *dared* to impose such a large escort unless his status had been significantly altered in the last few days.

Piasa, surely Morning Star wouldn't have ordered the marriage.

If so, she had the leverage to make him cancel it, that or he would appear ungrateful after her efforts on his behalf in the Underworld.

At the head of the stairs, the guards touched their foreheads respectfully. She took a moment, turning, looking back at the Great Plaza. It was mostly empty of people, but littered with trash: broken pottery, bits of clothing, corncobs, abandoned matting, and scattered refuse. The once-manicured chunkey grounds were stippled with tracks, the grass beaten and half-dead.

The remains of a single charred corpse, mostly bones, hung in the lone square at the foot of the stairs. No telling who that poor wretch might have been. The crowd hadn't been kind to him as they waited to learn the Morning Star's fate.

She met Fire Cat's eyes, gave him a slight nod, and strode through the gate. The courtyard was full, emissaries and chiefs waiting their turn to offer the revived Morning Star their best wishes and prayers for his speedy recovery. They went silent as they watched Night Shadow Star stride across the scuffed clay yard.

Word had traveled that she and Fire Cat had gone personally to the Underworld to retrieve the Morning Star's souls from Sacred Moth's clutches. That the Morning Star's souls had returned to Chunkey Boy's body was all the proof they needed that she had succeeded.

One by one they dropped to their knees, bowing, expressions awed.

After this I am even more removed from the world of men, she thought.

Piasa hissed and purred in satisfaction from behind her right ear.

"Beware, Lord," Night Shadow Star murmured. "One day this absurd worshipping and reverence may turn out to be a greater curse than a blessing."

But Piasa remained silent, though she could feel his presence like a building storm behind her right shoulder.

At the great double doors, Five Fists was waiting, a line of his warriors leaning against the palace's plastered wall. The lop-jawed warrior nodded, his eyes dark and glittering in the sunlight.

"Lady." He touched his forehead. "Given the Morning Star's weakened condition, I think it prudent that only you should be allowed in. We've just barely survived one assassination attempt." He looked meaningfully at Fire Cat, resplendent in his armor, strung bow, and quiver over his shoulder.

"War Leader, let us get something clear," she replied, crossing her arms, one foot defiantly forward. "If Fire Cat *ever* kills the Morning Star's host body, it will be at *my* order. A fact you should give some hard thought to. You know that the Morning Star and I serve different Powers, and for the moment, my master's goals are in alignment with those of the Sky World." She smiled coldly. "That might not always be the case in the future, War Leader."

"But, Lady," Five Fists protested, "the Red Wing's a heretic. His kind did more damage—"

"Where were you when the Morning Star was fighting for his very existence in the Underworld? Where were you when we were down there in the darkness, surrounded by the Dead? Did I see Five Fists leading the way into that burning cavern where Sacred Moth was sucking the Morning Star's soul away? Did *you* face the fiery light? It was Fire Cat who saved his life in the Underworld. All I did was get the Red Wing to the final chamber."

Every person in the courtyard gasped, eyes going wide as they stared incredulously at Fire Cat. For his part, the Red Wing stood at full attention, head high, eyes forward.

Five Fists' lips twitched with distaste and disbelief. "I'm to believe the heretic—"

"I wouldn't give a chinquapin seed for your beliefs, nor do I care. Open that door, or I will have your scarred and tattooed hide for a door mat."

Even as she spoke, she heard Piasa's voice meld with her own, felt the Underwater Panther's presence within her.

Five Fists' face seemed to change focus, to flatten and hollow under her vision. For a moment she could see his souls squirming uncomfortably as he went pale, stepped back, and shoved the carved doors open.

Well, no matter what Fire Cat remembered, or failed to, he was part of the legend now. He had once again saved the Morning Star despite his refusal to believe in the miracle of the living god's resurrection. The irony of it provided her with a dry sense of amusement.

She strode into the interior and crossed the great room, its eternal fire burned down so that only occasional flames leaped around the nearly exhausted wood.

A woman was seated at the foot of the Morning Star's dais. She wore a plain dogbane skirt; a hemp-fiber cape was draped about her shoulders. The thick tangle of her hair was in wild disarray. Ashes had been dabbed onto her cheeks and forehead, leaving her face pale and in contrast to the liquid darkness in her eyes.

Night Shadow Star stopped, blinking in disbelief. The woman fixed on her with an eerie stare. In her lap, she cradled the Tortoise Bundle, one hand patting it as though it were a pet.

In a thin voice, the woman said, "It no longer wanted you. It chose me."

Night Shadow Star nodded, finally feeling the rightness of it. "Of course it did. But are your souls strong enough to withstand the—"

"Sometimes, Sister, before a vessel can be filled, it first must be made empty." Sun Wing's Spirit-possessed eyes seemed to expand in her head. "I had to lose all of myself, be empty of everything that was Sun Wing before I could find the One."

"Whereas I was too full of things," Night Shadow Star told her as she gazed at the Tortoise Bundle, now so peaceful in Sun Wing's delicate hands. "Full of Piasa. Full of pain and anger. Crowded with voices and visions."

"You were driving each other to desperation." Sun Wing's hollow-eyed stare contrasted with the slight smile on her lips. Then her expression pinched. "Now we Dance with the One, struggling to Dream the harmony of the Spiral. Dissonant and chaotic. The balance is broken. . . . Needs to be brought back into harmony."

"I don't understand."

"How can you? You serve the dark world, Sister. The souls of the Dead still cling to you. Cobwebs. Filaments of the hopes and Dreams of colorless and bleached souls. Your fire draws them to you. Irresistible. You ache, pulsing with life, love, passion, and desire, but are bound to the Lord of the Dead."

Sun Wing paused, expression perplexed. "He thrives on that, you know."

"I know," Night Shadow Star whispered softly.

"That gives you your Power. You understand that, don't you? Give in. . . . Surrender yourself to that which you most desire." An oddly gruesome smile twisted her lips. "The crushing desolation will be unbearable."

"Lady?" Fire Cat asked. "What is she talking about?"

"You and me, Red Wing." Night Shadow Star closed her eyes, her souls keening within her.

"I don't understand."

"Of course you do." Then she added bitterly, "Nothing comes without a price. Piasa has played us well."

"Of course he has." The Morning Star stepped out from his private quarters, nodded his recognition to Night Shadow Star, and walked gingerly over to his dais. He added, "You cannot help being the woman you are. Nor can the Red Wing be less a man than he is. A fact that will eventually destroy you both."

In her ear, Piasa's hollow laugh was like a whisper.

Sixty-seven

Fire Cat knotted his fists as Chunkey Boy wobbled his unsteady way to his high seat atop its dais. The impostor actually looked as if he were back from the dead: his movements weak and still recovering from his poisoning.

He wore the scarlet macaw cape that had once belonged to the Itza agent Horn Lance. Had his choice been chance, or was he making some subtle point? With Chunkey Boy, a person never knew. His face was painted white with his traditional black forked-eye designs. He had pulled his hair forward into a bun and pinned it tightly to support a projecting black wooden-crescent headdress into which five small miniature arrows had been driven; his shell maskettes covered his ears.

Fire Cat started, recognizing the Morning Star's headdress: the same as the one depicted on his image in the Sacred Cave. Then he got a good look at the object Chunkey Boy clutched in his left hand: a familiar long copper blade.

Fire Cat gasped. "From my war club! But . . . How?"

"You gave it to him," Night Shadow Star told him dryly. "After your war club burned. Don't you remember? All that was left after the fire was the copper spike."

She gave him a sidelong appraisal, as if what he saw should have been as natural as daylight.

"You Dreamed that, Lady. One of your visions . . . spun by Sister Datura. As to the fate of my war club, I must have misplaced it in the dark. Perhaps while the datura addled my . . ." He blinked, shaking his head in disbelief. Rot it all, he just couldn't remember.

Chunkey Boy said, "Come here, Red Wing. Step up so I can see you."

Fire Cat gave Night Shadow Star a hesitant glance, but she nodded approval, inclining her head toward the dais.

Where she clutched the Tortoise Bundle, Sun Wing's eyes had sharpened, as if she were a spectator at some pivotal event.

Heart hammering, Fire Cat stepped forward. The tingling in his nerves was electric as he looked into the dark eyes of the man he'd waited all of his life to kill. Chunkey Boy stared back, gaze burning with fiery intensity behind his facial paint.

The supposed living god softly said, "You barely know the miracle. You have tasted the merest hint of the nectar upon your tongue."

"What nectar?"

"The sweet essence that sets the souls free. Metamorphosis. Evolving into something new. Fresh. As happened that night in the square when Night Shadow Star cut you down. Though it is but a shadow of what I have just experienced, it is still close enough to give you a glimmering of the reality."

Fire Cat ground his teeth, not sure how to respond.

Chunkey Boy smiled slightly. "I have just reawakened to a remarkable rebirth. Shed the cocoon after consuming the sweet darkness. The blood rushes. The Spirit is buoyant and airy. Embrace the miracle."

"What miracle?"

"The miracle of rising again from the blackest death, from the chill . . . the thundering silence of eternity." He touched fingers to his breast. "To feel the blood pulsing with each beat of the heart. To draw a breath, expand the lungs . . . and then walk out into warm sunlight again." Chunkey Boy closed his eyes, breathing deeply. "To emerge from darkness into brilliance."

Fire Cat held his peace, watching as Chunkey Boy savored the moment.

Then the dark eyes opened, possessed of an internal serenity quite out of sorts with any preconceptions Fire Cat might have had about the man.

From behind, Night Shadow Star demanded, "Why did you drink that woman's poison?"

Chunkey Boy's gaze never left Fire Cat's face as he said, "A being of light can only alter his nature by ingesting darkness."

What?

Chunkey Boy told him as if relishing his skepticism, "The immortal conflict. To become more than either light or dark requires a metamorphosis. Only Sacred Moth knew the secret way to the cavern—and only through the moth's defeat could the cocoon be spun."

"It was reckless." Night Shadow Star crossed her arms and glared as she stepped up to stand beside Fire Cat.

"What did you see down there in the darkness?" Chunkey Boy asked her mildly.

Fire Cat saw Night Shadow Star's lids thin as she said, "You and Sacred Moth locked in combat. You were losing until Fire Cat handed you the spike, and you stabbed Sacred Moth. Then, weakened as you were, darkness began to cocoon you. Enveloped you."

She paused. "On the way back to the surface, Piasa led me to the fragments of cocoon you shed along the way. I followed them to the cavern where you were freeing the souls from the bodies of the cavern Dead."

"And what did those souls do?" Chunkey Boy asked with a clever smile, as if he'd just had a revelation.

"They flew up to the images on the wall above their heads. Passed through the portal into the Underworld."

"I freed them?" Chunkey Boy said, almost as if asking himself a question.

Fire Cat watched Chunkey Boy's expression turn dreamy, eyes thinned to slits. Chunkey Boy's head tilted back, which let his beaded forelock fall down onto his nose. He said, "To think Piasa and Horned Serpent would have left them trapped forever with the portal so close. Those poor souls staring longingly at freedom." A pause. "You saw how I freed them?"

"With a touch to the head."

"I've heard the longing of their prayers, the very desperation of their pleas across time." Chunkey Boy's smile widened. "And you call my flight on the nectar reckless? I could have done nothing for them had I not lifted that cup to my lips."

"And had you died, the city would have come apart," Fire Cat growled, eyes on the copper spike. It *was* his. No doubt about it. But stained and corroded by some toxic agent. Sacred Moth's blood?

Impossible!

"It's not your city, Red Wing. Why would you have cared?" Chunkey Boy lifted an eyebrow. "If it is anyone's, it is mine. They came here for me. But do you have any idea how tiring it is? Trapped here? In this body? Listening to their endless pleas for favors? Watching their fawning prostrations? Playing their paltry chunkey games? And all those desperate young women quivering in excitement and expecting a miracle in my bed? Reincarnated Spirit or not, consider how satisfying you might find such an existence."

Fire Cat barely lifted an eyebrow. Unsympathetic.

Chunkey Boy shook his head wearily. "Whispering Dawn came reluctantly, honestly, without fawning and drooling anticipation. She was like a draft of cool fresh breeze on a hot and muggy day. The moment she was asked to slip the nectar into my drink, she did so with enthusiasm. Without her, I could never have opened that door."

Again he closed his eyes, breathing deeply, as if a being in rapture. "The sensations . . . I am born again into this life. Into this body. The adulation of the masses is once more a tonic." He paused. "And yes, Lady, I was able to free the cavern dead." Another pause, as if for effect. "As you saw."

Fire Cat shot her an evaluative glance, trying to read her expression. She saw what he was doing, didn't she?

"You doubt me, Red Wing." Chunkey Boy had again turned his calculating eyes on Fire Cat. Lifting the spike, he said, "To play the part of the living god, Chunkey Boy would have to be a master when it came to tricks, to sleight of hand and the arts of deception. I might have sent some agent down into the cave, perhaps one of the priests, to steal your vaunted war club. You might wonder why Chunkey Boy would go to such lengths on your account."

"I would indeed," Fire Cat agreed.

"Perhaps, Red Wing, it is because your skepticism serves my purposes. Perhaps it handicaps my sister's ambitions, or reminds others that skeptics end up as slaves. I might have orchestrated this entire assassination farce just to manipulate you."

Fire Cat had a look of utter disbelief. "As if *I* were important enough for such an elaborate hoax?"

Chunkey Boy's expression sharpened as he leaned forward, gaze fixed on Fire Cat's. "Perhaps I am preparing you—by the most cunning of means—for the day I will need you to do me some terrible service. Molding you so that when the time comes you won't hesitate to strike."

Fire Cat flinched. *Serve you? Not a chance.*

As if reading his souls, Chunkey Boy sat back, expression softening. "You only have two choices: Either this entire event was a trick to manipulate you, or I am indeed the Morning Star. Somehow I managed to obtain your war ax from the depths of the cave. Or your Spirit handed me this spike so that I could kill Sacred Moth, and the reason you can't remember handing me this spike is because you died down there. Sacred Moth killed you an instant after I grasped this from your trembling hand. Batted your dead body across the cavern." He paused. "Ask your lady."

Fire Cat shot Night Shadow Star a sidelong glance. Her slight smile, the lifted eyebrow and knowing, almost mocking, eyes, eloquently communicated what she knew she'd seen.

The Morning Star barely smiled at Fire Cat's discomfort. "Your souls were in a sack, so you don't know. Lady Night Shadow Star will tell you how Piasa, Horned Serpent, and Snapping Turtle were going to free me from Sacred Moth. How the battle would have shaken the earth. Brought chaos. She brought you close enough that your courage allowed you to hand me this."

He lifted the copper spike. "That, or it was indeed a clever deception, perfectly orchestrated in order to manipulate you for some arcane purpose."

"Stop it," Night Shadow Star snapped. "Why do you feed and promote his heresy?"

Chunkey Boy studied her thoughtfully. "Having Danced in the merging of light and dark, I now understand his Power. And yours. I finally know who you are. What you might become."

He fingered the spike lovingly. "We really do serve different masters, Lady. I had to embrace the darkness, free the souls . . . and see the future."

"What future?" Fire Cat longingly fingered his bow.

Chunkey Boy fixed on him. "Something is happening in the east. Beyond the Blue Mountains in the Cofitachequi colony. Some shaman stirring Power, accumulating it for his own ends. I learned of it on my way back through the Underworld. Took a detour to discover more, but found the way blocked."

Sun Wing—who had been watching quietly as she cuddled the Tortoise Bundle—suddenly cried, *"And among the People? Come the brothers. Born of Sun, one is slayed."* She paused, eyes going vacant before she added, *"Here, by the long trail, his corpse is laid."*

She blinked, lifting the Tortoise Bundle to her ear, whispering, "Yes, I hear." Then she looked at Night Shadow Star. "It is up to you. Lightning saved him. You must entice it to take him back."

Night Shadow Star spread her hands. "I don't understand."

"I had to be sure," the Morning Star told her. "You and the Red Wing, together, have the Power to defeat him. He hasn't given up, you know."

"Who?" Fire Cat asked under his breath.

Night Shadow Star took a deep breath. Her eyes had taken on that vacant look that indicated that Piasa was whispering in her ear.

Chunkey Boy's hint of a satisfied smile indicated that he, too, knew when Underwater Panther possessed his sister.

Night Shadow Star's expression blanched. Unsteadily she said, "And he's in Cofitachequi?"

Chunkey Boy nodded. "You are the last person he would expect to see so far from Cahokia."

"Who?" Fire Cat repeated with more emphasis.

Night Shadow Star shook her head, weary and disbelieving. "I am not going to Cofitachequi."

Chunkey Boy's lips twitched. "Spotted Wrist can't marry a woman who isn't here."

"Spotted Wrist?" she demanded irritably. "Surely after what Fire Cat and I just went through for your sake—"

"Oh, not me. Your clan matron. As an honor for the newly appointed Clan Keeper and Hero of the North. She—as leader of your birth clan—has ordered your marriage to the war leader."

"You had her appointed!" Night Shadow Star clenched a fist, jaws tight. "You *knew*!"

Face bland, Chunkey Boy said, "Curious how it all worked out, isn't it? Spotted Wrist will make a good match for you. Perhaps the only man in Cahokia worthy of your prominent position and authority."

Fire Cat felt the room sway, closed his eyes against the impossibility of it. Spotted Wrist?

"Entice the lightning," Sun Wing said absently as she stroked the Tortoise Bundle.

From Night Shadow Star's expression, Piasa was again whispering in her ear.

"Lady, please." Fire Cat knew something was being decided. *By Piasa's balls, anything but Spotted Wrist! Not in her bed!*

When her eyes cleared, a faint smile bent her lips. "We're going to Cofitachequi, Red Wing."

"Cofitachequi?" It was halfway across the world. And about as far as he could get from Night Shadow Star's despised new suitor.

She stepped forward, placing a hand on Fire Cat's armored breast. For long moments she stared into his questioning eyes. "My master tells me there may be a way."

"A way?"

"A way for us. For what we want more than anything. But know this, there will be a price."

"There is always a price."

"We are going to the far east to kill a man."

"Killing a man doesn't seem to be much of a price to pay."

Her eyes had gone hollow. "Depends upon the man, doesn't it?"

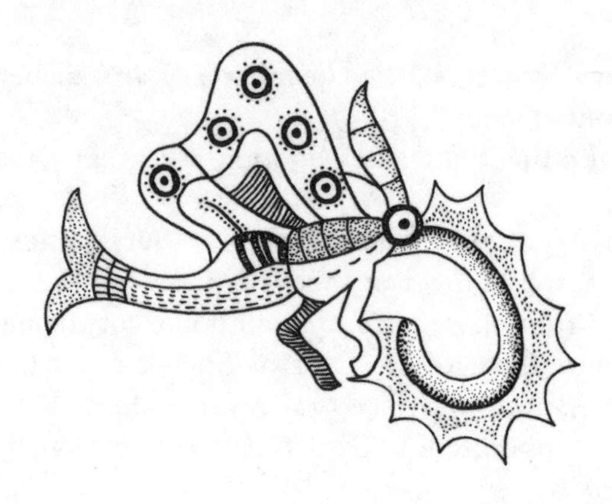

Reconciliation

The Great Plaza is busy as the morning sun beats down on my head. It is an unusually warm day for this late in the season. Behind me, the Morning Star's great mound and palace waver in the heat waves. Wooden Doll tells me that it is because a storm is coming. That it is always warmest just before the temperature falls.

That might be the theme of my life.

I look around at the hawkers and Traders plying their wares. On the chunkey courts, youths are grading and smoothing the trampled clay, repairing the damage done by thousands of feet as the people waited to learn if I had killed the Morning Star.

I glance up at the high palace, remembering that I am still the living god's wife. That I have heard no decree stating that he has divorced me. I think of the palace interior, of the benches, the wealth, the eternal fire, and of course I think of him.

The more I do, the more I'm sure he knew what I was about from the beginning. That he had been an almost willing partner in his poisoning. When I recall the look in his eyes as he took the mug of blueberry juice—how he held my gaze as he drank it—I am even more convinced.

I place my hand low on my abdomen, now fully aware that his child grows within my hips. Odd that it took Wooden Doll to ask "How long have you been pregnant?" after she caught me throwing up that first morning.

It is the Morning Star's child, of course. If my timing was right, on that first night of our marriage our coupling would have caught me in full heat. Perhaps that explains the passion with which I threw myself into his embrace. That deep inside, my loins hungered for his seed.

With that realization comes the belated knowledge that of all the men I have known, he was the kindest, the fairest, and most honest. For that I shall be eternally grateful.

I suck my lips in past my teeth and chew on them as I turn my eyes on the wooden square that stands across the Avenue of the Sun from the Grand Staircase. The charred remains of a man dangle inside the scorched timbers.

The head hangs, most of the hair and scalp burned away to expose the squiggly lines that mark where the bones meet. The hollow orbits in the skull where the eyes used to be are filled with char. The nose is gone, leaving only a triangular hole, and blackened teeth look garish where the lips were either sliced or burned away to expose the gaping jaw.

Just enough of the ligaments survived to hold the wrist and arm bones together and suspend the desiccated skeletal remains. The gut cavity is hollow, emptied of the intestines and organs that once resided there. Any trace of the genitals is a blackened ruin.

"What are you thinking?" Wooden Doll asks where she stands behind me by the waiting litter.

"Two Sticks told me that Straight Corn abandoned me. That he left with Hanging Moss and Wet Clay Woman."

"He was a liar. But before you torture yourself, you heard the news from the canoe landing."

I nod, feeling oddly hollow as I stare at what is left of Straight Corn. A sad and monotonous voice inside my head tells me that it wouldn't have made any difference if he'd run when his family did. Cahokian warriors caught up with them at the mouth of the Tenasee. Word is that seeing their capture was inevitable, Wet Clay Woman produced a powdered mixture of water hemlock, death camus, and morning glory seeds. They were in the throes of convulsions even as Five Fists' warriors drew up with their canoe.

"I loved him," I whisper to Wooden Doll. "Before he was my husband, he was my best friend. He came here for me."

"And asked you to poison the living god." She pauses for emphasis. "That is using you. Simple exploitation."

I nod. "Hanging Moss and Wet Clay Woman asked him to. That's what people do, Wooden Doll. Exploit each other."

Though I am still staring at Straight Corn's remains, I know she is studying the crowd, always wary.

She says, "That's the lesson I wanted you to learn."

"Why? Why even bring me here?" I am surprised that I feel no grief, no racking sobs for Straight Corn or the horrible way that he died. Instead I just feel hollowed out inside, numb.

Have I become wooden? Emotionless?

She says, "So that you will realize that even those who say they love you—and perhaps actually do—are still willing to destroy you for the right cause."

She indicates the passing masses of people, mostly dirt farmers come to stare up at the palace and perhaps glimpse the living god. "It's not a concern for them. For the most part they just have to live their lives, play their devotional chunkey games, fill their bellies, and pop out a child every other year. Oh, they'll have their little squabbles, the occasional fight and murder, perhaps an affair or nasty divorce. But barring catastrophe, they'll live out their lives in the interwoven mesh of relationships, successes, and tragedies."

"And I won't?"

Wooden Doll shakes her head, pointing at my belly. "You tell me the Morning Star's child is growing in your womb. Also, Two Sticks was right about one thing: You are the wife who betrayed and poisoned him. You were condemned to be different from the moment of your birth, Chikosi. You came here as a silly, headstrong girl, rapt in your own delusions of importance, love, and justice." She chuckled. "How did that work out for you?"

"What point are you trying to make?"

"Seven Skull Shield, for whatever reason, thinks you deserve another chance. I'm trying to slap it into your head that you have a choice to make. You can end up just like your beloved Straight Corn if you make stupid mistakes. You might still end up as fancy Trade, servicing strange men who want to drive themselves into the woman who betrayed the Morning Star. It would be so easy to become someone else's tool for the rest of your poor life."

"Or?"

"Remove yourself from the game for a while. Serve me. I offer fair Trade for food, shelter, and comfort until you have that child you're carrying. And while you're doing that, learn to stand on your own. To think. To be a full woman. You have time, if you'll use it."

I stare at the back of my hand, sore, scabbed, and aching where she had obliterated Sacred Moth's tattoo. "What's in it for you?"

"A well-kept house, the water jars full, cooked food, swept floors, folded clothing, and someone to tell clients that I'm occupied." She shrugged. "Do it well enough, I'll build you your own house after the baby is born."

"Why should I trust you?" I ask suddenly. "I could be worth a great deal were you to Trade me to Five Fists."

"Ah, now that's the kind of question you should have been asking all along. First, I'm the richest woman in Cahokia. Unlike even the tonka'tzi, *what I own is mine. Not the House's, clan's, or the lineage's, but* mine. *Second, I make my living by Trade. Whereas I Trade the services of my body to men, I will Trade you a bed, food, blankets, and fire. In return, you will see to the house. It's a simple deal. I need the work done; you need a place to stay."*

I consider this. "People are looking for me. What will they say when I am seen at your house?"

"I've had a constant string of foreign young women guarding my door over the years. You'll be taken for a slave I've purchased."

"A slave!"

"Hah, there it is. That's the arrogant stupidity flooding back. Would you prefer to be mistaken for a slave, or hanging there with your once-upon-a-time husband?"

I wince, glancing at Straight Corn's hideous remains. They are now swinging slowly back and forth on the ropes as the breeze teases the burned bones.

"After the baby is born . . . ," I remind her. "Well, caring for a newborn is complicated, time-consuming."

She smiles knowingly. "Back to Trade. Serve me well, and I'll hire help. Such can be had for little more than an engraved shell Traded every quarter moon or so."

I look into her eyes, seeing a woman who knows herself but expects little from the world. And what she gets is on her terms.

The sense of exhaustion, terror, and hopelessness begins to fade. I am a high minko's daughter, of the Chief Clan of the Sky Hand People. I nod slowly, and figure that I have learned my first lesson from this remarkable woman as I say, "We have a deal."

And I wonder what other lessons she is going to teach me.

She is smiling to herself as she turns back to the litter she has hired to bring us here.

I glance up at the living god's palace one last time. High on the bastion, where I know the Morning Star likes to stand, I see a man. Sunlight glints on the copper headdress, and even across the distance, I can see the bright red cape draping his shoulders.

Is it my imagination, or does he nod in recognition as his eyes meet mine?

An eerie premonition runs down my back like a shiver as I climb into the litter beside Wooden Doll. I am still looking up at him as I feel myself lifted. The porters call, "Make way!" and bear us back toward River Mounds City.

Not once do I look back at Straight Corn's remains.

Keeping my eyes straight ahead, I can feel the Morning Star's gaze as we are borne east.

Surely he has no use for me now. Had he, he would have sent Five Fists down the stairs with a squad of warriors to hang me beside Straight Corn.

No, I am free.

Which, after all, is the most self-deluding lie to tell oneself when the future is uncertain.